FINDING GRACE

FINDING GRACE

A NOVEL

Loretta Rothschild

ST. MARTIN'S PRESS
NEW YORK

First published in the United States by St. Martin's Press, an imprint of St. Martin's Publishing Group

FINDING GRACE. Copyright © 2025 by Loretta Rothschild. All rights reserved. Printed in the United States of America. For information, address St. Martin's Publishing Group, 120 Broadway, New York, NY 10271.

www.stmartins.com

The Library of Congress Cataloging-in-Publication Data is available upon request.

ISBN 978-1-250-38182-8 (hardcover)
ISBN 978-1-250-40906-5 (international edition)
ISBN 978-1-250-38183-5 (ebook)

Our books may be purchased in bulk for promotional, educational, or business use. Please contact your local bookseller or the Macmillan Corporate and Premium Sales Department at 1-800-221-7945, extension 5442, or by email at MacmillanSpecialMarkets@ macmillan.com.

First U.S. Edition: 2025
First International Edition: 2025

10 9 8 7 6 5 4 3 2 1

For my boys

CHAPTER ONE

The last time we were at the Ritz in Paris I had my fifth miscarriage at breakfast.

This Christmas, I was no longer in contention for the same bizarre privilege. Now that I'd had my ovaries confiscated by my doctor, I found myself oscillating between staring at my husband and daughter adoringly and wondering how long it would take to drown myself in the Seine. It had become an unwritten family tradition that we always came to the Ritz for Christmas. This year, as we drove to the hotel, with the moon beside us—a fine lick of chrome in an upside-down crescent—the driver pointed out landmarks I already knew well. I nodded, feigning interest before cutting him off to ask if he had a Motorola phone charger.

"*Non, madame, non.*"

"*Ce n'est pas grave,*" I said, sinking back into the front seat of the car. We drove past La Madeleine, lit up from below to emphasize its imposing Corinthian beauty. The few times I'd chosen to pray for my fertility, it had been in that church. Perhaps that's why my prayers for another baby had yet to be answered—maybe God could sense my secular proclivity.

The driver continued to prattle on about Napoleon, then Sarkozy. I gave him a tight-lipped smile; I wasn't really listening. The truth was I could've been in Paris or Putney, it didn't matter. Of course, I knew Paris was beautiful. Everyone did. But it was like I was trapped inside a snow globe that nobody was shaking. All I could think about was life back home. I kept hearing the doctor's voice in my head telling me the exact thickness of our surrogate Jess's uterine lining and wondering if she'd been taking enough folic acid in preparation for the embryo transfer.

We stopped at a red light, where a young couple crossed the road holding hands. The girl was laughing at something her boyfriend said, throwing back her head and playfully pushing him away. I rolled up my window. It had started spitting and my coat was cashmere. The hail came out of nowhere, pelting little wet bullets against the car's windscreen. I held down the power button again on my phone, but still nothing.

"Fuck," I said, which seemed to take the driver by surprise. *"Pardon, monsieur,"* I added, quickly returning to my French sensibility. I turned around to face Tom in the backseat. "Tom, is your BlackBerry working?" He was still in his suit but without the tie. His eyes were closed, his head resting against the window. Our daughter, Chloe, was asleep with her head on his lap, her little body curled up like a kitten beside him. On paper, the picture was idyllic. A healthy, happy child, born with a double set of lashes, safe in the lap of her father. But even the fortunate hand I'd been dealt didn't stop my longing for one more baby.

"Tom, can you check if your phone is working?" I said again. "Mine isn't."

"I'll do it at the hotel," he said, rubbing his face, his voice sleepy. "I don't want to wake Chloe up."

"Could you just check? Jess might've texted us."

"Oh, so now you *want* me to be on my phone. I'll get it once we're at the hotel." I clamped my lips tightly between my teeth. I jabbed at the button that switched off my heated seat; the sudden flare of concentrated warmth was making me want to vomit. Then I heard that familiar faint *dink* of Tom's BlackBerry.

"Can you see who that is?" I said, my throat slightly dry from the recycled air on the plane.

"Honor, we're less than two minutes from the hotel."

"I'm not asking how far we are from the hotel. I'm simply asking you to check your phone." A slight edge had crept into my voice, a tone I recognized as my mother's, sharp and unlikable. Chloe woke up then. She shot upright, like most four-year-olds discombobulated by not being in her own bed.

"Are we there yet, Daddy?"

"Almost," he said, pushing the hair off her face.

"Tom? The phone?" He didn't look at it, he just shoved it into my palm.

Our fertility doctor insisted we not take a pregnancy test for two weeks after any embryo transfer, but there was no harm in asking Jess how she was feeling; there might be early signs that the transfer had worked. Of course, it wasn't Jess who'd texted, it was the alarm company, duly followed by another from our friend Lauren, telling us she had accidentally put the code in wrong when she was picking up our dog Duke's lead. I replied, then texted our surrogate Jess on Tom's phone, trying to compose a message that seemed "happy-go-lucky" but most likely read "desperate." I knew I was teetering on overbearing, but at this point I had ceased caring about propriety.

The two-week wait for Jess to take a pregnancy test in tandem with my lofty drop into medical menopause at thirty-three had done little for my Christmas spirit. The irony of sitting in the waiting room at a fertility doctor's office to discuss having another baby when there was nothing in my arsenal wasn't lost on me. Nor was the fact that Tom and I hadn't had sex since Chloe's birthday six months ago. Apparently, infertility was an underrated but effective method of contraception.

By the time we pulled up outside the hotel, the rain had dwindled to a drizzle. The French flag draped above the entrance, catching ever so slightly in the damp breeze. Two bellhops dressed in Ritz blue stood by the door. They ran to the car, umbrellas up and at the ready.

"*Bonsoir, Messieurs-dames,*" said the taller of the two. There was a slight wobble to his voice. I didn't recognize him from previous years and his bumfluff indicated that this was a temporary job between life choices. They took our suitcases, and I watched Chloe and Tom trot away from me up the red-carpeted stairs, Chloe's velvet coat blending into the carpet's rich pigment, before they disappeared through the revolving doors.

The lobby was filled top-to-toe with the bustle of Christmas. The grand piano had been set aside to make way for the giant tree, a sparkling, verdant spectacle, decorated in the hotel's signature palette of peach and champagne, with a light dusting of Ritz-blue baubles sprinkled here and there.

I pocketed my gloves and put my bag down on one of the gilt chairs by the reception desk. Chloe was making the most of the empty lobby, pirouetting up and down the length of the foyer. It didn't matter how many years we'd been coming to the Ritz, I never got used to the height of its ceilings or the grandeur of its old-world beauty, a stark contrast to the dingy cottage my mother rented every summer in rural Normandy.

I stood breathing in the smell of amber and freshly dropped pine needles, trying to remember the last time we'd been in the lobby this late at night. It must have been before Chloe was even born, when we used to stumble in blurry-eyed after one too many dry martinis at Harry's Bar.

Tom turned and asked me for his BlackBerry. I walked over

and put it on the reception desk, making sure it slammed hard enough to make a point, but not hard enough to damage it. He didn't bite, though, which only wound me up more. We'd been having the same argument about my insistence on having another baby for the best part of two years.

I picked up my bag and marched off in an exaggerated huff before calling the lift. It was only when I pressed the button that I realized I should've left it for Chloe.

"You know she likes doing the buttons," Tom said as he joined me by the polished doors.

"She can press the ones inside," I said. "Chloe, come on. It's late!" But as soon as she saw the button illuminated, her bottom lip began to tremble. "I'm sorry, darling, I don't know what I was thinking. You can press the ones to go up. And all the other buttons that need pressing forever and ever, okay?" She nodded, but her lip was still turned down. The lift doors opened, and I squinted as we stepped inside. The light was unnecessarily bright and there were mirrored panels on all sides, dominoing us into oblivion. As the doors closed, the collar of my coat tightened around my neck. The lift suddenly seemed to shrink like an airless incubator.

Tom pointed to our floor, so Chloe knew which button to press. It was the little things with Chloe. I used to be the same about my coffee or starting a new notepad. But now my mind was in a constant fog of Jess's synthetic progesterone injections and phantom colostrum production.

I undid my top button and bent down beside Chloe, my long navy coat falling around me like a cape.

"Can I show you a trick?" I whispered. Her eyes widened. I took her little hand in mine and swiped her fingers down every brass button. Chloe let out a little giggle, knowing her mummy had just done something naughty. I stood up. Tom wasn't laughing, and when the doors opened on the next floor, he exaggerated his yawn for Chloe's sake and got out.

"Daddy needs some exercise, cherub," he said, before kissing her head goodbye but saying nothing to me—so different from when we'd role-played him chatting me up in this very lift before escorting me to his "room." Tom liked to take the stairs, but that wasn't why he was doing so tonight.

We were already in our suite when Tom walked in shortly after us, still visibly seething over my behavior. The rift continued throughout our bedtime routines, without a détente in sight.

"There we go," I said to Chloe as I tucked her into her adorable little bed. Her eyes were at half mast and her fingers were stroking her cuddly, Hedgie. We'd packed last year's white-and-pink-striped pajamas. They were big then; they were getting a touch too small around the ankles now. Nothing like a child to mark the passing of time. When Chloe was a baby, Tom would order a bottle of Pol Roger while I was getting Chloe to sleep. He would have a cold glass waiting for me as I crept out of her bedroom, being careful not to make a peep and wake her. But there was little chance of any champagne corks popping tonight.

My phone lit up as soon as I plugged it in. I held my breath anticipating Jess's name, but there was only a message from my editor, which I barely read. I texted Annie, my closest friend since day one of university.

> Tom is already in a mood, and I have to see
> my hideous mother tomorrow. I can't imagine
> why you didn't want to join us!

Annie texted me right back like she always did.

> How many more days until Jess takes the
> pregnancy test?

> Seven sleeps. Love you.

Call you tomorrow. And don't listen to anything
your mother says about surrogacy. Kiss my
darling goddaughter for me.

I flipped my phone shut and rubbed my thumb over the rain-bow sticker Chloe had stuck on during the flight. She'd already fallen asleep, making her little snuffly sounds, her breathing slow and rhythmic. I momentarily considered squeezing in next to her. It wouldn't be the first time in recent years. But that would mean I was declaring trench warfare, when the truth was I hated sleeping apart from Tom, even during an argument. By the time I got into our room, Tom was already in bed. A lumpy shadow beneath a duvet turned down in expectation of romance, but instead it got silent resentment.

"Tom?" I said, but he didn't answer. I blew my fringe off my face and put my coat over the back of the upholstered desk chair.

The bedroom was the quintessence of French taste: the canopy bed fit for a duchess, held together with layers of salmon-colored silk, the famous apricot sheets without a single crease. I used to go weak at the knees at the sight of this room, but tonight I didn't even pull back the curtains to look at the Place Vendôme. Instead, I had to fight every urge to scream into the nearest goose-down pillow.

I light-footed to the bathroom and closed the door. Running my finger over the neck of the gold swan tap, I remembered how many times Tom had bent me over this sink back when I was "fun." I splashed water on my face and let my mascara run down my cheeks, not bothering to wipe it on the towel. I just looked at the woman staring back at me in the mirror, wondering when she'd become such a shrew. I toggled off the bathroom light and stole a T-shirt out of Tom's suitcase. It was already open on the floor, and I couldn't face unzipping mine.

I took off my knickers and slid inside the cold sheets of our bed before clicking off my bedside light. Then I waited. I waited to see who would break first. I gave it another ten seconds. Then I slowly tiptoed my fingers over the hill of Tom's back onto his chest until they found his hands. He took them tight and held them against his body, the way I'd hoped he would. I pressed my lips up against his back. We were safe from one another in the darkness now.

"I'm sorry for being a dick in the lift," I said, as he kissed my fingers.

"Thank you for saying that," he said, turning his body to face me, our noses barely an inch apart. "Honor, I really want this week to be about us—me, you, and Chloe. I don't want to keep arguing all the time. It's driving me mad. I miss us so fucking much."

"I do too," I said, pressing the inside of my bottom lip up against his cheekbone.

"That means not talking about the baby." His tone was blunt, and I felt my body go rigid in his arms. "The baby we *might* have, or might *not* have, or the one we don't have—just while we're in Paris. Once we land back in London, I'll talk about it until the cows come home. But not this week, not over Christmas. I just want Chloe to hear us talking about *her* for once. I want her to hear us laugh with each other again." He held my hands tighter now, perhaps sensing my urge to pull away.

"Okay," I said, though my body conveyed otherwise, "I won't talk about it." I was glad the lights were off; had they not been, he would have been able to tell how inconceivable that idea was. He knew my intentions better than anyone. My nights at boarding school had been so desolate, and I couldn't bear the idea of Chloe experiencing even a whisker of the loneliness I'd felt as an only child.

Tom cuddled me a few moments longer, and we found our feet while talking about how wonderful Chloe had been on the flight and how tall she seemed in the lift in comparison with last year. Tom lifted his head off the pillow and found my lips. His hand began traveling up my thigh over my hip bone, following the familiar path to my waist.

"Say it," he said, his lips never leaving mine. I could feel Tom straining at the lead. "Say our poem, baby."

"Do you come from Heaven or rise from the abyss / Beauty? Your—"

"No, in French," he said, but I carried on in English, reciting the poem I always did whenever we made up after a fight: *Hymn to Beauty* by Baudelaire. I knew all too well that if I spoke French in the dark, especially that poem—the first words he ever heard me speak on the lawn at Annie's—it would inevitably lead to sex, and my brain was elsewhere, fixated on what was occurring between our surrogate's legs and not my own.

The following morning, I was still managing to nourish my obsession from the depths of a pearly-white bath. It seemed there was no tub deep enough, coffee strong enough, or martini cold enough that could distract me from the relentless yearning that a year ago a therapist had promised would eventually fade. In one of the many meetings with my fertility doctor, I'd been advised against not only carrying our next baby but also continuing to try with my own eggs. Such an unexpected turn of events, considering I couldn't even pinpoint the shag that led to Chloe, and now here I was, down with the IVF lingo and on a wait-list for an experimental implantation treatment in Sweden.

According to my doctor, I had developed too many fibroids, my eggs were of low quality, and "my oven wasn't hot enough." After I'd had my ovaries out just under a year ago, a surrogate and an egg donor became our only hope. Lying in the bath, I was so engrossed in my thoughts that I didn't hear Tom calling me from the bedroom. It wasn't until he came in and nudged my shoulder that I realized he was standing beside me.

"Babe?" he said again, his voice tentative.

"Yeah?" I said, looking up at him. His features were somewhat perturbed, but I pretended not to notice.

"Chloe's been calling for you. She wants to show you the card she's made for Annie and Oliver."

"Sorry," I said. I pushed myself out of the now tepid bath. Tom opened one of the thick, peach dressing gowns that was hanging on the back of the door and coaxed me into it. I pulled out my wet hair from the back and found the matching embroidered salmon slippers.

"I'm coming, angel," I called through the door. Chloe murmured something back, but I didn't quite catch it. Tom tightened the towel around his waist while I carefully avoided his reflection in the mirror.

"Let's just say we asked Jess to do a pregnancy test at home," I said. "If she was pregnant, she'd be showing as positive by now, wouldn't she? She must be."

Tom took a sip of his cappuccino and swallowed slowly, before putting the cup down just that little bit too hard on the lip of the sink. Our eyes met in the mirror.

"Baby, we said we weren't going to talk about this until we were home."

"*We* didn't," I said.

"I'm not going to rise to this, Honor," he said. His BlackBerry pinged beside him.

"Oh, that's convenient. Your phone's flashing. Go on. Start tapping away."

Tom forced shut the bathroom door. "Honor, you know what— and you aren't going to like this—but tough shit." I braced myself for what I feared was going to be a home truth. "If you spent half as much time with our daughter as you do obsessing over wanting another child, you might realize what we have instead of what *you* feel we don't."

The goose bumps rose on my neck like a dog's hackles and my eyes turned watery. I reached for my bottle of Chanel Sycomore and sprayed too much of it just to have something to do with my hands.

"Words land, you know," I said, my voice shaking. I wiped the one tear that had escaped onto my cheek.

"I *really, really* hope that's true," he said. "Because I need you to listen. This is the last time I'm doing this. I mean it. If this doesn't work with Jess and the egg donor, then I'm not—I'm not doing it again. I will not continue to do this to our family. To Chloe. You've lost sight of everything," he said, pointing his finger at me. "You say you want to be a mother, so be a mother. Be a mother to the child we actually have. Answer her. Answer our daughter when she's calling for you." His arms stiffened towards the door, like a flight attendant indicating emergency exits.

"Go fuck yourself!" I said, my fingers shaking against the soft laundered towel of my dressing gown. My breath had turned short and quick. He'd pressed the bruise. I picked up the shirt I'd worn the day before from the chair by the window. Then I tried to swing open the bathroom door, but it was heavy and unwilling.

Tom didn't follow me like he usually did. I just heard the door click shut. If Chloe hadn't been in the next room, I would've screamed until my throat bled. I stalled a little longer in the bedroom, still fuming but hoping he would change his mind. I could have fought about this topic forever. But instead, I heard his voice barely audible through the door.

"Yeah . . . Merry Christmas to you too, Honor."

I walked into the adjoining sitting room, where Chloe was on the floor. Thankfully, the TV was on loud. She was drawing with a red pencil, sitting with her feet pointed under her bottom.

"Look, Mummy," she said, lifting her picture. I came closer, holding my hands behind my back so she wouldn't see them shaking. She'd drawn the three of us in front of the Ritz, with a bright yellow sun in the corner and a navy-blue sky. I had to hold every muscle tight to keep my eyes from combusting. Never cry in front of your child. They never, ever forget it. My mother never did forgive me for the time I walked in on her hunched over her dressing table weeping into her forearms.

"It's beautiful, Coco. Well done," I said, kissing the peppermint shampoo of her crown.

She was beaming with pride, the way I was with guilt. "I'll put it just here, okay? We can post it to Annie later." I leaned Chloe's picture against the mirror on the demilune table by the door and pulled my jeans from the satin-pink chaise. "Right, are you ready for breakfast?" I said, buttoning my shirt.

"Can I have a crêpe?" she said.

"*Hmm* . . . Let me think about that?" I tied back my hair and glued on another smile. I could already feel the effects Chloe had at lowering my heart rate.

"I'll eat it all," she said.

"You promise?"

"I promise! I'll eat every bite." She wouldn't, of course, but I said yes, because when she looked up at me, all I saw was every preschool drop-off I'd missed because I was at yet another fertility appointment.

"And a milkshake!" I added for good measure. As I approached the door to leave our suite, I could feel Chloe stalling. I knew what she was going to say; this wasn't our style.

"What about Daddy?" she said. I ran my tongue over my teeth.

"He'll meet us down there," I said.

As soon as we left the room, Chloe sped down the grand hall-way, narrowly missing Jean, one of my favorite bellboys. "Careful, darling," I warned, but when Jean saw Chloe approaching, he put down the cases he was carrying and put out a white-gloved high five.

"*Bonjour, madame.*"

"*Bonjour, Jean. Joyeux noël,*" I said, but my eyes conveyed otherwise.

There's something about a strip of hallway that's irresistible to a toddler's turmoil. I watched as Chloe sprinted across the ornate carpet, her delicate fingers leaving an invisible trace on the blush-paneled walls behind her. Any other day I would've told her to slow down, but not this morning. I tried to block out what Tom had just said, but his words were playing in a perpetual loop in my head. All of it was so agonizing because I knew it was true. I hooked my navy scarf around my neck, wondering how I had become the person who shouted "Go fuck yourself" to her husband at Christmas. I glanced back at our suite, but Tom wasn't coming. Chloe excitedly pressed the button to call the lift. I squeezed her sweaty, warm palm in mine, watching her chest rise and fall, the way I had when she was a baby. When the shiny doors opened, I could see she was pleased to discover there were no other guests inside. Chloe remembered which button would take us to the lobby. I sat down on the blue upholstered bench, and she tucked in beside me.

"Mummy, we forgot Hedgie," she said, looking up at me.

"We'll see him right after breakfast, darling," I said. I couldn't face going back into that room. We were nearly all the way down when the lift stopped on the second floor and a woman joined us. Her hair was long, perfectly straight, a shade close to black. She looked at Chloe and gave her a warm smile.

"That's a beautiful color," she said. Chloe fanned out the edges of her emerald-green dress, her lily-white tights swinging joyfully underneath the bench. She looked up at me with her blushing cheeks. She was still quite shy with strangers.

"It's become a firm favorite," I said, smiling politely at the woman's interest. It was only when she readjusted her coat that I saw her burgeoning bump and felt that familiar angst in my gut.

"Do you know if you're having a boy or a girl?" I asked, wishing the question were being posed the other way around. She shook her head; there was that sweet smile again.

"No, it's going to be a surprise."

"Your first baby?"

"Yes."

"How exciting," I said. "It's such a magical time."

I pulled Chloe even closer, remembering the feeling of her body growing inside me. When I was pregnant, even though I had morning sickness breakfast, lunch, and dinner, I didn't care. We were starting a family.

When the lift doors opened onto the lobby, the already sizable baubles that hung from the ceiling had seemingly grown overnight. Chloe spun around in sheer wonder. The decorations were so grand that I half expected the Nutcracker himself to be doing a grand jeté across the carpet. The air was filled with the amber scent of French Christmas, and it triggered a pang of deep regret at how I'd left things with Tom upstairs; no one loved Christmas more than he did.

"Come on, Mummy," Chloe said, tugging at my hand. Though the lobby was busy, you could tell everything was in perfect order. There was never a hair out of place at the Ritz. I stretched my neck to see if I could make out Pierre behind the concierge desk. He was there, smiling as always, helping a guest among the bowls of pine cones and freshly foraged bracken.

Chloe and I walked towards the tree, majestically poised where it always was, at the bottom of the spiral staircase, every light twinkling. The glass-blown baubles looked like freshly dipped toffee apples waiting to be crunched. Chloe stood staring up at the tree with her ocean-blue eyes. Even amid our horrible fight, I regretted once more that Tom wasn't there. Was he right? Had I lost all perspective? Was my need for another baby going to cost me my marriage?

I'd dragged Tom along with my dream, never wondering what toll these failed pregnancies had on him. I spoke over his thoughts. I just went ahead, business as usual, as if he played no role, or had any voting rights. How many times had I rejected Tom's advances? How many times had I ignored him because I was reading posts from a stranger on an IVF forum who lived in Milton Keynes? And now I'd left him alone in the bathroom at Christmas. How had I let him believe that having another baby was more important than our family? More important than our marriage?

"Stand in front of the tree so I can take a photo of you. Then we'll go back and get Daddy," I said. "He'll be wondering where we went." I dug around in my bag for my camera, and pinched off the lens cap. By the time I was ready, Chloe had become distracted by the piles of wrapped presents sitting under the tree. "Coco? Look at Mummy," I said, holding my breath, a habit I'd picked up and never managed to neuter.

"Can you see me?" she said, looking straight down the lens, her presence magnified. I knew then I was going to remember this picture for the rest of my life. It was as if I was seeing her for the first time all over again. My happy little girl. The commotion of the hotel fell silent behind me.

I was about to press down on the shutter button when someone walked into the frame. I pulled the camera from my face and was about to say "Excuse me," when I realized it was the pregnant woman from the lift. I stalled for a moment. Something about her seemed vague, and I worried she might faint. But she didn't. Instead, she looked directly into my eyes and smiled. I smiled back, wondering why she was holding my eye. Then there was a soft click as she detonated a suicide bomb that killed me and Chloe instantly.

CHAPTER TWO

One Sunday morning, Tom and I were on Columbia Road sitting out-side our favorite café when I informed him of my recent purchase: two burial plots side by side in the churchyard next to my father, who died when I was seven.

"Don't I get a say in any of this?" Tom said, stretching up his arms with his fingers entwined. It was late summer, and the dregs of the last committed tourists filled the white, wobbly bistro tables. Duke sat be-neath my feet, content with his saucer of water in the shade of my chair, and thankfully Chloe was sleeping soundly in her pram. "Right. This is genuinely my last coffee and then I'm off," Tom added.

Tom had been prattling on about going for a run for the past fifteen minutes, while I was trying my best not to tease him about his rather questionable fluorescent shorts. I watched as he completed the rest of his coffee ritual: two white sugars, always torn open together, a boisterous stir, then a lick of the spoon on both sides.

"Shit. I burned my tongue," he said, never having learned to be

patient with food or drink. "So just to clarify, it's a flat no to crema-
tion?"

"It's a flat no," I said, before taking a sip of my cappuccino. I didn't
want to be cremated. I couldn't risk Tom leaving me in a cab, or being
sprinkled over some poor, defenseless dolphin's head at sea. I got seasick.
I would've hated it.

"Okay, so let's run through some scenarios," he said.

A woman in a pair of dungarees wearing a "Baby on Board" badge
threw me a look as if to suggest I might give her our table, a look which
I chose to ignore.

"What if I leave you for a much younger woman? Can she and I
bundle in there together? I imagine she'll be relatively small?"

"No. If you leave me, I'll be buried there with my new husband.
Your new wife will have to buy two different plots. Picture this: I'm your
landlord. I own all six feet and can sell the place from underneath you at
an hour's notice." Tom frowned; this wasn't a great deal for him. "And
let's be honest, who are you planning on leaving me for anyway? Like,
who's your top three?"

"That's a tricky one," he said. "I have a lot of options."

I rolled my eyes and wiped the cappuccino foam from my lip.
"Promise me one thing: If you do leave me for someone else, just
don't be a cliché. I wouldn't mind people saying, Yeah, that makes
sense, she's more interesting than Honor—younger, more intelligent,
better tits."

"No one has better tits."

"All I'm saying is, if you do have an affair, I want my replacement
to have Gisele's level of hotness, Marie Curie's intelligence, and Mother
Nature's maternal instinct. Marry someone you could see me being
friends with. An indoorsy poet with a disdain for socializing."

"You're actually giving me a hard-on."

"I strongly advise against that in those shorts," I said as Tom rearranged himself.

"In fact, if I die, make sure you do the same. Find a solid replacement.

Sure, I'd want you to be sad and incapacitated, but not for too long. You'd have to get your shit together. Chloe would need you." I glanced at Chloe, still sound asleep in her pram, seemingly immune to the sounds of the passing streetsweeper.

"Well . . . that was a short-lived semi," Tom said.

"You'd clean up, you know . . . pick of the litter. Women love a widower."

"Right. Okay. Well, thank you for giving me so many joyful topics to think about while I'm jogging, baby," he said as he stood up from the table. "Wait, who'd you pick? Let me guess: Jake Gyllenhaal? Or, that young agent at so-and-so, the Scottish one, what's his name?"

"Oh no, baby . . ." I said, twisting my head as he leaned down to kiss me. "If I leave you . . . I'm going oligarch."

*

Tom hadn't known the word for "coffin" in French until Chloe and I were killed. Even though he had successfully managed his own hedge fund for eleven years, he wasn't so good at life's logistics, household or otherwise. That was my department; I had a system, albeit an illogical one. Tom got into a muddle ordering two glasses of wine in French, never mind arranging two coffins and their transportation back to England. Tom was always doing a million things at once, his head filled with financial jargon about derivatives and market returns—things that, even after he'd explained them to me thirty-nine times, I still didn't understand.

After the attack, Tom came to lying on a gurney, with an oxygen mask strapped to his face, his body shrouded in thick gray blankets. As his eyes rolled open, a nurse in white overalls stood over him, her fist aggressively rubbing his sternum. She was speaking French, then English, while the blood pressure monitor beeped rhythmically beside him, as if to remind his heart to stay alive. With every intake of breath, Tom's throat felt like it was on fire. But the burning in his lungs was a welcome distraction from his memory, which suddenly returned with uncompromising clarity. He could see his bare feet running down the stairs towards the dining room, where he imagined us alive, huddled under a table. He didn't know then we were already gone.

Another set of paramedics slammed through the doors, piloting a stretcher with a woman wearing only a yellow neck brace and a peach Ritz robe, her eyes wide with shock. The blood pressure monitor beeped again as the Velcro strap tightened around Tom's arm. His heart throbbed. He could see me and Chloe at breakfast. I was drinking an espresso and Chloe was picking at her crêpe. He saw my veil in the wind on our wedding day. He heard the faint sound of Chloe's laugh, then the click of the bathroom door as I walked away from him.

Part of him hoped he might arrest right here in the hospital. If he took off the oxygen mask, would it all be over? Would he find us then? His teeth began chattering uncontrollably. Across the ward, a little boy sat crying in the arms of his mother, his face covered in soot. Lying there, surrounded by other unlucky survivors, it dawned on Tom that he was going to have to tell my mother that her daughter and granddaughter were dead.

After the Ritz had been evacuated, the police arranged vacant rooms at a nearby hotel for the survivors of the attack. Once Tom was discharged from the hospital, though, he couldn't bear the idea of being in an empty, sterile room without Chloe jumping on the bed and me complaining that the sheets were too itchy. The only place to go was my mother's apartment in the 6th Arrondissement. Hardly an appealing offer. Life with my mother had been a repeated stream of unsolicited opinions and digs at my choices, at my height, which was above average, and my decision to breastfeed in lieu of preserving my tits. I wore the wrong clothes. I gave my daughter the wrong name. I wrote the wrong books.

After Tom told my mother what had happened to us, she

didn't come out of her room for two days, leaving him alone in her apartment to manage the complicated logistics and the endless bureaucracy of bringing our coffins back to England. President Nicolas Sarkozy had temporarily closed the French borders, concerned a copycat attack would follow. Our closest friends— Lauren, Annie, and her husband, Oliver—couldn't fly out to hold Tom's hand or be there to help him in person. Oliver was calm and considered over the phone, whereas Lauren was climbing the walls, suggesting elaborate ways to infiltrate the border, which only stressed Tom out more. Everyone's reactions had been so varied that he couldn't begin to fathom telling his own mother, Judith, once a highly regarded art history professor who was now suffering from Alzheimer's in a care home. The news would only confuse and upset her, and inevitably, he would have to tell her again and again.

Maybe we could fly to Switzerland and drive down? Lauren texted, but Tom was so numb he didn't know what to say. He could barely tie his shoelaces, let alone figure out how to choreograph an intricate border crossing. He sat down at my mother's kitchen table and dropped his head into his hands, replaying our final exchange, the marble cold against his elbows. If only there were some way I could tell him I was there beside him, though no longer able to hold his hand. All through our marriage, and even more so before, I'd always wanted to know what Tom was truly thinking, and now it seemed I could.

*

Tom had just hung up the phone with the funeral director when my mother emerged from her bedroom, frail and sepulchral in her thin, white silk robe, her lip naked of its signature red. The call had been somewhat tricky, not just because of its subject but also because the gentleman didn't speak very much English. Tom was drinking a glass of water at the kitchen sink, steeling himself for the task ahead, as my mother came into the kitchen.

"I'm going to meet with the coffin—people, they are—they are helping with the flights, the organization of the—the coffins, back to London," he said. My mother padded past Tom and made her way to the stove, where she began putting coffee grounds in her little green-and-red Bialetti.

"Pourquoi?" she said. The pilot clicked, then ignited. Through the kitchen window, the neighbor watered her rosemary on the balcony, exhaling cigarette smoke into a cloudless blue sky. "To get back to England?" she said in perfect English. It was funny how my mother's capability to speak English was catalyzed by the idea of not getting what she wanted.

"I don't want them going back in some box," he said. "Honor—Honor would have wanted that for Chloe. For her to have a place to be."

"Non, non. That won't be necessary," she said, her voice rising. Tom's jaw clenched. As much as Tom didn't want to fight with my mother—not now, of all times—he knew I would've wanted him to stick up for me.

"Honor wanted to be buried in England. We—we discussed it. She bought two plots beside her dad, so that she could—so that she could be next to him." Just saying these words made Tom's innards contract. He knew how important those visits to my father's grave were. How I blamed myself for dreaming in bed that night while an aneurysm popped in his brain downstairs.

Tom hadn't eaten in days, and the sensation of his body clamping onto emptiness pained him. As the coffee percolated and boiled, the pervasive smell of burning grounds, reminiscent of the thick smoke that horrifying morning, made him woozy. He thought again of the moments after the bomb went off—the alarms blaring, the little girl in rainbow pajamas running down the stairs ahead of him at the Ritz. Someone else's little girl. Was that little girl alone in the world now too? Had she found her mother? Did her father manage to save her?

"My daughter is French," she said. "She should be buried here in France with her mother."

"Colette," he said. "Are you asking me to bury my wife and my daughter in a country that, as you might have gathered, I have very little desire to ever visit again?" Tom's voice broke. I could see the veins in his neck becoming strident. "Why can't we just do what Honor wants? For once? Would it be that hard? She wanted to be buried beside Richard." My mother looked up at him, stunned. The Bialetti shook in her hand as she poured coffee into her demi-tasse cup.

"And how will I see her?" she asked, as if Tom were suggesting I get buried on the moon. It was somewhat baffling watching my mother fighting for my company now that it was no longer available. When Chloe and I were alive, she'd never once joined us on our summer holidays, despite my numerous invitations, but now she couldn't get enough of me. Did she have big ideas of us convening at my grave on Sundays with a thermos of hot choccy and a packet of digestives?

"The same way you *always* could have, Colette, but never bothered to," he said.

"You're a very cruel man," she said. Tom took his coat off the stand and left, slamming the door behind him.

The bracing cold of the December air hit the back of Tom's throat as soon as he stepped outside. He zipped up his coat and put his hands in his pockets, finding a hair band of mine and squeezing it between his fingers. Adrenaline surged through his battered system. Though the funeral parlor was over a mile away, he decided to walk, telling himself to keep going, that each step and task might make him feel different. At every corner, there were hordes of armed police, who had seemingly sprung up across Paris overnight.

As he turned onto Avenue du Pere, he passed a billboard for Swiss watches showing an intact family all laughing in a fancy car. Other posters advertised antiaging creams promising to stop life in its tracks. The same thoughts kept penetrating his mind. Had I been aware of what was happening? Did I have time to pull Chloe towards me? It seemed just moments ago that we were in bed together at the Ritz. If he had only known it would be our last night. If only he'd taken my hand instead of sulking in the bathroom. If only he'd gone with us downstairs. And considering that my mother was of no help, was there somewhere on the way to the coffin maker where he could buy a French pocket dictionary, the one I always teased him about needing?

But walking that morning, Tom felt relieved at how little grasp he had of the language. He didn't want to overhear another recounting of the attack or read about it in a newspaper headline. He didn't want to imagine, even for a millisecond, how frightened we must have been at the moment of impact. With each stride, he kept trying to push away the image of Chloe and where she might have been standing when the bomb's shrapnel blew her into a thousand little pieces.

When Tom finally arrived at the funeral parlor, Alain, the coffin maker, shook Tom's hand and quickly ushered him into the front room. The furniture seemed intentionally sparse: a vinyl sofa against the wall and a large desk with a vase of lilies—my least favorite flower. They made everything reek of death. Tom sat down on the sofa, but didn't remove his coat; it was cold, and the fire, although laid, wasn't burning. He looked at the clock on the mantelpiece, more out of habit than interest. He no longer cared what time it was. It was as if he knew that from now on, there was just before and after.

"My English is not good," Alain said, opening his soft leather notebook. His tone was gentle now, almost a little self-conscious, which was rare in a Parisian. "But we will try."

"Thank you," Tom said, his voice gravelly. Alain coughed into the back of his hand to clear his throat; the loose-sounding spittle echoed in his chest. He looked as tired as Tom felt. His eyes were yellowing in the corners and his saggy jowl was cut with smoker's lines. He handed Tom a pencil and asked him to write down our names and birth dates as well as the flight number and time of departure back to London Heathrow.

Tom caught sight of Alain's hands—they were crinkly and sunspotted with little, if any, elastane left. It struck Tom, as it would for years to come, that my hands would never look like that, and that Chloe's would never finish growing. Tom picked up the pencil and somehow managed to write down our names without snapping it in two.

Alain put on his glasses and looked at the two names. "Which one was your daughter?" he said, the word catching in the back of his throat as he said it. No matter how many children's coffins one made, it clearly didn't get any easier.

Tom didn't say anything. He pointed to Chloe's name and Alain acknowledged it with a nod and put a star beside it.

"Do you know how tall she was?" Alain said. It took Tom a moment to realize why he wanted to know. Then he remembered that Alain would never know what our bodies once resembled. That to him, the customs officials, and the airline, we would always be that mother and daughter who arrived marked "HAZARD-OUS WASTE" in vacuum-sealed bags.

"No, but . . . I can show you?"

The furrow between Alain's eyebrows deepened. Tom stood up and measured us the only way he knew how.

"My daughter came up to about here," he said, his index finger resting on the fine navy corduroy of his trousers. Alain searched the table for his tape measure, while Tom stood still with his finger on the point where Chloe's head used to rest.

Alain marked the measurements down on the paper beside Chloe's name. "And your wife?" he said. Tom didn't say anything at first, wondering how after all these years he didn't know the answer to such a simple question about me, but that wasn't who I married. Tom only knew the important stuff, like where I'd left my glasses and to order me pad Thai if we were getting a takeaway.

Alain had probably expected Tom to point to a place on his arm to show how tall I was, but instead Tom dropped his head as if to kiss me and felt for a spot on his chest. He tried not to cry as he remembered me whispering *Hymn to Beauty* with my lips pressed up against his, our last night together. *Do you come from Heaven or rise from the abyss / Beauty? Your gaze divine and infernal . . .* Tom coughed to force himself to focus and readjusted his finger on his chest.

"Here," he said. "No, actually . . ." He closed his eyes. "Just— here." When it was clear there was nothing left to say, Tom thanked Alain for his time and turned to leave. Just as he reached the door, he heard the shuffling of feet on the worn wooden planks behind him.

"Sorry," Tom said. He shook his head in embarrassment for nearly walking out without paying. It was my fault really. I dealt with the bills, the taxis, the tips—everything. "How should I pay?" he asked, fiddling around for his wallet, which he found in the back of his trousers where it always was.

Alain went back to his desk and returned with a few stray pieces of paper. He seemed uneasy. Tom recognized that expression. In the days since the explosion, it was all he had seen on the faces of other people. Tom had never realized how much he loathed pity until it was all anybody could offer him. He understood why people opted to become recluses.

Alain passed the paper back and forth between his hands and peered over the rim of his glasses. "Credit card?" he said.

*

A few days later, Tom waited in the queue to check in for his flight to Heathrow. He stood perfectly still between the retractable belt posts, like any other traveler. He wasn't agitated like he normally was at airports, in a hurry for no reason, nor was he intermittently checking the stock market on his BlackBerry.

When the woman behind the check-in desk called "Next!" Tom approached the counter and handed her his emergency passport, the color of rich vanilla ice cream. Just then, an announcement came over the loudspeaker reporting a delayed flight and offering a subtle reminder for passengers not to leave bags unattended in the airport. The woman at the desk barely looked him in the eye. Tom had been anticipating having to explain why he was traveling on an emergency passport. His was cordoned off, trapped in a crime scene with Hedgie and my engagement ring. Only, the lady didn't ask him anything. Instead, she tapped away on her computer with gum-chewing insolence.

"You'll know thirty minutes before boarding if you're on the flight," she said, looking at her watch and ushering the next family to the desk with her long acrylic nails. The father, a red-faced man, carrying a suitcase of a similar color, barged into Tom, practically knocking him over.

"Wait, sorry?" Tom said, but the family behind him were already starting to load their suitcases onto the conveyor belt. The podgy father's T-shirt lifted slightly as he hoisted up the first suitcase, obviously belonging to one of his two little girls. It was baby pink and covered in stickers that Chloe would have liked. Tom stood still, holding his temporary passport, mumbling something that only I would've been able to translate. He waited for the family to finish checking in, then approached the desk again, but the woman was closing her computer now.

"The counter's closed," she informed him.

"Sorry, may I ask before you go? My ticket?"

"You're on standby," she said. She was up from her seat now, pulling the mandatory British Airways blazer off the back of her chair.

"But I can't be—I—I don't understand what you mean."

"It means you're on standby. It means you'll find out thirty minutes before the flight if you're on it. Like I told you before." Tom attempted to gather himself, but even his good looks couldn't hide how frail he was.

"Ermm . . . I'm sorry—but I really need to be on this flight." She leaned her head back with an audible sigh at Tom's simple request. "I have to be on this flight," he repeated.

"Everyone says that. Welcome to the world of standby," she said, pushing her chair under her desk.

"No, you don't understand. It's my family." Tom's voice was shaking now—the idea that we would arrive in England without him was nauseating. "You see, my wife—My child, they are on that flight. They—"

"They are welcome to not get on the flight too, sir. I suggest waiting until you get to the gate. There's nothing I can do for you. My colleague will take over now—if you want, queue up again in the line just there, okay?" And she slammed the CLOSED sign down hard on the blue countertop.

That's when Tom's bottom lip began to quiver, that start of a slow cry that I thought only happened in childhood. In all our years of marriage, I'd never once seen Tom cry, not even when his father told him he loved him for the first time as he was dying of lung cancer in the hospital. He tried to hold it in now, but the tears came anyway, short, choppy sobs streaming down his face in slow motion. The woman froze.

"They can't get off the flight," he said, the saliva webbing in his mouth as he tried to speak. "They aren't in seats. They don't have a ticket." He was gasping for air. "Please . . . please don't make me say it," he said.

The woman reached for the phone atop her desk. Tom shook his head in disbelief over the words he was about to say aloud to a stranger. He wiped his nose on his sleeve again and looked up at the woman with his bloodshot eyes. "They are in the hold. They were . . . They were at the Ritz," he said quietly, but the lady froze, the phone receiver squeezed between her shoulder and ear.

"Security?" she said, her eyes pinned on Tom. "Security? I need an escort, door-to-door." She slammed down the phone and put the lanyard back round her neck.

"I will reissue your boarding card, sir." Her nails were frantic on the keyboard. "And I will escort you personally to the gate."

*

Tom sat rigid on the flight back to England in a row designed for three. He was unrecognizable from the man I'd flown to Paris with nearly two weeks before. He looked feeble, his skin loose around his jaw. When the pilot announced that the crew should prepare for landing, Tom watched as seat belts were fastened and the galley loudly stowed. His body braced for something he couldn't comprehend. Landing. Landing would make it final. Landing meant driving home without us, leaving him perennially grounded, like a swift without flight. Tom's muscle memory hadn't caught up to speed yet; he still found himself habitually checking round for Chloe, reaching for my hand as the wheels touched down.

When the airplane pulled into its allocated slot, Tom's Black-Berry started to vibrate inside his bag. He'd forgotten to turn it off. He took it out, looking at it as if he had never seen a phone before, and without even checking to see who it was, declined the call. He sat waiting as suitcases were aggressively yanked from overhead bins. Tom used to be first off the plane, but not today. There was no queue jump or special treatment for people carrying dead family in the hold.

Tom was making his way down the aisle when a passenger behind him pointed out that a gentleman three rows back was attempting to get his attention.

"Sir! Excuse me! Excuse me! Your phone! You left it on the seat." The man waved Tom's BlackBerry proudly above his head, excited by his very public act of service. But he needn't have bothered. Tom looked back behind him and said, in something close to a whisper:

"I know."

*

When Tom arrived home, the whole house was silent, yet everything spoke. It was as if the house had been burgled but it wasn't the contents that'd been stolen, it was the context. Tom stood in the quiet of our hallway. But it wasn't our home anymore. Chloe's train set wasn't out to trip over, and her laughter wasn't echoing. There wasn't a wand to pick up in her wake, or a Disney film to negotiate.

Tom opened the door to the drawing room. The brass doorknob was cold in his hand. The sofa cushions were too tidy, and I wasn't propped in my usual seat with my feet on the ottoman, red pen in hand, looking over proposed illustrations for my latest book, or watching *Absolutely Fabulous*.

When he went into the kitchen, the fridge door resembled a shrine to a life he no longer had. There were lists everywhere, all in my handwriting, including my last one:

- *Book Louvre?*
- *Hedgie! DO NOT FORGET!*
- *Passports*
- *Order Duke's dog food x2*
- *~~DON'T FORGET CAMERA!~~*
- *Wrap Tom's present*

There's too much stuff on this fridge. I can barely open it, Tom could vaguely recall himself saying, though now he wished there were more clutter. The kitchen didn't look right. My half-finished cup of coffee wasn't on the table, nor was my navy cashmere jumper hanging over the back of one of the kitchen chairs.

It was as if Tom was only just noticing our house's grand proportions. The drawing room with its double-height Palladian doors leading out to the courtyard, the crystal chandelier in the hallway that I bought at auction in Paris. The Christmas tree I had decorated with Chloe, sequined stars and velvet baubles held on with tartan string. The rooms had never seemed quite so cavernous and austere to him when all of us were living there.

Tom walked up the stairs, noticing the absence of my usual pile of debris, odd socks of Chloe's, and fresh tubes of toothpaste, all waiting to be taken up on my next run. As he proceeded along the hall towards our bedroom, he avoided Chloe's room altogether, just as he avoided looking at the gallery of black-and-white photographs lining his path: Chloe in Corfu, her goggles askew; Tom and me in New York; Chloe and Tom, standing by last year's tree in Paris.

He opened the door to our bedroom. There were my reading glasses propped on my bedside table, exactly where I said I'd left them. He held them by their arms, careful not to touch the lenses and risk smudging away my fingerprints. I'd been so cross with myself for leaving them behind. How silly that all seemed now.

Rather than switching on my bedside lamp, he sat down in the waning daylight on my side of the bed and ran his fingers over the spines of a few of my books. Some of them I'd read; most of them I hadn't. He pulled out one of my favorites—*Stoner*, by John Williams. He'd told me to read it, told me I'd love it. I did love it. He was usually right about those types of things. He turned the pages and found my grainy leather bookmark inside, with the word "Mummy" embossed in Chloe's writing on the back, my final Mother's Day present.

He opened my bedside drawer. His eyes were immediately drawn to the little blue Smythson box patiently waiting for me to bring in the New Year. I'd had the same style of diary since I was seventeen. It was always bright red, with my initials stamped in gold in the bottom right-hand corner. The only change over the years was to my second initial after we got married. He unraveled the navy ribbon and removed the lid of the box, then peeled back the tissue paper doors; the ribbon tail was hanging loose, lost without a page to mark.

He held my diary in his hands. It felt so much like me, yet there wasn't a trace. He fanned the pages, but they were blank. No ink stains, smudges, or torn pages, the leather not yet beaten from a year's mileage. Not like my others. There would be no birthdays, no canceled meetings, no promises. Still, he couldn't help flicking through one more time. All it did was force him through a kaleidoscope of memories: when he tried to teach me to ski, our first date at the River Cafe by the bright pink pizza oven, my empty coffee cups left in every room of the house.

Tom closed my diary and walked into our bathroom, through our walk-in wardrobe where our clothes hung on either side, the wardrobe Tom had teased me about because I used Carrie Bradshaw's as my reference for the architect. My hats were piled high, my shoes the same. Tom didn't feel for my clothes or brush past the things he knew were my everyday favorites. Instead, he stood in front of the bathroom mirror, disturbed by the unfamiliarity of his own features.

His hand hesitated over my bathroom cabinet, barely opening it before slamming it shut. He tried to steady himself. When he opened it again, he didn't recognize any of the bottles by their appearance. Only by their scent could he intimately navigate every inch of my body. One by one he opened the lids. First was a little white pot with everything written in French: neck, nighttime, a mixture of almonds and *Newsnight*. Then, a bottle of yellow rose oil: Chloe, and the maternity ward. With the rose oil still in his hand, he picked up a porcelain jar with all the branding rubbed off. It was my secret antiaging cream. Night after night, when I was alive, I had looked at my deepening crow's-feet with such disdain before I went to bed. I hadn't realized just how lucky I was to have them. Aging had been marketed all wrong. The world seemed to prioritize a regimented skincare routine over the wonder of getting old.

There was one other bottle he tried hard to ignore, but whose presence drew him. It was every kiss, every night out, every night in, every day for as long as he could remember. Tom reached for my bottle of Chanel Sycomore and held it in his hands. It had lingered in the air that morning after I'd left him when he hadn't followed me. He could see me ripping off the lid aggressively during our last argument. Now, holding the bottle, anticipating the gut-wrenching reaction he knew he was going to have, he pulled off the magnetic top, but before he even had a chance to put it to his nose, he doubled over the sink, his body convulsing with an almost primeval yearning. Nobody on earth has the constitution to metabolize the sudden and terrific loss of unconditional love.

Tom didn't know how long he sat huddled on the bathroom floor, gripping the lid of my perfume, alternating between thoughts of murder or suicide, wishing that he'd been standing beside us and that the last thing he'd seen on this earth were my eyes and Chloe's button nose. The only thing worse than surviving our death was living with it. He looked up at the bathroom cabinet. How long would it take to be reunited with us? How quickly could he get there? How much paracetamol would it take? Tom had never been a religious person, but in that moment, huddled on the bath mat, he knelt and prayed:

"Please, God," he said, squeezing his eyes so hard they ached. "Please, please, please awaken me from this dream. I cannot take a single moment more."

*

A little after four o'clock, the phone rang in our bedroom. Tom didn't move, waiting for the answering machine to pick up. The voice that came through wasn't Lauren checking up on him for the ninth time, or yet another colleague calling to say how sorry they were. Instead, it was some woman, her tone so loud and upbeat that for the first few moments Tom assumed it was a cold caller. But then she said my name.

"Hello, good afternoon. I'm calling for a . . . Mrs. Honor Wharton? This is Hayley from London Fertility Partners." Tom's body didn't move. But ever so slowly his eyes began to drift towards the phone. "We've been calling your mobile—and I believe your husband's?—for the past few days but all the lines seem to be dead. We have some *very, very exciting* news from Dr. Chung about the results of your surrogate Jess's pregnancy test. She said she's been trying you too but had no luck either. Please call us back when you can."

Tom sat there stunned. The phone call I'd waited for all these years had come too late. The pipes groaned and clunked as the underfloor heating turned on beneath him. I had it set on an automatic timer for five o'clock, when I would lock the door to the bathroom and have my evening bath. Tom was going to have our baby, even though I was dead. He could no longer flirt with the end. Was this cruel or was this a saving grace?

CHAPTER THREE

The morning of the funeral, my mother arrived at Tom's house wearing a midnight-blue two-piece, smoking a cigarette. Even though it pained me to admit it, her dark brown eyes suited a mourning palette. She'd landed at Heathrow a few days before, and after spending one night at the house, had decided to check into Claridge's because the mattress in our guest bedroom wasn't hard enough. Caught in a puff of my mother's cigarette smoke, Tom was reminded of just how different we were. It never ceased to amaze him how two people could share the same DNA yet little else.

While Tom fixed his tie in the hallway mirror, my mother stood outside on the stoop in her dark glasses. It had rained earlier that day, and the sky was white with streaks of gray. Tom closed the front door behind him and put his keys in his pocket. He extended his arm for my mother, but she barely responded to his polite gesture, as if this attention were her right. She was the opposite of

Tom's mother, who had shared her carrot cake with me at Fortnum's the first time we met.

My mother sat despondent beside Tom in the car as it followed our hearses to the church. Tom stared at the black leather headrest in front of him. He was deathly pale, his face cadaverous, especially in comparison with my mother's, which had always resembled a carved marshmallow, plump and held high by finely sliced cheekbones, all carefully preserved with French moisturizers and a vampiric approach to sunlight.

Tom put down the window; the smell of my mother's perfume combined with the stale cigarette smoke clinging to her jacket was nauseating. He watched as the branches on the passing trees wrestled with the intermittent wind. How had our funeral arrived so soon when the days seemed to pass so slowly? It reminded Tom of a quote I'd often say when Chloe was teething and I was moody— *"The days are long, but the years are short"*—which used to annoy him. But now he'd learned the hard way just how true that was. Everything was just a click away from the past tense.

Outside the church, mourners had already started gathering in an accumulation of tailored black cotton and polyester. Tom stared into his lap, willing himself to move, before the undertaker opened the door, letting in the order of the day with a smack of Baltic air. My mother gathered her bag and pushed her glasses up the bridge of her nose. She unfolded herself out of the car, her face stern.

Tom and the other pallbearers stood by the hearse, waiting to receive Chloe's tiny coffin, which was covered in a spray of dusky pink hydrangeas. The world was silent. It was Tuesday, but not a Tuesday Tom knew, with buttered toast, and finding Chloe's lunch box and kissing me goodbye at the front door. It was the day he was burying his murdered wife and daughter.

Tom hefted the box containing his baby's body onto his shoulder, a spot she'd occupied a little under a month ago when she was still alive in Heathrow Airport and refusing to walk to the gate.

"I've got you, Coco," he said to the box, so quietly that only she and I could hear it. As Tom and Oliver and the other pallbearers proceeded through the arched wooden doors of the church, passersby on the other side of the flint wall stopped to remove their winter hats. Chloe's coffin was a horrific sight for anyone; you didn't need to know the little girl inside to feel it.

The church glimmered with candles and resounded with the lugubrious tones of an ancient, wheezing organ. Tom held himself rigid in the front pew, confronted by the unfathomable sight of his two girls in coffins, side by side. My mother was next to him, staring up at the crucifix hanging above the altar, a flat expression on her face, as if she were waiting for the 38 bus. Annie slid in beside her, followed by Oliver and Lauren. Annie's eyes looked dark, her skin pasty, especially in comparison with Lauren's, who always looked as though she'd been plunged into a trough of St. Tropez.

For the service, Annie had picked all my favorite flowers in Chloe's favorite colors. There were no lilies festooning the windows. Earlier in the week, she'd called Tom to say she was inviting the children from Chloe's class to her garden nursery to make their own flower baskets, which were now prominently displayed on the altar, each one a mix of white roses and Icelandic poppies, the sacred flower of the dead for the ancient Greeks.

"The flowers look beautiful," Oliver said to Annie, squeezing her hand. He took off his horn-rimmed glasses and cleaned them on the flap of his dark jacket. Annie fiddled with her gold necklace, which she always did when she was uncomfortable, her copper-brown hair in a low ponytail. Oliver was right: Whether it was flowers, clothes, or art, no one had better taste than Annie, something I'd admired about her the day we met in the library at Cambridge. She'd outdone herself today; my funeral looked better than my wedding, though there were a couple of attendees I would have chopped from the list.

The door to the church opened, letting in a rush of cold air as my agent, Eva, walked in followed by Angus, my favorite local bookshop proprietor, who sat down tentatively beside her.

"Do *not* let that ghastly Penelope Painter sit anywhere near me," she said to her husband as they took their seats at the back of the church. "What is she doing here anyway? Honor couldn't stand her."

It was a good question. Why *was* Penelope Painter at my funeral? When we'd met at the Hay Festival a few years ago, she'd been keen to tell me she would need to undergo a lobotomy to write a children's book about a family of ice creams. I nodded along through gritted teeth, listening to her tell me everything she thought I needed to know about my genre, even though *I* was the successful children's book author. She didn't appreciate the wonder of writing for children and seemed to be under the illusion that these stories could be knocked out before breakfast.

"Penelope's been ringing the office nonstop trying to get ahold of me," my agent said. "Maybe I'm missing the point, but I can't sell an eight-hundred-page book on the anatomy of a spoon."

As titillating as it was to discover that Penelope Painter had been on my agent's case, I was far more interested in what Annie and Lauren were going on about. Maybe they'd get on better now that I was dead and finally stop bickering like a pair of teenage siblings.

"I *really* didn't need to see Daniel today," Lauren said to Oliver. "Is he looking over? Is my mascara okay?"

"Yes," Oliver said, which was prudent, considering the industrial-grade application.

"Yes he's looking over or yes to my mascara? I told him not to come. Who wants to see their cheating soon-to-be-ex-husband at the funeral of their best friend? He's not with *her*, is he?"

Oliver looked at Annie for help, but all she did was roll her eyes. Though Oliver was probably the cleverest of Tom's friends, he was ill-equipped to engage with female nuance. Not that anything about Lauren was particularly subtle. In the early days of their relationship, we'd all rather liked Daniel. He doted on Lauren, but I'd find him to be a colossal drag at times. A frequent occupier of the middle ground, the ideal companion for an industrial entertainer like Lauren. But at least he was good with numbers. A typical square. So, it was quite a surprise when she discovered the second family he'd been procuring on the side.

"It's a strange thing to say, but Honor would have loved this so much," Oliver said. Annie's eyes filled with tears as the organ forced sour, moldy air through its pipes. "And let's be honest, she'd be so relieved not to have to write thank-you letters to all the attendees." Annie smiled weakly. Oliver was right: I did loathe writing thank-you cards, and often completely forgot.

But Tom wouldn't have to worry about life's formalities, the tedious protocols of being alive. The thank-you notes, the endless RSVPs, the small talk at cocktail parties. He would be excused from every convention moving forward. He had the widower card now.

"I can't look," Lauren said, attempting to navigate the stiff, lace veil of her pillbox hat as she blew her nose into a tissue.

Tom pressed the heels of his hands into his eyes until he saw spots. The door was still open, the cold air catching on his ankles. He could hear Lauren saying his name in that broken, pitiful tone. He needed air, fresh air, air that didn't contain our dead bodies. He stood up, and was walking towards the door just as Jess, our surrogate, was entering the church, in a dark trouser suit, her hair pulled tightly off her face. He could feel everyone watching as they embraced.

"I'm so sorry, Tom," she said, her face red. The organist paused, and a hush swept over the church.

"I'm really glad you came," he said. "Was the drive okay? Are you feeling all right?"

"Yes, I feel fine. The drive was fine. Thank you. Tom, I don't—"

"You don't need to say anything, but please come and sit with us," Tom said. "In the front." His voice was quiet. On any other day, Jess most likely would have protested; she didn't like any special treatment or attention. But what was the protocol for this particularly niche situation? Tom could hear the clack of his shoes and Jess's sensible heels echoing on the stone floor, like a clock in a Bergman film, which was a reference I would have made if I'd been there, and Tom would have laughed and pretended he knew what I was talking about. Would he always hear my jokes in his head? My incessant literary references and unsought opinions?

When Jess and Tom reached the front pew, everyone shifted to make room, including my mother, who reluctantly shuffled down the bench, mostly likely more concerned with what everybody else would be thinking than what Tom wanted. What was everyone going to make of this middle-aged woman sitting beside Tom at his wife and child's funeral? Did I have a secret sister? Was she a long-lost lover of Tom's? Tom didn't care. Jess was carrying the single reason he was able to get out of bed that morning.

As the service began, Tom didn't think of all the things we were no longer able to do. He couldn't. Instead, he thought about how fortunate he was to have known us at all. Every traffic jam and every bitterly cold, early morning school run we'd spent de-icing the windscreen had been anything but an inconvenience. How he longed to bicker with me about eating biscuits in our bed and to negotiate with Chloe about eating all her peas. How cold I would have been in the church, how much I would have loved Annie's eulogy and enjoyed hearing her stories of our salad days at university.

Somehow, Tom got through his own eulogy, even our make-up poem that I hadn't had the chance to recite after our fight that harrowing final morning. *Do you come from Heaven or rise from the abyss / Beauty? Your gaze, divine and infernal . . .*

When everyone rose to sing "Holy God, We Praise Thy Name," Tom tried his best not to cry. But as he heard the swell of voices joining together for "All in heav'n above adore Thee," he could no longer hold back his tears. He knew what came next. He didn't need to reference the order of service. Once we were in the ground there would be no more funeral arrangements or quiet, awkward meetings with the vicar about hymn selections. There were no paths back to us now.

After the service, Tom followed our coffins outside, where he was immediately beset by everyone competing to say the right thing in a different, more heartfelt way. Thoughts and prayers were offered in abundance, even though no one attending was likely to pray for him beyond this afternoon. He nodded and said "Thank you," shaking countless hands and looking into countless tearful eyes, at times finding himself comforting other mourners. These same people would go home and tell themselves to be more grateful for their mothers or more patient with their children. But they would all quickly forget and return to their ordinary lives as Tom's was buried deep in the earth.

As Annie and Lauren were leaving the church, they collided with Daniel, coming out of his row. He smiled, and Annie nodded curtly, hurrying along Lauren, who turned her head with dramatic flair and got her heel caught on the lip of a stone slab, almost tripping before she steadied herself on Annie's arm.

"It's going to be interesting to watch you navigate the terrain with those heels once we're outside," Annie whispered to Lauren, which made Lauren laugh despite the circumstances.

Lauren always looked as though she was wearing clothes she'd only bought the day before. Today's funereal "look" was likely intended to be *respectful yet sensual, fervent mourner,* but without a boyfriend to dictate the direction she had ended up looking like a cross between Nanny McPhee and a youthful, lamenting Pamela Anderson.

Tom followed the vicar into the churchyard, onto the grass. Everyone gathered round, squinting in the harsh, unflattering English light.

My mother never brought me to visit my father's grave. As far as I knew, she was only visiting him for the first time now. She didn't know that the most beautiful season here was early spring, when the churchyard was covered in drifts of white snowdrops and the swallows were nesting in the cracks of the flint wall. She had moved back to Paris after he died, promptly sending me to boarding school only three weeks after we buried him. Somehow, the cold, impenetrable fish had outlived us both. But she hadn't always been so chilly. It was only once my father was gone that something calcified in her, that she became skeletal and emaciated, a drastic shift that seemed to happen overnight.

Standing in the chalky soil, Annie took Lauren's hand, a show of affection that was rare between the two of them. I'd always been the common denominator in our triumvirate, the glue that held the three of us together, since we'd met at Cambridge. But now they would have to find their feet without me, discover a new equilibrium, which would be a considerable task in Lauren's heels, already sinking two inches deep into the ground.

Just as the sun broke through the clouds, Tom looked into the hole that would soon contain his entire world. Our wonderful housekeeper, Rita, stood alone with her head down, the order of service tucked in her bag. Annie and Oliver—who for such a tall man seemed so small today—bolstered themselves on either side of Tom as the pallbearers signaled that they were ready to bury us.

Tom didn't cry as we were slowly lowered into the ground. It wasn't because he had made a conscious decision to be strong or to move on in an orderly manner for everyone else's sake. But after the phone call with Dr. Chung confirmed that he was going to have a baby, it was as if airport-dad mode had suddenly been installed. There was no time to grieve. Had there not been that tiny sign of life, he would've climbed into the grave with us and never come out.

*

Eight months later, Tom stood with Jess outside John Lewis department store on Oxford Street, wondering if it had always been covered in so many lights. When I'd done the big baby shop for Chloe, he'd been standing outside too, only then he'd been on his phone, busy with an acquisition, not staring at the doors, unsure if he had the strength to push through.

"Come on," Jess said. "We've only got two hours in the car park." Tom followed her into the store and up the escalators to the baby department, a paean to the painfully privileged, shelf after shelf stocked to the brim with brightly colored landfill that would one day most likely wash up on a beach in Antigua. Tom must have walked by thirty different types of monitors, all insisting on high definition and reliability, sterilizers of all shapes and sizes promising to kill 99.9 percent of harmful bacteria.

"How is it possible to need all of this stuff?" he asked Jess, surveying the vast array of baby paraphernalia. It was a sincere question that any semiconscious person might ask standing among the supposed necessities for a baby's room. Lauren, Annie, and Jess had been taking on these preparatory tasks in turns—tasks that were tedious and exhausting at the best of times, but especially excruciating for Tom, given the circumstances. But still, he'd refused Lauren's constant offers to "do the nursery," and now he found himself here for the second time with Jess—kind, practical Jess, heavily pregnant, her ankles swollen, leaning on the trolley that was beginning to fill up with things Lauren had deemed essential and Jess considered utterly ridiculous.

"What is a Bumbo floor booster?" Jess said, consulting the list. "Who wrote this?"

"Lauren," Tom said, looking at the down escalator and wondering how quickly he could escape. He hadn't shaved in a few days, and his navy coat hung baggy on his shoulders, making him seem gaunter than he was.

"I thought so," Jess said. "You don't need half of this." She folded the list and put it in her pocket while Tom took over the trolley, doing his best to control its lack of suspension. The two of them had already attempted and failed at this expedition, and even in his fog Tom knew they were running out of time. The baby could come any day now.

"Let's just get the essentials crossed off. Pram, cot, and car seat," Jess said, counting the three on her fingers. Her nails were short and carefully manicured, painted a white shiny nude, the same shade she was wearing the day we met. She took off her puffer jacket and flung it inside the trolley before rubbing the base of her back.

"Do you want to sit down?" Tom said.

"No, do you?" Jess replied.

"No."

"Okay, so car seats," she said, waddling on. "I'll meet you over there—I need to pee again."

To a casual observer, Tom's lack of interest in his surroundings and seeming coldness towards Jess could have come across as any old boredom, or relative dickishness. These were the mundane errands of parenthood, but for Tom, every mum who walked by with a toddler was a reminder we weren't going to be there when he got home. I wasn't going to ask him if he wanted another cup of tea or tease him about how long it had taken to put together the pram.

"Good afternoon, sir! Can I help at all?" asked a member of staff appearing out of one of the aisles. She readjusted the badge on her T-shirt, which spelled out HEATHER: ASK ME FOR HELP! in bold letters. She was petite and smiley, with too much blush on her cheeks, and in the strip lighting her hair appeared as though it needed a good wash. Tom looked for Jess; she had the list.

"Erm, pram . . . ?" Tom said, reading her name tag.

"Perfect—follow me."

Heather led him to the pageant of prams, where she began talking at great speed about the various models, each promising a slightly different, nearly unattainable lifestyle no new parent had ever experienced, even with a squadron of nannies and both sets of in-laws.

"Did you have anything specific in mind? Pram-wise?" Heather asked. Tom didn't seem to understand the question; he just stared at her as though she were speaking Polari. The only thing he knew about prams was that Chloe's had been yellow. As Heather babbled on, Tom watched as a man walked by, thumb-typing on his BlackBerry, making the same mistake he had, looking at his phone instead of into his wife's eyes.

"Okay, so, we have this Bugaboo Cameleon," Heather said. "Very simple, very nice colors—fits in the car nicely too."

Jess reappeared from the loo and turned over the price tag of the pram Heather was suggesting. Her eyes briefly flashed, though she said nothing. An expectant mother rubbing her tummy in an orange jumper began considering one of the models, pushing it back and forth on the lino floor.

"This one is famous for an easy fold-down," Heather continued. There was something about the way she said it that made Tom think of all the times I'd complained about how difficult it was to manage Chloe's pram. I'd go on and on about how much I hated it, never once thinking to read the instructions to find out how it was supposed to go down. I got into the habit of just putting it in the car whole, too embarrassed to fail in front of other more capable mothers in the car park.

When was he ever going to stop thinking about us? Was every purchase for the rest of his life going to be this painful? Were we going to be there at every turn? I even occupied his dreams. Grief's iron grip never weakens. You just become accustomed to its hand around your throat, moving forward but never moving on.

"Right, there we go," Heather said, clipping the last of the supposedly easy levers into a formation requiring an engineering degree. "Do you want to have a go? Get a feel for it?" Tom hesitated but gave it a go anyway. "People love this one," she continued. "Very popular. Especially with the celebs."

"It's also two thousand pounds," Jess announced, before taking an apple out of her handbag and crunching a loud bite. The shop was getting busy, with smiley couples and bossy mothers-in-law taking a range of display prams out for a whirl. "Do you want me to show your wife how it works as well?" Heather asked Tom.

Her question hung there, suspended above them, unanswered. For a moment, it seemed as if the blunder were going to pass. Tom carried on, trying to dismantle the pram, neither he nor Jess saying anything, while Heather continued commentating from the sidelines: "Cup holder goes on the side too. That's extra but very handy. And it's got adjustable handles, so whether you or your wife's pushing, it's easy to change—"

"Please, could you stop saying 'my wife,'" Tom said, slamming the pram to the floor.

The color drained from Heather's face, leaving behind only the exaggerated streak of her synthetic blush.

The mother-to-be in the orange jumper looked on in horror at Tom's histrionic display. Perhaps he seemed like a man with unjustified rage losing his temper at a sales assistant in front of his pregnant wife. She would tell this story later to her friends, with her own narrative additions for dramatic effect about "the man in John Lewis who lost his temper."

"Stop gawking," Jess hissed at her. "Mind your own business." She put her hand on Tom's shoulder, but he shrugged her off. None of this was logical. Among all the parenting books peppered around the shop, there was no guide titled *How to Buy a Pram for the Surrogate Baby of Your Slaughtered Wife*. You couldn't grow out of it or sleep-train it away. Nothing could bring Chloe and me back to life.

Heather reached round her belt for her radio, most likely to call for security, but paused when she saw the tears rolling down Tom's cheeks.

"I'm sorry," he said to no one. "But I don't have a wife anymore." It was the first time Tom had articulated the horrible truth aloud. "And this pram, this impossible thing I can't even close, is for a baby we made together. He's not even breathing yet, and he's lost his mother and his sister." Tom stepped back from the pram, like a lion cub from a fire. "I don't want to do this. I can't do this. I can't do this fucking pram!"

Tom headed for the exit, narrowly avoiding two pensioners who had got off on the wrong floor. He made his way through the slow-moving hordes of dawdling Saturday shoppers, past the toasters and the table settings, until he was running down the escalators. Jess abandoned the trolley and followed behind, clearly fighting the urge to run, perhaps more conscious than ever of her precious cargo.

"Tom, wait!" she shouted, clutching the rubber banister. "Tom!" she said, pushing through the torrent of people, her eye on his head below as it moved towards the exit.

By the time Jess spotted Tom on Oxford Street, he had started to calm down somewhat and was standing on the edge of the curb, staring off into nothing. The sky overhead reflected the typical gray of a foggy London morning. Flashy cars shot past, their exhausts loud and obnoxious, something Tom used to complain about incessantly but now didn't notice.

"Tom," Jess said. "Tom," she repeated, trying to catch her breath.

"I can't do it, Jess. I can't do the pram. I can't do any of it," he said, shaking his head like Chloe refusing to eat her broccoli. His handsome face crumpled with despair while people moved all around them, oblivious and uninterested. Tom's coat was hanging off him and Jess did her best to bring it back over his shoulder. "I can't do this on my own. I don't want to do this without my family," he continued.

Jess paused, then said, "I promise you: You can." She took both his shoulders in her hands and forced him to look at her. "You will never fix what's been mercilessly shattered, and I'm so sorry for that. I wish I could fix it. I wish I had a magic wand to bring back Honor and Chloe, but I can't do anything for you besides this. This baby is coming. You've been given a gift, and you must take it. You survived, Tom. I don't know why, but what I do know is that this baby will change everything, because for some reason, they always bloody do. I don't know how, I don't know why, but they do."

The car park's lights came on as the two of them walked below the sensor. A pungent smell of urine lined the stairwell. Jess huffed as she reached the last step, having refused to take the lift. Tom opened Jess's door and took her bag as she got into his Defender.

"Are you sure you're okay to drive?" she said.

"Yes, thank you. I'm okay now," he said.

"Are you sure?"

"Yes," Tom said. "I'm sure."

"Good, because I think my water just broke."

CHAPTER FOUR

FOUR YEARS LATER

All through our marriage, women used to love telling me how good-looking my husband was. On the rare occasion Tom joined me to drop off Chloe at preschool, mothers who generally ignored me would come trampolining over to tell me how great he looked and how tired my eyes seemed. Tom was already a hot commodity on the playground when I was alive, so with the open position minus my presence, you had yourself an out-of-control equity. Tom would struggle to find a soul for miles who didn't know what happened to him in Paris, who hadn't been shown my obituary, or seen my photograph hanging in the bookshop. Nothing got the mums creaming their knick-knacks more than a grieving, handsome widower turned full-time single dad.

Henry ran ahead of Tom in his little winter blazer towards the shiny, red-painted school gates, his tractor lunch box bashing against his knee. One of the main reasons I chose Chloe's preschool was because I adored the uniform—the maroon blazers in winter

and the straw hats in summer. Since I died, Tom had been following my unwritten manual to a T; everything needed my seal of
approval. It wasn't just Henry's school that was the same as Chloe's.
It was my preferred milk, my brand of tea, and my Boston ferns
dotted around the courtyard.

For October, the weather in London was surprisingly mild, the
leaves on the trees like a thick orange sail catching in the wind.
Tom and Henry were the first to arrive in Henry's classroom, which
wasn't unusual for Tom—unlike Chloe and me, who generally inched
forward with the other slovenly latecomers.

"Good morning, Henry," Miss Rose said, pushing Henry's thick
chestnut hair off his forehead and smiling down at his cherubic
face. "I just checked on your painting! And guess what?"

"What?" Henry said, his eyes wide. If perfection existed, it was
Henry. It wasn't just his big-boy haircut now that he was four. It
was also his slight lisp and the way he pronounced the word "instructions" when he and Tom were building something with Lego.

"It's dry!'" Miss Rose said. "Shall we go and have a look at it?"
Henry nodded before saying goodbye to his daddy. Tom blew him
a kiss and checked Henry's cubbyhole to make sure he hadn't forgotten anything: a waterproof in case it rained, an extra snack, and
a tube of sun cream—which was optimistic for the time of year, but
Tom liked to be prepared for every eventuality.

After he said his goodbyes, Tom attempted to sneak out of Henry's classroom unseen, but the Vultures at the school gates had already started circling. Tom had heard enough from me over the
years to know about school-gate protocol. He knew how to avoid
coffee mornings and to recognize the telltale signs of being groomed
for weekend volunteering. But as he stepped into the car park, Tom
could see Luke's mother, Lily, coming in hot. Lily had always had
her eye on Tom, even when I was alive, but she was even more
blatant about her intentions now that I was dead.

"Oh, Tom?" she said as he walked by. London was on the

turn, the autumn leaves coating the tarmac in a carpet of copper and burnt orange. "I wanted to ask if I could bother you for your *scrumptious* chocolate brownie recipe." Lily was doing her best to catch up to Tom's pace, but the three-inch heels she'd chosen for drop-off were proving a little ambitious, even for her.

"I think it's Nigella," he said, pulling himself inside his Defender for safety. Duke sat panting on the front seat. "The book has a picture of a cupcake on the front. I think it's called *Goddess* something—*Domestic Goddess*! I'll scan it for you."

"Or . . . what are you doing now? I could pop over for a quick coffee and take a peek?"

I wasn't sure what Lily wanted to pop over to "take a peek" at, but I don't think it involved Nigella Lawson's cupcakes.

"I would, but I have to take Duke to the vet," Tom said, feigning disappointment. Duke's eyes widened and darted from side to side. "Another time maybe?" Tom turned on the engine and reversed out of his parking space. Cars and children were arriving at all angles. "I'll see you at pickup!" Tom shouted through the window as he drove off. "Sheesh, she's relentless," he said to Duke when they'd stopped at the lights. "Don't worry, my boy, there's no vet appointment."

Tom turned up the radio and hummed along to the Cranberries while Duke stuck his snout out of the window. His muzzle had started to turn gray, like the tips of Tom's hair. They were quite the pair. I couldn't blame Lily for taking a run at them.

The drive home from school had become almost rote. The wonderful tedium of the day—its banal rituals, the opening of Henry's half-picked-at lunch box after school, tipping out the crumbs and planning out dinner—grounded him. After our funeral, Tom had immediately sold his hedge fund, securing a comfortable financial future for himself and Henry. I'd quietly wanted him to sell it for years and do something he loved, like study contemporary art or open a gallery. But whenever I dropped what I considered to be a subtle hint, he would get overly defensive about the idea, so I stopped mentioning it.

Now, instead of working those hundred-hour weeks and losing sleep over a fragile market, all his focus was homed in on checking the ingredient lists on every product in Waitrose, scouring the World Wide Web to find a well-reviewed art class for toddlers, and checking the safety ratings for the newest car seat. He thought this devotion meant he was doing just fine; there was only the odd wobble, but so far nothing had rocked his strict adherence to routine or cracked his façade. Except at night, of course, when the house was quiet, or when he and Henry would go out for lunch and the waitress would innocently ask if it was "just the two of them?"

As Tom pulled onto the drive, our postman, Pat, was cycling on his bicycle on the opposite side of the road. Even though Pat knew the names of everyone on his route, he always insisted on addressing them by their numeric title. Pat swung his leg off his bike with practiced elegance and pulled the bundle of manila and white packages from one of the bike's pannier bags.

"Ah, good morning, Six," he said to Tom, his tone serious as ever.

"Good morning, Pat."

"Only three pieces for you today, Six," Pat said, passing them over.

Getting the post was so much easier now that I had been expunged from it. At first the letters of condolence poured in, but over time they slowed to a trickle and eventually dried up. Lauren had dealt with the bureaucracy of ceasing any receipt of my future mail, though occasionally the odd letter still slipped through.

As Tom stepped inside the house, he called hello to Rita, who was hoovering the landing upstairs. He hung up Duke's lead by the door and walked into the kitchen. Duke curled himself into his bed, before giving his paws a good going-over. Tom made himself a cup of tea, squelching the soggy bag against the side of a white bone-china mug before adding a generous splash of milk. He looked at the post and took a slurp of his tea. There was a letter from my mother addressed to Henry; I would have recognized that slope-y, French hand anywhere. She'd never sent letters to Chloe outside of birthdays and Christmas. But maybe the old bag was softening.

Tom put the letter aside for Henry and turned over the next letter, an invitation to an opening at an art gallery the coming Saturday. The next envelope was rectangular and white with a typed address sticker on the front. *A bill for something,* he thought. Henry's dentist, perhaps, or an invoice from the window cleaner. Tom slipped his finger under the lip and tore it open. He scanned the letter quickly, from a company called Effective Solutions, not recognizing the name of the agency from which I chose our egg donor. I'd spent hours dissecting the donor profiles, reading through medical histories, and listening to CDs of their voices, hunting for my replica.

As he sat there opening the mail, Tom didn't notice that the envelope he'd just received from Effective Solutions was addressed to him, but that the letter inside was not. In the top right-hand corner of the letter was the identification number of the anonymous donor I'd ultimately chosen for Henry—along with her name and address. I'd read that number over and over. I'd heard her say it on the accompanying CD time and time again. Tom and I had even nicknamed her "Dunkirk" because her donor number was 1940GG. But that private joke had been the extent of Tom's involvement. Now, here it was, her actual identity, laid bare.

By the time I'd landed on Dunkirk's profile, Tom had given me carte blanche to choose a donor on my own. He'd become so fed up with my monomania that he didn't want to read through any more paperwork or hear any more CDs of strangers' voices rambling on about their idiosyncrasies and weekend hobbies. So, he never listened to Dunkirk's CD nor looked at her baby photo, which was plastered on the case. At that point, his only stipulation was that whomever I chose had a clean bill of health, whereas my priority was that she resembled me as much as possible.

Tom put the letter aside and checked his notebook for the list of things he needed to do. He still had a shepherd's pie to batch and a prescription to pick up. He swigged back his tea before slicing three red onions at speed. He moved them around the pan, gently frying them in butter before breaking in the mince he and Henry had bought at the farmers market over the weekend. He didn't need to follow the recipe anymore; he knew this one by heart. It was Henry's favorite.

After Tom closed the door to the oven, he set the timer for thirty minutes, just long enough for the potato on top to get nice and crispy. Duke was staring out the back door at a family of pigeons gathering in the garden. Tom washed his hands and crossed off "shepherd's pie" in his notebook with a strike of satisfaction. "Book Henry's annual checkup" was next on the list. Tom sat down at the table and phoned the pediatrician's office.

"Hello, Dr. Anderson's office. Jane speaking," said the voice at the other end. "Can you hold, please?"

"Sure," Tom said, putting the phone on speaker. Handel played through the phone while he neatened the pile of mail, the misaddressed letter sitting on top. He picked it up again, noticing now that it was neither his name nor his address in the top right-hand corner, but a woman called Grace Stone. His eyebrows tunneled into one another as he tried to puzzle through how and why he had ended up with this stranger's letter.

As the music switched from adagio to forte, Tom checked the envelope. It *was* addressed to him. He picked up the letter he'd earlier dismissed as junk mail and read it again: Effective Solutions "DONOR BATCH NUMBER 1940GG." It was a statement regarding the storage of donor eggs. Why was he getting a letter regarding a woman's egg donation? Tom hadn't given a moment's thought to Dunkirk in years; there was just Henry, and besides, Dunkirk was a closed donor, meaning she had chosen to remain anonymous forever. That hadn't been a deliberate choice on my part. Of all the profiles I'd combed through, Dunkirk was simply the one that seemed most like me.

Tom sat there, baffled. Why was this woman's letter in an envelope addressed to him?

"Hello, Jane speaking. How can I help?" the receptionist said, pulling Tom out of his contemplation. He had forgotten all about Henry's doctor's appointment. "Hello?" she repeated. "Hello?"

Tom squinted at the paper in his hand, the lightness of its weight belying the gravity of its contents. Then it hit him: This woman *was* Dunkirk.

"I—I—I'll call you back," Tom said, nearly dropping the phone. From upstairs, he could hear the rhythmic sound of Rita running the vacuum up and down the hallway.

He folded the letter back up, feeling as if he was somehow trespassing. He took a blank envelope from the kitchen drawer and tried to steady his hand as he wrote out the name and address of the woman who was our anonymous egg donor, the woman who had given my husband a reason to go on.

> *Grace Stone*
> *40 Beales Street*
> *London*
> *SE1*

It was only when the timer went off for the shepherd's pie that Tom realized he was still holding the envelope, lost in thought. The very idea that he was in possession of the identifying details of Henry's egg donor was too overwhelming to comprehend. If I'd received that letter, I would have already fired up my laptop and been knee-

deep in an investigation. But Tom turned off the oven and placed
the letter in his jacket pocket to post to its rightful owner on the
way home from school pickup, then spent the afternoon trying to
concentrate on something, anything else. He walked Duke. Twice.
He picked up Henry's prescription. He booked theater tickets for a
show six months away.

He did everything to distract himself from the discovery of
Dunkirk, but it hung there in front of him, like a key to a door he
hadn't known was there. He thought about calling Annie to tell her
what had happened, but he felt protective of the information, and
he knew it would inevitably lead to a conversation about me, then
Chloe, then Paris, and he didn't want to dredge up any memories.
He could manage talking about me now—just about—but more
than three words about Chloe and his throat would close and he'd
end up in a ball of gulping sobs.

Tom looked at the clock on the oven. It was finally time to get
Henry; he would post the envelope soon and the details would be
gone. Dunkirk's name and address would fade from his mind—
this woman, this enigma, who was always meant to remain anonymous.

*

Tom loved arriving early to pick up Henry from school. He loved
catching a glimpse of him unawares with the other children. But
today, as he walked in, Miss Rose asked him if he had five minutes.
Her voice had that I'm-going-to-say-something-disconcerting tone.

"Of course," he said. "Is everything okay?"

"Everything's fine," she said. "But something has happened that
I feel we should discuss." She gestured for Tom to sit in one of the
chairs designed for four-year-olds, beneath a garland of hanging
finger paintings.

Tom immediately pictured Henry biting into the arm of one

of his classmates, and wondered how quickly he could whip up a batch of those Nigella brownies for the victim's mother.

"Henry is a wonderful boy," Miss Rose began. "I don't have favorites, but Henry is a *very* good boy, very interested. He is wise." Tom could feel a "but" brewing. "*Because* of that, he is going to ask a lot of questions. He's curious."

"Right . . ." Tom said. "Meaning?"

Miss Rose rubbed her hands together.

"Several times now, Henry has started calling me 'Mummy.'" Tom felt the floor drop from underneath him, his body subtly folding inward. "Of course, I corrected him, but it isn't a matter of him not understanding or knowing who I am; he knows I'm Miss Rose."

"I don't know where that could have come from," Tom said. He'd been so sure he had everything under control. The packed lunches were perfect. He was never late. He did five bedtime stories—never my bestselling book *The Ice Cream Zoo*, of course, which was tucked away somewhere in the basement. He cooked and took Henry to and from school. They ate their meals together and spent their weekends in lockstep. Had that not been enough? Had he missed a cue?

"He's an intelligent boy. He's going to continue to ask questions. I just want to make sure I'm following your lead on how you're choosing to speak to Henry about . . . what happened."

Tom looked across the garden at his son playing in the sand pit with his friends. In all the horror and grief, Henry had been his one salvation. He thought that by keeping Henry away from any memory or sense of what he had lost, he was doing the right thing. Had he made a mistake in swaddling him from consequence?

"I'll have a think about it," Tom managed, trying to clear the cement forming in his throat. He tucked the chair back under the little table and went to fetch Henry. Though pickup always gave him a surge of vital endorphins, Tom had never shed the feeling that he was forgetting something whenever he left the playground, that he had two children but was picking up only one. With Henry's pudgy hand safe in his right, Tom's left hand would dangle, limp and useless. Chloe would never fade from his mind; she'd remain four and a half forever with her Cupid's bow and her baby teeth intact. She didn't have any half-written books or unfinished business. She had no last wishes or regrets. She wasn't stuck in Limbo like I was.

*

That night, before bed, Tom read Henry their five stories without his usual zealous voicing of characters. His mind was a whir, processing the unexpected course his day had taken. He had known that Henry would eventually ask where I was, that the question would rear its head and he would have to explain what had happened to us. How do you tell your child that his mother and sister were murdered by a suicide bomber? There was no self-help book in Waterstones dedicated to that subject.

Mumma is . . . Mumma was . . . Your sister is . . . He couldn't even finish the thought.

After Henry was sound asleep, Tom closed the door to his son's bedroom and went downstairs, stopping by his coat to take out the letter he'd never posted. In all the commotion with Miss Rose, he'd forgotten about it. He walked into his office and opened the letter back up, more carefully this time, as if he might somehow accidentally damage its contents. Tom was only just realizing what I had known all along: There was a woman out there whom I had handpicked to create our son. A woman I had fiercely wanted not only to look like me but to be like me too. Only, unlike me, she was alive.

Tom placed the letter flat on his desk and put the hedgehog paperweight Chloe had made him one Christmas on top to hold it in place, then dissected every word of it like he was revising for his economics exams at Cambridge. He looked up at the shelves in the office where we kept our paperwork and began pulling down boxes and tipping out their contents on the desk. Expired insurance plans splayed out beside our mortgage payments, painfully large overseas phone bills, and rejected architectural plans, but that wasn't what he was looking for. All he wanted to find was the box filled to the brim with the physical evidence of my unceasing desire for another child.

Twenty minutes in, there was only one box left. Tom pulled it down. Here it was: The future I'd wanted but never got to have. He paused for a moment, swallowing the lump in his throat before rifling through every page of my failed fertility—unsuccessful IVF cycles, invoices that looked more like telephone numbers, consent forms, mandatory counseling—everything we'd ever had to do in our attempts to have Henry, including the CD marked 1940GG, with a baby photo of a little girl who looked just like Henry on the front. Miss Rose's words floated around his head, *"He's been calling me Mummy."*

Tom's breath became shallow. This was the longest Tom had let himself think about me in a long time. He had become so used to filling his day with household errands and papier mâché, anything to try to numb the sound of my voice in the heat of that final argument. My reflection in the mirror when he watched me walk out of the bathroom. If only he'd known Jess was pregnant with Henry. If only he'd told me to wait. If only he'd let it slide that I mentioned the baby yet again, we wouldn't have fought, and he wouldn't be alone. Alone in the aisles of Waitrose. Alone filling up his car with petrol, alone again on the sofa at night, falling asleep in front of the TV. Anything to avoid grief's tight bite.

Tom yanked open the CD case, but it was empty. He stared at it, gutted. Had I thrown the disc away? He crumpled, deflated at his desk, his hair ruffled, his face tired. There was one last place he could check, though he'd spent years avoiding it. A few weeks after our funeral, Annie had suggested the painful process of going through our things, but Tom had refused point-blank, choosing instead to put them in the basement, out of sight. If the CD wasn't here, perhaps it had ended up somewhere among all our clutter. Tom flicked on the light at the top of the stairs and went down to the cellar.

There it was, his former life, in total disarray. Unmarked cardboard boxes, black bin liners, and IKEA baskets stacked along the walls. The suitcase I packed for Paris but never unpacked, the luggage label stuck tight around the handle. He paused at the bottom of the stairs. He'd underestimated the sheer scale of the task. All the boxes and bags were unmarked, Chloe's things all mixed in with mine. Where would he even start? He opened a box at random, pulling at the flaps. It was full to the brim with Chloe's toys. The sight of her cuddlies en masse was too close to the image of her in bed at night, cushioned in by faux animals. It made him feel like someone was standing on his throat. He gulped for air, clenching his jaw, and slammed the flaps shut. Tears blotted the cardboard.

He peered into a random black bin liner next. It looked like my jumpers, scarves, and maybe some of my pajamas. He knew the CD was unlikely to be in there, but he dug through it anyway. By the fifth bin liner, he was close to giving up. Every bag triggered a different unwanted memory. *How was he ever going to find a single loose CD in all this stuff?*

By the end of it, all he'd managed to find was an organizer I'd used twice and my laptop. Tom hesitated for a moment; there was no object more sacred to me than that laptop. Tom often joked that it was more precious to me than my engagement ring. Maybe I'd stored information in a file marked "Dunkirk"? That seemed like something I would do. He had to try. Anything to get out of the bloody basement.

As Tom waited for my laptop to boot up in his office, he tried to push away the vision of me sitting at my computer, lost in thought, chewing the top of a pen, my legal pad beside me. He imagined leaning down, kissing my cheek, and nuzzling into my neck. After five minutes of looking at a blank screen with nothing to distract him from the image of me, he couldn't take it anymore and went to the kitchen. Maybe my laptop was bricked. Maybe there was nothing there anyway. This was not how he spent his evenings. Going down to the basement was a mistake. Bringing my laptop out of the basement was a mistake.

But when he returned to his office, the screen was illuminated, the cursor flashing on chapter nine of the memoir Tom had no idea I was writing. He sat down hard on his desk chair, his eyes trailing along the final line I ever wrote: *Let's hope it's a good egg.* This wasn't one of my children's books, which would have been torturous enough. It was us. Our story. In just that one line, he could hear my voice, my intonation, like I was standing over his shoulder reading it aloud to him.

He slammed my computer shut, ripped out the charger, then picked up my laptop from his desk, holding it by the sides like a monstrance. In his haste, the pad of his index finger accidentally bumped the eject button on the CD drive, and the caddy popped open.

There it was, the CD marked "DONOR: 1940GG."

Before Paris, this had been my world. I'd been secretly writing a memoir and listening to Dunkirk's voice on a loop. But she wasn't just Dunkirk anymore. She was called Grace Stone and she lived on Beales Street. Part of him knew it would be best to leave the CD where it was, hidden away like our artifacts in the basement, but a feeling erupted inside him like the one he'd had on realizing the significance of the letter. Listening to this CD, paired with confidential information, would be a choice, a premeditated violation, not a clerical error for which he bore no fault. He picked the CD out of its caddy, holding it carefully by the edges, telling himself he would just listen once. After all, what difference could it make? He dropped it into the drive of the CD player behind him and pressed play.

At first, there was the sound of white noise, a scratchy analog vibration emanating from the speakers. Then the room came alive with the sound of a woman's voice.

"Can I ask you to repeat your donor number?" she said. *"And can you speak up a bit?"*

"Yes. Donor number 1940GG." Tom froze, his eyes wide and un-blinking. It was her, Dunkirk. Grace. Grace Stone.

"Please confirm that you're a closed donor and you've requested to remain anonymous for the entire donation process."

"Yes. I'm a closed donor," Grace said.

"So, you're donating these eggs in Italy, is that correct?" the woman said.

"Yes."

Grace's CD had been different from all the others. She wasn't trying to sell herself like the rest of the candidates, who appeared to maintain a saintly lifestyle of long walks and zero consumption of alcohol. My choice hadn't solely been a matter of our matching physicality; I was taken by Grace's whole profile, which seemed unpolished and authentic. It was a visceral reaction that she was the one.

"Do you want to tell us a bit about yourself?" the woman said.

"I'm five foot eight on a good day. My eyes are blue. My hair was blond as a child. I don't know what you'd call it now. Brown-y blond maybe."

"Okay, that's helpful. Thank you. So, in terms of medical history, there are a few gaps."

"Yes," Grace continued. *"Well, I was adopted, so there are things I don't know about my biological family."*

"Okay. And before you read what you prepared: Is it a poem, or well-known speech?—that's what people generally do."

"It's a poem."

"Great. So, what about your likes and dislikes? It says here . . . you're about to start studying to become a master sommelier. Do you want to talk a little about that?"

"No, I'd rather not—is there a window open? Sorry. I'm always cold."
Tom willed his hand to press stop, but he was frozen, entranced by
these details, as Grace the human being started to take form.

Her voice faded, and the woman who was interviewing her
said, *"Do you want to share a little bit about why you decided to become an egg donor?"*

Grace took a breath, the depth of it audible on the microphone.

*"My circumstances . . . changed and—actually, I'd rather read the
poem, like I was advised to? I studied this in university—and I don't
really know. It just seemed fitting . . ."* There was a pause, accompa-
nied by the sound of flicking pages, then she began to recite, *"Do
you come from Heaven or rise from the abyss / Beauty? / Your gaze,
divine and infernal . . ."*

Tom pushed his chair back from the desk, stunned. I'd had the
exact same reaction. Here it was, our obscure poem. He couldn't
get his head around it. As Grace spoke the words, Tom saw only
me, pacing up and down the lawn at Annie's the day we met. He
could smell the freshly cut grass and hear the distant hum of a lawn
mower as I ambled beneath a duck-egg-blue sky, my hair streaked
with bad honey highlights. I seemed so sure of myself as I recited
these same verses, pretending not to notice him. Now here Grace
was, repeating verbatim the last loving thing I ever said to him
before I was killed. If this wasn't a sign, how could God be so cruel
twice?

> *. . . Whether you come from Heaven or from Hell, who cares,*
> *O Beauty! Huge, fearful, ingenuous monster!*
> *If your regard, your smile, your foot, open for me*
> *An Infinite I love but have not ever known?*
> *From God or Satan, who cares? Angel or Siren,*
> *Who cares, if you make,—fay with the velvet eyes,*
> *Rhythm, perfume, glimmer; my one and only queen!*
> *The world less hideous, the minutes less leaden?*

Tom pressed play again and again, captivated by the sound of Grace's voice as she recited these words. It was only when Rita popped her head into his office to say she was leaving that he was able to press stop. The room, without Grace and the poem, suddenly seemed desolate and empty.

"Duke has walked for miles," Rita said, detaching the lead. "He has eaten. Why do you look so pale? I will make you a sandwich."

"No, no, it's not that. I just realized I've forgotten something," Tom said. But I knew that gleam in his eye. I'd been on the receiving end of that relentless determination. I knew when Tom was going after something, and there was not a single doubt in my mind where he was headed. "Are you all right to stay just one more hour? I'll pay you double."

"You already pay me triple."

"Thank you," he said, grabbing Rita's face with both hands and kissing her forehead. "I'll be back in an hour. I promise." Tom swiped the letter with Grace's address and ran out the front door.

CHAPTER FIVE

It was one of those cold English mornings that felt like the prologue to winter. Lauren, Annie, and I were sitting in Annie's garden, a bucolic haven where plants lived respectfully beside one another on a handshake rather than in neatly defined parameters. Annie was wearing her long wax jacket and her green felt winter hat, painstakingly pulling up her dahlias, the leaves blackened from the first autumn frost. Lauren and I sat on the silvered teak bench, Chester beneath our feet, wet and panting from our walk in the park, while Duke barked incessantly at a squirrel hiding in one of the oak trees.

"Right, so—Jess carries the baby, but she's not the mum?" Lauren said, her mouth full of shortbread, a few crumbs sprinkled onto her hugely pregnant tummy that I tried not to take as a personal affront. With the back of one of her gardening gloves, Annie pushed her hat a little off her face and threw me a glance. As well-meaning as Lauren was, she tended to run a few pages behind.

"No, I'm the mother," I said. "And I'm not explaining this again without a very strong Bloody Mary."

"But won't she think she is?" Lauren said.

"No."

"But how can she carry the baby if it's not her baby? What part of it is hers?"

"None of it! Surrogate: one person. Egg donor: another person. Mother: me."

"It's very confusing. I wonder if it might be easier to adopt." My jaw clenched, and it took all my strength not to snap at her. If there was one thing that drove me bananas about Lauren, it was her unsolicited advice. For some reason, people were under the impression that adopting a child was the easy solution, but adoption was an equally long and rocky road, filled with just as much disappointment and heartache.

"Has Chester farted?" Annie interrupted. "It smells like his brand."

"No, he has not—Well, maybe, but don't embarrass him—Wait, so Tom doesn't mind having a baby with another woman?" Lauren said. The implication enraged me. Was this what people were going to think—that Tom was having our baby with "another woman"? Lauren meant well, she always did, but if she'd given that question a few more seconds of thought, she wouldn't have needed to ask it.

"Lauren," Annie began. "Remember the other day, I told you to take three breaths before blurting out the first thing that comes into your head?"

"Baby brain," Lauren said, pointing to her forehead. "But what if the baby comes out and you don't feel connected to it at all? Or what if the mother finds out how rich you and Tom are and tries to take the baby's inheritance or kidnap the baby?"

"For fuckssake, Lauren. Stop saying 'the mother.' I'm the mother. And besides, the egg I've chosen is coming from Italy. The laws there aren't the same as they are here where it's mandatory that the donor reveal their identity when the child turns eighteen. I'll never know who she is, and she'll never know who we are."

"Wait. You're going to Italy?" Lauren said.

"Christ! No. The agency matches you with eggs all over Europe."

I didn't want to fight with Lauren, but I could tell from Annie's *expression that she agreed with me entirely. "Look, sorry to snap. It's just that questions about potential kidnappings and inheritance seem a little tone-deaf," I said. Lauren nodded and forced a smile.*

I glanced over my shoulder across Annie's garden, noticing how jagged the flint wall looked now that the creepers were barren. It was only when I thought I'd come to terms with all of it—that some women could just gaze at the sky to get pregnant (Lauren with twins, no less), while others (like me) had to have their ovaries removed—a bone-deep, biological sadness would usurp my whole being. But I wasn't going to let myself wallow when I was in the privileged position to pick out an egg donor and borrow a uterus.

*

Tom was halfway down the stoop when he heard a familiar voice call his name. It took him a moment to register that it was Lauren, waving at him from across the road. Lauren lived only a few doors down. She'd always loved this street—everyone did—so when I found out Number Eight was coming up for sale, I told her immediately and she and Daniel bought it the next week. There wasn't a day that went by where I didn't see her. Whether it was unloading the shopping or taking out the rubbish, Lauren was never far away. Even though bumping into her wasn't particularly out of the ordinary, tonight Tom felt caught out, as if his mother had just discovered the secret stash of porn magazines beneath his bed.

"I was *just* about to knock for you," Lauren said. "Henry left this at the house yesterday." She passed Tom one of Henry's beloved tractor toys, then tucked her bouncy blow-dry behind her ear. In the amber light from our house, Lauren's hair seemed a few shades blonder than usual, and her frown lines a little less pronounced, making me mildly suspicious that she'd been at the Botox again. It could've just been that she'd finally changed hairdressers; we both did get the feeling our colorist, Olivia, had gone a little off-piste ever since she'd started the Jenny Craig diet. It was something we'd discussed ad nauseam on our evening dog walks when I was still alive—both of us dressed in pajamas and duck-down coats, huddled beneath an umbrella.

"Ah! Thank you," Tom said. "I've been cross-examined about its whereabouts all afternoon."

"I bet," Lauren said, laughing. She wasn't wearing her pajamas tonight. She had on her favorite blue jeans, which always gave her bum a great shape. Her coat was slightly open, showing a tight cashmere jumper underneath that made her look like she had a C cup when she really had no tits at all. "Where are you off to in such a hurry?" Lauren said, pulling Chester away from an oncoming jogger. Due to our road's clever one-way system, joggers were about the only traffic we ever got; we could hear the birds all day, not just in the morning. It was one of the things I loved most about the house.

Tom unlocked the car and continued walking round to the driver's side. When he'd put Grace's address into Google Maps, a wine shop called Sprezzatura popped up. It made sense, considering Grace was studying to be a master sommelier. If he dropped by and glanced at her through the shop window, he wouldn't be breaking any rules, would he? He was only going to satisfy his curiosity, a look from afar, without any intentions of going inside.

"Tom?" Lauren said.

"Sorry," he said, getting into the car. "Say it again?"

Lauren crinkled her nose slightly, a shadow of worry passing over her features. "Oh God, did I forget something going on at school? Is that where you're going?" Her eyes widened. "Wait, is tonight the pumpkin carving?"

"No, no—I'm just going to get some petrol—to save doing it tomorrow, and—get some milk—for Henry, for his porridge . . . for the morning." Tom always began to waffle when he was cornered.

"Okay. Phew," she said, with her hand to her chest. She loved

nothing more than coordinating or managing a crisis. Despite Annie's impatience at her constant flapping, Lauren had been such
an incredible support since I died. Always ready to bat away Lily
at the school gates and protect Tom from the other birds of prey.
She helped him with all Henry's birthday parties and guided him
through the correct handling of a soaring temperature.

"Do you want some company?" she offered, even though Chester was pulling incessantly on his lead.

"No!" Tom said a little too emphatically. "I mean, it's late. Chester's raring to get on and I'll only be a minute. But what's the plan
for tomorrow? Shall we drive to Annie's together?"

"Yes, perfect. What time do you want to leave? Annie always
takes the mick out of me if I arrive too early. I'm making cheesecake, and I don't want to take it out of the fridge until absolutely
necessary."

"Twelve-ish?" he said, turning on his Defender, hoping Lauren would get the hint, but she gestured for him to roll down the
window.

"Does that mean twelve, or just after? I'm always so confused
with 'ish.'"

"Twelve," Tom said. "On the dot."

Even though Chester was still pulling, Lauren leaned her forearms onto the frame of the car's window. She'd definitely been at the
Botox. There was barely a line on her face. Her eyes seemed too wide,
like she was trying to be emotional but her face wouldn't allow it.

"You okay?" Tom said, his hands gripping the wheel.

"Yes, yes. I just always—I just miss Honor. Especially around
this time of night when we'd walk the dogs together. The way she'd
ring the bell even after I'd told her fifteen times not to. Always with
a packet of crisps which would leave crumbs all up and down my
hallway. I remember once—"

"Okay. Yeah," Tom said. He moved one of his hands off the
wheel and tightly clenched his fist out of sight.

"Sorry," Lauren said. She dabbed at the corner of her eyes with her knuckle. "I can't believe it's been nearly five years," she said. "I thought it would get easier, but it doesn't, does it? I was thinking about going to one of those groups where they talk about life after death, things like that. We could go together if you wanted?" Tom's body stiffened. He'd just unwillingly excavated all Chloe's soft toys, my laptop; it was all too much.

"No," he said, looking down at his lap. "I don't want to sit around with a bunch of people that are chronically sad."

"Sorry," Lauren said again. "I didn't mean to—" Seeing Lauren's face morph from earnest to crestfallen made Tom soften his tone a touch.

"Nothing to apologize for, all good." He smiled to reassure her. "I just mean—I have Henry to think about. I haven't got time to dwell on all that stuff. Or talk about it. I'm fine, Lauren, really. I have you. I have Annie. I have Oliver. I don't want to poke the bear. Nor do I want to pull it apart. I want to keep things simple for Henry. I can't risk any change. At least for a little bit. I'm fine." He put on his indicator and released the car's handbrake. "See you tomorrow. Twelve o'clock. On the dot," he said, pulling out of the drive.

Lauren watched Tom's brake lights disappear as Chester halted to inspect one of the lime trees lining the pavement. For a few minutes after Tom had gone, she stood looking up at our house. A wistful smile crept over her lips—maybe she was remembering that final dinner party we'd all had. Oysters from our local fishmonger. She'd made her famous citrusy vinaigrette. Annie and Oliver had overseen the drinks, resulting in painfully strong margaritas and Tom spraining his ankle during an appalling game of midnight Twister. The following morning I'd woken up to Chloe's elbow in my armpit, and what felt like a terminal case of dehydration, yet somehow Tom didn't have even a glimpse of a hangover.

"I'm never drinking again," I said to Tom, who was standing

over me on my side of the bed. Without me having to ask, he passed me a Coca-Cola and gave me an ice-cold flannel for my face. That Sunday, the three of us didn't get out of bed until dinnertime. I drifted in and out of sleep with the two of them beside me eating toast and singing along to *The Jungle Book*. It was worth the hangover just to watch them. The following week, the doctor performed the oophorectomy procedure that slammed me into early menopause.

When Tom pulled onto the main road, he didn't listen to BBC Radio 6. He had enough noise in his head as it was. He drove by Saint Paul's Cathedral, stopping at a pedestrian crossing to let a rush of commuters pass. He looked at the mass of strangers going about their lives, wondering if they had ever done something perhaps they shouldn't have. He watched one man who took a final drag of his cigarette, before flicking it into the road and leaving it there like a smoking gun.

At the lights, a flash of heat came over him. Tom opened the window and unzipped his coat. He needed some air. He could hear the brakes of a bus and a woman's cackle as she nattered some meaningless dross into her phone. Tom tapped his thumb on the wheel in anticipation, wondering if his breathing always sounded this loud without the radio on. The light had barely turned green before he was off, the acceleration throwing fresh, cold air on his face.

As the car in front of him slowed down to make a left turn, Tom took the opportunity to check the map on his phone, which said the shop's location was fewer than five minutes away. He tried to steady his breath, repeating a series of calming mantras that had no discernible effect until he found a parking space a few doors down from the shop. The moon was bright behind the clouds, making the sky appear a dark shade of silver. For a Friday night, Beales Street was surprisingly quiet. The famous *fromagerie,* where it was rumored the Queen bought her cheddar, and the French baker both had their awnings up. Grace's shopfront was just as it would've been in the nineteenth century, with black lacquered paint and a polished brass knocker. A hand-painted blade sign swaying in the breeze read SPREZZATURA. Out of the row of quaint, independent shops, only Grace's was open. But it was far busier inside than he'd anticipated. A glitch in his otherwise perfect plan. The panels in the windows were lined with Christmas-style condensation, making it difficult for him to see fully inside without going right up to the glass and pressing his face against it like the Little Match Girl.

If this hullabaloo was a sign that Tom was meant to give up and go back, he chose to ignore the message. Instead, he crossed the road, awash with nervousness. After all, how would he ever be able to tell Grace from Tara from Emily? All he'd seen of her was her baby picture. As Tom got closer to the shop, he reassured himself that no one in their right mind would ever guess the true reason for his visit, which, when you really thought about it, was barely a blip in the trajectory of his life. *One tiny peek at Grace and then he would be off. She wouldn't even know he'd been there at all.*

The clouds had passed, and the moon was full behind him, giving his shadow a sinister appearance. Tom was bang opposite Grace's shop now, unable to ignore the red letter box conveniently located in front. Its insistent presence, a warning that this was where his folly could, and possibly should, end.

Post the letter—she never has to know, he thought. *Respect this woman's wishes to be anonymous. You can't make a river run backwards.*

Though I'd always been the more literary, Tom's mind flashed to our Baudelaire poem. My breath on his face, my lips so agonizingly close. After I died, he told himself that he never wanted to hear it or any other French poetry again. But it was too late. This poem wasn't a white flag anymore. It was a siren. It was as if for the first time he understood the couplet about heaven and hell: *Do you come from Heaven or rise from the abyss / Beauty? Your gaze, divine and infernal.* But still, this insight wasn't enough for him to take out the letter and post it. Rather, he ignored the envelope with all its secrets and stepped onto the pavement with a purposeful gait, narrowly missing a puddle.

When he was right in front of Sprezzatura, he could see, through the glass-paneled door, a drinks party in full swing. Inside, people were packed cheek-by-jowl, holding glasses and mingling, one of my least favorite pastimes. Women in roll-necks and matte nude lipstick, alongside men, husbands, maybe brothers, bobbing on the balls of their feet, accepting a top-up of their wine. So far, there wasn't a soul who looked like me. Not even close. Had I overindulged a resemblance between us? Blue eyes and blond-brown hair and similar height guaranteed nothing. Tom scanned every face in the room, searching every profile. There were at least five women in that room who fit the bill, and not one of them looked like me.

The wind had picked up now, but Tom was sweating as though he was getting a temperature. Just as he was coming to accept the possibility that he'd never recognize Grace, that he would never set eyes upon this woman and know it, which was fine, maybe even preferable, a man in a herringbone coat stepped aside, and there she was. A woman who was indistinguishable from me. I'd always hoped she'd be a close match, but I could never have imagined a near–carbon copy. This woman could only be Grace, standing tall in a sheer black dress, seemingly looking back at Tom with my bottomless blue eyes. She shook her hair off her face, before smiling with her tongue between her teeth.

The merger of life and death slammed into Tom like a speeding car. He stumbled backwards, nearly falling off the pavement. Time seemed to stretch, then narrow, the way it had when we'd first met at Annie's house and he'd scooped me off the lawn and ferried me to lunch. Tom's heart was charging, though to him it felt like it had stopped altogether.

The pendulum didn't swing back after that. Magnetized by an unseen force, Tom reached out to twist the knob, but the door wouldn't open. He tried again, jiggling the handle until his attempts caught the attention of a man inside. The gentleman, clearly in an advanced state of inebriation, put down his champagne flute and began fiddling with the door. He opened it narrowly, his skin resembling something like carpaccio, an unlit cigarette balanced between his fingers. "Closed for a private event tonight, I'm afraid," he said in a somewhat pompous rumble, before shutting the door in Tom's face.

In the split second Tom pulled his eyes away from Grace, she'd disappeared into the mix of people. Our extreme likeness hit him again with full, disturbing force. Having those eyes—*my eyes*—blinking back at him, as if I'd been hiding here all along, was too much for him to bear. Tom fled back towards the world he knew was real, and the simple safety of the car.

His skin burned hot, then broke out in a cold sweat as he crossed the street. He was still walking when his mouth filled with saliva. He realized too late he was about to be sick as he vomited beside the curb, retching up his insides. When he finally finished, he leaned onto the car and dabbed at his mouth with the cuff of his jacket. For so long, he'd prayed to God to awaken him from this dream. But he never thought I would manifest in another person's body in a wine shop on Beales Street on any ordinary Friday.

Nor did I. Though this comedy of errors was my own doing, I wasn't a fortune teller. I'd merely hoped that a passing stranger would presume my second child had my eyes.

That night, Tom sat at his desk, shaky and wired. He took the letter out of his pocket and put it on his desk next to the CD. The Tom I knew wasn't sentimental. Nor was he a hoarder. But since we died, every pen cap, pair of socks, and even my last tube of toothpaste had assumed an inflated sense of meaning.

But he couldn't face going back down to the basement tonight. He didn't want to see my suitcase again, or my name written on the luggage tag. The only place Tom could think of to keep these things was beside Hedgie and my engagement ring in the safe. Tom used to joke with me and call it "The Vault." Accessing it couldn't get much more straightforward—the code was my birthday—but somehow my analogical brain always got the hash in the wrong place and then it would start flashing. Thankfully, Lauren had the same safe, so if I got locked out, she would always come and reset it for me, a favor I'd had to call in more than once.

Tom turned off the lights and made his way upstairs. He passed by Henry's room, checking in on him briefly, careful not to wake him, before going into our bedroom. He walked into my Carrie Bradshaw wardrobe, where he pushed his shirts aside to get to the safe, his fingers automatically tapping in my birth date. When it opened with an automated whir, he pushed the CD and the letter to the back, averting his eyes from Hedgie, as he clicked the door shut.

Later, Tom found sleep even more elusive than usual. Since the first time we shared a bed, Tom had always insisted on having some part of his body touching mine. I thought it would phase out, like spooning does when you just need a decent night's sleep and you're far enough down the road in your relationship that turning your back can no longer give off the wrong impression. But it never did. Whether it was his knuckle against my thigh, or a pinky beside my ankle, there was always some part of us anchored. And no matter how deep his sleep, if I moved away, he would always find me again.

Tonight, Tom found himself in the belly of a waking fever dream, only rather than trying to claw his way to the surface, he was burrowing deeper and deeper down the rabbit hole. He'd expected the sight of Grace to quell any further interest. So why was he now lying in bed thinking of her? Thinking of us. My hair spilled across the pillow. My naked body beneath the white sheets. The way I writhed around in pleasure beneath him.

But when Tom closed his eyes, he saw her face, not mine. The dimple on one cheek that had caused him to stumble backwards because I had the one that matched it on the other side and her Cupid's bow, that delicate shade of a rose in bloom. He didn't realize it at first, but as he allowed himself to concede to baser instincts in the secrecy that only darkness can offer, his mind began to wander into suggestive territories. He found himself wondering what perfume she wore, and what the crease of her neck smelled like after a day of wearing it.

Over the past few years, the need to pleasure himself had been a matter of simple physical release that had been robotically executed in the shower, but this was different. If he ever thought of me, he could never finish. But that wasn't my hair he was imagining on his pillow. Those weren't my all-seeing blue eyes he was locking onto. Tom's body convulsed in a way he'd forgotten it could—the reaction of unvetted pleasure. As he inched closer, he thought about the way Grace clamped her tongue between her teeth when she laughed. Tom never missed a detail like that. The smile had shown off the scar she had, which went from the crack in her lip to her cheekbone—the most beautiful part of her.

Tom didn't imagine slowly unzipping the black dress Grace was wearing that night. He didn't feel ready, nor have any desire to stray into a world of make-believe. Now that he knew the shape of her body, he had neither craving, nor need for elaborate fantasy. As he thought about the moment her lips broke into a smile, revealing the poppy-seed gap between her teeth, Tom's head hit the back of the headboard. His eyes closed, right at the moment he was at his most vulnerable, the final few seconds just before he came.

CHAPTER SIX

When I first met Tom, I was sauntering up and down Annie's parents'
garden in Richmond beneath the wisteria-covered pergola, frantically
memorizing Baudelaire for my exam. At the time, I fancied myself a
mix of Jane Birkin and some sort of French intellectual who churned
out dense, unreadable poetry. I didn't go anywhere without my strate-
gically placed, dog-eared copy of The Second Sex *that I never actually*
read. I just wandered around with it like it was a clutch bag or left it
noticeably propped open wherever I went. The whole thing was laugh-
able, because what I really did when I got home was eat Kit Kats and
read Jackie Collins.

"Annie, who is that?" I said, looking over my sunglasses at an un-
deniably attractive man. The garden was in full bloom, the air choked
with pollen. I could hear the bees buzzing in the wisteria. I hadn't had a
shower since the day before or a pedicure since the previous summer—I
wasn't remotely Birkin-esque. The hot weather had sprung on us with-
out warning, and like all good English people, we'd made a large jug of
Pimm's and refused to go inside.

"Oh, that must be Tom," Annie said. *"Oliver's friend. The one he tried to set up with Lauren, but she said no. Apparently, she's now exclusive with that Harry Von Wankerface,"* Annie said, *licking the tip of her finger and turning the page of* The Times.

"Did she know he looked like that?*" I said, trying to lengthen my posture.*

"I doubt it. The only thing Oliver told me was that he worked in finance—"

"Uch, finance. Such a cliché. Let me guess. Daddy heads up JP Morgan in Germany?"

"If you'd let me finish, you would have heard me say that his mother is that wonderful art historian Judith Shelley who writes for the Sunday Times *and his dad is Brice Wharton as in, yes, Brice Wharton. The artist. An old chum of Picasso's, no less. But please, do go on with your sweeping generalizations?"*

I rolled my eyes. "Well, anyway, he thinks he's Tom Cruise in those glasses."

Annie looked up at me, squinting, an unlit cigarette stuck between her lips. She was slathered, head-to-toe, in Hawaiian Tropic, her knockers pert in a chic, cranberry-colored swimming costume.

"You might wanna tone it down a touch," Annie said.

"Tone what down?" I said, though I knew full well.

"That ridiculous trot you're doing."

"Oh, be quiet. What do you know about flirting? You're basically already married to Oliver." I was wearing my round tortoiseshell sunglasses with the blue lenses, thinking I was doing my very own sexy rendition of La Piscine. *I upped the volume of my animated French poetry recital, hoping to attract admiring glances from Oliver's guest, who I'd soon find out over lunch was a fellow Etonian—as if we needed any more.*

"You look constipated, walking like that," Annie said, blowing a plume of smoke out of her mouth.

I was about to kick her in the shin when I trod on a bee. It took me a moment to register that the searing pain in my foot was a bee sting, and I collapsed in a heap on the grass. Later, I would learn that the most likely colors to attract bees are purple, violet, and blue. I would also learn that Oliver's friend was called Tom Wharton, and he was funny and charming and not at all boring for someone who worked in finance.

To my horror, while I was keeled over on the ground, assuring Annie I was fine, Tom came rushing over. My foot had swelled to the size of a small tabby cat. Tom's first impression of me, rather than a gamine, fabled French beauty, was a cursing, English wuss with an unsightly, bulging foot, greasy hair, and coffee breath.

"I'm Tom, by the way," he said, bending down to examine my foot close up. "Can you walk?"

"I'm fine. I just need a little ice."

"It really does look awful." Annie said. "Awful, awful, awful."

"I can carry you to the table," Tom said.

"She'd love that, wouldn't you, Honor?" Annie said.

"No. I'm absolutely fine," I said, then yelped as I tried to stand and put pressure on my foot. Tom didn't ask me again if I needed him to carry me. He just hoisted me over his shoulder like I was a rucksack and schlepped me to the lunch table.

"I haven't showered yet," I told his arse as we walked across the lawn. "In case you can't tell. I'm revising for my exams. French literature."

"Excellent," he said. "Then we should probably sit next to one another. I've just finished The Second Sex *myself and I'd love to know all your thoughts." I found out in bed a few weeks later that he hadn't read it either.*

*

It was still raining when Lauren and Tom arrived with the children for lunch at Annie's. Annie opened the door wearing a thick, butter-yellow, woolen skirt landing just above the ankles that looked effortless but moved like couture. Both Jarvis and Basil,

Lauren's twins, and Henry greeted Annie with an excited, trailing hello. Annie just about managed to kiss the crown of Henry's head as he whipped by, following the older boys down the hall to the back garden to explore the puddles.

"Here, I'll take that," Tom said, gesturing at Lauren's soggy trench coat, putting it on the back of one of the entrance-hall chairs.

"Thank you, Tom," Lauren said, shimmying it off her shoulders.

The rain outside made it feel later than it was. Tom stood for a moment with his back to the fire, pleased to be out of the wet.

On the round table in the hall, Annie had filled a large blue Wedgwood vase with sweet chestnut leaves and last year's dried hydrangeas. No matter the time of year, the hall always had a wicker basket overspilling with logs for the fire. The house had been in Annie's family for generations. Like her floristry, the rooms had a sense of theater, each with its own dramatic flair. The paneled walls were covered floor-to-ceiling in pictures, silly prints she'd bought among drawings she'd inherited. I was always amazed she found space to hang any more of them. But as grand as this house seemed to an outsider—and it was the grandest house in Richmond—to Annie and Oliver it was home, and that meant that dogs went on the sofas and soggy children were treated supremely, and if anyone ever asked for a coaster, Annie would always say, "Whatever for?"

"Miserable fucking weather," Annie said, trying to pry the cheesecake from Lauren's hands. "I can be trusted with a cake, you know, darling. Just because I chose not to have a child doesn't mean I don't know how to hold shit." She really did have an unrivaled way with words.

"I didn't say—" Lauren said.

"I know you didn't, darling. You didn't need to. Anyway, I'm winding you up. Don't tell me you've left your sense of humor at home again," she said, winking at Tom.

"Why do you always do that? Do you know how long it took me to make that cake? It hasn't got a single crack."

"Right, let's get you a nice, strong drink."

Lauren and Tom followed Annie into the kitchen, where they were greeted by the familiar Sunday smell of roast chicken and honeyed parsnips. Oliver was standing in his usual spot by the Aga, meticulously thickening the gravy, his immaculate apron tied twice around his lanky frame. Lauren kissed him hello, while Tom went to occupy his usual spot at the kitchen island.

"I thought it was Daniel's weekend to have the children?" Oliver said, offering his expectant cheek, his glasses steamed up by the boiling carrots.

"Yes, but he's in Frankfurt," Lauren said. "*Again*. Anyway, did you get my invitation to the Halloween Street Party?" Lauren said. "I designed it myself."

"Yes, I loved the unexpected green glitter that I'm still finding now," Annie said.

"'Wicked Witches is the theme. I'm going to Hobbycraft on Wednesday if anyone wants to get their costumes with me."

"You're very sweet to ask. But I'd rather be eaten alive by a clowder of feral Greek cats than go to Hobbycraft," Annie said, making Tom laugh.

"Can I do anything?" Tom asked, stretching his arms above his head.

"Yes," Oliver said. "Get a pen. I've nearly finished the crossword. I've only two spaces left." Tom took Oliver's pen, folded over the newspaper, and looked at the clues.

"Right," Tom said, reading. "Ship for cold seas, ten letters."

"Here you are," Annie said, passing Lauren and Tom each a Bloody Mary. Annie always made the best Bloody Marys. Her secret was a whole lemon, sometimes two. It was a trick she'd learned from her father.

"Thank you," Tom said as he accepted the spicy red concoction. Sitting in the warm, familiar confines of Annie's kitchen, Tom let an untroubled serenity fall over him. In recent years, much like everything else in his life, this house had lost its luster. It had dimmed or hardened over, but today every flower seemed like it was in full bloom. Had the kitchen always been so flooded with light? Had the jasmine creeper by the window always smelled this rich?

While Tom looked out of the Palladian glass doors, any casual observer would have presumed that he was gazing into the garden at his son, but at that moment, he was remembering the previous night. What he'd done in his bed thinking of Grace. He hadn't thought about another woman in years. How could he? Sitting at the kitchen island, he wasn't thinking of anything untoward, just the way Grace stuck her tongue between her teeth when she laughed.

Suddenly, Henry appeared at his knee, wiping his runny nose on Tom's jeans.

"Daddy, can I sleep over tonight?" Henry asked. Before Tom had a chance to respond, Lauren jumped in,

"Are you sure you don't want to sleep over at my house with Jarvis and Basil? We could watch the Lego movie?"

"No. I want to sleep in the roof," Henry said. Chloe had been similarly obsessed with the attic at Annie's house. It was a children's dream—a sturdy fort, lined with fabric and fairy lights.

"Of course you can, my angel," Annie said. "Your bed is already made up." Henry clapped and ran back out to the garden with the answer he'd wanted to hear, happy that there was Oliver's hot chocolate and a late bedtime in store.

"Are you sure you don't mind?" Tom said.

"I'm not answering that," Annie said. "You know how much we love having Henry."

As Tom took another sip of his drink, it occurred to him that it didn't feel wrong, per se, to be thinking of another woman. He didn't feel like he was polluting the waters of his and Henry's life. After all, she wasn't some stranger. She had my ultimate seal of approval.

"Midsummer!" Lauren shouted, jarring Tom out of his thoughts.

"Not ten letters," Oliver said.

"Midsumm . . . *ers?*" Tom suggested.

"Middlebrow," Annie said, then busied herself with the table-scape. Today there was a train of nasturtium leaves down the center and fruit-filled cucamelon vines entwining the porcelain candelabras, ready to be picked by the children after dinner.

From the garden, a high-pitched yelp erupted, followed by barking. Lauren jumped up and looked out the doors that opened onto the lawn, but it was just the twins jumping in puddles.

"Two minutes and then it's time to sit for lunch!" Lauren shouted.

"Tom, are you all right?" Annie said. "You seem a bit out of sorts."

"What? No, I'm fine," he said. Her question made him aware he'd been unknowingly pulling at the edges of the newspaper, leaving a pile of confetti on the wooden countertop. He swept the shreds into his hand and walked them over to the bin, wondering if there would ever come a time when everyone would stop asking him how he was. Would it be when he went from "single-dad widower" back to "someone's husband" again? Would he ever just be Tom, Henry's father?

The children came running in, sweeping past the large, untamed jasmine creeper framing the doorway, lacing them with a honey-like scent. Tom and Annie helped Henry as he shook off his yellow Wellingtons and left them in a heap by the door.

"Okay, let's wash hands, everyone," Lauren said, marching the children off to the downstairs loo.

"Are you sure you're all right?" Annie said. Tom tried to picture broaching the subject of Grace's existence, momentarily considering what it would be like to tell his friend the story of the misaddressed letter and his impromptu visit to Grace's shop on Friday. Maybe if he told Annie what happened, she could get him back on track. "Tom?" Annie said, holding Henry's yellow Wellie.

"I don't know if I am." Annie motioned for Tom to follow her into the pantry and closed the door behind them. The shelves were stacked high with Kilner jars in no discernible order, some labeled, some not.

"What's wrong?" Annie said.

"Nothing's wrong. Well, I don't know. It's—I got a letter the other day, and this is going to sound strange, because it is strange, but the letter that was in the envelope addressed to me wasn't for me."

"That is odd. You know, these things happen."

"They do. But the letter was sort of confidential."

"What the fuck are you talking about, Tom? What are you trying to tell me? Spit it out."

"No. Sorry. I—the letter was addressed to Henry's egg donor, and now I know who she is."

"Jesus," Annie said, playing with her necklace. "That's quite a cock up."

"Before you say anything else—I know—it's insane, but honestly, Annie, when I saw her, she looked—she looked exactly like Honor."

"Wait. Hang on a second. What do you mean 'saw her'? You just told me you got a letter." Tom said nothing; he just stood there unable to respond. How could he admit to acting on some bizarre whim?

"I did get a letter. But then I went to the address on the letter."

"Oh my God, Tom. I think that's illegal. You cannot tell *anyone* you've done that, especially Lauren. You and Honor signed all those documents. Jesus Christ. Please tell me you haven't told anyone else about this?"

"No, just you."

"Lunch!" Oliver called from the kitchen.

"Coming!" they both said quickly.

"Did you tell her who you are?" Annie said.

"Of course not. I didn't even speak to her. I just saw her through the window of her shop."

"Promise me you'll never tell anyone you did that?" Tom said nothing. "Look, you were curious. You're human. I get it, but draw the line here. This is serious. You need to get rid of that letter, okay? You never got it." Tom looked past Annie's shoulder at the tins of Heinz baked beans stacked on the shelf.

"But I did get it. And when I saw her—"

"Tom. Let me stop you right there. You didn't get this letter. You didn't see her. You didn't go to the shop," Annie said. "It didn't happen." She grabbed a needless can of beans from the shelf and stormed out of the pantry. Tom stood and covered his face with his hands. He should never have said anything to Annie.

When Tom emerged, Annie was visibly tense. He busied himself by helping Lauren take the warm plates off the Aga and carrying them to the table. He tucked in Henry's chair and sliced his chicken, wishing he too could sit at the kids' table, but instead he took his usual spot opposite Annie, who had gone mute. But just as everyone sat down for lunch, there was a knock at the door.

"I'll get it!" Oliver called out theatrically, before anyone had a chance to offer.

"Are we expecting anyone?" Lauren said, indicating the extra place setting at the table.

"Yes, as a matter of fact, we are," was all Annie replied, taking a sip of her drink. She hadn't looked Tom in the eye since he came back into the kitchen.

After a few moments, a striking woman with auburn hair and brown eyes followed Oliver through the kitchen door. In my estimation, she must have been nearly six feet, with impressive legs and a seemingly natural marcel wave in her short hair. Lauren glanced up from her plate and took in the woman's long limbs and chic minimalist style. She was the opposite of Lauren, whose clothes tended to broadcast the amount of effort that went into their selection and application, as though she were dressing for the TV version of her life rather than her actual life, most notably during the Christmas bazaar at school.

"Lauren, this is Zara; Zara—Tom; Tom, Zara, and of course, you know Annie," Oliver said.

"Hi again," she said to Annie, who responded with a deranged smile and an unnatural-sounding "Hello."

Tom put out his hand. "Hi, lovely to meet you," he said, rising from his seat.

"Likewise," she said.

When Oliver began acting peppier than usual, Tom quickly figured out what was going on. Between Oliver's animated behavior and his eye contact with Annie, it didn't take a genius to interpret that this was a setup, especially when Zara was artlessly plonked next to Tom at the lunch table. Had everyone been in on this from the start? Lauren hadn't uttered a peep on the way over, and now she seemed to be studying Zara as though she were the subject of a life-drawing class.

"Zara—*do* tell Tom about what you've been doing in India for the past few months," Oliver said from the head of the table, sharpening his carving knife.

Zara began regaling everyone about her recent work in Mumbai. She was highly intelligent but not lacking a sense of humor, something Tom and I had always doubted about lawyers. Tom wondered what his reaction might have been had this attempt at a setup occurred even a week ago. Would he have been receptive? Was he receptive now? This woman beside him was undeniably impressive and attractive by anyone's standards. Even I was warming to her. Tom circled the rim of his glass and mulled over the notion of that possibility—trying to drum up an attraction for Zara. How hard could it be? he wondered. After all, he hadn't met Grace in real life. Perhaps *this* was the real opportunity—to build something on sound architecture with no secrets in the mortar.

"Tom used to work in finance," Annie said, masticating a roast potato.

"Used to?" Zara said.

"Yes. I concentrate on Henry now. I guess I'm a sort of stay-at-home dad."

Zara nodded. "But what about when he's at school?" she said. "Don't you ever fancy doing a mixture of both? As much as I love my kids, I can't imagine being with them twenty-four seven."

Tom looked around the table at his friends' expressions. Oliver obviously hadn't filled Zara in on the grim details. "Yeah, it—it was a pretty easy decision for me," he said. "And, no, I don't miss the long hours at all."

"Tom is a great dad," Annie said, leaning into the table. "He's not irresponsible. Or an idiot. He has morals and he doesn't act on a whim, do you Tom?"

"Darling? Are you all right?" Oliver said. "You're not blinking."

"I'm fine," Annie said through gritted teeth.

"I don't know how you do it," Lauren said to Zara. "I could never leave Basil and Jarvis for months on end. Don't you find it hard to leave the children like that? For those long stretches of time while you're away?"

"Sometimes I bring them with me," Zara said, drawing her knife and fork to a close.

"To *Mumbai*? What do they do about school?" Lauren said.

"They have schools there," Zara said.

"I suppose," Lauren said. "I read that children need routine, especially after a divorce. When my husband left, I decided as a single mother to keep Basil and Jarvis on a strict schedule. I read that any deviation from stability can lead to severe trauma and potentially walk them into a life of homicidal choices, bad partners, and intravenous drug abuse."

"Lauren, can you help me with the cheesecake?" Oliver said, bolting up from the table, his chair bumping along the wooden floor.

"Can I pour you some more wine?" Tom asked.

"Please," Zara said, sliding her glass towards him.

"You barely touched your chicken," Lauren said as she collected the plates. "Are you vegan? Is that how you stay so slim?"

"Lauren, help. Please!" Oliver shouted from the fridge. "The cheesecake."

"Annie, where can I find your loo?" Zara asked.

"I'll show you," Tom offered, already standing.

"Yes, Tom," Annie said. "Show Zara the loo!" Zara's face broke into a smile, catching Tom a little off guard. She really was very pretty.

"Thank you," she said.

As they walked through the hall, Zara was quick to inform Tom that she had no idea about the setup.

"You and I both," he said, laughing.

They stopped by the Wedgwood vase in the hallway. Zara slid her long, elegant fingers into the back pockets of her black jeans as the two of them stood facing each other for a moment. A painting hung above the chimneypiece, of Yeats in his later years, looking genial and mellow. Beneath Yeats' beady eyes, Tom thought how much simpler it would be to do things the right way round, starting from true north with a woman like Zara who was sanctioned by his friends. It could also be helpful to have a lawyer at his disposal.

"Did you want to go for a drink?" Tom asked, at the same time Zara said, "I feel like I should just come right out and say this."

"Okay . . . ?" Tom said, belting up for another peculiar conversation.

"Can we sit for a moment?" she said. They sat down on the upholstered club fender, the fire crackling behind them. "I think Oliver might have the wrong end of the stick about me. My fault entirely. I haven't exactly been honest with him. Or with myself, really," she said, pulling her sleeves farther down her wrists. "I don't know. Over the course of our friendship, I've always been married, so it's not Oliver's fault that he thinks this is my thing. We bumped into each other at Frieze the other day, and when he asked me to lunch, I didn't think anything of it. I hope it's not uncomfortable for you."

"Not at all," Tom said.

"Truth is, I'm actually in love with someone, and it's a disaster."

"Why a disaster?" Tom said, crossing his arms. He felt strangely relieved at the prospect that this wasn't going to go anywhere. "What's wrong with him?"

"*She's* my daughter's nanny. And she hasn't a clue."

"Ah," Tom said in that short, clipped way that always used to make me laugh. "Yes, well, that is rather a pickle." Zara laughed and put her hands up to her mouth.

"Sorry. I think I'm a bit tipsy. I don't usually drink at lunch. It's just . . . I'm going to go home after this, and she's going to be there, being adorable, and kind, and to be blunt, I don't know how much more of this secrecy I can take." Zara leaned her forearms on her knees and dropped her head. "*God.* It felt so bloody good to come out and say that," she said.

"I get it," Tom said. "I've got myself in a pickle too. I think I like someone I shouldn't." He looked back at the kitchen door. The fire let out a bang, making Zara jump as a log fell into a rearranged position. "I do wonder, would it really be that bad? To tell her?" Tom said.

"Well, it would blow up my entire life, and maybe hers too."

"Would it though?"

"I don't know. I suppose I've just gotten so used to keeping secrets." Tom looked down at the coral-colored rug on the floor before lifting his eyes to meet Zara's expectant gaze.

"Maybe we're both overthinking things," he said.

"I can't help it. I'm a lawyer." For a moment, Tom was tempted to ask Zara's legal advice on his own recent postal conundrum. Maybe she'd know the immediate ramifications or any potential loopholes, but he couldn't find the entry point to the story. Instead, he showed Zara the door to the downstairs loo and made his way back to the table. At the very least, thinking about Grace wasn't a crime, was it?

The table was quiet when Tom reappeared in the kitchen, the thick silence suggesting that everyone was waiting for him to say something.

"I know what you're doing," Tom said to Oliver.

"I'm not *doing* anything," Oliver said, decanting another bottle of red. "Quite a girl, though."

Lauren scrunched her face. "Who?" she said. "Zara? Tom doesn't like girls like that. She's very scrawny. What is it with you and setting Tom up with people? I mean, you tried to set us up. Do you remember, Tom? Remember, Oliver wanted to set us up? How crazy is that?"

No one said anything. The wax from the candle continued its slow, inexorable drip, hardening on the foliage of the vines. It was so odd hearing Lauren refer to their non-setup. She'd never once mentioned it to me when I was alive. She'd dated Harry Von Wankerface for two years after Tom and I got together and barely came up for air before landing on Daniel.

"When are you going to take Zara out?" Annie said as Oliver put a cheese board down on the table.

"I'm not taking her out. It's not going to work," Tom said.

"I think it will," Annie said, picking up her phone. "Why don't you two have dinner tonight? I can book you a table at Le Caprice."

Oliver had his mouth full of cheese, but it didn't stop him from replying, "What do you mean 'It's not going to work'? You haven't even tried."

"I've got Andrew on the line," Annie said. "What time do you want the table? Seven? Eight?"

"Annie, stop it. He's not keen," Lauren said. "And besides, Le Caprice has gone off terribly."

"Annie, hang up the phone," Tom said. "I appreciate the thought. It's very lovely. And Zara's lovely. If I do ever find myself in an international humanitarian crisis, I shall call on her, but I think I like someone else."

"Tom," Annie said. "No, you don't." Her eyebrows looked like they had shot up into her hairline. "Zara's here now. There's no baggage. There's no *harm* in going out with Zara!"

"Annie. You're shouting," Oliver said.

"You like someone?" Lauren said, her eyes like saucers. "Who? Is it Margaret? From Mummy's Music Class? The one who always wears those dotty leggings?"

"No. It is most certainly not Margaret from Mummy's Music Class," Tom replied. "And on that note, as Henry is staying here tonight, I'm going to have to rain-check that delicious-looking cheesecake."

"What?" Lauren said. "But it hasn't got a single crack!"

Before any of them could ask any more questions, and much to Tom's relief, Zara chose that moment to return to the table.

"What did I miss?" she said. For the first time in ten years, Lauren was speechless.

CHAPTER SEVEN

It was early spring, and Tom and I were walking along the Wiltshire Downs, humoring each other with the idea of one day moving to the country. It was only our first morning visiting with some friends of Tom's, so the novelty of unpolluted air and a distinct lack of people hadn't quite worn off yet. Those first few hours away were always the most heavenly, before Duke's coat became crisp and matted with mud and I hadn't yet been forced into any group culinary participation.

Even though we were going on and on about the idea of uprooting, we were both aware that neither of us would be capable of a move like that; after twenty-four hours, we always started checking the train times back to London. Tom struggled with the lack of decent phone signal, and I was plagued with the looming anxiety that one of our friends was going to ask me to dice an onion. Still, we continued to point out houses we might one day buy and imagine ourselves in them growing old and gray.

"I'd have a subscription to Farmers Guardian, *and you'd make friends*

with all the locals in the pub, who'd invite you to pick wild garlic in the woods with them," Tom said, weaving his gloved fingers through mine.

"Is that a euphemism for dogging? Or taking mushrooms?" I asked.

"We'd have to learn the local vernacular too, you know. And you couldn't be pootling around in those Hermès 'walking' boots. You'd have to wear proper Gore-Tex ones, fully waterproof, by Merrell. And you'd have a raincoat that you always kept in the car."

"Do I pootle?" I said, waiting for Duke to get out of the sheeps' water trough.

"You really do. It's sexy, though." My nose was starting to run, and I could feel the cold creeping into my toes.

"Would you swim in that dirty old lake?" I said, lifting our held hands to gesture towards it.

"Baby, that's not a lake, that's a pond."

"What's the difference?" I said. Tom took me in for a moment. I couldn't tell if he was concentrating on the answer, had spotted a hair poking out my nostril, or was appalled that I'd asked such a simple question.

"A swan can only take off on a lake. If a swan can't take off, then it's a pond." I didn't care if it was true, it was the most romantic theory I'd ever heard.

*

Even though it was only late afternoon, a warm, buttery light emanated through the windows of Sprezzatura, the blade sign catching ever so slightly in the wind. As soon as Tom opened the door, the butler's bell rang overhead, triggering a muffled female voice from somewhere inside to call, "I'll be right up!"

Tom stood alone in the shop, like an anxious schoolboy waiting for the reply of a girl he'd just asked to dance. He used to have so much confidence—a little too much, in my opinion. He longed to tap back into it, like in the days when he'd enter a conference room with his dick swinging and lay it all out on the table without a moment's thought. Telling Zara to stop overthinking things had seemed so easy. He'd left Annie's with a spritely step. But driving over, the reality of the letter had burned a hole in his pocket. The right thing to do was return it. Grace had a right to know that her anonymity had been breached. But what would happen if she wasn't receptive to the news? Or, worse, angry? Would she throw him out? Or call the police?

Tom hovered by one of the mahogany shelves, hoping Grace might appear any second so he could finally put this matter to bed. He picked up a bottle of Brunello and feigned interest in its label. The expanse of Tom's wine knowledge was minimal at best. He knew he liked his white dry and his red on the lighter side, but that was the extent of it.

A few minutes went by, and she had still yet to surface. Tom fumbled by the reds, trying to figure out his opening line. During all the faffing, Tom hadn't noticed a table draped in a neatly ironed white tablecloth set with candelabras. Out of the corner of his eye, he saw the cellar's trapdoor propped open behind the counter. He inched closer, past the table, towards the hatch, causing the floor-boards to creak beneath him—a woman's voice quickly followed. "Make yourself comfy! We'll be up in just a minute!"

Now that he was within decent earshot, he knew it was her. He'd listened to that CD enough times to recognize that voice—*her* voice. Tom froze in front of the counter, his heart slamming in his chest. His mind went blank. As he stood there, rattled, he reminded himself that none of this was originally his doing. It wasn't his fault the letter had been incorrectly sent to him; *he* hadn't mixed it up. Maybe if he took the approach that the letter was a funny coinci-dence, they would laugh about it and take it from there?

Would he leave out the part about Henry for now? Leave out the part that because of her egg, he had managed to survive the most horrific event that could ever happen in a father's life? That seemed too gargantuan an introduction. He couldn't even fathom himself articulating it. *Hey, so, funny thing. I got the wrong letter in the post. My wife and I made a child with a surrogate using your egg and then she got blown up with my daughter. And I was left holding the baby and HERE I AM!* It was hardly the most amorous kindling.

I shouldn't be here, Tom thought. He'd just decided to leave when the shop's door swung open and a gaggle of women—all a certain age and reeking of patchouli—barged in, chatting as they found seats around the table with routine precision, like regulars in a smoky bingo hall.

Tom was so taken aback by the unexpected stampede of females that he'd failed to notice Grace emerging through the trapdoor to the cellar holding a decanter filled with red wine. She pushed herself off the final step of the ladder and greeted Tom with a parted smile. For a moment, they were just inches apart. Their eyes met. This time, Tom didn't stumble back.

"Oh," she said, as though surprised to find someone like Tom standing there. *God, she's even more ravishing up close.* "Sorry, I didn't know we had a customer." She nudged her fringe off her face, then passed the decanter to a woman with electric-pink highlights who'd just climbed up the ladder behind her. "Can I help you find something?" she said, looking at her watch. "Hi, Marjorie. *Someone's* been to the hairdresser."

"I know," she replied. "It's a bit too short, but hey ho."

Grace's proximity was making Tom lightheaded. Her lips had a sheen to them, captured beneath her defined upper lip. Tom had always thought Henry had got that from him, but clearly, he hadn't. "Can I . . . *help* you with anything?" she said again. "Or can my assistant, Nellie? We're about to close the door for a . . . sort of . . . tasting," Grace said, then gestured at the petite woman with the pink hair.

"No. Yes," Tom said. "That's why I'm here. Sorry, I was . . . in another world for a moment. I'm—just—here. For the . . . for the tasting." Tom's eyes were still wide, but at least he'd started blinking again.

"The tasting?" Grace said, cocking her head over to the left ever so slightly. Nellie glanced over at Grace and shrugged. Every time Grace's lips parted to reveal that irresistible poppy-seed gap between her teeth, Tom had to curtail his mind from returning to the other night when he'd thought about those lips in the private darkness of his bedroom. "You're here for Sunday Blues?" she asked.

"Yeah, I love the blues. I love . . . blues music." Nellie snorted, pushing up the sleeves of her purple hoodie to reveal a plethora of tattoos.

"Right," Grace said. "Can I talk to you for just a moment?" She beckoned him over to the shelves, which were lined with golden-colored dessert wines. "I think there's been a bit of a mix-up. This isn't a regular tasting per se. It's more of a gathering I run. For widows?" Though they were standing alone, Tom got the distinct sense that ears had pricked up.

"Right, I see," he said. "Silly me. I'll be off." He felt for the letter in his pocket. Should he just pass it to her and leave? Then he played back what she'd just said. *A group for widows? Was Grace a . . . widow? Was it too forward to ask?*

"But I haven't closed the register yet, so if there's anything you wanted to buy—"

"What about widowers?" he said. "Are they welcome?" The room fell silent. Now she was the one who looked as if she'd seen a ghost.

"Yes," she said. "Yes, of course. Sorry. I shouldn't have assumed. I'm Grace."

"Tom," he said, taking her hand and shaking it. As if he didn't already know, not only her name but her dislike of cold weather and the fact that she'd been adopted and used to live in Italy.

Grace extracted her hand from Tom's. She pulled a chair from behind the counter and gestured for him to sit down, then took her seat at the head of the table, identifiable by a pile of things that

Nellie had just set out: a stack of warm printouts and her notepad, open with a black Biro in its trench.

"Right then," Marjorie said. "I'm Marjorie. Husband, Robert, died of lung cancer."

"Blanche," the woman next to her said. "Skiing accident."

"Jenny," said the next one, a handbag the size of a suitcase on the table in front of her. "Parkinson's. Hello."

"Edith," said a woman who looked remarkably like Olivia Colman. "Heart attack." A pause ensued.

"As I said, I'm Grace," Grace said. She looked down at her wine notes. "Pietro. Heart attack in the bath."

"Your turn," Marjorie said, gesturing at Tom.

"Right," Tom said. He swallowed. The room held its breath. "Honor. Suicide bomber." He waited for the collective gasp or the chorus of "I'm so sorry," but none came. The last time he'd seen those words had been when he signed our death certificates. The articulation threw him straight back onto that gurney in Paris.

"Right then," Marjorie said. "You've come on a good week, Tom. We're opening a wine my Robert absolutely loved. Barolo. He was a real snob about wine, so it's the good stuff."

As Grace passed around the printouts, Nellie began pouring wine from the decanter into tasting glasses. It was nearly dark outside, and the streetlights were gently warming up to white. Tom undid the buttons on his woolen peacoat and put it on the back of his chair. He didn't generally lead with the widower card. Yet here he found himself at a widows' convention, wedged between Blanche, in her mauve cardigan, rubbing a heavy-scented cream into her veiny hands, and Jenny, who seemed to be constantly staring off into the middle distance with a permanent smile. Grace closed the latch on the shop door and Nellie lit the candles on the table, until Blanche complained that she couldn't read the printout and Grace turned the dimmer up.

Even though Tom had felt more at ease with the dimmers on low, he was glad for the light. He would have preferred every light in the shop to be on high, so that he could closely examine every bit of this woman. But was this genuine attraction or his mind playing tricks on him? Some sort of muscle memory at odds with his brain, trying to tell him that every double take was just old habits dying hard.

"Right, has everyone got a glass?" Grace said from the head of the table. As she spoke, Tom took full advantage to observe her unencumbered, nodding as though he knew exactly what she was talking about, laughing when the other women erupted in titters about some wine joke he didn't get. "Let's start with color," she said. Everyone glanced down at their printout.

"Whoop, better spit that back in. I've already started," said Jenny, who had cracked on regardless of the color. Tom tried to appear as if he were interested in the contents of his glass as opposed to Grace's lithe fingers, which were long like Henry's. He put the glass up to the light, holding it like a chalice.

"It's always useful," Grace said, coming over to him, "to hold the glass against something white, so you get the true color—against the tablecloth, for example." He watched as she rolled the stem between her fingers with the glass at an angle.

"How do you do that?" Tom said. "How do you roll the glass between your fingers like that?" Grace put her hand on Tom's, demonstrating the motion, her fingers gently rubbing over his. Her touch was electric.

"Like that," Grace said. "Exactly. You've got the hang of it."

"A bit heavy for my taste," Blanche said, clearly the downer of the group.

"So, what are we getting for color?" Grace continued.

Tom tried to pull himself back down to earth. That simple touch had knocked him sideways, his mind overanalyzing whether her hand had lingered on his and, if it had, what it meant. He looked at

the wine again, then back up at Grace, who was swirling her glass
in her hand with practiced elegance; he took a beat and said,

"Red."

Grace laughed along with the rest of the women. It was a joke
he always used to make at restaurants when asked to taste the
wine.

"Yes. Very good," she said. He wanted to do it again—to make
her laugh. He'd forgotten how wonderful it felt to make a woman
laugh.

"Can we taste it now?" Tom said, clearly eager for the Dutch
courage. A bird never flew on one wing, after all. It was something
Oliver always said.

"Ooh, someone's eager," Edith said.

"Not yet. Patience. Now we smell." Grace held the glass by its
stem. She swirled it once more before closing her eyes and putting
her whole nose into the bud of the glass. Tom did as he was told
and followed suit. "And remember, you can't get it wrong. You
could tell me it smells like the inside of your fridge, and I can't say
it doesn't—that's what I love about wine. It's never just one thing.
It's complex."

"I'm getting a lot of red currants and shoe polish," Marjorie
said. "How about you, Blanche?"

"It just smells like a headache to me."

"Okay, thank you, Blanche, for that," Grace said.

"I smell chestnuts," Jenny said. Tom couldn't concentrate on the
smell of the wine or the gradation of color. He was so used to being
the disarmer. Now here he was, disarmed.

"Gosh, just, that sniff," Marjorie said. "I feel like I'm back on
the train from Florence. Robert was so excited to get back on the
train. We were over an hour early. I think this was the most expensive bottle on the menu." She paused. "May I take a sip?"

"Yes, of course," Grace said. She didn't pretentiously aerate the
wine in her mouth, or if she did, Tom didn't notice.

"Just as I remember it," Marjorie said. "And, in other news, my Louise is having another baby. A girl this time. Robert always said she would make a great mother. He was so good with the children." Jenny put her hand on Marjorie's.

"Have you thought any more about going back to Italy, Grace?" Jenny said, still with an odd, fixed smile.

"No, I haven't," Grace said, sitting up straight in her seat and focusing on something written on the printout. "Right. Let's move on . . . Tom?" Grace said. "You didn't try the wine." Tom swigged back a gulp, then pushed the glass away from him.

"What do you think?" Grace said. He fixed his eyes on her, the candlelight reflecting in those bottomless blue eyes as she met his gaze. The wave caught him and pulled him under.

"I think I like it," he said, causing the blood to rush to his neck. She quietly cleared her throat and looked away. I could tell from the way Grace was fidgeting that Tom wasn't the only one feeling something. She seemed flustered. Grace snapped the cap on her Biro and realigned her papers.

"Excuse me for a moment. I—I think I left a window open in my flat."

"Oh," Nellie said. "I can get it . . ."

"No. I'll go."

Grace walked behind the counter through the door that led to her flat upstairs. As I expected, there was no window open. While Sprezzatura was like a Nancy Meyers set, with a perfectly worn-in, wooden counter, stacks of freshly pressed tissue paper, and a vase of peonies, Grace's flat was austere, verging on a corporate rental. The only personal touch I could see was the wallpaper, a waterfall of fluorescent pink Post-its, but these weren't positive affirmations, encircled in a love heart. They were her wine notes, covered with factual minutiae. She stood facing the wall, her eyes charging across regions, dates, and questions as if she were trying to piece together some sort of a homicide.

"Describe the location of the Cotes de Duras," she read aloud, shaking her head. "Don't know," she said, then turned over the Post-it. "Southwest France. Due east of Bordeaux. Oceanic climate." She crumpled up the note and threw it on the floor before taking to the wall and swiping in every direction, Post-its flying everywhere, stopping only when Nellie appeared beside her in the sitting room.

"Everything okay?" Nellie asked, surveying the carpet of pink Post-its on the floor. "Jenny's after some crackers."

"Fine, why?"

"You've got a Post-it on your arm." Grace ripped off the Post-it and stuck it on the counter with the others, then opened the cupboard, pried the lid off a tin of Jacob's crackers, and slammed them onto the board.

"I wasn't expecting an extra person, and now I don't know if we have enough Brie," she said.

"Right . . . You mean for the hot guy downstairs that clearly fancies you?"

Grace's face turned red. "No he doesn't," she said.

"Yes he does. He hasn't stopped looking at you. You're basically on a date."

"Don't be ridiculous."

"Oh, I forgot. Silly me. You don't 'do dates,'" Nellie said, making quotey fingers, a gesture I loathed, but it was justified here. "Can I give you a bit of advice?"

"I would really, really rather you didn't." Grace shoved the board into Nellie's midsection. "And on that note, after tonight, the group goes back to being just women." Nellie narrowed her eyes. "This is a serious group. I am all some of these women have. I can't have any of them getting distracted with what you call 'hot guys.'"

"I don't think they're the ones getting distracted." The two of them faced off over the tin of crackers. "And if you think I'm going down there to tell a perfectly nice man whose wife was killed in a terrorist attack that he's not welcome, you've got another thing coming. *You* tell him, if you feel so strongly about it."

"Maybe I will," Grace said. Nellie hesitated, then left with the crackers. Grace stood alone in the room. Once Nellie was out of sight, she began picking up the Post-its, her eyes welling up as she stuck them back onto the barren wall. "Fuckssake," she said.

While Tom anxiously waited for Grace to return to the table, he made small talk with Jenny, who was angling to set him up with her daughter, a car insurance broker, an offer he politely declined.

"So, Tom, how did you find us?" Marjorie said.

"I got something in the post," Tom said, which was more or less true. Even though he was indeed a widower, he was there under false pretenses. While Grace was upstairs, Tom was away with the fairies trying to figure out how best to orchestrate a moment alone with her without it seeming peculiar. He was in such a swirl about it that he didn't notice his phone ringing in his pocket.

"Do you prefer Tom or Thomas?" Jenny said.

"Sorry?" Tom said. His mother was the only person who called him "Thomas."

"Is that you? That buzzing? Is that your mobile telephone?" Jenny said.

Tom glanced down and pulled his iPhone out of his jeans pocket. When he saw Annie's number on the screen, his complexion went milky as he imagined Henry with a broken limb or something much worse, the place my mind used to go when the school rang in the middle of the day. He leaped out of his chair, knocking over his empty glass. He hoped he wasn't over the limit to drive to the hospital.

"Hello? Is everything okay?" Tom said into the phone as he pushed through the door and onto the pavement, bracing himself for the worst. A flash of that day. The acrid smell of smoke. The feeling at the back of his neck as he ran down the stairs at the Ritz to try to find us.

"Daddy?" Henry's chirpy voice on the other end. The chilly evening air hit his face.

"Hi, Tootle." He tried to sound relaxed, but it was almost impossible to calm himself in moments like these. "Are you about to go to bed?"

"Mmhmm," Henry said. Across the road, a newsagent closed the shutters of his shop and rattled them to check they were locked.

"Did you watch a film?" Tom said, pacing up and down the pavement.

"Yes," Henry said. Tom could hear Annie whispering something to him in the background. "Good night, Daddy," he said. There was a rustling sound, and then Annie's voice on the other end.

"Hi, he's been wonderful. Going to finish watching *Brambly Hedge* now and then stories." I knew that tone. Annie didn't beat around the bush; Tom was going to get an earful after Henry was asleep.

"Okay, great. I got scared for a second—when I saw your number."

"I did text you, to say we would call when it got close to bedtime. Anyway, where are you?"

"Not far from home," Tom lied. He was already feeling a thousand times lighter. He could hear Oliver in the background counting to twenty for pre-bed hide-and-seek. In his peripheral vision, he sensed someone had come outside—Grace, holding out his coat. She walked towards him with the glow of the moon behind her and passed it to him.

"You forgot this," she said, then turned to go back inside.

"Who is that speaking?" Annie said. "Tom?"

"I'll call you tomorrow," he said before hanging up the phone and calling, "Grace?"

Grace stopped in the doorway and looked back at him; her

fringe had fallen slightly onto her face. "Thank you. For letting me stay," Tom said. Through the window, he could see the women, gathering their coats. "I really enjoyed the company."

"Of course," she said.

"I'm sorry I ran out like that," he said. "It was my son. He was calling me to say good night. He's staying over at his godparents. It's just the two of us. His mother died. Before he was born." Grace tilted her head to the side. "Long story. But he—he was born via surrogate." Tom avoided telling this story at all costs. After the funeral had squeezed the life out of him, he'd promised himself he would never talk of it again. But as Grace stood in front of him, it felt natural to tell her. It felt natural to say, "He's called Henry. His mother and sister died—in the attack." Grace pinched the collar of her shirt and looked at the pavement.

"I'm so sorry," she said. The way Grace said these three words landed in a different way than it had the countless times Tom had heard other people utter the same sentence over the years. For the first time that winter, he could see his breath as he spoke. Now was the time to tell her who she was to him. It was just the two of them beneath the sodium streetlights, just as he had wanted. Just as he'd imagined.

"There's actually more to the story," Tom said. "If you can believe it."

"Oh?" Grace said.

"This is a—this is a tricky one." Grace crossed her arms, looking back over her shoulder towards the shop. She was clearly cold without her coat. "I came to your shop tonight because a few days ago—Well, it's a bit of a funny muddle, really, not ha-ha-funny, but strange-funny and—Okay, hang on, I'll start again."

Just then, the door opened, and the ladies poured onto the pavement, scarves tightly wound around their necks.

"Right," Marjorie said. "We're off to the pub. Gracie, go inside and fetch your coat and lock up. We'll wait for you."

And just like that, Grace was gone. The window had closed. A crowded Sunday pub was not the right place to tell her.

Edith extracted a Werther's from her handbag and unwrapped it noisily. "Tom, will you be joining us?" she said.

"Maybe next time," Tom said.

"Welcome to the gang," Marjorie said. "Same time next week?"

"Same time next week," Tom said.

CHAPTER EIGHT

"Mummy!" Chloe called. I'd been sitting at the kitchen table for nearly two hours in a state of creative constipation. I'd got down a total of nineteen words of my memoir and was under some strange delusion that if I wrote about my longing for a child, an actual baby would have to appear at some point. The only glitch was that my agent had told me not to bother. The publishers had rejected my memoir idea outright. I was a children's author, tethered to the adventures of Madame Choc Chip and Mr. Mango Sorbet.

"Mummy?" Chloe said, clomping over to me in a pair of heels I'd only worn once. Her hair was on top of her head in a topknot like mine, only she'd finished hers off with a tiara.

"Yes," I said, not taking my eyes from the screen. "Coco, please don't pull at my pocket like that."

"Will you dance with me, Mumma? You can be the hedgehog and I'll be the worm?" She pushed a bobbly hedgehog costume into my lap, accidentally knocking it against my keyboard.

"Chloe, be careful. This is Mummy's work. I'm just finishing this page. Can I have half an hour?" I said, convinced I could break through this wall before bath time.

"How long is that?" Chloe asked, pressing play on my iPod. Suddenly Stevie Nicks was serenading me with *"If I could turn the page"* from every corner of the room.

"Thirty minutes. I just need to finish this. Mummy will get in trouble if she doesn't finish." That was a lie. There was zero demand for my story. But I carried on sitting there, beating a dead horse, writing about my desire to mother differently from Colette while my three-year-old daughter danced in the other room without me.

*

The gate to Annie's was already open when Tom arrived to pick up Henry the following morning. There was still dew on Richmond Green, where it had rained most of the night, the wet glossy blanket broken only by a track of early morning dog walkers. Annie's wooden trug was by the front door, piled high with rosemary, Henry's adorable little Wellies like fallen dominoes beside it. Nothing to suggest Annie was out buying the newspapers like Tom hoped. He reached for the knocker, bracing himself for a further onslaught of self-righteous monologuing from Annie. He wasn't in the market for any unsought opinions, even though she and I both knew the only thing he needed to do was tell Grace about the letter. He knocked at the door, which Annie opened almost immediately, a cup of steaming tea in hand.

"Morning. Where's Henry?" Tom said, Duke plump and panting at his heel.

"With Oliver. Listen to me," Annie said, closing the door behind him. "I haven't slept a wink. I know you went there last night. I can feel it. I can feel what's happening." Annie took a sip of her tea and tightened her paisley robe.

"I shouldn't have told you," Tom said. He looked over his shoulder; he could hear the *PAW Patrol* theme tune coming from the red room, where we all used to watch television.

"No. But you did. And now I do know, and I wish I didn't. The woman Honor chose was a closed donor. I heard her say it with my own ears. I heard her say it on that CD. She was meant to be anonymous, Tom. Please don't borrow trouble," Annie said.

Annie and Lauren had spent as much time listening to those CDs as I had, discussing details and dissecting hobbies. But this was different. I could see with piercing clarity how much Tom was falling for Grace. I'd seen him scramble for words and blush over red wine. I'd spent more time than anyone looking into those eyes. There was no greater cheerleader for this relationship, but Tom had given himself a false start. I knew too well how stories like this ended.

"I should never have told you. I should never have told you I liked her."

Annie's eyebrows jumped up in tandem. "You *like her*? You didn't tell me that. Jesus, Tom." Annie stepped in closer, her eyes wide and bloodshot. But before she could berate Tom any further, Henry ran into the hallway, throwing himself onto his father's legs.

"Daddy!" Henry said.

"Well, if that's the case, when are you going to tell her, Tom? When?" Annie said, tracking his eyes.

"At the next available opportunity." Tom scooped Henry into his arms. "Just leave it, Annie. I know what I'm doing."

*

Tom spent the following week as usual—school run, walking Duke, music class, a visit to the butcher, extended bath time, stories, bed. He ordered some new books for himself and Henry and had them posted to the house, still unable to step inside my favorite bookshop.

He didn't want to rifle through the children's section and risk stumbling across the new editions of my book. He didn't want to see the dates I died in black-and-white or read the dedication to Chloe, "our Coco." There were certain odd roadblocks of grief. Tom remained in our home, but the bookshop seemed too excruciating.

Only during the evenings now, instead of flicking through TV channels on an endless loop or changing lightbulbs that weren't out, Tom studied the wine books he'd bought earlier in the week with great agency——*Wine for Dummies* and *Windows on the World: Complete Wine Course*—reading about grape varieties and the white wines of Burgundy.

By the time Sunday came around, he'd watched *Sideways* four times and felt confident he'd be able to hold his own if questioned. He'd been reading about pairings and even bought a mature cheddar to take with him for the group, something I would have strongly advised against—turning up to see the girl you like with a large wheel of smelly cheese. He made it through Sunday lunch at Annie's, happily grazing like a hungry mule, doing his best to pretend that Annie wasn't being a little icy. Lauren even commented on his peppy mood over the sticky toffee pudding.

Later that evening, when Rita arrived to babysit Henry, Tom got in the car and sped off to Sprezzatura, arriving a painful twenty minutes early. He sat in the car deliberating whether to just rock up now or revert to the etiquette he'd had rammed down his throat at Eton, where they told him it was considered bad manners to be even a minute early. The analog clock in his Defender ticked, but the hands weren't moving fast enough so he opened the door and got out.

Within moments, the sound of the butler's bell rang overhead, and he was back in Grace's world. Unlike last week, the table in the shop wasn't covered with a white linen tablecloth. Instead, it was a collage of till rolls, accounting books, and crumpled receipts. A steaming cup of tea sat beside an open diary crammed with stray papers and a red pen. Had he got the wrong night? He wasn't *that* early.

"Oh hi, *Tom,*" Nellie said, coming up from the cellar.

"Hi," Tom said, unbuttoning his coat. "I know I'm a bit early. I brought this cheese." Nellie stood there awkwardly looking between the cheese and Tom. Something was off. Where were the glasses and the wine? Where was Grace?

"Thank you," she said, grunting as she received the cheese, which was clearly heavier than she anticipated. "So . . . a bit awkward. Funny thing—we canceled this week. The girls got through to the semifinals of their bridge tourney. We didn't know how to get hold of you. Otherwise, we would have let you know. Sorry." Tom fought to keep his face from falling.

"Oh, right. No big deal. Erm . . . I think I'm just going to leave the cheese then, and I'll come back next week," Tom said. "It looks like you've got a busy night ahead. Is it that time of the year already?" He dreaded the drive home and the thought of not seeing Grace again for another week. Tom didn't read romance novels. He'd forgotten just how quickly you could become tangled in another person's existence.

But he needn't have fretted, because the door that led to Grace's flat swung open, and she walked straight through it.

"Well, I've lost that box and—Oh, Tom. Hi."

"I'm just hearing about the bridge tournament," Tom said. "Sounds promising."

"Tom brought us this cheese," Nellie said. They all looked at the ill-fated cheese. Its looming, withered presence made it look like it had grown in the last five minutes.

"Oh, thank you," Grace said, putting the box on the counter.

"Grace, I was wondering if I could have a private word," Tom said.

"Right now?" Grace said. "We've kind of got an evening of accounts ahead of us."

"Actually, I was just leaving," Nellie said, fiddling with her nose ring.

"You were just leaving? *Really?*" Grace said. She looked at Tom. "Can it wait? It's just . . . I'm *really* behind on my accounts, and, as you can see, it's not my strong point."

"Well, can I help? It kind of *is* my strong point. I used to work in finance."

"I thought your coat looked expensive," Nellie said, giving Tom the once-over.

"You're offering to do my accounts?" Grace said. Nellie slid a chilled bottle of Riesling and two crystal glasses onto the table among the receipts.

"Yes," Tom said. "It wouldn't take me that long, I don't think."

"That's smashing, that is," Nellie said. "I'm a Pisces moon, so I'm utter shit at this stuff anyway. And she's hopeless, obviously."

"Thank you, Nellie, for your support," Grace said before turning to look at Tom. "You really wouldn't mind?"

"Not in the least. If we can have a chat after it's done," Tom said.

"Right, banging," Nellie said. "In that case, I'm going home to play *Call of Duty*." She put on her puffer jacket and dimmed the lights a smidge before locking the door behind herself.

"I need a glass of wine for this," Grace said.

She poured two glasses of wine and handed one to Tom. They sat down at the table amidst the debris of Grace's questionable accounting. As she pulled in her chair, their thighs lightly bumped, sending a jolt through Tom.

"It's not as messy as it looks," Grace said. "I have a system." Tom studied the table for a moment.

"Right . . . Well, it's definitely not a system I'm familiar with," he said.

"This was the part of owning a shop I hadn't factored in. I thought it would all be trips to meet winemakers across Europe and California and endless, glorious tastings, yet here I am back in England on a Sunday night doing my accounts."

"Back in England?" he said, though he knew full well from the CD that she used to live in Italy.

"Yeah, I moved back a few years ago. I was living in Italy. With Pietro." She searched the papers on the table the way I would have flipped through my notebook if Tom had brought up a topic I'd been trying to avoid. "What do you think of the wine?" she said.

"I think it's working," Tom said.

"Do you always have a smart-ass response for everything?"

"Only when I don't know the answer." She laughed and topped up Tom's glass.

The second glass tasted different from the first, light and fresh, or maybe that was just because he was drinking it with her. Tom had long ago hung up his spurs with no plans to get back in the saddle, yet here he was, sitting across from a woman, hoping she might like him or, at the very least, find him charming.

"Is this a system that's verbally explainable?" Tom said.

"Isn't it obvious?" He laughed; his eyes fixed on the point where her scar met the crease in her lip. Grace put on her glasses and picked up a pile with an orange Post-it marked "Invoices." "So, this yellow pile is money in, and it goes over here," she said, plonking it down. "Then I take *that* pile, which is money out, and I subtract it from this pile, so that I can figure out what I need to write in this column ... here, marked 'Deductions.' That's these receipts over here. Are you with me so far?" Tom passed a hand over his forehead and looked on, wide-eyed but utterly charmed. "Then, these"—she lifted a folder of till rolls above her head—"go over here with these. No—wait. That's wrong. This is payroll. *These* receipts—whoops," she said, dropping them on the floor.

As she bent down to retrieve them, Tom's eyes landed on her

diary. It felt strange to investigate it, but he couldn't help himself. He wanted to know everything about this woman. He wanted to know that she was playing tennis on Friday at half past nine and she was meeting with someone called Louis to discuss Château Lafon-Rochet tomorrow. But what was most interesting in that diary was that on Wednesday at ten o'clock, she had plans to go to Hobbycraft with Marjorie to get Halloween costumes. Hadn't Lauren also said at Sunday lunch that she needed to go to Hobbycraft? The very idea that my husband might be plotting a trip to a craft store during the lead-up to Halloween showed the extent of his growing infatuation.

"These were in order, but now, obviously, I need to do a bit of shuffling," Grace said. "I'm never going to get this done tonight. I'm already so behind."

"You obviously didn't play shops as a child."

"No. Not really. Playing shops never really appealed to me. I preferred playing on the allotment. My mum grew all sorts of things. But maybe if we'd played shops instead, I wouldn't have ended up doing it now and saved myself a lot of trouble," she said, flattening a curling bunch of till receipts.

"Luckily, I played a lot of shops. And I just need more wine, a piece of that cheese, preferably atop a cracker, and this chair and I can do this in an hour."

"An hour?"

"Maybe two."

Grace poured them both some more wine and leaned on the edge of the table while Tom mapped out a battle plan with the finesse of a blackjack dealer in Vegas. Every now and then, their eyes met, tempting Tom to slow down the whole process. Whether Grace was acknowledging it or not, this looked awfully like a date. To anyone walking by the window, the dim lighting, the half-drunk bottle of white, and the obvious chemistry would have ticked all the boxes.

"Numbers are clearly your thing," Grace said. "How come you don't work in finance anymore?" Tom braced himself. This line of questioning was never pleasant.

"I wanted to be there for Henry. Not just show up at the tail end of bedtime with my phone in my hand like I used to. I wasn't exactly 'Dad of the Year' before . . . everything," he said. Tom reached for a pile of receipts he'd already shuffled three times and straightened their edges. "Please tell me to stop if I'm going on about Henry too much."

"Don't be silly. You're not," Grace said, wiping the crumbs off her hands. "He's a lucky boy. My mum was really hands-on too. She made such a fuss of every little scratch. She once pretended to call an ambulance when I got stung by a stinging nettle." Tom paused, searching her face.

"Don't get me wrong, some evenings at home . . . I rattle around a bit. You can only watch so many episodes of *Curb Your Enthusiasm*."

Grace laughed. "I'm not sure that's true. I love Larry David. Do you need a paper clip for that pile? You've shuffled it quite a few times."

"Have I? I hadn't noticed." Grace rose from the table and grabbed a saucer of paper clips from beside the till. "I suppose I just don't want to make the same mistake twice or get distracted with work all over again."

"Avoid becoming a master sommelier then," Grace said. "I could literally spend the rest of my life studying and still barely scratch the surface."

"That's quite the task you've set yourself," Tom said, "All I know about that exam is from that documentary on Netflix."

"*Everyone* talks about that documentary."

"I bet. When do you take the dreaded exam?" Tom said.

"November, next year." Grace glanced around the table at the depleted pile of receipts. "Marjorie thinks I'm mad, of course."

"You're very sweet with her. How did Sunday Blues even come about?"

"Marjorie, of course. She came into the shop one Sunday looking for—you guessed it—Barolo. She told me that every year on the anniversary of her husband's death she bought his favorite wine and cracked it open with her girlfriends. The idea seemed so romantic, so at odds with what I thought you were supposed to do. We chatted for hours and ended up finishing the whole bottle. She said I'd helped banish what she called 'the Sunday Blues.' Then she came back the following week, this time with Jenny in tow, and a snack pack from Marks & Spencer. Then they just kept coming, and Sunday Blues was born. I can't believe that was six years ago." Grace smiled to herself; this serendipitous meet clearly moved something in her. Tom felt his gut clench, longing for the privilege of stumbling on Grace by chance like Marjorie had. "Can I ask you something or are you concentrating?"

"I can do both at the same time," Tom said, closing a paper file. "Talk and concentrate."

"How did you end up coming to Sunday Blues?"

Tom paused. She'd teed him up. They were alone. The conditions were perfect. Tom slid his hand towards Grace's until the sides of their fingers met. She glanced down at their hands and didn't pull hers away.

"I saw something I liked in the window," he said.

Grace looked up at him, her lips parted, framing the poppy-seed gap between her teeth. Tom leaned towards her. But even in this heightened state, in the back of his mind, he knew that this kiss wouldn't be a simple kiss. They were only inches apart, so close he could feel the heat from her skin, when Grace suddenly pulled away.

"Right then, I really have to get the rest of these accounts done by tomorrow," she said, rising, her face red. She moved to the other side of the table, away from him. "What's next? Payroll?" *Why did she pull away? Did I misread her?*

"Nothing's next. I—I finished an hour ago," Tom said, embarrassed. Was this divine intervention or a war of attrition? When Tom turned to leave, Grace scooped up their glasses and thanked him for all his help, before passing Tom his coat and locking the door behind him.

CHAPTER NINE

The morning of our wedding started off seamlessly. The weather was sub-lime, a perfect summer day for a garden ceremony. Tom and I had decided to get married in the exact spot we met—beneath the wisteria-covered pergola at Annie's house. I was fresh-faced, a bridal paragon, with just the lightest touch of a tan and a nude lacquer finish to my nails. My dress was long, vintage McQueen, with hundreds of satin-covered buttons up the back. The delight and awe on Tom's face when he saw me as I came down the makeshift aisle imprinted on my brain forever, much like my mother's comment when she saw my dress for the first time and said I could have used one more fitting.

The day was going so well until the champagne took a turn with all the red wine in my stomach and I had to be propped up during the speeches. Annie was equally sozzled. Lauren didn't touch a drop, wor-rying it might interfere with her bridesmaid duties, there at the ready in case anything went wrong.

When Tom and I crawled into bed at Annie's later that night, I could

barely string a coherent sentence together, but nonetheless insisted on
the consummation of our marriage. Tom was struggling with the buttons on the back of my dress. In all the commotion of getting ready, I'd
managed to lose the tool that undid the bloody things. In the end, I kept
the dress on and settled for what I thought was a very sexy blowjob. I
was midway through when I felt a jolt of pain in my jaw so severe, I
thought I'd had a stroke. Even in my drunken state, I knew something
had gone terribly wrong. I tried to close my mouth, but my jaw refused
to shut. I squeezed Tom's thigh with my nails to alert him to the crisis.
All I could do was make these "ahh, ahh, ahh" sounds, which he must
have initially confused for sexual enjoyment, because he remained mo-
tionless on the bed.

"Arrr, arrr, arrrr," I said. When Tom opened his eyes, I was looming
over him in my wedding dress, minus the veil, drooling everywhere like
a Saint Bernard. "Arrrrr, arrrr, arrrr."

At that moment, I think Tom couldn't separate his blurry, drunken
wedding-night fantasy with the reality that my jaw was wide open and
stuck that way. Was I trying something new? Something special for the
big night?

"Honor, what the fuck are you doing? Close your mouth. This isn't
funny," Tom said, "I don't feel safe. I think we should institute a code
word. I'm giving us a code word. Purple, purple, PURPLE!"

"Arrrr, arrr, arrrrr!"

"Wait, is your jaw . . . stuck?" I nodded, at this point fully crying.
I grabbed Tom's boxer shorts from the bed and stuffed them into my
mouth to absorb the drool. "Oh my God, Honor," Tom said, standing.
"I'm so drunk. I can't drive you to the hospital. We'll have to wake up
Annie or Lauren—Lauren seemed sober." Stepping into his trousers, he
fumbled out of our room and into the hallway to get Lauren, but in the
process crashed into a demilune table, knocking over a rare amphora,
and woke up the whole house.

An hour and half later, we were still at A&E with Lauren. For the
sake of propriety, I had replaced Tom's boxers with a tea towel, and was

now sitting on a gurney in my wedding dress when a doctor who looked like George Clooney came in to check my chart and examine my jaw.

"Do you want the good news or the really good news?" he asked, pulling the blue curtains closed around us.

"How can there possibly be good news," Lauren said. "I'm Lauren, by the way—the best friend."

"Arrrrr, arrrrr," I said, twisting round on the gurney to nod at Tom. The tight space was beginning to give me vertigo. On the other side of the blue curtains, someone's monitor beeped alarmingly.

"I think we have to ask yes-or-no questions here, Doc," Tom suggested.

"Okay, I can fix your lockjaw right now without anesthesia. At this point we have little option, unless you want to wait six hours until you sober up," George Clooney informed me. "It will hurt quite a bit, but it should work." Tom looked at me. Lauren looked at Tom.

"Tom, you seem a little peaky," Lauren said. "Are you all right? Do you need some Nurofen? I've got some in my bag. Or at the very least some Calpol sachets."

"Arrr, arrr, arrr," I said. My IV continued its slow, inexorable drip.

"We'll do it now," Tom said. "What's the really good news?"

"Well, congratulations," the doctor said.

"Congratulations?" Lauren said, foraging in her bag.

"Thank you, yes," Tom said. "Newlyweds. It's a very special time, as you can see."

"Yes, that too," George Clooney said. "But I meant congratulations . . . on the baby. You're pregnant."

*

"It's slightly concerning how well you know this place," Tom said to Lauren as they stood in aisle six of Hobbycraft. In all his dubious social engineering, he had drastically underestimated the sheer horror of a place like Hobbycraft, a big-box supply mecca designed to stop time and trap you in a windowless hangar. It had never occurred to him, until now, that these places even existed, or that once inside, it was as dog-eat-dog as the trading floor. For the whole of my friendship with Lauren, I had mostly managed to avoid these crafty outings. I had no need for a ten-pack of cocktail napkins printed with "*Mrs.*" in cursive or posters reading "THIS KITCHEN IS FOR DANCING."

Tom was doing his best to hurry Lauren along as she expertly navigated the Halloween section, filling up her trolley with orange and black paraphernalia. When he'd put this plan together, he'd envisioned Hobbycraft to be like the art shop on Carnaby Street with one till and two eager members of staff, but this place was more like IKEA. It would be so easy to miss Grace. How was he ever going to find her, moving at this tortuous pace with Lauren scrutinizing every item she picked up? He hadn't exactly planned on being a human coat stand, his arms akimbo with plastic trick-or-treat buckets hanging off them like lanterns on a scarecrow. It was five past ten. *Is Grace going to be on time? Is she parking? Is she in aisle 27?*

Lauren had been ecstatic, albeit flabbergasted, when Tom rang to ask if he could join her at Hobbycraft. He'd never attended the Halloween street party while Chloe was alive. He was always too busy with client dinners and spent most of the following day complaining about the mess on the street, but now Tom loved every bit of it—the slime, the cheap sweets, the plastic crap, even tidying up the street with Lauren the following day.

"Excuse us, coming through," said a pendulous-breasted woman, wearing a bright green T-shirt. Tom shimmied out of the way as a troop of oncoming craftspeople marched by, nearly knocking him over.

"I think we've got enough now, don't you?" Tom said. "Let's try the next aisle." He tried to look at his watch, but the pumpkin buckets were making his intended task less than straightforward. "Can I put these down for a second? I'll keep an eye on them."

"Do *not* put those down! If you turn your head for even a moment someone will nab them. The people here are ruthless. RUTHLESS. Trust me on this," Lauren said, looking round as if for a military sniper. "You won't believe the lengths people go to in these places," she whispered. Tom looked where Lauren was indicating to find a small octogenarian woman with an aggressive dowager hump trying to decide between two identical packets of purple sequins.

"Yes, she seems ruthless," Tom said as Lauren trotted on.

In the harsh, white light of Hobbycraft, it was hard not to notice the substantial amount of makeup Lauren was wearing, especially for a trip to a retail park on the outskirts of London. Since her divorce five years ago, she'd taken to wearing hair extensions every day and too much blusher, which under the wrong light left her looking a little like Mr. Blobby.

After Daniel had left, Lauren had made a point of being "fine" whenever asked. She continually told anyone who would listen that his departure had been a "blessing in disguise." But I knew that was rubbish. Lauren wasn't someone who could interpret divine messages. The idea of independence terrified her. She knew neither how to do solitary strolls nor enjoy dinner alone with a gripping novel. Her identity was a flat arc: down to her history of plateauing with men.

"Should we do pin the tail on the donkey or bobbing for apples?" she asked. "Fun fact! Did you know that it's not originally a Halloween game? It used to be that girls would bob their heads in water attempting to bite into apples named for their male suitor?"

"I find that game slightly odd, like some sort of voluntary waterboarding exercise," Tom said, raising his voice to compete with the Adele cover blaring from hidden speakers. "Do they always play this music here?" he asked.

"Yes, isn't it great?" Lauren said, picking up a bat-shaped streamer. "By the way, after the party on Thursday, I'm going to do dinner at my house—once the kids are asleep, obviously, if they ever go to sleep after all that sugar."

"Sounds good," Tom said, his arms starting to ache from holding all the jack-o'-lanterns. "I'll check if Rita's available to babysit."

"Brilliant," Lauren said, then whipped her phone out of her handbag. "I'm making Indian, your favorite. Cheese naan and saag aloo," she added, stifling a chuckle as she read something to herself off her phone. Tom didn't pry into Lauren's correspondence; all he could think about was finding Grace. The idea of not seeing her, after being trapped here, was incomprehensible. But when Lauren laughed again, this time a little bit louder, he felt compelled to ask.

"Oh, this? Nothing," she said, pushing her hand through the air. "It's just this guy I've been texting. I think he *really* likes me. He's not exactly my type, but I get so lonely sometimes. You know how our houses can feel? So big and empty. Don't you find that? That your bed just feels gigantic? Alone?" She paused. "The winter is the worst. It gets dark so early. We're so lucky to have each other." Lauren's voice broke, and for a moment Tom feared that she might cry. "I'd be lost without you."

"I'd be lost without you, too. This is a very large Hobbycraft. I'd never find the exit." Lauren snorted.

"You're always making me laugh," she said. "The guy I'm texting is not so funny."

"Yes, well. Should we split the list and get this going?"

"No. Let's stick together. Hey—look at this," Lauren said, stopping mid-aisle.

"I thought we had a long list to get through. Come on," Tom said as Lauren reached up for an oversized, tawny owl mask. After a fair amount of effort, Lauren contorted it over her face and hair and turned around. "Cooo, coooo, coooo," she began, flapping her arms. I think her intention was to make Tom laugh, but aside from Tom's phobia of birds that he liked to keep quiet, he was only interested in finding Grace. The owl's round, infinite eyes reminded him of a dream he had as a boy of an owl carrying off his mother.

"Lauren, can we wrap up the mask? My arms are going dead."

Lauren nodded and began tugging at the elastic edges, to no avail.

"Can you help me? It's very hot in here," she said after a moment, becoming somewhat flustered. "I think—I think it's stuck in my hair. Can you look?" As she tugged, Katy Perry singing "Firework" began blaring through the store.

"Okay . . . but I'm going to *have* to put these buckets down in order to do that successfully."

"No! Do *not* put those buckets down! Oh my God. I can't see anything."

"Okay, just give me a second," Tom said, plastic pumpkin baskets clanking as he attempted to release Lauren, but her hair extensions were caught, and the task was proving to be more arduous than he'd anticipated.

"What are these strange clippy things?" Tom asked, fumbling around in her hair.

"Don't pull on those—ow."

"We might have to cut it off," Tom said.

"What?!"

"Not your hair. The elastic. What aisle are scissors in?"

"Four."

"What aisle are we in now?"

"Thirteen. I'm getting claustrophobic. Tom? Are you there?"

"Follow me, Papageno," Tom said, unable to hold in his laugh.

"I don't think this is a time to joke about pizzas," Lauren said, following behind Tom, the feathers of the mask catching in the breeze as she walked.

As Tom explained his joke to Lauren, that Papageno was the half-man, half-bird of Mozart's *Magic Flute*, Lauren's panicked breathing escalated. He remembered something I always told him about his esoteric jokes, that if you had to explain it, then it wasn't a joke, but as they rounded the corner on their way to aisle four, Lauren collided with Marjorie from Sunday Blues, nearly knocking her off her sensible shoes.

"Marjorie!" Tom said, his arms still outstretched like Jesus on the cross. "Are you—are you all right?" The sight of this pensioner filled Tom with joy. Grace had to be close by.

"What's going on?" Lauren said, facing the opposite way.

"I'm fine," Marjorie said. "I'm made of rather tough stuff."

"Who's fine?" Lauren asked. "What's happening?"

"Did you get through to the finals of the bridge tournament?" Tom asked. "Grace mentioned that you had made it through the semis."

"What?" Lauren said.

"You know, as a matter of fact, we did. Thank you," Marjorie said, and Tom wondered if he detected a knowing smile. *Has Grace been talking about me?* After their aborted kiss, Tom had spent his evenings deconstructing the scene and concluded that to pull away, you have to lean in first. "She's here, you know."

"Who's here?" Lauren said just as Grace came around the corner laden with Halloween decorations. Even beneath Hobbycraft's aggressive lighting, Tom couldn't believe how staggeringly beautiful she looked in her red duffle coat with horn buttons, her hair tied high off her face. "Who are you talking to? Tom?"

"Look, Gracie, it's your accountant," Marjorie said, looking between them with a delighted expression.

"I can see that," Grace said. "Thank you, Marjorie. I told her you helped me the other day. Thanks again. For all the . . . adding up."

"It was my pleasure," Tom said. "Any time." Their eyes caught. Behind Grace, an employee crouched beside the display shelves, restocking baby skeletons.

"Can someone please tell me where I am?" Lauren said, her hands outstretched like a mummy. "I'm stuck in this mask, and I can't see."

Tom had forgotten all about Lauren, but now he registered Grace and Marjorie looking slightly puzzled, quite rightly, at his friend, the owl.

"Lauren, I want you to meet Grace and Marjorie," Tom announced into the depths of the owl mask.

"Who? Who?" Lauren said. The employee stood and wheeled his empty trolley down the aisle.

"I like your mask," Marjorie said, tilting sideways. "I was going to go as Willy Wonka, but maybe I should go as a crow. What do you think, Gracie?"

"Did they turn the heating up in here?" Lauren said. "I can't breathe."

"Tom. You've got your hands full," Grace said. "Maybe we should leave you to it." When he noticed that Grace was avoiding his eye, he worried she might be under the false impression that Lauren was his girlfriend. The only way to clarify any misinterpretation was to announce Lauren as though she were arriving at a ball in a *Bridgerton* novel.

"My friend here—Lauren, who is my *friend,* a very old, old, old friend and wise, is nevertheless stuck in a mask, which in retrospect is most likely designed for a child aged seven to nine. We are having something of an avian emergency. I don't suppose either of you are ornithologists?" Tom joked, and luckily Grace laughed.

"I'm worried about my hair!" Lauren shouted, in the direction of Grace and Marjorie. "I do not want Tom going at it with a pair of sewing scissors."

"Gracie, look, she's getting in a right flap," Marjorie said. "We can't leave her like this, poor love."

Grace looked from Tom to Lauren, then put her pile of decorations down on a display of flashing lanterns. Marjorie went off to find a pair of scissors while Tom, Grace, and Lauren chatted aimlessly. Tom longed for another opportunity to be back in the shop, just the two of them, getting to know each other, not exchanging small talk about the weather (bad) and the traffic coming out of London (worse).

By the time Marjorie returned with the scissors, the three of them had touched on every English small-talk milestone known to man. Marjorie, with her nimble fingers and crafty ways, seemed the obvious candidate to perform the extraction, but she'd forgotten her glasses and couldn't differentiate faux hair from natural, so Grace ended up taking over.

"Scalpel," Grace said, holding out her hand for the scissors.

"What?" Lauren said. Tom laughed. Was she leaning in again?

"Count down from a hundred," Grace said. "You'll be back with us in no time."

"Oh, you're joking. You're making a joke. Ha-ha. I feel like I'm on *ER*," Lauren said.

During the surgery, every so often Grace asked for Tom's help, and their fingers would touch and their eyes would lock. It took the best part of half an hour, but when the mask finally fell away, Lauren and Grace were standing within centimeters of each other. Lauren gulped her first breath of fresh air as she took in Grace's remarkable resemblance to me.

"Oh my gosh," Lauren said.

"There we are, pet. You're free to fly off to a wooded glen," Marjorie said.

"Right. Thank you, yes," Lauren said. Her hand went to her hair, as if to check it was still on her head, then she looked at Tom. "I just—Tom, doesn't she look so much like—"

"Lauren," Tom said. "Didn't you say we had loads on that list?"

Grace smiled, preening at the owl mask. "I'll put this back on my way out. Unless you want it?"

"No, thank you." Lauren's eyes were wide, and I could tell it was taking all her strength not to say exactly what was on her mind, that Grace was my doppelgänger.

"I'm actually starving—Lauren, you said we'd be eating by now?" Tom said.

"I feel a bit strange from the mask," Lauren said. "I think I'm seeing double."

As they all walked towards the exit, Tom kept to the middle, holding his pumpkin buckets, literally keeping Grace and Lauren at arm's length. But that didn't stop Lauren from staring incessantly at Grace. All the while, she prattled on about the children's Halloween street party and how she and the Council had shut down Lansdowne Road for the event. It had been *so* stressful and taken longer than it should have. At the till, Grace helped load Marjorie's Halloween paraphernalia onto the conveyor belt.

"How old are your children?" Lauren said, gesturing at the children's costumes.

"Oh, no," Grace said. "No. These are for Marjorie's grandkids. I don't have children."

"So, what are you doing for Halloween?" Lauren said. "Are you going to a big party?"

"I'm not going to a party this year," Grace said. "I have so much going on at the moment." She picked up a pile of decorations from the shopping trolley. "I usually just leave a big bowl of sweets on the counter at the shop."

"She sells wine," Marjorie said. "We're in a sort of a wine club."

"Ooh, fun! I want to be in a wine club," Lauren said.

"It's not that sort of club," Tom said.

"Are you in it?" Lauren said. "I thought you only liked vodka on the rocks?" I could see the gears in her mind shifting. "I'm in a book club, but the books are always so heavy going. I can never finish them. I like wine so much more." The idea of Lauren somehow trying to elbow her way into Sunday Blues or getting wind of it was giving Tom the sweats.

"What are *your* plans, Tom?" Marjorie said. Before Tom could answer, Lauren butted in.

"He's having dinner at my house with our friends. I'm cooking saag aloo. It's Tom's favorite. After the street party, of course."

"Oh, that sounds splendid," Marjorie said. "Grace, you should join them. You could do some lovely wine pairings, couldn't you, Gracie?" She turned to Tom. "She never does anything, this one, except study." Grace shot Marjorie an extreme wide-eye and began shoving Marjorie's purchases into a complimentary plastic bag.

"That's really not necessary," Grace said. "I'm sure Lauren's got her dinner party well under control."

"Oh . . . well, if you have no plans . . ." Lauren said, though she looked less than enthusiastic. "Of course you can come. It can be my 'Thank you' for setting me free."

"Isn't that a lovely idea," Marjorie said. "She'd love to." When Grace began to stammer, Marjorie intervened, adding, "You don't want to miss a good saag aloo." The music suddenly stopped—Mariah Carey's "Always Be My Baby"—and a raspy voice made a completely inaudible announcement. Tom edged closer to Grace slightly, his core tightening in anticipation of her answer, watching as she nibbled the inside of her cheek.

"I'm well and truly cornered, aren't I?" Grace said, the slightest smile appearing on her lips. "What time do you want me?" she asked.

"Eight o'clock on Thursday," Lauren said. "Here's my number and my address. Text me if you have any trouble finding the house." She ripped off a page from her notepad and passed it to Grace. "And please don't ring the doorbell. It wakes the children." Watching this whole exchange, Marjorie swiped her credit card to pay, grinning like the Cheshire Cat.

"Eight o'clock on Thursday," Grace repeated, taking the shopping bags from the belt as she turned to walk away. Tom couldn't believe what was about to transpire—a potentially memorable evening with the woman he liked, or a banquet of consequences?

"Tom?" Grace said, turning back, her gold hoops catching in the light. "What's Henry going to be for Halloween?" Tom was floored.

She'd remembered Henry's name. I could never remember half the names of the other children in Henry's class, but Grace had remembered Henry's. If he wanted a sign, there it was.

"He's going as Humpty Dumpty," he said.

CHAPTER TEN

I woke up one morning to a pain in my stomach so severe I thought someone had stabbed me in my sleep. When I looked down, the sheets were so drenched in blood it was as though someone had ritually slaughtered a Paschal lamb in our bed. I glanced at the clock. Tom was still on his flight to Berlin. He'd left early that morning while it was still dark outside, and I'd barely kissed him goodbye.

"I'll call you when I get there," he said, both of us oblivious to the catastrophe occurring in my womb.

I rang Annie from my bed. I had to dial her number three times because my hands were shaking so much.

"Hi, hi," I said.

"What's wrong?" she said.

"I think something's happened. I think—I think it might be okay, but there's a lot of blood." I'd started crying then—choppy, shaky cries for help while doing that thing where I spoke in a jolly tone as if I'm talking to a child. I was trying desperately to ignore the brutal fact

that our second baby was now staining the sheets and seeping into the mattress pad. Our baby who would later end up in the washing basket among my knickers and Chloe's polka-dot pajamas.

I don't know how much time passed after that phone call to Annie. I didn't move, worried it might somehow make things worse. I just sat there in the blood. Then I heard Annie's tires screeching along our road. I got out of bed and dropped my keys out the window, leaving a bloody trail along the rug.

Annie appeared behind me so fast I barely had time to get back into bed before she was beside me. She was still in her pajamas, her wax jacket thrown over them.

"I've lost it, Annie," I said, "I've lost the baby. Haven't I?"

"I don't know. I think so," she said, helping me take off my clothes. She sat me on the Howard chair before wrapping me in Tom's dressing gown. I couldn't speak. I could barely think. My head was pounding. I didn't know then it was a side effect of a miscarriage.

"I can't do the nursery run," I said.

"I'll take Chloe to nursery," Annie said. "I'm going to run you a bath in the guest bathroom. While you're there, I am going to deal with the sheets, and I'll call the doctor."

Later, I would remember sitting on the bathroom floor, Annie's heart against my ear, and breathing like I had hiccups. She'd tell me a few months later that she'd never been so scared in her life. That if she could have one wish, it would be to make sure I never, ever felt that frightened again.

*

Tom must've changed his shirt three times before landing on the one he'd picked out initially. White, Charvet, with a navy-blue cashmere jumper over the top. He walked down the stairs, making sure that all the windows of the house were fully closed before scrutinizing the deadlock. In our absence, he'd developed a routine of sorts. The most important part, of course, was double-checking that the monitor was plugged in. For Tom to leave the house, there needed to be a risk assessment. Though he knew that Rita would call if anything happened, he always felt understandably frightened leaving his son, even to go the two doors down to Lauren's.

Tom studied the grainy picture on the monitor; there was Henry, peaceful in his bed, Pudding right beside him. Henry's Halloween costume had worked out well, and they had enough chocolate in the fridge to last until Christmas. Watching his son sleep, Tom considered, like he always did, taking the monitor with him. He wished the signal would reach Lauren's so he would be able to keep an eye on Henry, but then he shook his head and told himself he was being neurotic. Rita, whom he trusted implicitly, had come over to babysit. Besides, it was only a ten-second dash if something happened. But tonight wasn't a straightforward dinner party. He was terrified Annie might have one too many and spill the beans or that Lauren would blurt out how much Grace looked like me and pique Grace's interest.

Lauren had asked Grace for eight o'clock, and Tom got the sense that Grace was the sort of person who, unlike me, always ran on time. He didn't want to risk being late and miss her entrance, leaving Annie alone with her. He thought back to the moment she'd appeared in Hobbycraft. Her hair swept off her face, her freckles visible on the bridge of her nose, the same gold hoop earrings she'd been wearing on Sunday. *Did she wear those every day?* He wanted to know her habits, such as how she took her coffee in the morning and what time she liked to go to bed. Did she fall asleep with a book propped open on her chest like I used to?

"Are you going anywhere nice?" Rita asked. She was sitting in the drawing room watching *Coronation Street* with the volume on low, knitting yet another hat for Henry.

"To Lauren's. I won't be back late," Tom said, passing Rita the monitor, then threading his arm through his coat. He pulled the front door shut and waited until he heard Rita put the chain on before jogging down the stoop. The cold air shocked his face. The moon was high, but there were no stars visible. Instead, London had been cloaked in a heavy fog. Tom, the least superstitious person I knew, tried not to take it as some sort of omen. That was my department as a writer, to infuse everything with metaphor and meaning, while Tom took the world at face value.

The street seemed quiet without the ambient cackle of hyperactive, trick-or-treating children, now home in a sugar stupor. Somewhere up the road, a couple of teenagers threatened the neighbors with half a dozen eggs, but aside from their harmless revelry, the street had returned to its usual quiet state. Tom had never been trick-or-treating with Chloe. He knew she had been a vampire, a witch, and a tabby cat. He'd seen the photos before and after, but there was always something "urgent" at work, always a "next time." Yet another thing to regret.

As he walked the short jaunt to Lauren's, Tom wondered if there would ever come a time when he wouldn't constantly hear my voice in his head or second-guess himself, thinking about whether I would have approved of his choice of Tennis Tots over Soccer Tots for after school. He hoped that now that Henry had surpassed Chloe in age, his constant ruminating and comparing his two children would diminish. Maybe Henry's having outlived Chloe could be the true starting point of their new life, free of the past, even though Tom knew that was impossible. Henry didn't even know he'd had a sister, and the mummy issue had yet to be broached. Every time he carved out time to tell Henry about me, he couldn't find the words.

Tom turned up the stone path to Lauren's house, his stomach dipping, the way it does when you drive over a steep hill. The door was ajar, which was Lauren's usual form when she was entertaining, not wanting to risk someone ringing the bell and waking the twins, whom she had on a rigid sleep schedule. Chester doddered

up to Tom with his usual swagger and gave him a gentle sniff
around the back of his knees before returning to his basket. Tom
took off his coat and hung it beside what looked like one of Oliver's.
In the antique hallway mirror, he ran his hand through his hair,
which was nearly dry. His cheeks were flushed from the shower,
with two strips of red like the ones he often got after sex.

Tom walked past the drawing room, which was lit with candles
and peppered with white orchids. The marble fireplace was crackling and the music playing low—to his astonishment, something
good: Wings, "Let Me Roll It." The layout of Lauren's house was
somewhat like ours, though our taste differed. When Daniel left,
Lauren had redone every room as if she'd been in consultation with
Gwyneth Paltrow, all in a bid to extinguish any remnants of Daniel's personality. The only color was in the dining room—if Farrow &
Ball Elephant's Breath can be considered a color.

Tom followed the murmur of voices into the kitchen, where
all of Lauren's pointless appliances gleamed bright white beneath
dozens of spotlights. Lauren and Annie had their backs to the door
and didn't turn when Tom walked in. Instead, they stayed huddled
over a cast-iron pan like the witches in *Macbeth*. Annie pulled at
the sleeve of her black silk dress and touched her hair, which was
pulled back in a tight, low bun. She was never one to entertain the
idea of "fancy dress."

"I'm telling you, it's *unbelievable*," Lauren was saying over the
fragrant crackle of mustard seeds. "They look close to identical,
just wait—"

"Wait for what?" Tom said, putting the bottle of wine he'd
brought on the kitchen table.

"Tom! *Hi*," Lauren sang. She was still wearing her Cruella de
Vil costume, only without the black-and-white wig and the cigarette holder.

"I was just saying," Lauren began, wiping her hands on a tea
towel, even though they appeared dry. "How similar Camilla looked

to Morticia tonight. Such a great wig. And the dress, the long black dress, it was just *so* good. And having the children be Wednesday and Thing was so perfect. I love a coordinated costume, don't you?" This fictional discussion, about a mother from Henry's class whom Tom couldn't recall, went on for the better part of five minutes until Annie interrupted.

"Tom," she said. "I called you earlier. Did you get my message?"

"Honestly, I can't remember. Busy day."

"Mmhmm, can I borrow you for a minute?"

"Well, I'm just going to say hi to Oliver," he said. "Is he in the drawing room?"

Annie looked at him over her glass of wine as he walked backwards down the hallway.

"I'm right behind you," Annie said, swiping the bottle of wine off the island.

When Tom walked into the drawing room, Oliver was standing by the grog tray, a cocktail shaker in hand, wearing a mustard corduroy dinner jacket.

"Good timing," his friend said. "Usual?"

"Yes. A double," Tom said. Annie put the wine bottle down on the ottoman, staring daggers at Tom as Oliver emptied the contents of the cocktail shaker into a tumbler.

"Annie dragged me to the Tate earlier. I know you two love Kusama, but honestly, all those dots. Enough to give you a migraine." But Annie wasn't nibbling at Oliver's back end tonight with an alternative opinion. Instead, she was slumped on the sofa, staring straight ahead. "You're quiet, darling," Oliver said to her.

"I've got a lot to think about," she said.

"It's probably all those dots. Made you go a bit hazy." Annie rolled her eyes as Lauren came in through the double doors with her phone in one hand and a fresh ice bucket in the other.

"Bloody Daniel," Lauren said. "Thinking he can change the schedule for some poxy romantic weekend with his girlfriend at a moment's notice. Hang on, he's ringing again now." She passed the ice bucket to Annie and put the phone back to her ear as she walked out of the room. Tom blocked out the noise spilling in from the hallway as Lauren carried on with some hideous custody disagreement.

When he heard the latch, then footsteps on the beechwood floor, he shot up, banging his shin on the coffee table, but he needn't have bothered because it wasn't Grace. Instead, it was Lauren's date, Jimmy, a twenty-nine-year-old personal trainer who was built like a Greek sculpture. Tom stood to greet him, putting out his hand.

"Evening, gents," Jimmy said, as if Oliver and Tom were three hundred years old. Tom winced under the grip of Jimmy's crushingly strong handshake.

Tom and Jimmy sat together on the sofa. I could see Tom wonder, as he studied Jimmy's pectoral muscles threatening to split the seams of his shirt, if he should start doing push-ups. Tom never felt insecure about his looks. He didn't need to. He was tall and good-looking by any standard, with hair as full as a young Montgomery Clift's.

Oliver offered Jimmy a drink, but he didn't "imbibe alcohol," one of his few topics of conversation besides something called "meal-prep" and another thing called CrossFit that sounded utterly hideous. As it drew nearer to Grace's anticipated arrival time, Tom found it difficult to listen to anything.

"Do you know what time we're due to eat dinner?" Jimmy asked Tom, just as Lauren came into the drawing room with more nibbles.

"Jimmy?" she said in a high-pitched voice. Her face was a bit sweaty from being by the oven. "We're still waiting for Tom's . . . friend or date—what are we calling her?" she said, looking at Tom. The music changed and Tom downed his drink.

"Well, this is exciting," Oliver said. "How did you meet her?" Annie cleared her throat and shoved a handful of pistachios into her mouth, although I knew she didn't like them.

It occurred to Tom that this decision to bring Grace into his life wouldn't just mean lying to her; it meant lying to everyone, all under the watchful eye of Annie, who, regretfully, knew full well how they met.

"It's a bit of a funny story, really," Tom said. "I don't even know if it's a *date* date."

"I'm really hungry," Jimmy said. "And I can't eat all these carbs. I need macros."

"Then have some more nuts," Lauren said, passing him the silver bowl of pistachios.

*

At a quarter past eight, Grace still hadn't arrived. Tom was almost at the end of his second vodka on the rocks and Annie was halfway through a bottle of wine. The drawing room felt muggy and close; between the fire and the candles, the atmosphere was sweltering.

"I normally eat a lot earlier than this, because I'm in training for the CrossFit Games," Jimmy announced. Lauren lit one of the scented candles that had gone out on the mantel, then perched on the tasseled white ottoman. When Lauren left this mortal coil, I was convinced, she was going to come back reincarnated as one of those Jo Malone candles.

"I think we should go through to dinner," Annie said. The Lighthouse Family crooned "Lifted" through the Sonos. "She's clearly not coming." Oliver gave Annie a look. "What? I'm just saying she's half an hour late."

"Someone's hungry," Oliver said, passing her the olives.

But Tom couldn't care less what anyone was saying. *Did something happen to Grace?* Though he tried not to go there, his mind slid to all the possible worst-case scenarios: Grace in a ditch by the side of the road. Grace held hostage in Barclays Bank. Grace blown to bits by a terrorist in a suicide vest.

By quarter to nine, Tom could feel everyone's eyes on him, waiting for him to make some kind of decision, as if he were a surgeon calling time of death. Grace had Lauren's number. If she was running late, why hadn't she called instead of standing him up in front of his friends? If this was the romantic arena he had to look forward to, he'd rather stay home with Henry and watch *PAW Patrol*.

"Well, more curry for us!" Tom said finally, attempting to hide his abject disappointment. He hadn't smoked since his twenties, but he found himself jonesing for a cigarette. He tried to scavenge for any positives, but there was only one: If Grace was a no-show, he would never have to fess up and tell her the story of how Henry came to be. *Infatuation is so misleading. A solitary existence is better.* If Tom had been alone, he might have flopped facedown on his bed, but he wasn't. He was in front of all our friends, humiliated. If Grace wasn't coming to Lauren's, unless he went back to Sunday Blues, their paths were unlikely ever to cross again. He should forget about Grace and focus on surviving this dinner, and then go back home and hunker down to an honest life with Henry.

A little before nine o'clock, everyone was sitting around the table. Lauren put the saag aloo down beside Tom, along with her homemade mango chutney and popadam. She was using her best plates tonight, so she must have really wanted to impress Jimmy, who seemed to notice only his own caloric intake.

"I'll just clear this place setting?" Lauren said, looking at Tom. "Or . . . ?"

"She's obviously not coming," Tom said. He picked at his cheese naan, trailing it through a burnt-orange puddle of chutney.

"Delicious curry, darling!" Oliver said, shoveling a spoonful of rice into his mouth. They ate in silence for a few minutes. "Did it take you long to get here?" he said to Jimmy.

"No," Jimmy said. "I took the Tube." Tom knew that the small talk at the table was for his benefit. The curry was hot; it was burning his throat, but Tom didn't care. He had no appetite. "Lauren," Jimmy continued. "You should do wild rice instead of basmati. It's better for digestion." Lauren smiled tightly. Just then, the doorbell rang, and for a nanosecond Tom dared to imagine Grace on the other side of the door.

"Oh, crumpets," Lauren said through a mouthful of potatoes. "I forgot about Tilly's mum. She's dropping off the boys' P.E. kits. I only told her four times not to ring the bell." The pitch of her voice was a few notches higher than usual, a giveaway for when she'd had one too many.

"Have you ever considered a sign? 'No bell ringing after eight o'clock'?" Annie said.

"Tom! Eat more," Lauren called from the hallway.

Tom heard the latch spring up, the door open, words exchanged. He looked at his watch and rearranged his napkin. Maybe this was his opening to beat a quick retreat in the shuffling. If he left now, he could walk Duke and still make it back in time for the evening news. When Lauren returned, however, it wasn't with Tilly's mum. It was with Grace.

The sight of her standing there in Lauren's kitchen, clutching a bottle of white wine, after he'd thought he might never see her again, was more intense than when he had first seen her at Sprezzatura.

"I'm so sorry I'm so late," Grace said as Tom rose to greet her. "I was just telling Lauren I was calling and calling her phone, but it kept going straight to voicemail."

"Oh shoot, I must have turned my phone off without thinking when I hung up with Daniel," Lauren said. "Sometimes I think if I turn it off, all my problems might suddenly turn off too. It's stupid, I know."

"There was a problem with the alarm at the shop," Grace said. "I couldn't get it to set." She turned to Tom. "I didn't have your number. To let you know. Otherwise, I would have."

"It's okay," Tom said, scrambling for his bearings. "We're just getting started. Everyone, this is Grace."

In that moment, it wasn't just that Grace looked so much like me, it was that Tom looked so much like Tom again. While Tom took Grace's coat, Lauren mouthed *"I told you"* at Annie. If Annie and Oliver were trying to conceal their astonishment, it wasn't working. Oliver looked like he'd had the wind knocked out of him and Annie's mouth was agape. The only noise in the room was Jimmy's fork scraping on his plate as he separated the sauce from his chicken.

Only Tom didn't care what anyone thought. He felt as though his head were underwater. He wasn't drowning; it was quite the opposite, that glorious, terrifying feeling of swimming too deep.

CHAPTER ELEVEN

An hour later, the stripey orange-and-black candles had nearly melted, and everyone was still sitting around Lauren's kitchen table. Tom was ten clicks into a story about when he and Oliver broke into Tom's house at Cambridge one New Year's and managed to get arrested in the process. The part where Tom fractured both of his wrists climbing up the drainpipe made him laugh in a way I'd forgotten he could, loud and carefree—a window into the world we once had. Oliver was in top form, bantering back and forth with Tom. Grace dabbed at the tears in her eyes, not in the least bit appalled at Tom's story.

Lauren had made a tiramisu, which she began portioning out in generous mounds. As soon as Jimmy saw the dessert, he made a beeline for the exit, citing an early training session and sending Lauren into a spin. Once he was gone, she kicked off her heels and sulked at the end of the table, pouring herself a huge glass of wine as she watched Grace with seemingly begrudging admiration.

There'd been no sparks flying over the tikka masala between her and Jimmy, which, knowing Lauren, had to be a huge disappointment. She'd obviously been anticipating a sleepover. I watched Annie struggle to reconcile her moral quandary; the actual woman sitting beside Tom in Lauren's kitchen was no longer a huddled discussion in the hallway. This is what everyone wanted: for Tom to move on, to find someone to share his life with. If only their genuine connection weren't born of a lie.

"I know exactly where your shop is," Oliver said. "There's that marvelous cheese shop just along. How long have you been open? I've always gone to Berry Bros. & Rudd."

"About seven years now," Grace said.

"I watched this documentary recently about master sommeliers," Lauren said, chiming in from the head of the table. Tom and Grace exchanged a knowing glance. "Did you know there are only three hundred in the world and that they can tell any wine by taste and smell?"

"There's a little more than three hundred, I think, darling," Oliver said.

"No, she's right. There are two hundred ninety-eight," Grace said. "Hopefully two hundred ninety-nine soon." Annie played with her dessert spoon.

"You can do what they do in that documentary?" Lauren said. "You can taste any wine and know what it is?"

"Well, not *any* wine," Oliver said.

"Yes," Grace said. "Eventually. Any wine."

"Wait," Tom said. "If I pour you a glass of wine from that decanter, you can tell us—"

"Grape variety, vintage, region, and maker," Grace said.

"She already knows it's red," Lauren said.

"I love this," Oliver said, getting a fresh glass and pouring Grace some wine. Annie looked at her watch and said, "We'd better leave after this, darling. It's getting late, and I didn't sleep well last night."

"Late? Do we have a train to catch?" Oliver said.

"Okay, ready," Grace said. She picked up the glass and swirled the contents before putting it to her nose and sniffing deeply, like a Shepherd on the scent of a truffle. The corners of her lips lifted as she asked, "How long do I have?"

"Two minutes," Oliver said.

Grace took a sip and aerated the wine through her tongue, then put her nose in the bud of the glass again. "This is a great wine. I know this wine." Tom found the change in the tone of her voice seductive. "I'm impressed you have this, Lauren. It's a great vintage." They all looked at one another. She took another taste. "Twenty-seven thousand, five hundred bottles produced. It's a Bordeaux, Château Gombaude-Guillot, 2015."

Lauren got up from the table and opened the drawer to the recycling, where she retrieved the green bottle, slamming it a little too hard in the center of the table.

"That's quite the party trick," she said. Everyone applauded, even Annie.

"Very impressive," Annie said. She stood abruptly and pushed in her chair. "Okay. Home time. I said I would meet Willow Crawley for lunch tomorrow."

"But it's early," Tom said. The night couldn't end here. Not now that Grace was relaxed and even laughing at most of his jokes. "Let's do another one. What if that was a fluke?"

"Does anyone want any leftover curry?" Lauren said. "I made too much." But the room was on the move. Lauren was rifling through a cupboard for lids to her Tupperware even though she didn't have any takers.

"It sounds like we're off then?" Oliver said.

While everyone got up, picking up stray bowls and glasses and putting them in the sink, Tom continued firing unintelligent questions at Grace. Even though he knew the night had to end sometime, he didn't want it to end here. Lauren clicked shut the thick plastic tops on her individual Tupperware and turned up the lights.

"I think that's our cue," Grace said, rising from the table. She and Tom walked to the front door, past the drawing room, the candles still flickering, though the fire had burned out. Lauren was quick to follow, padding after them on her bare feet.

"Thank you for having me," Grace told Lauren. "I had a great time."

"I'm so glad you made it," Lauren said, blinking incessantly. Oliver reached for Annie's emerald-green jacket with the velvet collar. He was helping her put it on when Lauren said, "Honor, which one's yours?"

When the group fell silent at the misuse of my name, it was clear from Grace's pallor that she realized exactly who "Honor" was.

"I don't know why I said that," Lauren said, turning red. "I'm so sorry. It's just—It's just habit."

"Don't worry about it," Tom said quickly.

"I think that's our taxi outside," Annie said.

"I've never known Tom with anybody else," Lauren continued. "And Chloe was like a daughter to me." Grace froze, a stunned expression flashing across her face. Lauren looked around as if for some sort of lifeline. "This is all so new. We're all adjusting."

"It's an honest mistake," Tom said. Annie coughed and fumbled around in her bag. Tom worried that if they lingered another second, Lauren might say, *You look so much like her,* something he knew our friends had been thinking all night long. It was a thought that often crossed his own mind, although he pretended it didn't. "This one, isn't it?" Tom said, holding up Grace's red woolen coat. Grace slid her arms into the sleeves and Tom pulled it up over her shoulders.

Lauren stood holding the door as everyone left. She was trying to catch Tom's eye, but he was pretending not to notice, which was what he did when he was avoiding an uncomfortable topic. "I really am sorry," Lauren said. "Please don't think anything of it."

"It's fine," Grace said, holding the lukewarm tikka masala. "Really."

Tom prayed she meant what she was saying. He knew I would have said "No problem," then ruminated on it for days on a loop. He was relieved that Grace appeared unfazed by Lauren's mistake. Then again, she was completely in the dark about our likeness and probably just put Lauren's slip down to context. The crush of tragedy often ironed out these awkward moments.

Lauren shouted from the door that she would see Tom tomorrow—they were walking the dogs after the school run. Tom stepped onto the pavement with Grace, fighting a desire, or was it an instinct, to take her hand. From the backseat of the taxi, Oliver wound down his window and bid adieu. He was visibly animated, enjoying his friend's renaissance after nearly a five-year hiatus. The cab disappeared round the corner. Suddenly alone with Grace, Tom began to panic. He didn't want the night to end. He had so much he needed to say.

"You know, I'm still convinced it was a total fluke," Tom said.

"What do you mean?" Grace said. Autumn leaves skittered across the pavement.

"I think you spied the bottle in the recycling."

Grace laughed. "Oh really?"

"Yeah," Tom said. "I need to be sure."

"You can test me all you want. I'm confident in my abilities."

"I've got a bottle at home. I only live just there," he said, pointing. The moths fluttered around the light of the streetlamp, as if they perceived something shifting. Tom wished he lived farther away, wanting to revel in the simple pleasure of walking beside Grace, each stride filling him with a nervous energy. But Grace didn't seem nervous at all. Unlike Tom, I could pick up on subtle female nuances; this wasn't the same Grace who'd pulled away from him at the shop, nor the one he had "bumped into" at Hobbycraft.

"And if I get it wrong, I can blame it on the saag aloo," she said as she followed Tom up the stairs to the front door. Tom's hands began to clam up as he inserted his key into the hole and pushed open the door, Grace beside him. When they crossed over the threshold, the fire was still burning in the hallway, though Rita had drawn the mesh metal curtains. When Tom walked through the door with Grace, I could see Rita's lips momentarily twitch, but in true Rita fashion she put on her coat and discreetly left the house, saying nothing besides "Good night."

"Your house is quite something," Grace said.

"It didn't look like this when we bought it," Tom said. He couldn't believe that Grace was here, alone with him in his house, and that they were about to have a drink—this woman who had occupied all his thoughts for the past week. He'd wept over her, he'd vomited, he'd perspired, he'd masturbated, he'd laughed, he'd drawn out the blueprint for this moment so many times.

"I love these Harland Millers," Grace said, gesturing to some paintings in the hallway we'd bought years ago, one of his vintage Penguin book covers that read "I'll never forget what I can't remember."

"I wasn't convinced about the pictures at first, but Honor loved them. She was a writer."

Grace followed Tom past the fire in the hallway into the kitchen before sitting on one of the barstools by the counter. Tom wished he could teeter on this precipice as long as possible—the delicious, all-too-brief time when everything is just beginning. Tom and I called it "The Island," when the rest of the world became inconsequential overnight. We sealed ourselves into Tom's flat for days on end, having sex and eating leftover takeaway.

"You know," Grace said, "you're making this easy for me. Normally I do these tastings blind."

"Right, well if that's the case," Tom said. He jogged upstairs to fetch a cravat. It was navy and finely striped and he hadn't taken it out of the box since I bought it for him in Vienna years ago. He took a moment to gather himself in the wardrobe. The green indicator light on the safe flashing rhythmically. Once he took out the CD and showed her the letter, their rapport would change, and Grace would never look at him in the same way again. Why couldn't they be just Tom and Grace, two people without a past who met at a pub or a party? But there was no such thing as "just Tom and Grace." There was no such thing as a life without a past.

*

While Tom dilly-dallied in the wardrobe, Grace took her phone out of her bag and checked her teeth in the camera. There were three new messages from Nellie: *How is the non-date going??? Does he look sexier than ever? Do NOT kiss and run this time.* Grace shook her head and was rapid-texting her response—*You're ridiculous. I don't*—when Tom returned to the kitchen. From the back, she could have been me at my laptop, writing into the night, chewing on the tip of a black felt pen. But then Grace turned around, and he saw her scar, her fringe, our difference.

"Ready?" she said, setting down her phone facedown on the counter.

Tom folded up the cravat and placed it gently over Grace's eyes, taking care not to catch any of her hair as he looped the knot at the back of her head. He was immediately struck by the intimate, tickly feeling of her hair on his hands and the back of his wrists.

"How does that feel?" Tom shouted.

"You don't need to shout. I'm blindfolded, not hard of hearing."

"Sorry," he said. Tom paused. He felt like a teenage boy in his parents' house in Chelsea, sneaking his first girlfriend up into his bedroom. "I'm nervous."

"Tom?" Grace said, taking off the blindfold. She looked at him. "I won't pull away this time." Tom moved her hair off her face. He knew it wasn't just his own pulse he could feel racing as he traced his thumb over the delicate skin of her scar. Her eyes softened and her lips parted, revealing that poppy-seed gap. All he could do was lean in and kiss her.

With Grace's lips pressed against his, Tom was surprised when the memory that popped into his mind was the first time we'd kissed. He tried to stay present and block out my voice, but these weren't my lips. This wasn't my skin. When their lips parted, he panicked for a moment that Grace could read his mind. That she knew he was having thoughts about me.

"Grace, before we go any further—" But Grace continued kissing his neck and biting at his earlobe. It was hard to concentrate. "You know, just before, at Lauren's, the minor kerfuffle when Lauren said 'Honor.'"

"You don't have to say anything," Grace said, beginning to undo her jacket. She made up the space between them as she leaned in to kiss Tom, her lips open and insistent.

"No, I do. Because the thing is I really like you. And it's not just—there's no avoiding the fact that you do look similar. Not the same, but similar."

"We all have types," Grace said. "It doesn't bother me." Tom could feel his head thumping. He always got a headache when he drank too much red wine. He wasn't in the right frame of mind to tell her just how similar we looked and the more pressing reason why. His mother always told him never to broach important subjects late at night. *We all make our best decisions first thing in the morning with a clear head.*

"I think I've had too much to drink," Tom said. He pinched the bridge of his nose.

"Is this because of what happened at the shop?" Grace said. "I told you I'm not going to do that again."

"Of course not. Grace. I—"

She looked so forlorn. He couldn't stand the idea of her overthinking his motives or second-guessing his feelings for her. He pulled her in closer. "Have coffee with me tomorrow morning?"

he said, his hands finding the subtle flare of her hips. "Let me take you somewhere before you open the shop?" he said. "I'll buy you a piece of cake."

"You want to take me to a tea shop at nine o'clock in the morning for a piece of cake?"

"Not exactly a tea shop."

"This better be good cake," Grace said. Tom took her chin in his fingers with unwavering self-assurance, finding her lips and kissing them gently. She pressed her body into his as he pulled her off the barstool and in between his thighs, his hands firm around her waist. As her soft hair fell across his face, he could smell the slightest trace of her tuberose perfume, and there was no thought of me after that.

CHAPTER TWELVE

It was pouring rain when Tom walked in the front door a little after eight o'clock. He wiped his feet on the mat, then loosened his tie. I was sitting at the top of the stairs with Chloe limp in my arms. She'd just fallen asleep after projectile-vomiting all over the bathroom floor. Duke was beside us, his jowls resting on my thigh. The large antique chandelier was set to dim, the halogen circle glowing hot like a halo above us.

Tom passed by the fire I'd long since neglected in the entrance hall. He threw a log on its orange embers, then carried on towards the kitchen. I could hear him put on the kettle, then crack open a beer. The cap landed on the marble island and then the opener. Tom had a habit of leaving things just above or just beside where he'd found them, which I always found highly irritating. It fascinated me that he could find everything he needed, yet never the time to put it back where it belonged.

*

From the top of the stairs, I watched him through the tall, wide kitchen door as he unbuckled his belt and pulled the leather strap from the loops on his trousers. He coiled it up like a snail and left it on the long kitchen table where my laptop was open, my glasses resting on the keyboard.

For a moment, I envied my husband. If only I could be more like Tom and put myself first, no matter what—maybe then I would finish my memoir. But my career was secondary. I think Tom believed that because my calendar wasn't blocked with back-to-back meetings, my job equated to some sort of glorified hobby. Apparently, hours slogged over a laptop writing dialogue for a family of ice creams wasn't a currency Tom valued. He seemed to think my deadlines were random, self-imposed, and plucked from thin air; it was as if what I did with my day was of no consequence, even though I'd published four books in rapid succession and The Ice Cream Zoo *had been on* The Sunday Times Bestsellers List *for 122 weeks.*

"Fuck," Tom said, dropping his BlackBerry on the stone floor, but thankfully Chloe didn't stir. I wondered how long it would take Tom to come and look for us, so unlike my father, who would be calling my name before he even took his keys out of the door. After what seemed like half an hour but was probably only two minutes, Tom came into the hall, typing on his BlackBerry.

"There you are," he said, looking up, as if nothing were out of the ordinary. I shook my head with my eyes squeezed tight to indicate the need for inside voices. He unlaced his shoes and untucked his shirt as he walked up the stairs towards us until he reached the landing, where he sat beside me, making a face when he caught the sour smell.

"What happened?" he whispered. Duke lifted his head and, sensing it was Tom, lowered it back onto my thigh.

"You're late," I said, like a harpy. "She was sick, everywhere. I never knew two-year-olds could be sick like that." Tom ignored my dig at his tardiness and kissed the top of Chloe's head. Of course he'd arrived on the scene now that she was pale and peaceful, the violence of emptying her insides having tired her into submission. I'd lived through The Exorcist, *and he'd made it home in time for* Heidi.

"You two looked like the Pietà sitting there," he said, but as sweet as the reference was, I was glad I couldn't raise my voice, because I would have lost my temper. Why did he get to swan in when the sick had been mopped up and Chloe was already asleep? *"Is she okay?"* Tom said, and something in the stupidity of that question triggered me.

"I want her to sleep in our bed tonight," I said.

"Fine. I'll take her. Then I need to decompress for a moment," Tom said, just as the red light on his BlackBerry began to flash and his attention was once again diverted.

"Decompress? When do I get to decompress?" I whisper-shouted, standing with Chloe in my arms, her head lolling. *"When do I get to rock up after bedtime? I have deadlines too, you know. But sure, enjoy your decompression."*

"Wow," he said, not looking up from his BlackBerry, *"you're really making the idea of having another child seem appealing."*

I was so taken aback by the cruelty of his comment, I couldn't respond. Every argument these days boiled down to my desire to have another child and Tom's ambivalence about starting a third round of IVF. Just as I was trying to think of something equally horrible to say in response, he apologized.

"I'm sorry. That was below the belt," he said, then kissed my cheek and peeled Chloe from my arms and carried her to our bedroom.

*

The Kusama show at the Tate Modern was unusually empty for a Thursday morning, the industrial galleries echoing like a derelict train station. Tom and Grace stood staring up at the collection of paintings that comprise *Love Arrives at the Earth Carrying with It a Tale of the Cosmos*. At first glance, the primary colors and linear brushstrokes appeared jolly and childlike, but on closer inspection the paintings evolved into something hallucinatory. I never liked the Tate Modern. I always thought it was too big and that the location was awkward. I was pregnant the last time we were there, trying my best to conceal my appalling gas. On seeing the size of my ankles, Tom suggested we call it a day and have lunch at the Wolseley instead.

Grace smiled as she listened intently to his impassioned soliloquy, her nose still red from the cold walk to the museum, her long black-and-white checkerboard coat cinched tight at her waist with a brass button. Tom took after his mother in the art department. He was never more in his element than when he delivered an impromptu monologue on pop art, getting highly irritated when I didn't concentrate hard enough or went off-piste. I secretly found Tom an unbearable museum date and generally tried to send Annie with him instead. He stopped at every picture, reading every legend. My attention span was limited, and I got hungry after an hour.

But today Tom was the one struggling to maintain focus, finding himself more and more distracted the longer they walked around. Every now and then, when Grace gestured to something with her arm, he could smell her perfume. Each time he caught a whiff of it, he'd instantly be thrown back to their kiss the previous night. The thought of the way her body felt up against his groin, and the way his mouth continued to taste like her long after she was gone.

"What I love is that no one art movement defines Kusama's oeuvre," Tom said. "When she is asked to define it, she says her style is 'Kusama art.'" He realized Grace was stifling a chuckle. He wondered if it was his pompous use of the word "oeuvre," which always used to make me cringe. "Why are you laughing?" Tom said, his arm outstretched, as he gestured at the large, red, all-seeing eye in one of the paintings near the top.

"You've got a tractor sticker stuck on your arse," Grace said.

"What? This?" Tom said, turning to inspect his behind, his arm still raised. He left the sticker where it was. "That's a backhoe loader. Very different. May I go on?"

"As you were," Grace said, continuing to study the picture.

"When Kusama was young, her mother would send her to spy

on her father, who was having all these affairs, and it had a trauma-tizing effect on her," Tom said. "She was in a field of flowers one day on her family's farm and began hallucinating an infinite river of dots. That's where her obsession with dots began."

"Really?" Grace said. She looked again at the fifteen panels. "I always think having an 'obsession' is just a prettier word for a 'dis-traction.' It's staggering to think of the damage that can be caused, just like that." Grace clicked her fingers. "Sometimes I just want a picture to be a picture," she continued, homing in on a striking pho-tograph of Kusama as a little girl, looking straight at the camera. "I don't want to know the whole story. Does that make me terribly unsophisticated?" she said, turning to Tom with her hands in her pockets.

"Not in the least. I hope I haven't ruined it for you," he said.

"The artist looks so sad in this photograph," she said. "It's bru-tal. The domino effect of what a little girl sees playing out like this." Tom was quiet for a moment.

"I sometimes worry that Henry knows subconsciously what happened to us, even though he wasn't alive yet," Tom said. "That he can feel I'm hiding something. That he knows there's something I'm not telling him."

Tom looked pained, his eyes unblinking. The Tate was vast, but Tom suddenly felt like he was in the middle of a dark, collaps-ing tunnel. Even though he was technically lying, he wasn't a liar. He had always been honest to a fault. He told me if I had chives in my teeth or if a coat didn't suit me. He had been so blunt that morn-ing in the Ritz when he'd told me that under no circumstances did he want to try for another baby. How, in the space of two weeks, had he become a liar by omission?

"If I've learned anything in my life—and I don't have kids, so maybe I'm speaking out of turn here—it's to be honest. Look, I'm adopted, so you know, it's not the same as Henry by any stretch, but I always sensed there was something I didn't know. On paper, I had a perfect childhood. I was happy, but I always had this feeling that there was something being discussed in hushed voices after I went to bed—sorry. Tom?" she said, touching his forearm.

He looked as though he'd just been pulled over by the police for speeding. He hated himself for nodding along as she told him that she'd been adopted and pretending it was the first time he'd ever heard it. "Tom?" she repeated. "Maybe I'm not the right person to ask about parental problems. I never know if I'm saying the right thing. Pietro used to say, *Fatti i cavoli tuoi*—Mind your own cabbage." Tom nodded and uncrossed his arms. *Would a conversation ever just be a conversation? Would every seemingly innocent exchange reroute to the importance of honesty?* It was too dangerous to talk any more about Henry until he told her the truth.

"How did you two meet?" he said.

"Not the most romantic story . . . I got in a car accident in Italy—hence the scar."

"You met Pietro in a car accident?" Tom said, his eyebrows raised, wrinkling his forehead.

"Sort of. It's not as dramatic as it sounds. I used to go to Alba every year with my family in the summer—you know, where they hunt for white truffles? Anyway, I was on my bike, and a car was driving on the wrong side of the road. And when I swerved to avoid it, I fell into Pietro's family's vineyard. I would love to say he scooped me up in his arms and sped me to the hospital, but our only method of transportation was the farm's tractor." Grace laughed at the thought. "I didn't know it at the time, but Pietro had a very severe phobia of blood, and I was covered in it."

"I thought you were going to say you found him truffle hunting. But yes, you're certainly right. That is not the most romantic way of meeting someone."

They headed to some of Kusama's earlier paintings and were standing in front of one called *Lingering Dream*, a bright, nightmar-ish landscape, the foreground crowded with fallen red sunflowers, their stems broken and contorted. A docent standing close by, with a broad Scottish accent was telling a group of secondary school pupils about Kusama's early childhood in provincial Japan.

"He was paler than me when we got to the hospital. By the time the doctor had given me stitches, his whole family was in the waiting room . . . *Lingering Dream*," Grace said, just barely audible. She moved closer to the painting. "I like this. It feels more real. Less pretty." She slid her hands in her pockets and turned around to Tom. "Your turn. How did you and Honor meet?"

"Also not the most romantic. She trod on a bee." Tom looked at the floor. He didn't get that tight feeling in his throat he often felt when he pushed my name against his vocal cords. With Grace it was different. She knew the dialect of lost love; there was no head tilt of pity or projection. "She was in Annie's garden revising for her exams, and she trod on a bee. She took so much Piriton that she just kept repeating herself and laughing. She was just irresistible. You know, I haven't come to this museum since Honor was alive. We used to come here all the time, and quite frankly, I'm not sure she ever liked it."

"Is that what she used to write about? Art?"

"No. Actually, that was my mother. Honor wrote children's books, but she loved art. She had a great eye. She was like a magpie. She could spot a great picture in the back of an old antiques shop."

"Pietro had that. That gut instinct. He knew so much about wine without even trying. I didn't appreciate then just how incredible that was, until I gave it all a go. I am literally banging my head against a wall trying to learn something he intuitively understood. Italians. They just know how to do everything." She stared off into the middle distance. Her expression was hard to read, though Tom recognized the longing. "One day he was there, the next he was gone. And I was alone. Just like that. I thought widows were old women in all black with dowager humps in Taormina, but apparently not."

"Well, I can confirm you definitely don't have a dowager hump."

"Why didn't Pietro tell me he felt off? Why did he take a bath? Why did I have the radio on so loud? I think about that day so much, and I still can't get my head around it. How the weather can be so perfect outside and the tomatoes are in the garden, growing in abundance, and you're cooking for two and then you're not. How someone at such a young age can just drop dead like that. He was thirty-two years old. How does that happen?"

Tom knew full well this constant rally with hindsight. No matter how hard he hit the ball over the net, the image of the back of my head as I walked away from him came rocketing back with brutal force. It pained him to the marrow.

"Do you want to sit down for a bit?" Tom said. "There's a cafe upstairs."

"I'm fine. And besides, we're right by the 'Infinity Mirrored Room,'" Grace said. "Isn't this why we came?" She pointed to the small queue for the exhibit.

Tom weighed his options, knowing she needed to head off soon to open the shop. But everything would be compromised until he told Grace about the letter. He could feel the words accumulating in his throat and picture himself saying them, and even imagine her response. He could already feel himself stalling, relishing the last few untarnished minutes with Grace, forty-five seconds of which were going to be alone in a darkened, mirrored room surrounded by hundreds of small, twinkling pinpricks of light, reflecting into infinity.

The last time he'd seen "Infinity Mirrored Room," I was pregnant with Chloe. On entering the exhibit then, he'd expected to have some sort of mystical experience, a cosmic connection with the great beyond. Instead, he'd been confronted with the grim reality of extinction, that death was imminent, a cold, dark thing. Had that palpable awareness of mortality been some strange harbinger of our future? He couldn't say. But standing in the queue with Grace, behind a man in a houndstooth jacket and matching cap, he began to feel claustrophobic, fretting that the experience would repeat itself, that he would be pulled back into the vast well of darkness. Maybe he was just nervous to admit to Grace that he'd been keeping a secret from her and that their relationship would end before it even had a chance to begin.

As they began to shuffle forward, a voice shouting "Grace!" startled him. He turned, and to his surprise, he saw Zara, the unsuccessful setup from lunch at Annie's, marching towards them in a long camel trench coat. Watching her approach, he felt like he might combust, though he wasn't sure why.

"Tom?" Zara said, her pointer finger flicking between him and Grace. "You two know each other?"

"Zara?" Grace said, leaning in to hug her. "Are you here by yourself?"

"I'm with Katie," Zara said. "She's in the loo, but we're going to pick up Rebecca after this. I didn't know you knew Tom. Small world."

"Well—we just met and . . . he's a new . . . friend," Grace said, glancing at Tom.

"How do you two know each other?" Tom said, trying not to read too much into the word "friend."

"We've been best friends since primary school," Grace said. "I'm godmother to her daughter." Zara's eyes tennis-matched from Tom to Grace.

"I didn't realize you were talking about *this* Tom," she said finally. Grace shot Zara a look much like the one I would have given Annie. "This is the Tom I was coerced into the setup with."

"That was you?" Grace said to Tom.

"He's the one who told me to go for Katie," Zara said.

"How did you manage that? I've been telling her that since her divorce."

"I can be very persuasive," Tom said.

"Looks like we both followed our own advice," Zara said.

"What advice?" Grace said.

"Oh, wait. There's Katie," Zara said, waving. "I've got to go. Don't forget we've got Rebecca's tennis tournament Saturday morning. Don't try and get out of it," Zara said.

"I can't wait," Grace said.

"See you again, Tom?" Zara said, a knowing look in her eye. "Let's all have dinner, the four of us."

After Zara walked off, Grace said. "I can't believe you got set up with Zara. She and Rebecca are like family to me." There was something he relished about these nuggets of information that he learned about Grace directly from her. They were next in the queue to go into the exhibit "Infinity Mirrored Room."

"How old is Rebecca?" he said.

"She's nine. Ten in August," Grace said. "She's much more than a godchild; Zara came and lived with me for a month after everything happened, and Rebecca was just a baby. Pietro and I were in the middle of doing IVF when he died. I was so wired on synthetic hormones. And even though the worst thing ever had just happened to me, I still needed to do the egg retrieval. The doctor said it was dangerous otherwise, and Zara made sure I wasn't alone. I was a zombie. I wasn't myself, and I made some bad decisions. Zara talked me off a cliff, I guess."

Tom's breath stalled as he absorbed the meaning of what Grace had just said. Did she regret donating her eggs? Had she just told Tom what I couldn't read between the lines? Henry wasn't her child, but without Grace's egg, there would be no Henry. Even if Grace were to say that she understood why he'd tracked her down, even if she nodded her head as she listened intently over a cappuccino as Tom explained, "Oh by the way, that batch of eggs you were planning to use for your own family resulted in my son," she would most likely find the whole dynamic too fucked up and bolt.

"Are you okay?" Grace said. "You've gone a little peaky." They were practically on the threshold of the exhibit.

"Are you two coming in?" the museum coordinator said.

"Yes," Tom said.

They stepped into the room and waited on the floating platform as the museum coordinator closed the door behind them. Standing still in the vast, twinkly darkness, Tom anticipated the dreaded grip of extinction as he took in the sight of himself and Grace in the mirrors. But when the door closed behind them and the lights came on, the fractured images felt limitless, as though he and Grace were coasting together towards a very particular kind of heaven. He wasn't sure if it was real or a dream, but looking at Grace in that small room full of stars and seeing her face reflected millions, no, trillions of times, was like a window into a universe where wives don't suddenly die. A universe where children go down to hotel lobbies for crêpes and get to eat them. A universe of second dates and second chances.

The idea of stepping back into the real world beyond this miraculous chamber without Grace terrified him. The thought of losing her made him feel catatonic and alone all over again. His marred heart wouldn't be able to take the pain of another loss. During the forty-five seconds he stood there, every eventuality of this conversation went through his head: Grace crying, Grace misunderstanding, Grace nodding, Grace touching his arm as he wept in front of her, the back of Grace's head as she walked away from him.

But, at a certain point, would enough time have passed that this secret would seem a blip, a pinprick in their long, hopefully wonderful history? It was too big a gamble now. Maybe he didn't need to tell Grace she was Henry's anonymous egg donor after all.

The pinpricks of light changed to a purple hue, illuminating Grace's peaceful face. In the mirrors, reflected infinite times, Tom saw what he wanted, and then everything went dark, and the door flung open.

CHAPTER THIRTEEN

"When someone describes themself as outdoorsy, does that mean they climb Helvellyn at the weekend or take pills at Glastonbury?" I called, watching Tom as he peeled off his socks and left them beside the washing basket. I was lying on our bed, sifting through egg donor profiles, listening to the sound of the water from the tap hitting the bathtub. It was already dark outside, but through the crack in the curtains I could see the streetlamp polluting the obsidian sky. I tucked my feet under the apple-green blanket that was always draped at the end of our bed—a wedding present from Lauren.

"Read another one," Tom said. He turned off the faucet and walked back into the bedroom with his toothbrush in his hand.

"Right, listen to this," I said. "'Big reader,' it says, then she fails to mention a single book." I knew I sounded pernickety, but I couldn't help it. I wanted details: nail length, hat size, and inseam. Did they buy one thriller on holiday, or were they working their way through the collected works of Shakespeare? Tom went back into the bathroom and spat his toothpaste into the sink.

"*Come on, baby, you've got to be realistic,*" *he said. I knew what he was getting at, but it wasn't just the physical symmetry I wanted to replicate, or even literary taste. I was searching every line, trying to find nuances that most likely couldn't be expressed or didn't exist.*

"*This one is clearly a congenital liar,*" *I said.* "*I'm writing her off. I don't believe anyone actually likes Coldplay.*"

"*What's wrong with Coldplay? Read another one, this time with an open mind, perhaps?*" *Tom said, coming back into the bedroom in his dressing gown.*

"*Okay, blue eyes—good start—similar height. 'I like to cook most evenings and enjoy spending time with friends. I have a master's in finance and statistics,'*" *I said.*

"*She sounds hot,*" *Tom said, crawling into bed next to me. I could smell his minty breath as he started to kiss my neck before taking the pen out of my hand.* "*Tom,*" *I said.* "*Please be serious.*"

"*I am being serious. Deadly serious.*"

"*You're not, you're—you're kissing me.*" *Tom stopped and gazed up at me, his face open and boyish.*

"*We've been looking at these for nearly six months.*"

"*I know.*"

"*We're not looking for your twin, babe,*" *he said, shifting onto his elbow.* "*It doesn't matter whether they prefer Hitchcock or Spielberg, you're never going to find one that says, 'I can't stand being outdoors. I read all day long and leave coffee cups wherever I go, even beside the bath,'*" *he said, kissing me again.* "*'I'm utterly adorable even though I am shackled to my laptop. I'm an atrocious cook and consider a family pack of salt and vinegar crisps to be a balanced meal.'*"

It was lucky he slipped in the "adorable" part, but it didn't deter me from my hunt. I was convinced that if I looked hard enough, for long enough, I would find the one, the person who clicked, the usurper of my throne.

It wasn't till four months later that I found Dunkirk. Her profile ticked every box. But by then, Tom was fed up. He was only interested in a donor's medical history, if anything at all, so I refrained from mentioning that she was adopted. Or that, of all the poems in the world, she'd read Hymn to Beauty. *I'd already become protective of her; I couldn't bear the idea of him dismissing my choice because of the gaps in her medical history. This was kismet. It had to be.*

In the end, like this memoir, I kept the details of Dunkirk to myself.

*

If any other person had suggested a walk up the Downs on a freezing Sunday in November, Tom would have physically recoiled, politely declined, and continued reading the *Financial Times* in bed while Henry watched cartoons. But today he bounded up the hill like Shackleton against the westerly gale, leading the ladies from Sunday Blues like his life depended on it.

"Beautiful, isn't it?" Grace said, her hair blowing wild in the wind. Red kites wheeled overhead. The one day between Sunday Blues and their visit to the Tate had seemed so endless. Henry had been at a birthday party and then gone to Lauren's to play with the twins, so there'd been little to distract him. But now Tom gazed out over the South Downs, the fields below undulating in patches of yellow and racing-car green. Where Tom came alive on country walks, like Fraulein Maria in *The Sound of Music*, I almost invariably bypassed the outdoors, preferring instead to experience the elements through the pages of a Brontë novel.

"I haven't walked the Downs in a long time," Tom said, battling the Baltic wind. As Tom and Grace strolled along, he tried his best to block out the sounds of Blanche and Edith, who were squabbling over the map like a pair of siblings. Though he did enjoy the camaraderie of the women—helping Blanche with the quote for her new roof and listening to her prattle on about her neighbor's low-hanging apple tree—he was desperate for more alone time with Grace.

"I have to say, as beautiful as this is, I wouldn't personally have chosen to climb up here in November," Tom said, slightly out of breath. He'd managed to set a swift pace on the climb and successfully, albeit briefly, break from the herd and get Grace alone, but the gap was shortening; he probably had only three or four minutes with her before the group reconvened and *Wuthering Heights* quickly became *The Best Exotic Marigold Hotel*.

"Oh, come on. It's good for the lungs," Grace said.

"They used to say that about menthol cigarettes."

Grace laughed, shaking her head. Watching her laugh was as good as kissing her. His mind kept flashing back to the last time they kissed, her warm body up against his.

"You can't just walk when the sun's out," she said. Tom looked back at Blanche, clutching the map, cackling at something Edith had said. Grace continued, "We live in England. And besides, the pub where we parked has a great wine list."

Alongside them, in a neighboring field, a shepherd was herding his flock with the help of a couple of well-trained border collies. The last time Tom had forced me to go for a walk, it hadn't ended well. I'd been so lost in thought about a character arc for Madame Choc Chip that I couldn't hear him warning me to put Duke on a lead. It wasn't until I turned around and saw the farmer wielding a shotgun and Duke chasing a limping ewe that I realized the urgency of the situation.

"I haven't been on a walk like this since my dog nearly got shot," Tom said.

"Nearly got shot?" Grace said. "How did you manage that?"

"Honor plus exercise plus farmer—bad combination. Turns out farmers don't appreciate their sheep being chased by weekenders. It only got worse, because we then had to chase Duke, our dog, across eight fields, all of which had just been doused with fresh fertilizer. It was my fault. I shouldn't have torn her away from the fire and her book but—sorry—I digress . . . What were we talking about? Dogs? The wine list?"

"Oh my God, I know that smell. It feels like it gets in your pores. We used to use it on the vines in Italy," Grace said, her lips full and reddened.

"Sexy stuff." Tom glanced behind him, then preened a stray hair from her face.

Seeing Tom with that familiar smile, I couldn't help but wonder if it was the shared vernacular of grief that was bringing them closer. But grief doesn't pardon you from telling the truth. I'd told him in no uncertain terms: *Find a solid replacement. Marry someone you could see me being friends with.* He had my indisputable blessing. But not at all costs.

"How much further till we hit the pub?" Edith called, Marjorie and Jenny walking alongside her. "I need to use the loo!"

"Not long—another five minutes or so," Grace said, jumping away from Tom as though she could conceal their flirtation, which was a fool's errand. It was clear, even from space, that these two were what Nellie referred to as "vibing," but Grace seemed unsure about being overly affectionate in front of the girls.

"I told you not to drink all that water," Marjorie said, suddenly beside Tom in her Harris Tweed cap.

"Doctor Bunbury told me I needed to stay hydrated," Edith said.

"Tom, look at you. You've barely broken a sweat," Jenny said, feeling for Tom's muscles as Grace rolled her eyes at him. The clouds sat low beneath a surprisingly blue sky, and a flock of starlings flew by overhead.

"Let's wait for Blanche," Grace said. They were reaching the bottom of the Downs now, the stile in sight, the wooden steps bolstered by an old flint wall.

"What a view," Marjorie said.

"I could have done without the gale-force winds," Tom said.

"Please. You'd have come out in a blizzard," Marjorie said, giving him a wink.

"You're right," Tom said, his eyes on Grace. Her cheeks were ruddy from the cold. "I would have. But may I be so bold and suggest the next outing?"

"Sounds like you're going to . . ." Grace said, her tone playful. She readjusted the snood around her neck and tightened the strap on her rucksack.

"We do these walks up the Downs in the summer and perhaps a nice, cozy ceramics class in the winter?" Grace laughed. "I can't feel my hands."

"You want to do a ceramics class?" Grace said. She sounded unconvinced.

"I would be open to discussing it," Tom said before Marjorie interrupted.

"Oh, I like that idea. Why don't we do that, Gracie? That would be great. What's the film where they do ceramics?" Marjorie said, adjusting her cap.

"*Ghost*," Tom and Grace said in unison.

Tom looked over Grace's shoulder. He could see Blanche in his periphery. She'd lagged early on but had nearly caught up now.

"Is she all right?" Tom said, gesturing at Blanche.

"Oh, she's fine. All she does is complain," Jenny said, collapsing her stainless-steel walking poles.

"Blanche? All okay?" Grace called, her hands cupping either side of her mouth.

"She'll only bite your head off for asking," Edith said. "Do we know if it's chicken or beef today? I'm absolutely famished. Gasping for half a bitter." But Grace wasn't listening. She had already started to walk briskly up the gravel path towards Blanche. Grace was just a few meters away when Blanche appeared to lose her footing and collapsed, dropping like a stone to the ground.

"Blanche!" Grace cried. Tom ran up behind her, his pulse racing. The sound of Grace with worry in her voice put his teeth on edge. Grace took off her rucksack and sat on the ground.

"Will you stop fussing!" Blanche said. "I must have tripped on one of those blasted molehills." Tom recognized the look on Grace's face as she frantically rustled in her bag. He knew first-hand the sensation of helplessness and abject panic that overtook him at Henry's every tumble. He was no longer the shock absorber he once was. Every little pop was a bang, every stumble was a fall from a great height.

"I'm fine," Blanche said, sitting up. "My knee just gave way, that's all."

"I asked her three times if she was okay," Edith said as she arrived beside them. "I could hear her wheezing, but she just kept telling me to get lost. Silly woman."

Grace tried to get a grip on the lid of her bottle, but her hands kept slipping. Without asking, Tom took it from her hands and twisted it open, bending down so he could hand it to Blanche.

"Drink some more," Grace said.

"Will you stop it, Grace?" Blanche's tone was sharp. Jenny and Marjorie exchanged a look. "Tom can help me down to the pub. Can't you?" she said.

"Yes," Tom said. A slight hint of apprehension laced his voice. She was rather frightening even when she wasn't disgruntled. The gaggle of girls carried on with Grace, while Blanche hobbled down the hill, her arm draped over Tom's shoulder. Every so often Grace would turn to check on the two of them and Tom would perk up, trying to reassure her that things were fine.

"I never wanted to come on this poxy walk," Blanche said, her distinctive northern vocals sounding a bit thinner than when they'd first set off.

"No?" Tom said.

"I've got better things to do on a Sunday," she said. He'd never really looked at Blanche until now, never really noticed her light green eyes, nor her hair, which was thick and curled at the edges like an elderly ram's horn. "And I'm getting a little fed up with all the fussing, if I'm honest, when it's her who should be fussing with herself."

"I think she's just worried about you. You did torque your knee."

"I'm not talking about my bloody knee." She paused. "You've got no idea, have you? That we all meet like this for Grace?"

If Tom were me, he would have asked Blanche to expand on what she'd said, asked for the context, but instead he said, "You mean Sunday Blues?"

"Well done, Poirot. You weren't truly thinking we want to sit around talking about our husbands? The last thing I want to do is sit around talking about mine, I can tell you." Blanche dabbed at the sweat gathering on her brow. "If Marjorie hadn't gone in that day when Grace was hunched over the till bawling her eyes out, I wouldn't be stuck here, week after week, under false pretenses, trying to shake Grace back to life. Marjorie said we'd do this Sunday rigamarole for six months max, but it's been six years, and she hasn't even let someone take her out for lunch!"

Tom squinted, readjusting Blanche's arm slightly on his shoulder. Sunday Blues had a different birth in Grace's mind. *Why hadn't she told him she'd been upset that day Marjorie walked in? Why had Grace left out that part of the story? Why didn't she feel like she could tell Tom the truth?*

"It's not simple, you know," he said. "Lunch. Dinner. Questions. People."

"Hanging around with us lot every Sunday doesn't do it. You can't boycott grief, unless you want to boycott happiness with it. You don't get the meat without the bones." The bracing air stung Tom's throat.

All the while Tom had been attending Sunday Blues, he'd never once clocked onto its being a ruse to get the youngest widow moving, nor picked up on its rather therapy-adjacent style. He was never one to suspect that things weren't kosher. Tom's favorite film was *Taken 2*, and he was pathologically punctual. When I would go deep on a post–dinner party debrief, he'd look at me as though we'd been sitting at different tables, much preferring to talk about the creamy dessert than about who was on their way to another divorce or who wasn't paying their taxes on time.

But now he wondered what else he'd missed. Did Annie and Lauren think the same about him that Blanche thought about Grace? Had Sunday lunch unknowingly been his weekly therapy session? Even Oliver, who was emotionally stunted to say the least—a man who would rather be hanged from the neck by piano wire than have a "meaningful" conversation—had suggested Tom "speak to someone." Their exchange had been awkward, but he'd mentioned it all the same. Tom had managed to cushion himself between Black Hawk helicopter parenting and the rhythm of Henry's routines, abruptly shutting people down if they attempted to talk about Chloe, thinking the pain of losing us would weaken the longer he looked in the other direction. But grief isn't an oyster—you can't swallow it whole.

Blanche and Tom were quiet the rest of the walk down. The bitter cold persisted, and fog was rolling in. Tom helped Blanche clamber over the stile, noticing that she was wincing with every step.

"Nearly there," he said. "When we get to the car, I'm driving you straight home." They weren't far from the pub now; the first signs of modern life were finally beginning to appear—a postbox and a red bicycle, the distant laughter of a child on the swings.

"Don't be silly. I'll be fine on the train," Blanche said.

"I'm not arguing with you, Blanche."

Grace was waiting outside the pub, leaning on one of the ring-stained picnic tables by Tom's car. She waved at the two of them as they made their way across the road. Behind her, Tom could see the rest of the gang taking off their coats as a spritely young waiter handed round the menus. The idea of Grace crying, alone, hunched over the till, gutted him.

"I've got you a bag of ice," she said, holding up the Ziploc as Tom and Blanche approached.

"I'm going to drive Blanche home to Battersea," Tom said. "It's worse than she's letting on."

Grace looked at Blanche, who shrugged and continued sulking. But eventually, after what felt like an endless negotiation, she gave in and allowed Tom to help her into the front seat of his car.

"And I thought *I* was stubborn," Grace said, as Tom closed the door to his car. Through the pub window, three pairs of eyes were riveted on the scene unfolding outside as if it were *Bridget Jones*.

"We've got an audience," Tom said.

"I owe you," Grace said. "How about I make you dinner tomorrow night?" Tom was struck for the umpteenth time not just by our physical similarity, but by a visceral longing so strong he almost moaned. He ached to step closer and kiss her.

"Ah. I'd love to but I can't," Tom said. "Blanche's asked me to go Jet Skiing." Grace laughed, her big, beautiful teeth offset by her dimple. Blanche's words tumbled around his mind, but one thought prevailed: Grace had asked to have dinner with him. This wasn't Sunday Blues. This was a date. Their first date. Their first date in years.

"Why don't you come to mine, though? Maybe eight-ish? After I put Henry to bed. I'll cook, you bring the wine," Tom said.

"I'll see you at eight," Grace said.

CHAPTER FOURTEEN

"Can I do anything?" Grace said, watching Tom aggressively whisk his famous peppercorn sauce. Air was playing—a band I loathed, and Tom adored. Tom had laid the table, using the olive-green linen napkins that hadn't come out of the drawer for years, and the candles were lit, their amber light bouncing off the crystal water glasses.

"You can cut the ends off these broad beans," Tom said, passing a wooden cutting board and a sharp knife across the kitchen island. He opened the fridge and pulled out the steaks to take the edge off. Grace shimmied off her blazer and put it over the back of one of the mahogany kitchen chairs before folding up her cuffs. Her silk shirt was champagne-colored and slim-fitting, and her nails were shiny and freshly polished, a deep shade of aubergine. A long gold chain, looped once, hung around her neck. Grace shuffled the green beans into line, then quickly topped and tailed their curling ends, her chunky gold bracelets clinking together as the knife hit the wood board.

Watching Grace chop, then prepare the salad, Tom was surprised at how easy it felt to have her helping him in the kitchen. After all those nights of ordering takeaways alone, or eating Henry's leftover fish fingers, here he was, with the table laid for two, trying to navigate the vast array of emotions: excitement, fear, guilt, infatuation. He'd thought he would step right back into his former self, but that man no longer existed. In the back of his mind, something Grace had said at the Tate overshadowed the edges of what was shaping up to be an otherwise exceptional evening: *I made some bad decisions. Zara talked me off a cliff, I guess.* Was Grace talking about her eggs? Had she wanted to keep them after all? But who was he to go digging for information when he was omitting such a whopper?

This cyclical anxiety quickly dissipated the moment she brushed past him to reach for the corkscrew or to run the fennel for the salad under cold water. She was a natural in the kitchen, opening drawers with confidence as opposed to asking where things were, navigating her way around Tom as he stood over the Aga.

"Make sure mine's rare," Grace said as he salted the steaks. "I don't want any shades of gray."

"Listen, you know wine. I know steak. So why don't you sit down and have a glass and just compliment me on my food, especially the salad dressing. It's my specialty."

"Yes, chef," Grace said, her face lit from the bronze lanterns that hung above the island.

Tom put his hand over the pan to check the heat before laying the meat on the grill.

The rain began to pour, hitting the Palladian skylight. The house always felt so alive in the rain. The sound of the raindrops pelting the glass traveled the entire length of the staircase, like cantering hooves on dry soil. I found it so comforting, as did Tom, like being under a protective dome that no malignant force could penetrate—which was why, when his phone screen lit up and he saw Annie's number flash across it, he chose to decline the call. Grace got up from the island and hovered by the fridge, studying Henry's paintings, an invitation to a party for a puppet show, and a picture of Tom and Henry at a nearby farm. Tom watched as she bent down to inspect one of Henry's recent drawings, signed in the corner with his name. He was doing so well with his letters.

"Is Henry left-handed?"

"Yes," Tom said, astonished. He could feel himself start to sweat under the natural fibers of his jumper. "How did you know that?"

"Takes one to know one," Grace said, lifting her wineglass with her left hand.

"Right—yes," Tom said, his shoulders dropping in relief. "So was Honor; she was always talking about it. How left-handed people are different, better and so on," Tom went on, waffling into another lie. I wasn't left-handed. Was this his life now? To be a good liar, you need a brilliant memory, and Tom's had always been questionable. It demanded perfect conditions, which life never afforded. Would he have to feign surprise when she pulled my *Baudelaire Volume II: The Poems in Prose* from the shelf, thinking it was Tom's? When she said "You like Baudelaire too?" would he say "Does that surprise you? Do I seem more the type to wallow in the Romantics?" How many fibs was he going to have to tell to stay afloat?

"He's very cute," Grace said. Her ring dinked on the glass as she took another sip.

"He's rather fond of tractors. I thought it would phase out, but apparently not," Tom said. The flesh of the meat sizzled on the cast iron. "I promised I would take him to see a John Deere combine harvester. It's all he's willing to talk about—you know, the spout and how it has that warning light that comes on when it's nearly full."

"A real little country boy," Grace said. "I see he has a tractor lunch box too." She followed Tom over to the table with the salad, picking out a leaf of rocket with her fingers. "Good dressing," she said. "But mine's better."

"Oh yeah? I look forward to being proved wrong when you cook me dinner," he said.

Tom pulled out Grace's chair and thankfully turned off Air, who were midway through another electronic drone. His show-off meal, which he hadn't made for years, was a galloping success and tasted even better than he remembered. Grace even liked his peppercorn sauce, which I'd always thought was too rich but ate anyway. Tom hung on Grace's every word, whether she was talking about the shop and how helpful Nellie was even though she was kind of bonkers or how time-consuming it was to prepare for her sommelier exam.

"Why is the shop called Sprezzatura?" Tom asked. "Am I saying it right?"

"Not bad," Grace said. "It's what Pietro used to call me. It means something like 'effortless grace.' At least that's what he said."

"Seems fitting," Tom said.

"He made up nicknames for everybody, and they always stuck. I'm pretty sure half the people in Alba didn't know my real name was Grace."

Tom and I never exchanged stories about our past loves on our first dinner date, but he looked at me just like this. He listened. He was fully present. He was interested. He was falling.

They were unable, even for a moment, to pull their eyes from each other. Tom didn't eat with his usual alacrity; the steak sat untouched on his plate. Watching her lips move as she spoke, he was in another world, his body aching to get closer. The more she said, the more he wanted to know.

After dinner, Tom took Grace's plate to the sink and pulled the tart he'd bought from the patisserie out of the fridge.

"That better have chocolate inside," Grace said. Tom opened the box and Grace peeked in to find a lemon tart sitting atop a doily.

"Ah, not smooth on my part," Tom said, turning back to the fridge. "Let's try again." He brought out another white paper box, this time revealing a chocolate Nemesis Cake he'd ordered specially from the River Cafe, just in case she fancied something chocolatey.

"Impressive," Grace said.

"I always have a plan B."

Grace's smile dissolved as she looked down at the cake. "Right . . . good old plan B. How well do the two of us know that one?" She put down her wine and crossed her arms over her body.

"Sorry, that was a bit tone-deaf," he said.

"No. It's fine. I just—it's stupid really. Sometimes the oddest things set you off. I just need a sec," Grace said. "Can I use your loo?"

"Yeah, of course. It's just at the end of the hall to the right." Once Grace had left the kitchen, Tom looked at the cake, still in its glossy white box, wondering if he should slice it. He knew first-hand that "the stages of grief" were a myth. It was disobedient and unruly. This was grief—being hit from the side by unexpected tur-bulence. Would she prefer to be left alone? Or would she like a soft knock on the door like I would have?

When Grace still wasn't back a few minutes later, Tom pan-icked that she might have legged it without saying goodbye. He decided to check on the drawing room fire. He hadn't put a log on it since Grace arrived, he reasoned.

But as he opened the kitchen door, he was surprised to hear the gentle timbre of Henry's voice coming from the top of the stairs. Outside, the rain had picked up, the percussive sound of it on the skylight practically drowning out what Henry was saying. Then he heard Grace's voice. He stopped in his tracks and hid behind one of Annie's grand winter arrangements displayed on the entrance hall table. Normally, Henry was so shy with strangers, but he was midway through a very impressive and detailed description of a combine harvester. Tom crept closer to the stairs and there they were: Grace with her legs outstretched, and Henry smiling back at her with dimples she didn't know were hers.

At that moment, all Tom's fretting ceased. Grace and Henry had stumbled across each other, an untainted chance meeting. The sight was so pure, Tom wanted to be snowed into it. The fire let out a bang, and that's when the two of them spotted him, hovering by the foxglove.

"Henry told me he heard us laughing," Grace said. Tom inched closer. He didn't ask Henry why he was out of bed, or hurry him back to his room, which was his usual practice. He just sat down beside them. "It woke him up. That's why he's out of bed," she said, her eyes bright beneath the glow of the chandelier. Grace's arms were no longer crossed tight. Her air of openness had returned; the momentary glitch in the kitchen had passed.

"I'm sorry, I didn't mean to wake you up, Tootle," Tom said, resting his hand on Henry's knee. But Henry's eyes were transfixed on Grace. If Tom needed confirmation that this was the right decision, what better vignette than this tableau?

"I think he's been sitting here for a while," Grace said. "He also said he had an itchy label."

"Come on, little guy," Tom said. "I'll look at the label." Tom took Henry in his arms. As Grace rose to make her way back downstairs, Tom said, "Oh, Grace—I thought we'd eat dessert in the drawing room. The fire's on."

"Great. I'll start slicing."

*

After Tom put Henry back to bed, he took a moment on the landing to gather himself. When he walked into the drawing room, Grace was standing with her back to the fire. She'd cut and plated two slices of Nemesis Cake, which were sitting on top of the ottoman, one piece already with a bite missing.

"I hope I didn't startle him by going up and talking to him," she said.

"Quite the opposite," Tom said, throwing a log on the fire from the big woven basket. "He asked if you will be coming back to-morrow." Grace smiled and readjusted one of the thin gold chains around her neck.

"Tom," she began.

"I'm sorry," Tom said. "I wasn't thinking."

"No. It wasn't justified."

"Of course it was. But just so we're clear, if there is a plan B, if such a ridiculous thing exists, I want it." Tom held her eye, the fire making her cheeks flush.

"I'm getting really hot, standing here," Grace said, moving over to the sofa. "And I want more of that cake." She parted the cushions to make space for Tom as she sat, crossing her legs towards him. The way they both landed meant Grace's knee grazed his hand, but she wasn't moving it away. Sitting beside Grace, it was as if every nerve in Tom's body was on high alert. The only light in the room came from the fire and a few carefully placed table lamps, masking the volume of the vast, double-height ceilings. Grace took a bite of Nemesis Cake.

"That *really* is good," she said with her mouth full.

"I forgot how dangerous this cake is," Tom said. "I haven't had it for years."

"I can tell you're enjoying it," she said, laughing. "How have you managed to get chocolate on your nose?" She passed him her napkin and Tom wiped the chocolate from his face before putting the plate down on the ottoman.

"Do you have any coffee?" Grace said.

"Coffee?" he said. "I never had you down as an evening coffee drinker." He rose to make some, but Grace put her hand on his arm to halt him.

"I was thinking more for the morning," she said.

Tom didn't say anything in response. His mind shorted out; for a moment every limb felt paralyzed. He hadn't been with a woman in five years, and before that our sex had become scientific and sterile, an outcome-driven, joyless affair. When Grace's shoes hit the floor, one after the other, Tom knew what to do. Without any thought, he found himself moving towards her.

"Can I kiss you?" he said, and Grace replied with two distinct nods. They sunk into the sofa. Grace's fingers slid through Tom's thick hair and locked around the back of his neck as she pulled him in closer. They kissed each other slowly at first, but soon Grace's hands found their way underneath his shirt, turning Tom's skin bumpy and tight. Her body wrapped around his, the silk of her shirt the only barrier left between them.

When Tom could feel himself begin to lose composure, he tried to pull away, conscious of overstepping the mark, but Grace only pulled him back in, wrapping her legs around him a little tighter each time. When their mouths naturally parted and he was able to look at her fully, her hair loose, falling off the edge of her shoulder, his euphoria was so extreme that he almost felt guilty. But love isn't finite. One doesn't take from the other. It's not a number or an equation. It's an open field, and here he was, charging through it.

"Do you want more dessert?" Tom said, his hands on Grace's hips, their bodies touching. He knew he was stalling. What he wanted to say as he looked at her, her cheeks rhubarb pink, was that he'd fallen in love with her. But Tom now knew that she could spook like an unbroken horse, and he couldn't risk her running away again—not now that he also knew the softness of her skin on the curve of her hip or the sensitivity of her scar when his lips brushed over it. Still, no matter how much he wanted to go further, something stopped him. It wasn't fear or nerves, though both were there, but an urge to tell the truth.

"Grace," he said, his voice just audible, "I haven't done this since, since Honor . . ."

Grace didn't say anything. Instead, she loosened her grip around his neck and then began unbuttoning her shirt. By the time it had fallen to the floor, she'd started to kiss the space between his Adam's apple and collarbone, her skin warm against his.

They didn't rush things that night. They simply explored each other's bodies, knowing this would be the first of many chances. Both acutely aware that after a certain age, no one ever gets into bed alone. There's always someone else in the room in some form or another. Whether it's holiday memories or drunken mistakes or ghosts, the past cannot be rewritten. But whether Tom opened his eyes or kept them closed, all he saw was Grace.

CHAPTER FIFTEEN

I never thought I'd be happy to see my husband in bed with another woman.

Just before six o'clock, as Tom fumbled for the monitor on the bedside table, it was clear he'd followed my instructions: *Find a solid replacement.* He scrutinized the grainy, pixelated screen, comforted to discover the familiar lump of Henry under his covers. It was still dark outside, but there was enough light from the streetlamp creeping in through the crack of the curtain for Tom to see Grace, her bare arm resting on the white duvet. He watched her until the sun rose, shining through the oatmeal-colored curtains, lit up like a ship's sail crossing the sea at sunrise.

"Hello," she said, waking up. "Was I snoring?"

"Yes."

"I really do snore loudly."

"You don't need to tell me," Tom said, as Grace covered her face with the duvet.

"Do you have a spare toothbrush?"

"Unlikely. But if I do, it will probably be a very small, soft-bristled number with Snoopy all over it." Tom got out of bed, noticing her silk shirt draped on the back of the chair as he walked to the bathroom. "It's not Snoopy. It's Winnie-the-Pooh," he called, rifling through a drawer. "I hope that's all right?"

He broke open the toothbrush and set it in the holder on what used to be my side of the sink and returned to the bedroom. Grace moved across the bed on her knees, letting the bedsheet fall away from her. Here was the confirmation in front of him that it hadn't all been a dream. This beautiful woman, alive, naked in his bed.

Tom listened to the sounds of Grace brushing her teeth in the bathroom. He'd learned in the most appalling of ways how to appreciate all the daily activities he'd never thought to savor. Every predictable outcome now felt like a gift to relish—the sound of Grace's feet as she padded across the floor, the sound of the bristles as she brushed her teeth, even the inevitable sound of the toilet as it flushed. There was something so exciting, so invigorating about the thought of Grace's daily rituals intertwining with his: her tissues crumpled in the bin, her knickers on the floor.

She came back into the bedroom, wearing Tom's faded blue-and-white terry cloth dressing gown, and picked up her bra from the chair by the window.

"I hope you aren't planning on putting that back on," Tom said, moving towards her.

"I should sneak out before Henry wakes up. And besides, I don't think leaving your house in a dressing gown is a great look for your neighbors," she said, her bra hanging limply in her hand.

"Henry will be thrilled you're still here. He'll insist you have dippy eggs with us. And in terms of the neighbors, they're going to have to get used to it." He felt for the break in her dressing gown and slowly traced his fingers down her torso, before putting them

inside her with excruciating slowness, the way he'd learned she
liked the previous night.

"You sound confident," she said.

"Am I wrong?" Tom asked. Grace began to moan in response.
He could feel himself getting hard, his need to have her eclipsing
every rational thought.

"You didn't answer," Tom said, his voice barely audible as Grace's
body tightened around his fingers, causing him to push faster inside
her. But when she reached out for his boxers, he pulled away. He
could tell she was close. Her shoulders started to curve in and her
eyelids grew heavy. Her toes gripped the rug. Something about this
new intimacy, their closeness in the light of day, made him even
more excited. He undid the tie of her dressing gown and bent down
in front of her, pressing his mouth against her clit, her body stiffen-
ing in response as he slowly worked his fingers deep inside her until
she came in his mouth.

*

Later that morning, Tom pulled a slotted ladle from the kitchen
drawer and gently dropped three eggs into the boiling water, careful not to let them bounce too hard on the bottom of the copper pan.
Lauren had continually advised me against those pans, prattling on
about how high-maintenance they were, but obviously I ignored
her and bought the set. In general, I tended to count out practicality,
always favoring aesthetic over function.

Tom took the milk out of the fridge and turned down Radio
4. As the blue flame engulfed the base of the pan, Tom set the
timer for four and a half minutes, every now and then glancing at
Henry and Grace sitting at the kitchen table, as if to keep double-
checking this sight wasn't a figment of his imagination: Grace
wearing one of his jumpers, her hair wet and pulled back off her
face, and Henry sitting opposite in his school uniform. The image

of the two of them together in the kitchen felt both familiar and new; it wasn't just the extra egg in the saucepan and three slices of bread in the toaster.

While he made breakfast, Tom found himself having flashbacks of the night before—the successful steaks, her body warm and receptive beneath him, loading the dishwasher, the unfortunate lemon tart, finding Henry and Grace on the stairs. But nothing was better than now: making her coffee with a splash of milk before Henry was off to school. Grace didn't force herself on Henry like so many people did. She drank her coffee and every so often glanced over at him as he built his Lego set at the end of the table. A tractor, of course. The Bialetti whistled and Tom poured Grace more coffee.

"Wow, full service," she said.

"We like to impress, don't we, Henry?" Tom said, wanting to kiss Grace but treading lightly around Henry, of course. The timer for the eggs went off on his phone just as the doorbell rang.

"Do you want me to get that, Julia Child?" Grace said.

"Please. It's probably Pat."

"Pat?"

"The postman," Henry said.

Grace laughed as she walked out of the kitchen past the drawing room, where the fire had turned to soft gray ash. She took the chain off the door and pulled it open. Annie was standing on the doorstep. I could tell by the way Annie's eyes flashed unnaturally wide that she wasn't expecting Grace to be opening Tom's door with wet hair first thing in the morning.

"Annie," Grace said.

"Grace," Annie said.

"Come in. We're just having breakfast."

Annie followed Grace to the kitchen, her hands in the pockets of her wax jacket. Whenever Annie was uncomfortable, she reacted in one of two ways, with silence or excessive fidgeting. Today was the latter. She took off her felt hat before putting it back on, then did a lap of the kitchen, all while taking her hands in and out of her pockets.

"Annie? I wasn't expecting you," Tom said, cutting Henry's toast into soldiers.

"I tried ringing last night," Annie said, looking at Grace and Henry, who were building something out of Lego on the table. "But I see now, you were busy." Annie kissed Henry hello and handed him a copy of *The Slightly Annoying Elephant*.

"Do you want something to eat?" Tom said.

"No, I've eaten, thanks. Did you forget I was taking Henry to school today? It's reading week. I'm reading to his class."

"Shit," Tom said, just as a burning smell pervaded the kitchen. "I totally forgot."

"I can see that. You seem to be forgetting a lot of things these days."

Tom picked the blackened toast out of the toaster with a pincer grip and dropped it in the bin.

"Yuck, Daddy," Henry said. "Can I have cold toast, please?"

"Cold toast?" Grace said. "Do you mean bread?" Henry laughed.

"I really don't want to be late," Annie said, not looking at Grace. "You know what the traffic's like at this time in the morning."

"Annie, I'm going as fast as I can," Tom said.

"Are you? Because it feels like Sunday morning in here."

Grace didn't need to be Agatha Christie to pick up on the tense atmosphere between Annie and Tom. When Henry asked her if she'd seen his John Deere trailer, Grace snatched the opportunity to excuse herself and offered to help him look for it upstairs. They'd barely left the room, their footsteps moving along the landing, when Annie accosted Tom.

"Are you expecting me to just go along with this?" she whisper-shouted.

"Please. Don't start, Annie."

"Me? I didn't start anything." She checked behind her. "I didn't ask for this information. I didn't want to be in your bloody lie. But I am. And now Henry is too apparently."

Tom began clearing the table before turning to Annie, who was leaning up against the island.

"Even Honor, of all people, with the most far-reaching imagination, would not be able to convince herself to keep this a secret," Annie said. "She would want you to tell Grace the truth."

"Can you keep your voice down," Tom said through gritted teeth. He snapped shut Henry's lunch box and passed it to Annie across the island. "It's not that simple."

"It's not fair to Henry. Or Grace. You have to tell her. Otherwise, I can promise you one thing, this is all gonna end in shit."

As Tom slammed the pan on the range, turning to Annie, Grace and Henry were making their way back downstairs. Henry stopped for a moment in the entrance hall to roll his tractor along the jute rug while Grace took the opportunity to rub yesterday's mascara from beneath her eyes.

"I haven't had anyone to make breakfast for besides me and Henry in five years," Tom said. "And if you can't be happy for me, then I don't know what to tell you."

"Oh my God. You're falling in love with her, aren't you?" Annie said, no longer whisper-shouting. The house had never been good acoustically. Every sound traveled. I could sometimes hear the dishwasher running when I was in the bath. There was no chance Grace had missed a word of what Annie had just said.

"And what if I am?" Tom said. Grace stood frozen by the mirror as if someone had just given her an electric shock while Henry pushed his trailer towards the kitchen.

"You're not listening to anything I'm saying," Annie said. "But if you're going to hear anything, hear this: She's not Henry's mother. Honor is. Don't get your wires crossed."

"I don't want her to be Henry's mother," Tom said. As Grace

listened by the kitchen door, she began to breathe more quickly, short bursts pushing through her nose.

"Tom, you can press it down all you want, but this is not going away." Annie looked at her watch and shouted, "Henry! Let's go!"

Henry pushed open the kitchen door and Grace followed right behind. The kitchen was spotless, but the tension hung there like a leg of dry-cured ham.

"Grace? Do you want to play with me after school?" Henry said, swiping the trailer wheels up and down his palm.

"Maybe. Let me speak to your daddy first," Grace said. Annie shot a look at Tom.

"Good to see you, Grace," she said, then hustled Henry out the door. The atmosphere didn't leave with them. Tom's mind was in a scramble trying to resuscitate what had been a divine domestic morning.

"All okay?" he said.

"I overheard you talking with Annie," Grace said. Tom's stomach fell through the floor. "I'm not going to get my wires crossed."

"Annie didn't mean it like that," Tom said. He gripped the island.

"I know. I know she's just looking out for Henry but—can we sit down?" Grace's tone wasn't sharp. She wasn't running. That must mean something. He'd thought once she found out, she'd run for the hills, but she hadn't. Tom felt as though he could hear every step he took towards her at the kitchen table. A mixture of tinnitus and a thumping of his heart. "I know it's different because I don't have my own children," she said. They sat down at the kitchen table, the sky glum through the window. "But I'm not going to get confused and think I'm Henry's mother."

The blood rushed to Tom's stubbled cheeks. "Grace, I—"

"Let me finish. The other day when I told you about having my eggs retrieved, after Pietro died, what I didn't tell you is that I didn't keep those eggs. I couldn't handle the situation. Every part of myself felt so entwined with Pietro. I wanted to go under the duvet and never come out. I donated them to a charity in Italy a few days later. Anonymously. Thinking that would change everything. It was a rash decision, to be honest. Do I regret it? Maybe. Do I wonder when I see children in a restaurant if they could be from those eggs, or if I'd recognize them in the park? Yes. But even if I did, or if those children exist, do I think that those children are mine? Absolutely not. Those children have mothers. Henry has a mother. It's Honor. I mean, you must see her in him every day, right? I'm not going to get my wires crossed. Ever. I'm not going to overstep with your son."

Tom felt a Gordian knot form in his stomach. He teetered, trapped between Grace's wish to remain anonymous and his lie. It was all very well for Grace to feel this detachment when the child was nowhere to be seen. But would she feel differently if she knew we used her egg to make Henry? That she wasn't just any-body's egg donor, but ours? I'd chosen her. Amidst all the possible choices, her authenticity had shone through. Now I knew why she sounded so straightforward. Why she hadn't been trying to sell herself; in that moment, her world had been in turmoil.

"Tom. Say something." Grace took his hands in hers. "Your lips have gone white."

"Sorry, yes," Tom said, squeezing her hands like a lifeline. Even though Henry wasn't biologically my baby, Grace was right: Henry was my son. He was as much a part of me as he was of Grace. Something Tom had always known. "Honor lives on everywhere," he said. "Not only in Henry. He exists because of her. He breathes because of her. It's like she's preserved in amber because of Henry."

Tom couldn't tell if his hand or his entire body had gone numb. The truth was out. Only it was her truth. His truth was still locked away in the safe at the back of the wardrobe with Henry and Chloe's birth certificates, his dad's Rolex, and Hedgie.

"I've never told anyone that I donated my eggs. Except Zara,"

Grace said. "But I feel like I can tell you things. I feel like you see me as Grace, not the girl who found her husband dead in the bath at thirty-two. You don't pity me or look at me like a project. I hate fate and star signs and all that bollocks, but I feel like I'm meant to be here with you and Henry—I think I'm falling in love with you."

"Grace, I already fell."

CHAPTER SIXTEEN

For most English people, February is by far the most depressing month of the year. A predictable four straight weeks of horizontal rain, potentially sleet, threats of snow, and bitter wind. But it was my summer. The days were so short that the hours of socialization were limited, and I could have every fire burning in the house without Tom complaining. I'd wake up in the morning when it was still pitch-black outside and write at the kitchen table before Chloe and Tom woke up. After I dropped Chloe off at preschool, I'd decant myself into a chair and stay put until pickup.

When I didn't have a vestige of energy left, the only break I could invariably justify was a visit to the White Horse Bookshop. It had everything, from first editions in a locked glass cabinet along one wall to a round table right as you walked in that was always blazing with fresh treasures. I spent hundreds of hours in that higgledy-piggledy store. I'd done so many signings there, met so many readers, and read to so many children. When I died, the owner, Angus, filled an entire window with copies of *The Ice Cream Zoo*.

That particular nippy February morning, Tom and Grace were walking along the High Street on their way to lunch when the heavens opened, soaking the two of them almost instantly.

"Quick, run in here!" Grace said, squinting as the rain hit her cheeks.

Tom flipped up the hood of his jacket and looked at the gray-and-white-painted sign reading THE WHITE HORSE BOOKSHOP. His blood turned to bronze. This wasn't any generic Waterstones. It was my parish. "Quick, come on! You're getting soaked!" Grace called from the doorway, the rain running off her duffle coat.

The past three months with Grace had been magic. In a bid to avoid Annie's moral finger-wagging at Sunday lunch, Tom had started making it at home. They went on long walks with Henry and Duke, before Rita came over to babysit and then they went off to meet the girls at Sunday Blues. Grace and Henry started an herb garden on the windowsill, and the basil in particular was thriving. Grace slept over so often that Tom and Henry had secretly cut her a key to the house. When Tom had asked Henry if he liked the idea of Grace's moving in with them, Henry had said, "Can she stay in my room?" and promised to keep the key a secret from her until the personalized Smythson key ring they'd chosen together was ready to be picked up.

During the evenings, once Henry was tucked up in bed, if Grace wasn't revising for her exam, the two of them would settle in the drawing room and watch a film. Much to Tom's unwavering aston-ishment, Grace had never seen *Die Hard*, and Tom had never seen *The Philadelphia Story*. They gave it a good go. Only they never got to the part where John McClane talks to his wife, Holly, on the phone or where Macaulay Connor rescues Tracy Lord from the pool. A kiss always led to more, and there was a lot of kissing.

"I might as well look in the chapter-book section for Henry

while we're here," Grace said, following the hand-painted arrow for the children's section at the back of the shop. Tom felt as if he'd just been dropped into a session of exposure therapy. Standing on the fawn-colored carpet, he lifted his hand to Angus, who thankfully was busy helping a customer by the till. Tom didn't want him coming over and making a big fuss. Although he spoke to Angus quite frequently when ordering books over the phone, they hadn't seen each other since my funeral.

Tom paced the length of the bookshop, meandering about like a deer in a stagless herd, before finally settling in one of the battered, upholstered chairs by the window. He picked up a lone, discarded book: a collection of love letters between Georgia O'Keeffe, a painter he'd always admired, and Alfred Stieglitz, a photographer whose pictures we adored. The rain was easing but still heavy. He tried his best to engage in the pages, homing in on the words and repeating them under his breath to moor him, but the suffocation wasn't ceasing. Why couldn't they have run into the antiques shop next door? Why hadn't they made something at home like Grace suggested? Tom was still stuck on the same page when Grace sidled over.

"Boo," she said, coming up behind him, holding a brown paper bag of her purchases, her hair still soggy from the rain. "What's that you're reading?" she asked. The weather was beginning to clear; soon they'd be back in fresh air. He held up the book to show Grace. "*My Faraway One: Selected Letters of Georgia O'Keeffe and Alfred Stieglitz*," she read. "Are there any juicy bits?" She perched on the arm of Tom's chair, then took the book and began flicking through the contents. "It says here they wrote to each other three or four times a day. They're the original texters."

The phone in the shop rang and Angus quickly answered, straightening the complimentary bookmarks that sat in a pile by the till. "We should go to the Ghost Ranch," she said, not realizing Tom was already there.

"The what?"

"Georgia O'Keeffe's house." She showed him the photograph in the book. "It's in New Mexico. It looks beautiful. It says here, 'You can embark on a spiritual, transformative journey.'" Tom looked at the picture, recoiling at the idea of any type of journey, spiritual or otherwise.

"It's about to stop raining. Here, let me take your bag?" he said.

"Hang on. What's the rush? Let me show you what I bought first."

Grace passed Tom the brick of love letters and turned her body towards him. She dove her hand into the shopping bag and held up a copy of *Fantastic Mr. Fox,* one of Chloe's favorites. "When I was getting this for Henry, I saw the display they have for Honor's books." Tom paused, watching a woman in a yellow raincoat by the front table have a heated disagreement with her umbrella. "You know, I sometimes think we would have really gotten along." Tom fought to keep his face cheerful. *Marry someone you could see me being friends with . . .* "I think she'd be happy we found each other, don't you?"

"I don't *think*—I know she would be," he said, sliding his hand across her cheek. "I know this is what she would have wanted." *Marry someone you could see me being friends with . . .*

"Even though I can't make up a story to save my life?" Grace said. Tom's throat felt like hot asphalt.

He wasn't well-versed in dishonesty. He was learning on the job that once a lie erupts, you forever live in the psychological aftershock. He hadn't foreseen his secret becoming inflamed and impinging on yet more subjects he couldn't share with Grace. "I saw they have a picture of her doing a signing here," Grace continued. "I was thinking it might be nice to get a copy. For Henry?"

"Oh? Yeah—sure," Tom said. How was Grace to know this bookshop was Tom's Achilles' heel? Tom and Grace talked about me all the time. There were photos of me dotted around the house.

But this was different. What if she suggested, in her loving way, they read my books to Henry? Then what was he going to say? Talking about me to Grace was one thing, but hearing Grace read my words aloud to Henry, a child we would never have had without her, felt like another irretrievable deceit. It was too close to the bone.

"Am I overstepping? You don't look convinced. I just thought it would be nice," Grace said. The brown paper bag rustled as she tucked it under her arm.

"Of course not," Tom said, reaching for her hand. He obediently followed her to the children's section, feeling ill at ease. They stood in front of my photograph. I was sitting behind a small mahogany table with my Sharpie poised over an open copy of *The Ice Cream Zoo*. Angus was leaning beside me, his rimless glasses perched on the end of his nose. The sales for my book that week had shot up three places on *The Sunday Times* Bestsellers List. After the signing that evening, we'd brought Angus back to Annie's house for oysters and champagne. Obviously, my turn to cook.

"It's a great photograph," Grace said, looking at Tom. "She looks so happy."

"Yeah, she was. I remember," Tom said, looking across at Angus, who was still on the phone. "Let's come back tomorrow. Angus is busy." Grace held Tom's hand tighter. "I'm starving, babe. Shall we go?"

"Wait," she said, glancing at the photo one more time. "I thought you said Honor was left-handed?" Tom drew a short breath. The books lining the shelves felt like they were closing in on him. "She's signing with her right hand. You told me she was left-handed, like Henry. Like me?"

"Sorry?" he said. It was all he could think of to say. Tom screwed up his face slightly, a clear indicator that he was fibbing. Like when I'd ask him if he had turned off all the lights downstairs or put the loo seat down. His lip would curl up dramatically and he would say, *Yeah, course,* and I'd know he'd done neither.

"Well, she was ambidextrous," Tom said. Grace narrowed her eyes. Where was Tom keeping track of all these lies? Whereas I was used to keeping notes for a fictional family in my notebooks, Tom hadn't developed that practice. He wasn't keeping a spreadsheet, and this was a moving train, gathering passengers at rapid speed.

"Ambidextrous?" Grace said. "That's very—I don't remember you saying that."

"Didn't I? I didn't think much of it. Should we go to Ottolenghi?" Her suspicion sat there uncomfortably, like droplets of water on cashmere.

"Sure," Grace said. "But please not Ottolenghi."

*

As they drove to lunch, Tom replayed their conversation, observing Grace's profile in his peripheral vision. Sitting beside him, was she doing the same? Was she going over her own spreadsheet of everything he had said up to now? Tom had just read in one of Stieglitz's letters, *All I want is to preserve that wonderful something which so purely exists between us.* Tom longed for a day when he and Grace could be just like us: two people who met, fell in love, and had a baby.

But what was he worrying about? Grace didn't outwardly appear that concerned. Instead, she turned up the radio. Maybe he was being paranoid. Or would the question of my ability to be ambidextrous come up again, like an itch following a brush with poison ivy? Grace sang along to Alanis Morissette and continued rustling through her paper bag of books, looking at what else she'd bought. I have to say, I was rather envious that she could read in the car. At the mere sight of a sentence, I became irretrievably carsick.

Outside the car window, a man with a large, shaggy dog flagged down a taxi. Tom turned his eyes from the road to Grace, doubletaking the book she was holding. Tom would have known that sepia portrait on the front cover anywhere. For a moment, he thought he was imagining it. It was *Les Fleurs du Mal* by Baudelaire.

"Tom. The lights," Grace said. He shot another furtive glance at the cover. The all-too-familiar image of Baudelaire's portrait glowering at him made Tom's innards seize. He could hear Grace's voice on the CD reading the poem contained in these very pages. *My voice reciting it on the lawn at Annie's.* It was as if someone had tripped the fuse in his brain and his mind had gone dark. Was this how she would find out? Would he be forced into confessing because of obscure French poetry?

"Can I read you something?" Grace said, adjusting her seat belt to turn her body slightly towards him. They'd stopped at another set of lights and a bus pulled up beside them, advertising a mediocre action film with yet more Jason Statham. Every passenger was staring intently at their phone screens, but Tom could see only one thing: Grace's book, held open on *Hymn to Beauty*. *Our poem.* Was this a test? And if it was a test, what was the test, exactly?

"Of course," Tom said, though there was a hint of hesitation that only a well-trained ear could pick up, a nuance in inflection that was detectable only after years of marriage. I knew from personal experience that Tom didn't like this sort of listening exercise. I would read something aloud, stressing certain words with zeal in the hope of eliciting a specific response. Then, when I didn't get the reaction I sought from him over a passage I thought was especially resonant, I would become unjustifiably frustrated and slink off in a huff.

"I studied Baudelaire at university, and I used to think he was so romantic," Grace said. "It's amazing how context changes everything."

Tom nodded, hoping she would move on to another book, or that he would get pulled over by the police.

"When I donated my eggs, one of the requirements was to do a recording of my voice—either a famous speech or a poem, or a song, so that potential families could hear me, and know I was a real person, I guess. I felt like such an idiot."

"That makes sense," Tom said. His hands had grown sweaty on the steering wheel.

"I grabbed the nearest book as I left the house. I used to think this poem was about love, but maybe that was only because I was *in love* and inexperienced. But when I read it again that day, newly widowed, I felt like I finally understood that it was about how merciless time is more than anything else. Things read so differently now. Do you find that?" She trailed off.

"Yes. Very different," Tom said in a voice not his own. His face was turning a shade like those terra-cotta tiles you see all over sun-dappled roofs in the South of France. He gripped the steering wheel tightly, knowing that the only person he could blame for where he was right now was himself. What was he supposed to say? *That poem was one of the last things Honor ever said to me before she died.* The idea of hearing it made him want to weep. But this seemed utterly impossible to articulate, so instead Tom lied and said: "I—I'd love to hear it."

"*Do you come from Heaven or rise from the abyss / Beauty? Your gaze, divine and infernal . . .*" As Grace read our poem aloud, Tom's knuckles tightened. There was no escaping the words. They floated around the car like flakes of fresh snow. Tom opened the window, letting in a rush of air, but Baudelaire's words remained present and clear. Hearing the poem on the CD was one thing, but having Grace recite it beside him in the car was quite another. It felt like a betrayal, but who was he betraying exactly? Or who wasn't he?

"*And one may for that, compare you to wine. You contain in your eyes the sunset and the dawn; You scatter perfumes like a stormy night,*" Grace read, before she stopped somewhat abruptly. She closed the book, using her index finger as a bookmark. "Are you all right?" she said. "You're gripping the steering wheel incredibly tightly."

"I'm fine." Tom faked a very bizarre laugh. The rain had picked up again, the drops violently pelting the sunroof, the windscreen wipers swiping back and forth like a metronome set to the wrong song. He wondered if this was an indisputable opportunity to tell

Grace it was our poem she'd just recited. Would Tom say, *This poem has huge significance to me, so much so that it was what justified my tracking you down?*

As he was taking inventory of the mounting lies he'd told to cushion himself from consequence, his phone rang. Normally, he wouldn't have picked up while he was with Grace unless it was Henry's school, but it was Arcot House, his mum's nursing home.

"Sorry, I have to get this," he said. "It's my mother . . . well, her nurse."

It had been a couple weeks since Tom had visited Judith, and even though calls from the care home weren't unusual, they always startled him.

He pressed the green button on the dashboard and braced himself for news that his mother might have taken a turn, or worse, fallen. Judith had grown frail. Every time he drove home from one of his visits, he feared it might have been the last time he would see her. When the doctors had initially told us Judith had Alzheimer's, I'd been convinced it was a misdiagnosis.

"Mr. Wharton?" The voice of his mother's nurse emanated through the car, her tone somewhat upbeat.

"Yes? Speaking. Is everything okay?" He glanced over at Grace, and she responded with a look of such warmth.

"Everything's fine. Is this a good time?"

"Of course," Tom said, unzipping the top of his coat.

"Great. Well, your mother's had a good couple of days. She's been quite lucid and talking about you a lot and telling all sorts of wonderful stories."

Grace rubbed the back of Tom's neck, and he was able to give way to her touch, like a kitten to a dangling hand. The poem had stopped, its lines no longer strangling him.

"I'm pleased to hear that," Tom said.

"You can't come for a visit today, by any chance? These moments can sometimes be so transient. We're about to sit down for tea."

Tom looked across at Grace. She nodded and gave him two thumbs-up. Her eyes were bright, her smile broad. "Of course. I'm not far." Tom looked behind him before performing a U-turn.

"I'll tell her you're coming," the nurse said.

Tom ended the call and glanced over at Grace. She knew about Judith's condition, of course, just as he knew about her parents—who lived in Brighton and fished for mackerel on the weekends—but that didn't mean he'd be meeting them anytime soon.

"Do you mind?" he said. "If we go? My mother's so rarely like this."

"Mind?" she said. "I'd be honored. Unless you want me to wait in the car? Do you think it would confuse her if I was there?"

"Of course I want you there," he said. "I just wish you could've met the old her. She was wonderful. Everyone wanted to be with my mum. She had such a brilliant mind. If you thought *I* talked a lot about art . . . Most of my quotes are stolen from her."

*

In the car park of Arcot House, Tom turned off the engine and pulled the keys out of the ignition.

"Before we go in, it's important you know I never told my mum about Paris." A heavy swelling occurred in Tom's throat, which he knew, however hard he fought, he could never swallow. He'd never told anyone, not even Annie, that he hadn't told Judith what happened to us. "If I had, it would have meant having to tell her again and again, and I just couldn't do that to myself. To her. Undergo that shock every time I came to see her. Thinking about it is excruciating enough, let alone reliving it out loud. I let Honor and Chloe walk out of that room."

Tom didn't wipe away his tears; instead he let them stream down his face. "My mum is the only person in the world who doesn't know. Who sees me as I was. It's not just that she didn't recognize Honor anymore—though she hadn't for years—it's that when I walk into that room, I'm not a widower. Just for half an hour. And I can't bear or justify changing it for either one of us. It's too cruel."

Grace dropped her book into the car's side compartment and reached across the middle console for Tom, his tears penetrating her coat as Baudelaire observed them from the door.

"Tell me what you want me to do. I don't have to come in with you," she said. Tom looked at her, his anxieties momentarily allayed by her warm presence.

"No. I want you beside me," Tom said.

"Then that's where I'll be."

When they walked into Arcot House, they found Judith in her room, watching *Sky News*. Someone had done her hair and even painted her nails, which would not have been her idea. She wasn't one for nail varnish and she couldn't stand being fussed over. She would have complained about that even a year ago, but now she didn't seem to notice, though her face lit up when she saw her son. Tom kissed his mother hello and squeezed her hand while Grace hung back by the door.

"I like the flowers, Mum," Tom said, gesturing to the dahlias in a yellow ceramic vase by the window. He gestured for Grace to come and sit down on one of the two cane-back chairs Judith used to have in the hallway of her old house.

"Thomas," Judith said. "Why didn't you tell me you were coming? Your father didn't say anything. I've been marking dissertations all day. Piles of the things."

"Have you?" Tom said. He didn't remind her that his dad had died of lung cancer two decades ago. He tucked in the edges of his mother's blanket and moved her glass of water a little closer. Grace put her bag down beside the chair and slid her hands underneath her thighs. "Mum, I want you to meet Grace," Tom said, knowing that his mother would remember neither Grace nor this moment. But he wasn't going to treat his mother any differently because of her disease

or the fruitlessness of introducing new people to someone with virtu-
ally no short-term memory.

"Hello," Grace said, standing up. "It's so lovely to meet you."

They shook hands, only Judith wouldn't let go. She held on, her
eyes focused on Grace. When Judith had moved to Arcot House,
Tom had decorated her room to make it look as similar to her own
living room as possible. That meant building bookshelves and lining them with her beloved books and artifacts that she'd collected
over the years. Grace examined the photographs on the side table—
Chloe and me in Athens holding gelato, Tom as a little boy in his
school uniform, Judith and I on my wedding day, the four of us in
New York. I was everywhere today.

The three of them had tea and biscuits in the conservatory,
where Judith looked out at the birds and occasionally informed
Tom of the habits pertaining to a certain family of blue tits.

After they'd finished their tea, Tom and Grace walked Judith
back to her room.

"I'll come and have lunch with you Wednesday, okay?" Tom
said, but Judith seemed tired and didn't respond.

"It was so wonderful to meet you, Judith," Grace said, laying
her hand on the end of the bed. Judith's head turned slightly.

"I like your hair like that, Oni," Judith said. Tom held his
breath. He hadn't heard his mother's nickname for me in over a
decade. Neither had I. While hearing it evoked a certain nostalgia,
it was the last thing he would have wanted her to say now. Should
he jump to correct his mother? Would Grace be upset if he didn't?

He was about to say, *This isn't Honor, Mum. This is Grace,* when
Grace shook her head at him, perhaps to indicate his mother's con-
fusion was understandable. But privately was she wondering if
there was ever going to be a day when she wouldn't be taken as my
understudy?

As they walked back to the car, Grace took Tom's hand and
thanked him for bringing her to see his mother.

"You have your mum's eyes, you know," she said. "And the same mouth." The freshly mowed lawn seemed almost too green, like a film set. He tried not to let Grace's sweet compliment be clouded by the endless familial comparisons that had become the bane of his life. Wouldn't people have said the same thing about me and Henry? Would Grace have said Tom resembled his mother if Judith and Tom had been two strangers in the street? Would Grace eventually start to recognize her own genetic similarity to Henry? Henry and Grace got the shivers in the exact same way, a full-body, top-to-bottom wriggle. They sneezed the same way. Their yawn was the same. They were both left-handed.

The clerical error that had led him to Grace had removed any chance of serendipity. What did Grace see when she looked into Henry's eyes? Was their love becoming more and more powerful, or was it there from the start, an unspoken, visceral connection? All of this could have been a coincidence, except that it wasn't. Was Henry growing every day to be more like Grace or more like Tom?

But while Tom was wrestling with these questions that should've been theoretical, Grace began talking about where to go for lunch. The secret he was keeping was so unbelievable, so far from the realm of possibility, that unless she got a letter intended for Tom, there was no way Grace would ever figure it out.

CHAPTER SEVENTEEN

I was just about to leave the house for the school run, one boot already laced, when Lauren started knocking at the front door. To call it "knocking" would be a bit of a misnomer—she was slamming the solid brass knocker so loudly that it made the crystal pendants on the chandelier tinkle. It was the tail end of winter, and a soggy tea towel of clouds was hanging over London. Between the miserable weather and Lauren's relentless banging, I felt like I'd suddenly been dropped into the opening sequence of a Hitchcock film. I looked at my watch: I had three minutes before I needed to leave, otherwise I'd be late for Chloe.

When I opened the door, Lauren was standing there disheveled, her shoulders limp. Strands of hair were sticking to the salty residue on her cheeks and her upper lip was blotchy from crying.

"What's happened?" I asked, as she barreled past me.

"He has a child with her," she announced, "It's not just an affair. They have a child."

Though I wasn't shocked, my nostrils flared. We had become suspicious of Daniel, Lauren's soon-to-be-ex-husband, when he'd taken a fancy to "night fishing" and begun seeing a dermatologist. When Lauren had found illicit emails on his computer, Daniel had admitted to having an affair and agreed to go to couples therapy. But during those sessions, it appeared, he had conveniently left out the part where he'd spawned another child.

"If he thinks he's getting the twins, or Chester, he has another thing coming!" Lauren said.

"Should we discuss this in the car?" I said, doing up the buttons on my coat. I had less than a minute to get out of the house before gridlock traffic. I already had two late strikes against my name, and a third meant I was immediately nominated to set up the school fête the following weekend. Starting at 7 A.M. On a Sunday. But Lauren was already in the drawing room, having thrown herself onto the sofa.

"And to think I had all that anal sex with him," she declared, just as Rita walked by the drawing room door with a large pile of folded washing.

"Right," I said, momentarily numbed by the very image.

"She lives in Manchester," she added. "I saw her leave the house today, holding the baby." I could hear Duke pacing up and down in the hallway, his lead clinking as it dragged along the floor.

"You just drove back from Manchester?" I said, passing Lauren a tissue. "To look at the outside of her house?" She nodded and blew hard. Manchester was a good three and a half hours away, and with Lauren driving, probably four.

"You're so lucky to have Tom," she said, blowing her nose again. "He would never do a thing like this. It's just not in his nature to be deceitful."

"Let's not get carried away with giving out any prizes for basic fidelity," I said. "It's kind of what you sign up for. And besides, Tom's so in love with his work that I'm not sure he would have the mental capacity to hatch another family, especially one all the way in Manchester."

Watching Lauren wail on the sofa, I cringed remembering the way

I had spoken to Tom that morning about leaving all the drawers open in our bedroom. It was all so meaningless; we should have just been grateful that neither one of us was nurturing a secret second family in the north of England.

"Should we call your lawyer on the way to school, then?" I said.

"I'm not calling the lawyer!" she said, sitting upright. "Not yet."

At times, reasoning with Lauren was like stepping back into the eighteenth century. For her, somehow, a man was always the solution. At university, while Annie and I were more concerned with getting a First, Lauren endlessly hosted dinner parties in a bid to get herself wedded off as quickly as possible.

"Lauren," I said. "If you don't ring your lawyer, then he will." She nodded like a toddler admitting defeat, then yanked the blanket off the back of the sofa and arranged it meticulously over herself. "You stay here. I'll pick up the children. If you don't want to see them when we get back, just get in my bed. I'll take care of everything else."

*

The school gates were rife with chatter over the upcoming Easter break when Tom's car pulled into the car park. It was the first warm spring day and winter coats had been shed for goose-down gilets. The sky was Wedgwood blue, and the familiar faces at pickup were taking full advantage of the first hint of sunshine. It was still early enough in the spring that the British habit of complaining about the weather—our incessant need to discuss in detail those days when the Tube became so hot it could set the vase you made in your evening ceramics class—had yet to kick in.

Lauren, the doyenne of the school playground, was ensconced in her usual circle of raptors, her cropped, red denim jacket like a flare in a sea of black Alo leggings. She was deep in a discussion with Camilla, a mother I always found highly entertaining. They were talking about the price increase of uniforms and trying to pinpoint patient zero of the school's recent head lice outbreak, topics I tried my best to avoid. I mostly found the whole school-gate scene intolerable, not because I thought I was above it—some of the parents I quite liked—but because in aggregate, the vibe was reminiscent of everything I hated about my snobby, overrated boarding school in Dorset. Eleven years of an unsisterly cooperative of little breeding gangs, each with its own agenda.

No matter how often Lauren assured me that everyone was *obsessed*—her word—with *Mr. Mango Sorbet*, when other parents approached me with questions about my next picture book, I always detected a slight uppity air. Some dad would ask me if I was going to write another "story," or go into great detail about the "serious novel" he was thinking of writing with a tone that implied my little books were specious bits of fluff that randomly became bestsellers because of some sort of zeitgeist in the frozen food aisle.

"My shaman Heather said this morning that if you don't incorporate holotropic breathwork into every Yogilates session, you aren't tapping into the power of your true core. Do you want her number? She's amazing," said Julia, a mother whose towheaded child I always thought was reminiscent of Draco Malfoy.

"I have no comprehension of anything you're saying. I think I'll pass," Camilla said. She pried the lid off her coffee. "The last thing I need is to accidentally get hog-tied in one of those springs half an hour before work."

As Julia and Camilla prattled on about the quality of the recent school photos, Lauren continued to glance over in the direction of Tom's Defender. He was later than usual, only five minutes early instead of his customary fifteen. Normally, Lauren would have taken great pleasure in sharing any number of opinions about boutique exercise, one of her topics. But when the door sprung open with an energetic bounce, it was Grace, not Tom, who stepped out. A short, barely audible gasp escaped Lauren's lips, causing Camilla to stop talking and turn around.

"Crikey," she said, looking over the top of her sunglasses. "Well, he's certainly got a type."

However, it wasn't just Camilla and Lauren who were tracking Grace, but the school gates in their entirety. The unexpected arrival of a woman getting out of Tom's car—a woman who looked so much like me—had hushed even the most obnoxious parents. One of the dads, whom I used to find a lech, ogled Grace the way he used to ogle me, that staggered glance over my body that always made me feel like he was undressing me with his eyes. A sporty mother in her tennis whites even stopped stretching her hamstrings to get a glimpse.

What Grace most likely didn't yet realize as she walked across the tarmac for her very first school pickup was that as simple as this errand seemed, it was anything but, especially for her. She had insider information on the only currency that mattered, and she didn't know that she had just stepped onto the trading floor.

"Grace! Grace!" Lauren shouted, waving frantically.

"Do you think your Yogilates woman could contour me a pair of legs like that?" Camilla said, laughing, only Julia didn't have much in the way of a sense of humor.

"I suppose he has to move on sometime," Julia said, crossing her arms. "I doubt it will last. I mean, what are the chances the first woman straight out the gate happens to be the perfect replacement— even if she does look the part?" Needless to say, Julia was one of the mums I did not miss.

"Grace, what a nice surprise," Lauren said. The two women hugged hello, but when Grace tried to pull away, Lauren held on as though Grace were the door at the end of *Titanic.* Lauren looked back over Grace's shoulder at Tom's car as if he might still emerge from the passenger side. "Where's Tom? What happened?" she asked. "Is everything okay? Why isn't Tom picking Henry up?"

"He's visiting Judith," Grace said. "He hadn't been going to see her as much because of the early pickup."

"You met Judith?" Lauren said.

"Hello, I'm Camilla," Camilla said, stepping forward. "And this is Julia. We were just marveling at the length of your legs."

Grace looked down as though she'd never seen her legs before.

"So, you're gonna do early pickup every week?" Lauren said, pursing her lips. "Why didn't Tom ask me? I'm here anyway."

"I'm not sure," Grace said. "I mean, I offered."

Lauren's eyebrows contorted. She'd become such an integral part of Tom's life since I died, it was only fair for her nose to be a bit out of joint. She was the emergency contact on Tom's passport. She knew the alarm code. She received all Tom's missed packages. This was her territory. She and Henry were so close. She was probably already worrying about potential ramifications if Tom's relationship with Grace went tits up. In some bizarre way, I wish Lauren knew Grace's identity. If she had been in on the secret from the get-go, she would have been so gung ho. She would have loved to head up Bletchley and help Tom break the code to track Grace down at the shop.

Just as Lauren was about to say something, Henry spotted Grace and broke from the throng of uniformed children. He ran over, holding his latest treasure—a hot-pink, polka-dot Easter egg covered in green feathers. I used to call these things "dust gatherers," and would slowly thin them out on bin day, hoping Chloe wouldn't notice, whereas Lauren's garage was an organized trove of Henry's and her twins' artistic clutter.

"I made this for you!" Henry said, passing Grace his fluorescent egg.

Grace bent down to Henry's level, and as she took off her sunglasses, her eyes lit up at Henry's gluey gift. Around them, the playground had started to empty, leaving behind a few stragglers who were trying in vain to hurry along their charges.

"Wow. Did you paint all those dots on by yourself?" Grace said, pushing Henry's hair off his face where it needed a trim.

"I think I just spotted mine over there," Camilla said, breaking from the group. "Nice to meet you, Grace. Hopefully see you around."

"Yes, definitely," Grace said.

"I see Orlando," Julia said. "I'm coming with you." From inside the school, the bell rang. A minute later, Lauren's twins bounded over, Basil dragging his school bag along the tarmac, his tie askew.

"Oh, Basil, you look a state," Lauren said, trying to flatten his hair. Even though the twins were ambushing Lauren with repeated requests for ice cream, she stood rooted to the ground as the other parents dispersed at Olympic speed. Now it made sense why they all wore those Alo leggings.

"Look! Here's Miss Rose. I'll introduce you," Lauren said, as Miss Rose appeared at the front door with another gaggle of children. "She's by far the best teacher."

"Actually—" Grace began.

"Miss Rose!" Lauren called, and the children's teacher marched diligently over. "Miss Rose, I want you to meet my friend, Grace!"

"So good to see you again," Miss Rose said as Grace got to her feet.

"Wait, what?" Lauren said. "You've already met?"

"Yes, but only briefly," Grace said. "I had to fill out a form last week so I could pick Henry up." Miss Rose's face broke into an awkward, animated smile.

"We hope to see you at the Easter egg hunt, Grace," Miss Rose said. "It's going to be our best yet, thanks to Lauren here, our wonderful head of events." Behind them, a feral child swung upside down before falling off the climbing frame.

"I'm sure Grace has better things to do than chase after a bunch of other people's wired children on a Sunday," Lauren said. "I know you have so *much* work to do for your exam. Grace is training to be a master sommelier."

"Oh, how splendid," Miss Rose said. "Maybe you could have a

wine stall at the summer fête this year?" With that, perhaps sensing
a moment to escape, Miss Rose looked at her watch and added, "I'll
leave you two to natter then. See you at the hunt!"

"Grace, please can we go to the egg hunt?" Henry said, playing
with the feathers on his egg.

"Of course we can," Grace said. "You know your dad can't resist
a Cadbury Creme Egg."

Lauren's eyes flashed watching Henry slide his pudgy little
hand into Grace's. I wished I could be there to reassure Lauren that
she had nothing to worry about, to tell her that Tom adored her,
that she was like a sister, like family, and nothing in their relationship was going to change.

*

Tom had been so willingly stranded on "The Island" with Grace
that he'd managed to forget that my mother was coming for Easter.
When she turned up at the door one evening during dinner, to say
Tom looked surprised would be like saying Liberace wore the odd
feather. My mother's sudden desire to visit a few times a year now
that I was dead was still unfathomable, considering she'd barely
come once when I was alive.

Tom was zesting a lemon for pasta al limone when the doorbell rang. Grace was sitting with him at the counter, leaning over a
book on Burgundy, her glasses poised on the end of her nose. Tom
glanced at the clock behind him.

"Bit late for packages?" he said. "I hope that doesn't wake
Henry."

"I'll get it. You keep zesting," Grace said. She straightened the
jute rug in the hall on her way to get the door. Duke trotted behind her, barking. "Duke, quiet, that's enough. We know you're
extremely intimidating, you don't need to overdo it."

Grace opened the door to find Colette, her luggage down by

her feet, the same trunks she'd had since I was a little girl. The same ones she'd packed when she'd moved back to Paris. The same mother, wearing dark glasses and a knee-length maroon two-piece. The early evening sky behind her was brushed with lilac. As soon as she saw Grace, a woman who looked exactly like her dead daughter—smiling and alive in an oversized shirt I might have worn—my mother's mouth nearly hit the floor. If it weren't for those glasses, what would I have seen in her eyes at that moment? For Colette, even a glimmer of surprise on her face was on par with anybody else screaming at the top of their lungs in the middle of the High Street.

"Hello," Grace said. When my mother didn't say anything, Grace added, "Can I help you?"

"*Où est Thomas?*" Colette said, clutching her handbag to her body as though she suspected Grace might mug her.

In the kitchen, a jolt of shock charged through Tom when he heard my mother's thick accent all the way from the front door.

"Colette!" he called, charging down the hallway, nearly surfing to the front door on the rug. "I was *absolutely* expecting you," he lied. He kissed my mother hello on both cheeks while she stood there immobile. "You met Grace?" he said, picking up my mother's trunks and lugging them inside.

"We did, yes," Grace said, raising her eyebrows at Tom. "We've been . . . waiting for you all evening, haven't we, Tom?"

"Yes, and we've made pasta, your favorite!" Tom said.

"*Je ne mange pas de pâtes,*" Colette said.

"Right, well, red wine for dinner, then," Tom said. My mother moved past them into the kitchen.

"*Je ne savais pas que tu avais des invités . . .*" she said on cue. She folded down the arms of her sunglasses and waited for Tom to pull out her chair.

"Grace isn't a guest," Tom said.

"*Je vois . . .*" Colette said.

"Est-ce que vous voulez un verre de vin?" Grace said. *"Où du champagne?"* On discovering Grace could speak perfect French, my mother naturally spoke only English after that, nursing a large glass of red and picking at a few chunks of Parmesan rind from the table. She eyeballed Grace for the entirety of the meal, watching her every move around the kitchen—the way she held her fork, the way she sipped her wine, the way she gazed across the table at Tom. Grace either didn't notice or was far less bothered than I would have been by Colette's disapproving eye. Grace carried on as usual, engaged, interested, asking about the political mood in Paris after the recent protests.

As Tom shaved some more Parmesan onto his pasta, my mother spotted Henry's nursery photos he'd had taken the week before, sitting in the bowl of gubbins in the middle of the table. She picked up the larger of the two prints.

"He looks so much like her," she remarked. Tom's appetite evaporated before she'd reached the end of the sentence. Not wanting to seem perturbed, he carried on eating, shoveling spaghetti into his mouth.

"Yes," he said, spooling the pasta around his fork.

"No. But really. So much." Colette went into the hallway and came back in with her bag. She took out her wallet, the same one she'd had for years, brownish lamb's leather, somehow still without a scratch. Tucked behind her credit cards in a plastic slip was a picture of my parents and me, taken in those wonderful years before my father died. I was probably younger than Henry, but no older than three. I'd never seen the picture before. I don't remember the photo being taken, though I do remember the eye-burning yellow T-shirt I wouldn't take off. My father was making a silly face, and my mother was smiling from ear to ear. I was kissing her cheek with force, my dimple taking up half my face, the same as my mother. I always thought I got my dimple from my dad, but there it was.

Tom studied the picture, wondering what I would think if I could see this. Had that photo been in my mother's wallet my whole life, quietly sitting there out of sight? Was my mother showing him the photo just to put Grace's nose out of joint? While he was deciding how to react, my mother slid the photo across the table for Grace to see.

"She was very beautiful," Grace said. She pushed the photo back to my mother, then carried on twirling her pasta. "Tom was telling me the other—"

"Can you see it? The resemblance?" Colette said, sliding the photo back once more.

"I do, yes, so similar. Just like Mumma. We say that all the time, don't we, Tom?"

Tom continued eating though he felt intensely nauseated. Grace set her fork down on her plate and dabbed at the corners of her mouth with her napkin.

"And also like you," Colette said to Grace.

He could feel it coming, like *Jaws* under the water.

"Have people told you? How do you say this in English, Thomas—doppelgänger?" Tom suddenly got that feeling when you think you've lost your passport, a wave of sickness that lingers until you've laid your hands on it and even still the sensation remains, as if the passport itself were a figment, as if it might slip through your fingers and you would follow it down the rabbit hole. He slammed his chair back and pretended to search for something on the kitchen island.

"Sometimes. Yes. Actually, people say it a lot," Grace said. "More wine?"

"The eyes," Colette said. "Incredible. Very blue, like hers."

My mother sat back then. For the duration of the evening, no matter how many times Tom tried to change the subject, my mother reverted to me, truffling out endless parallels. It was like watching Mrs. Danvers give the second Mrs. de Winter an unsolicited tour of Rebecca's room. *Just as she always had it.*

When Grace drew the curtains in Tom's bedroom later that

night, she was unusually quiet. Tom could tell she wasn't herself. Before my mother arrived, she was dancing around the kitchen, testing the saltiness of the pasta water, taking the piss out of Tom for turning up Taylor Swift on the radio.

"Christ. I'm so sorry," he said. "I totally forgot she was coming." Grace plopped down on the bed and began untucking the edges of her white shirt from her jeans.

"I figured that out pretty quick."

"I'm sorry she kept comparing you to Honor." Tom sat down beside her on the bed.

"Honestly, I just don't get what the point of it is. I get it—we look alike. Next question." Grace took a hair tie off her bedside table and began gathering her hair in her hands. "The annoying part is that I don't mind feeling Honor's presence around the house. It's nothing you do at all, but everyone else telling me 'Oh, Tom has a type.' 'Oh, you look just like Honor,' like that's the reason you're with me. What do people want me to feel when they say stuff like this to me? I don't know. Maybe I'm a bit tired." When Tom didn't respond, Grace pressed him on it. "But it's not, though, is it? The reason you're with me?"

"Of course not," he said. "I love you. *You.*" Grace's eyes softened, and Tom pulled her close, nuzzling her neck. The streetlamp shone through the window, casting a swath of pale light across the duvet. Tom held Grace tighter, glad she couldn't see the concern on his face.

*

Even with the unexpected showers and soggy bottoms, the Easter egg hunt was a triumph. Henry spent most of the day yelping with excitement at every egg he managed to find. Tom ate more chocolate than anybody else and spent the rest of the day baffled that he had a tummy ache. My mother was there ducking out of the rain in the Pimm's tent, trying her best to keep away from every passing child. It seemed that Henry was the only one who had the magic touch. She even played hide-and-seek with him at one point, which was a first for her. I'll never forget how much I loved Chloe's first egg hunt and how cute she looked in her buttercream cotton dress. The whole picture had been like a scene out of Beatrix Potter, with fluffy rabbit tails bouncing around, wicker baskets overflowing with treats, and gingham bunting lining the inside of the drinks tent.

During the hunting escapades, Lauren had underestimated the strength of the Pimm's and had one too many. She'd carried on, hopping around in her oversized pink, fuzzy polyester Mopsy costume, but by the end of the afternoon, she'd clearly tipped herself over the limit to drive. It was decided that Tom and Colette should take Henry to the swings—which, to my amazement, didn't throw my mother into a state of recoil—and Grace would drive Lauren's car home with the twins.

Lauren babbled on and on the entire drive. By the time they arrived at Lauren's, the sky had turned from white to a lifeless silver and Grace had heard at length about her dream the previous night and the plot of an entire episode of *Poldark*.

"I'm not letting you get away without a cup of tea," Lauren said as the twins bounded upstairs. "Do you like shortbread? I made some just this morning."

"That's so kind of you, but I really should be getting back to Tom. I'm sure they're home by now. Colette's leaving this evening."

"I insist," Lauren said. "Please, sit. Sit, sit, sit, sit, sit." Lauren took one of her many teapots down from the shelf and a little jug for the milk that intentionally didn't match the rest of the set. She was back where she liked to be, holding court in her domestic precinct. Grace looked up at the ceiling in the direction of the excessive banging, which seemed to go unnoticed by Lauren, who was more taken by portioning out the shortbread evenly than the chaos of her children.

Before I had Chloe, even the sound of a child breathing in a cafe while I was trying to write drove me bananas, but it didn't seem to bother Grace. Besides a few concerned glances, she sat unaffected at the oval kitchen table beneath the two large windows through which you could watch all the comings and goings of Lansdowne Road. As much as I didn't care for Lauren's overly femme taste, the painfully glossy cream paint, and the upholstered, mushroom-colored banquette, I loved being around that kitchen table. I'd cried there, breastfed, ruminated, and spilled my tea. I even passed out there once after Lauren's birthday party, when Annie had overseen the martinis.

Lauren slid into the banquette holding a tray adorned with lavender shortbread and hot tea.

"Shortbread?" Lauren said.

"How can I say no," Grace said.

"Henry *loves* it." Lauren seemed transfixed by something on Grace's face. "Who cuts your hair?"

"My hair? A woman called Tracey. Near my shop. I could introduce you if you want."

"Really? Oh, that would be wonderful. I've been meaning to do something a little more subtle with mine. I'm too old to be this blond."

"What are you talking about? It suits you."

"Thank you," Lauren said, inspecting the ends. "I could probably tone it down a touch. But what's the point?" She nibbled her shortbread. "I'm pretty sure Jimmy's gay and every Tinder date is a disaster. I barely know how to use the app and I don't understand any of the lingo. Do you know how long it's been since I've had sex? Sorry, is that TMI?"

"No, that's okay. Delicious shortbread, by the way."

"I usually make it once a week, for Henry and Tom. They love it. So, how are things over there at Number Six?" Lauren said, doing some weird dance with her shoulders.

"They're good—I mean, they're great. Tom's great."

"He really is. You landed a salmon there. Did Tom ever mention that he and I were originally meant to get set up, not him and Honor? How crazy is that?" I could see Grace having the same reaction I might have had to this somewhat odd, tricky information. Lauren had never once brought this up in all the years of our friendship. It was a nonstarter.

"Funny. No. That never came up," Grace said.

"It was a million years ago. I was already with someone anyway. A German aristocrat. He ended up marrying a Spanish princess and I ended up with Daniel, who thinks he can just rock up to my Easter egg hunt with his hot lactating girlfriend, *Sarah*. He didn't even tell me he was bringing her. I would have worn the sexier bunny costume if I'd known, not the oversized fluffy one."

"I don't think turning up as Bridget Jones would have made you feel any better."

"I even find their new baby cute!" Lauren said, the groove of her upper lip speckled with sweat, which always appeared whenever Lauren had too much to drink. "I loved when the twins were babies. Everyone's always in such a rush to hear their first words, but I love that helpless, gurgling stage. When Henry was little, my God. His neck smelled like prawn and avocado toast, and he was such a mush. He looked indistinguishable from Honor, even as a baby. It was crazy. You know how people say that babies always look like the dads at the beginning so that the dads know that they're theirs? Maybe it's the same psychology when you use an egg donor, to help the mothers bond or something?"

Grace sat back on the upholstered banquette and crossed her arms.

"What do you mean?" she said. I'd watched Lauren put her

foot in it in the past, but this wasn't her usual gait. She was trading on my private life with little regard. As if my infertility were the weather.

"I cannot tell you how many discussions we had about different egg donors," Lauren said, pulling the bunny ears out of her hair. "It took me so long to understand the ins and outs of that whole dynamic. The who, the what, the how. Between the surrogate and the egg donor . . . who knew it was so complicated? Even up to the day they did the embryo transfer, I was still asking questions. Honor got so fed up with me. We looked at *so* many donor profiles and *so* many baby pictures before she finally settled on one. I tried to tell her, 'Why don't you just adopt? It would be so much easier.' But Honor kept pushing and pushing and pushing to have a baby at any cost."

Grace went rigid.

"Honor and Tom used an egg donor with Henry?" she said.

"Yes. Wait, you didn't know? I thought Tom would've told you. Oh shit. I always put my foot in it. Well, it's none of my business. I just assumed he would've told you."

"No. Tom didn't tell me," Grace said, scooching out of the banquette. She made her way over to the island and began gathering her things. "I should get going."

"Grace. Forget I said anything. Here, have some more shortbread." Lauren attempted to stand, but the giant bunny costume was proving somewhat restrictive.

"He probably just doesn't want to talk about it. The baby was such a bone of contention when Honor died. I told her so many times that it wasn't fair. Tom was working hundred-hour weeks, but she didn't care. She was relentless, even though she already had everything; she just couldn't see it. They were fighting about it all the way to Paris."

A loud bump came from upstairs, followed by silence. This wasn't the Lauren I knew. The way she was detonating these little knowledge bombs seemed almost intentional. The way she was talking about me with such refined judgment, a whole new take on the dynamics of my marriage, a take she'd never aired to me, pouring out of her. It wasn't that what Lauren said was untrue, per se, but the pointedness of the way she delivered the information. It wasn't news to anyone that Tom and I hadn't been at our best when I died. But the use of an egg donor was not Lauren's story to share, and she knew it.

"I have to help Tom with dinner," Grace said. The wan afternoon sunlight cast dappled shadows across the kitchen floor.

"Please don't tell Tom I told you," Lauren said, grabbing onto Grace's arm.

"I don't like secrets," Grace said, wrenching her arm free to rifle through her bag.

"Please just keep this between us. I wouldn't want to be the cause of friction between the two of you. I'm sure he'll tell you himself in time. It's obvious he really likes you."

Grace finally found her keys on the island. "Thank you for the tea," she said.

Standing alone in the kitchen, Lauren watched Grace walk back to Tom's house. She stretched her arm behind herself to unzip her costume but couldn't reach the clasp. After a few futile attempts, she lost her temper and began cursing and yanking at the neck, her face mottled and blotchy. When she couldn't get free, she picked the milk jug off the table and hurled it across the kitchen, where it landed on the Sub-Zero and smashed into a hundred little pieces, spilling milk across the floor.

"Fuck," she said, her hair matted and askew. "Fuckity, fuck, fuck, FUCK."

"Mummy?" Jarvis called from upstairs. "Basil hit me with the lightsaber."

"Coming, sweetie," she called, patting down her hair and snapping back into her customary upbeat character. In nearly sixteen years of friendship, I'd barely heard Lauren raise her voice, let alone swear. If Lauren had been an egg donor, her profile would have looked perfect, but I could see between the lines now. I had a trained eye. Something wasn't right. And I couldn't help but wonder how I had missed it.

CHAPTER EIGHTEEN

My mother dropped me off at boarding school three weeks after my father died. She was already dressed when I woke up that morning, my half-packed suitcase spread-eagled on the biscuit-colored eiderdown. When I saw my clothes stacked in neat piles, I naively assumed we were going to Normandy, but once we got to the car, I noticed there was only one suitcase in the boot.

"Where are your things, Maman?" I said, my fluffy red rabbit hanging in one hand and a few of my favorite storybooks in the other. The wind whipped around my ankles, raising goose bumps all over my skin.

"We'll talk on the way," she said. She slammed the boot down so hard that I rocked back on my heels.

But we didn't talk on the way. As we drove deeper into the countryside, the car remained deathly quiet. There was no sound of my father affectionately teasing my mother in the front seat or telling loosely plotted stories to me in the back. I was seven. I knew my father was gone, but I assumed his absence was temporary. He wasn't going to leave me in this world alone. Dads don't do that.

"It's not forever," she said, coughing into her handkerchief. *As we drove through the wrought iron gates, I placed my hand over my mother's, which was shaking against the polished-walnut gear stick.*

"What isn't?" I said. Her hand felt cold against my palm.

She looked across at me, swallowing back whatever was stuck in her throat. "Boarding school."

I could feel the heat charging up from my feet. "I'm sorry I haven't been doing my bed, but I'll do it now. I promise. I'll do it forever. Please, Maman, don't you love me anymore?"

"Of course I do. What are you saying?" she said, though her voice lacked conviction.

"What about teeth? What if I get poorly? What about bedtime?" But there was no complex brokering. I was staying. She was leaving.

"I can't read you stories forever, Honor. You have to learn to be alone," my mother said, her eyes wet. "I wish I could be here, but I can't." What had I done? Why was everything changing? Was this my fault? Had I become an inconvenience?

But even then, I knew: Something had cemented in my mother the day my father died. A door had slammed shut between us that I could never find the key to unlock, leaving me alone in a world I didn't know how to navigate.

At least that's how I remember it.

*

When Grace walked back into the house five minutes later, she didn't take off her shoes by the umbrella stand like she normally did. She headed straight to the kitchen, where Tom was unloading the dishwasher, meticulously lining up the glasses in the cupboard.

"Where are Henry and Colette?" she said.

"He's having a nap. He's on a come down from all that chocolate," Tom said. "Colette's having a bath. I might have a kip myself.

How's Cottontail doing?" Tom ignited the burner under the Bialetti. "I'm making coffee. Do you want some?"

"No, thanks," she said, fiddling with one of her gold hoop earrings. Tom could hear my mother running the water upstairs. "Can we talk about something?" Grace placed her bag on the island and surveyed the kitchen.

Tom froze, sweat gathering in the gap between his shoulder blades. If you're feeling guilty, "Can we talk about something?" is one of the most terrifying questions. Was this how it would all start, calm and collected? *What could possibly have transpired in the time between the jolly egg hunt and the ride home with Lauren?* Was this the confrontation he'd been dreading, the one that had been waking him in the middle of the night?

"Of course we can. What's wrong?" Tom said, moving towards the island, where Grace was leaning, but not in the loving way she had been that morning, when she kissed his bottom lip and he was hard up against her. She was the one standing firm now, unapproachable, biting at the inside of her cheek. "Grace, what's going on? You're scaring me."

"We should close the door," Grace said. Tom did as he was told, his head beginning to throb at the prospect of this conversation. Duke approached him, sensing the change in atmosphere, and Tom reached down to pet his head. "I don't know how to say this," Grace continued. She placed her index fingers to her mouth. "At Lauren's just now, out of nowhere, she told me you and Honor used an egg donor with Henry."

"What?" Tom said. Hearing those words spoken sequentially out of Grace's mouth spiked his heart rate. The moment stretched out before them, long and wide as Flanders Field. "Maybe I'm being a little bit presumptuous, but I would've expected you to tell me, given what I'd shared with you about being an egg donor. And other people know, so it's not a secret. Lauren brought it up assuming I knew. So why don't I know?"

"Grace, honestly," Tom said, pacing around the kitchen. I could see him trying to process this information and decide how to navigate this turn of events. "It's not that I wasn't telling you—"

"But it was, though. Because I told you that I donated mine. There's no way the thought didn't cross your mind, considering your son was made using an egg donor."

"Lauren is bang out of order. I'm ringing her right now." Tom reached for his phone on the kitchen table. In all my years with Tom, through every argument and bitter dispute, I'd never once seen him crumble like this.

"That's missing the point, Tom. This isn't about Lauren." The Bialetti whistled, a horrible, high-pitched scream. Tom pulled it off the stove, scalding his fingers on the handle.

"Shit!" he said, flapping his hand.

"Here. Run it under the tap." Grace turned on the cold water and held Tom's hand beneath it. Though the pain was agonizing, he was glad for the momentary diversion. Grace was so close; he could smell the rosemary of her shampoo. He wished this were any other Sunday, and they would put a dressing on the burn and have a roast before Sunday Blues and everything would be fine.

"I'm really sorry," Tom said. "All that egg donor stuff was Honor's territory. I just did what she told me to do, when she told me to do it, and signed whatever she asked me to sign. It was a very sore subject, so I just went along given how strongly she felt. And thank God I did." He pulled his hands from the water and dabbed them dry on a tea towel. "But you're right. I should have just told you."

"Why didn't you want me to know?"

"Grace, I made a mistake. It's just that the story's so much bigger than that and one day I'm going to have to turn around and tell Henry everything from beginning to end and I'm petrified. I just lock it away with everything else because I can't do it."

Grace crossed her arms and looked at the floor.

"I told you everything about myself. Things I've never told anyone. Nice things and less nice things. And sometimes, I feel like you've told me nothing. Like, you were gonna get set up with Lauren, for example?"

"Wait, what? Lauren? This is insanity. It's not the way it sounds. Not in the least. Lauren? And me? I met Honor before I ever even met Lauren. Grace, I want you to know everything about me."

"So, tell me something."

"You want me to tell you something? Now?"

"Yes."

"Okay. I'll tell you something," Tom said, looking around the kitchen. Where could he even start? "Wine gives me a throbbing headache, but I love it because you do. I want to cry when I see you with Marjorie and Blanche and how caring you are towards them. I fell in love with you the moment I heard your voice. I melt when you speak Italian. I sometimes just ask you what day it is on the weekend because I love the way you pronounce your esses. I sometimes think I'm going to stop breathing when I hear you and Henry laughing. You are the only person I have ever told about the shame I feel every second of my life because I let my daughter die. I failed at the one job a dad's meant to do. Before I met you, I hadn't even admitted that to myself, let alone anybody else. And I will tell you something else as well."

Tom got up from the kitchen table and walked over to the junk drawer where we kept the screwdrivers and obsolete currency. He pulled out the freshly cut house key on the red leather Smythson key ring and slid it across the island. "I want you to live with us."

Grace looked at the key, then at Tom. Though she didn't gush or blush, or immediately acquiesce, she couldn't argue with this talisman. I could see her scrutinizing the evidence.

"How do I know you're not just saying that now?" she said. Tom turned over the key ring, which was embossed with Grace's initials.

"Because I'm not," he said. "I'd planned to give this to you on Friday night, but then we had company."

"I'm not going to give up my flat," she said.

"I'm not suggesting you do." Grace eyed the key that sat between them, her face inscrutable.

"Is there anything else you're not telling me?"

"Nothing," Tom said. "Nothing at all."

With that short answer, I no longer had eyes on the man I married. He'd lied so matter-of-factly, these sweet nothings turning into hard evidence. For a split second, when Grace's fingertips landed on the key, Tom thought she was going to push it back across the marble. But then her face changed, that unrivaled smile, her dimple, her poppy-seed gap. She took it in her palm and moved towards him, sliding her hands under his top, the key cold and hard against his skin. He could hear his heart beating, loud and clear. Grace traced the key down the dip in his back and pressed her lips against his. Not in the gentle style that had become their custom, but primal now, fast and rough. Tom lifted Grace onto the kitchen counter, her legs naturally wrapping around him. She reached for Tom's belt, finding the buckle, and pulling down the zip. Tom didn't take off Grace's shorts, he didn't undress her slowly like he usually did, button by button, tracing her torso with kisses, until she was so wet that she begged him to take her. Instead, he pulled her shorts aside, followed by her knickers. She took his cock in her hand and guided him inside her, their mouths open, gasping for air.

"I fucking love you so much," she said, her hands tight around his face.

"I love you more," Tom said.

*

That evening, Grace asked my mother to help her with dinner: fresh ravioli and an artichoke salad. I couldn't remember a time when I'd asked my mother to help me with anything. Had I just assumed she'd say no? But watching her peel the leaves of the artichokes while Grace and Henry rolled out the pasta, I wondered what else I'd assumed about her. Colette set the table and played endless rounds of musical statues with Henry while they waited for the pasta water to boil. She even ate two pieces of ravioli with extra Parmesan.

After dinner, Tom was loading the dishwasher when Grace came into the kitchen, buttoning her coat. "Should we go?" Grace said.

"Go where?" he said.

"It's Sunday. We're going to the shop?"

Colette's arrival on Friday had thrown Tom through a loop which had been compounded further by Lauren's decision to reveal my use of an egg donor over lavender shortbread. By some miracle, Tom had managed to steady Grace and himself during the squall, though the boat had listed. Unbeknownst to Grace, in the past few days Tom had sailed through every type of sea, and while he hadn't drowned or sunk, he lived in fear of an oncoming storm.

"Right," Tom said. "Sorry. My head's all over the place—I forgot to ask Rita to babysit . . . I don't have anyone to watch Henry."

"What are you talking about? I thought you hadn't asked Rita on purpose because Colette is here." Tom shook his head and mouthed the word "No."

"I'm perfectly capable of watching a monitor or tending to my grandson while you go out," Colette called from the drawing room. My mother's ability to register human emotion was minimal at best, yet her ability to pick up on pantomime through a half-meter-thick nineteenth-century wall was clearly impeccable.

Grace ushered Tom into the drawing room and followed behind him.

"Well, that's a suggestion," he said, staring at the floor as if an oracle might appear in the weave of the carpet. We never left Chloe

with my mother. Not that we wouldn't have, but she'd never offered. Or had I never asked? My mother closed her book and took
off her reading glasses.

"I know how to look after a child. I had a daughter, you
know," my mother said, though I didn't *quite* agree with her on
that point.

"Yes, right. Yes. Great, great idea. Just give me one second,"
Tom said. "I'll get the monitor." Tom gestured at Grace to come
upstairs. Grace rolled her eyes and followed Tom up to his bedroom, which a few short hours ago had become theirs. "What am I
supposed to say? She wants to watch the monitor?" he said.

"You say yes. And put a coat on. She's his grandmother. We're
not splitting the atom." In Grace's defense, all she'd seen was this
upgraded version of my mother, one who peeled artichokes for dinner and scurried along after Henry looking for chocolate eggs.

"It's just not like her. That's all."

Grace touched his arm. "Look, if you don't feel comfortable,"
she said, "I'll go without you. I'm just saying, she's not that bad.
She's been looking after Henry basically all day anyway."

"Henry does seem to like her. It's funny, because—"

"Babe. Tell me along the way. I don't want to leave the girls
standing outside the shop."

At the front door, Tom went through his usual ritual before
leaving the house. My mother reassured Tom that she would ring if
anything happened, even as Grace was pulling him down the stoop
and into his Defender.

The whole ride to Sprezzatura, he chatted endlessly about how
strange it was to leave Henry with Colette and how strange time
was, the way it could whittle down even the hardest rock. Still,
he doubted his decision. Should he have bought Henry along with
them? Was he being a bad dad leaving Henry alone with Colette?
What if Henry got a temperature? What if she didn't hear him go
downstairs and out the front door?

When they arrived at the shop, Marjorie and Jenny were already there. But Marjorie wasn't her usual self. She'd had a disagreement with her daughter, something to do with her son-in-law. As they stood on the pavement, Grace put her arm around Marjorie and pulled a tissue from her bag.

"Thank you, pet," Marjorie said, taking the tissue. "I was only asking her if he was going to get another job." Tom took the keys from Grace's hand and opened the door, noticing that the alarm was blinking. They filed into the shop one after the other, but when Tom toggled the light switch, the shop remained dark. Tom turned on his phone light and crept over to the fuse box while Marjorie carried on about the soaring rise in her granddaughter's school fees.

"Sorry to interrupt, but I think there's been a power cut," Tom said. Jenny looked out into the street.

"The whole street's pitch-black," she said. "There must have been an outage. Oh, that is a bore."

Though I'd had nothing to do with the electricity board, it was coincidences like these when Tom would sometimes wonder if I was still calling the shots. But my powers didn't reach that far. Even in the darkness of the shop, he could sense Grace's concern for Marjorie. He was no longer under any illusion that this was any old wine club. It was therapy, but chic and loosely inebriated.

"That's such a shame. I was so looking forward to tonight," Marjorie said. "I always feel better after being with you girls. Even Blanche. That old bag."

"Hang on," Grace said. She followed the beam of Tom's phone light over to the fuse box. "I don't want to leave Marjorie. Can we go back to your house?" Grace whispered.

"No, we can't," Tom said. "We can go back to our house, though." It was the first time he'd said that aloud. *Our house.* Had he forgotten that my mother was there having tea in the drawing room? She barely said hello to her neighbors in Paris, whom she'd known for thirty-two years, let alone unexpected strangers who arrived unannounced on a Sunday evening.

Tom slammed the fuse box shut. "I'll bring the car round."

*

My mother was on her way back to the drawing room with a fresh cup of mint tea when Tom pushed open the front door, slamming it hard into the chain.

"*Attendez,*" she said. She put down her teacup on the hallway table and released the chain before opening the door, revealing not just Tom and Grace but the unfamiliar profiles of Jenny and Marjorie.

"The electricity was out at Grace's shop," Tom said, barreling in.

"I thought you two were going out for dinner . . . ?" Colette said, looking at Jenny like she was some sort of rare fish.

"No, we meet at my shop every week," Grace said. "It was how Tom and I met." She stroked Tom's arm.

"You met at a wine shop?" Colette said. "*How modern.*"

"Yes. We were all there," Jenny said. "Having a little tipple and a chin wag."

I couldn't work out whether it was Jenny's familiarity or my mother's aversion to Jenny's choice of synthetic leather handbag in a very bright blue that had struck my mother mute. She passed Tom the monitor and was about to excuse herself when Marjorie stepped towards her.

"You must be Rita!" Marjorie said, bustling forward and putting out her hand. "Grace has told me so much about you. Do you want me to take off my shoes?"

"*Pardon?*" Colette said, her eyebrows burrowing into her hairline.

"No, no. This is Colette," Grace said. "This is Tom's mother-in-law."

"Oh. *Oh,*" Marjorie said. "Pardon me. Will you be joining us?"

My mother was just about to respond when Tom interrupted her.

"No, I'm sure Colette's exhausted," he said, but my mother didn't look tired. "She's not a sit-around-and-chat kind of person."

"That's not true. Colette and I sit and chat all the time," Grace said. "Colette, would you like to join us?"

"Of course she doesn't," Tom said. "Do you?" My mother pulled closed her cardigan and looked at the friendly faces of Jenny and Marjorie.

"I planned an early night," she said, then turned on her heels to go upstairs, clutching the banister, averting her eyes as she walked past the photos of me and Chloe in the hallway. When she got to her bedroom, she closed the door behind her and made sure it was safely locked. She went into the en suite, turning the taps on full blast. My mother looked so tiny as she sat on the marble lip of the bath. She undid the buttons on her cardigan, followed by her white shirt, draping them over the bathroom chair, then she took off her bra, which fell to the floor with a thud. That's when I saw them, two thick, jagged scars on her pale skin where her breasts should have been.

I thought back to my childhood, trying to place this new information into context. *I can't read you stories forever, Honor. You have to learn to be alone.* Was this the reason she sent me to boarding school? Had she been too ill to take care of me? Was it possible that my father had died and my mother had been diagnosed with cancer all in the space of a few weeks? Was this why her skin had turned sallow and her hair looked so different when she picked me up for summer holidays in Normandy? One day she was my mother, the smiling picture in her purse; the next, she was Colette, and her hugs had turned to handshakes. But all I knew was that my dad was dead, and my mother had turned as cold as a corpse. *"When sorrows come, they come not single spies but in battalions."*

What sort of mother would I have been if I had known my days were numbered? Would I have written Chloe long, loving letters to open every year at Christmas as she grew up, or would I have suddenly turned frosty, in a bid to protect her? However you want to dress it up, every mother lies to her child. Father Christmas, the tooth fairy, "Everything is going to be okay." I covered Chloe's eyes when Bambi's mum got shot. Was I lying to her then, making her think we all live forever, that she would never lose me? Of course not. We all protect our babies in the way we think is best.

I'd never told my mother I'd had my ovaries removed, because I was worried that she might say something awful or, worse, say nothing at all. If I'd given her the chance, though, would she have surprised me? Would she have reached for my hand and told me she understood? She'd had a part of herself removed, too. Just as it had never occurred to me that my mother could have been ill, she'd never foreseen a future where she'd outlive me. Had her ability to mother been stolen from her like mine had?

Once the water turned tepid, my mother pulled the plug and got out of the bath, wrapping her dressing gown around her waist. She brushed her teeth and washed the makeup off her face before getting into bed. The sudden sound of everyone downstairs laughing erupted through the floorboards, a joyful, acoustic overspill. My mother turned off the light and didn't move again till morning.

CHAPTER NINETEEN

When Miranda gave birth in Sex and the City, *the worst thing that happened was her water breaking on Carrie's Louboutins. She didn't kick Steve in the head or call him "the c word." She pushed for five minutes, holding her best friend's hand, until a fully formed, gorgeous six-month-old baby popped out.*

When I gave birth to Chloe, it took thirty-eight hours, start to finish. I was a whisker away from needing an emergency C-section; plus, I shat myself in front of Tom, who took it all in stride, including the fact that Chloe initially came out looking like the Hobbit. Before I knew anything about giving birth, I'd talked a big game about having an all-natural situation. I'm not sure why. I took paracetamol. I ate deep-fried food. The doctors even told me the medicine wouldn't harm the baby. What was I trying to prove? I needn't have made any preliminary plans, because after that first contraction tore through me, I begged for all the drugs on offer, including an epidural.

"Are you sure those drugs are kicking in?" Tom asked the nurse

*between contractions. "She doesn't seem to be dealing with this quite as
well as she did in rehearsals."*

    *"Shut the fuck up, Tom," I said. "Shut the fuck up and hold up the
fan."*

    *Lauren had gone on and on about Tom staying at "the head," as if
he were the one in stirrups and I was accommodating his preferences.
But I'd ignored her, and Tom eventually pulled Chloe out of me. He was
beside himself with happiness, even when I birthed the placenta shortly
thereafter. He seemed besotted, but I couldn't see anything apart from the
tubular shape of our baby's head. Why hadn't Lauren mentioned that?*

    "Is her head gonna stay like that?" I said, between galloping tears.

    *"It's temporary," said the midwife, a wonderful woman who had
the work ethic of a police dog. "If I had a pound for every time someone
asked me that," she added, taking Chloe to the scales. Tom followed behind them, while I lay there, crying, with my feet still in stirrups.*

    "She's getting cuter," Tom called from the scales.

    *Birth had been the Battle of the Somme. I hadn't stopped weeping,
but lying there with Chloe barely ten minutes old, I was already fretting
about the fact that she didn't have a sibling.*

*

A week or so after Colette returned to Paris, it felt like Grace had
been living in the house for years. Unlike me, Grace didn't arrive
all at once with two removal vans and Lauren coaching from the
sidelines with a vanilla latte and a topknot. Instead, she brought
her things in one by one, book by book, box by box, until the house
organically became theirs. She put her wine books on the shelves
and Tom gave away his old suits to make room for Grace's clothes
in the wardrobe. Every time he left the house, the simple sight of
her trainers beneath her raincoat in the hallway filled him with
indescribable happiness, as did her little pot of almond nail oil that
popped up around the house the way my coffee cups used to.

Until Tom watched Grace unpack her clothes, he hadn't realized how much he wanted to belong to someone again. To have someone to wait in the car for and spar with about what to eat for dinner, fish and chips or curry. The bits they don't show in films because nothing happens. The scene where Grace runs her bath. The part where they drop off Henry at school. The montage where Rita is clucking to babysit so they can go out on date night, beaming when she sees Grace come down the stairs with her hair blown out and a new dress. All of it.

It was midweek when Grace came home from the shop with some framed pictures wrapped in butter-colored tissue paper. She unwrapped each of them carefully and leaned them against the wall in the kitchen just below a collection of Albert Oehlen drawings of trees and roots. I'd bought three of them for Tom for our first wedding anniversary. Whenever Tom and I picked out pictures, we always tended to agree on what to buy, but when it came to hanging them, we bickered about what should go where—sometimes for days. But there was none of that friction now. I could see him taking in Grace's architectural drawings of a Florentine palazzo with interest.

"We can move these other pictures if you want," Tom said. "I think those drawings would be wonderful there, if that's what you're thinking." He picked one up and turned it over, looking at the label with the artist's name, the title of the drawing, and the gallery on the back. "Where did you get them?"

"In this charming little shop in Florence. Pietro chose them. He was very proud of himself for haggling down the price." Grace looked at her picture, then at Tom's. "Are you sure you don't mind? We can find another spot."

"I'm quite sure. Let's try it."

Grace took the Oehlen drawings down one by one, placing them on the floor until she was holding the last of them. The picture side was facing her, and the back of the picture was facing Tom where he stood by the kitchen table. That's when he saw it—in Sharpie, my inscription, a line from *Hymn to Beauty*: *Darling, Your gaze, divine and infernal . . .*

As soon as Tom caught sight of my handwriting, my words, our poem—the poem Grace had read to him in the car, and he had pretended not to know—he froze. If Grace turned the frame around now to look at the label, she would see the inscription and he'd be trapped. If Tom were the sort of person to believe in telepathy, he would have enlisted every synapse in his brain to mind-meld with Grace to not turn the picture around, to hang it back on the wall, never to be lifted off again.

"I'll find another spot for it," Tom said. "Here, give me that. I'll get these out of the way." He took the drawing from her hands, holding it to his torso like the Shield of Achilles. He had to hide the evidence. As he was on his way up to the loft, clutching the picture, the landline rang, and without thinking, he picked it up.

"Tom? It's Oliver. You're so bloody hard to get hold of these days. It's almost as if you're trying to avoid us," he said.

"Yeah, sorry, it's been a bit . . . hectic." From where Tom stood, he could see Grace in the kitchen tilting her head back and forth, assessing the height of her pictures.

"What about lunch, Sunday? Liverpool's playing and Lauren's bringing the boys. I'm even threatening to make bread sauce."

"Right, yeah, sounds good." Tom said, his voice at a strange pitch, the drawing I bought him practically vibrating in his hands. Oliver had caught him on the back foot. Between Lauren's big mouth and Annie's moralizing, the absolute last thing he wanted to do was have Sunday lunch. Would Lauren "accidentally" drop another corker over the bread sauce, or would she be playing a different game? He couldn't think about it. He'd rather spend time in a confessional, listing every mistake he'd ever made.

"Great, we'll expect the three of you," Oliver said. "Twelvish, usual." Grace began making her way towards Tom.

"Twelvish," Tom repeated, hanging up the phone. Grace was just a pace away from him now. He tightened his grip around the drawing, my words pressed against his chest, the jagged edges of the tree roots facing Grace.

"That was Oliver," Tom said, stepping backwards. "I said we'd go for lunch on Sunday."

"Oh, okay. Henry will be happy. Will you just come and look at these pictures for me? I don't know if they work. You might end up wanting to put that back."

"No! No need. I mean—I'm sure they're perfect."

"Daddy!" Henry called, just as Grace was about to say something else. "Come and look at my Hot Wheels. Daddy!"

"Can I just try the picture back where it was?" Grace said, reaching out for the frame.

"I don't want the picture back up," Tom said. Grace pulled her chin into her neck and pressed her lips together. "I better check on Henry."

As Tom shot up the stairs under the guise of answering Henry's call, he fretted about how many more of these little landmines were planted around the house. He'd forgotten about my battered copy of Baudelaire, hiding in plain sight on the bookcase, marked on every page with my silly collegiate scribbles, notes, and Post-its. *Eternal collision of love and death? There is beauty in all things, even wretchedness.*

When would Grace nonchalantly ask Tom to open the safe so she could put her passport inside along with his and Henry's? Now that Tom was discovering these hidden snares, would he finally get rid of the CD and the letter instead of holding on to them? Along with the rest of my things, it seemed these belongings had assumed a divine significance beyond their mortal hardware. But whether he was willing to admit it or not, in keeping them, he'd loaded his own gun.

In the end, Sunday lunch at Annie's wasn't much to write home

about. Tom managed to get through it unscathed. Annie didn't
corner him in the larder by the baked beans, and there were even
subtle hints at a fresh effort towards Grace. Tom smiled on cue and
laughed through gritted teeth at Lauren's Instagram memes. But
below the surface, every time Lauren put her hand on his shoulder,
he felt his body tense, wondering what her motivation had been in
sharing something so private with Grace with such disregard, as if
she were reading a joke out of a cracker.

The week shot by without incident. Grace and Henry had a
playdate after school with Camilla and Atticus at Pizza Express
and Tom went to a gallery opening off Bond Street with Oliver.
But most nights were spent at home. Once Henry was in bed, Tom
would light the fire and the two of them huddled around the ottoman, Tom ready with Grace's flash cards to test her for her upcoming exam. Though he was still in awe every time she got the
wines correct, her discernment worried him. Grace's palate was so
refined. If she could sniff out a rare French grape and know its
vintage before declaring the region it was grown in, then how hard
could it be for her to recall every little fib he'd told? Could she smell
a rat the way she could smell a 1997 cabernet?

*

Grace's birthday fell on a Saturday in May. Tom and Henry had
spent the morning doing their best to stay quiet while Grace slept
unawares upstairs. Henry slathered a slice of sourdough toast with
salty French butter, while Tom frothed the milk for Grace's coffee.
A little after eight o'clock, the two of them crept up the stairs and
into the bedroom. The morning light traversed the muted kilim
rug, illuminating the apple-green blanket and Grace below the
duvet. Henry clambered onto the bed, clutching the presents with
excitement as if they were his. Tom followed, holding the breakfast
tray, laden with cards and his present.

"Happy birthday!" Henry shouted, shoving the presents at her, both wrapped in recycled brown paper and a crooked silk bow. Grace turned over, her eyelids still heavy with sleep, and beamed at Henry as if he had just presented her with the Oscar for Best Picture.

"I feel like Barbara Cartland," Grace said. She sat up in bed, moving the pillow behind her back so she could take the breakfast tray from Tom. The curtains billowed in the May breeze, bringing with it the musky scent of wisteria in full bloom.

"Happy birthday, baby," Tom said. Grace poured a dash of hot milk in her coffee, being careful not to spill its dark contents on the crisp, white covers. Henry was beside her, keeping a watchful eye over the presents, insisting repeatedly that she open his over Tom's first.

"Let Grace have her coffee first, Tootle," Tom said, rubbing Grace's leg over the duvet.

There was something so sweet about the way Henry had taken to Grace since that night they'd met on the stairs. I wanted them to be a family, but the more in love Tom and Grace fell, the more nerve-racking the scene became. Tom knew that at some point he had a responsibility to tell Henry how he came into the world as we went out of it.

But the simple fact of being born with the help of an anonymous egg donor was no longer quite true. Tom had put them both in the grip of an ethical dilemma. During one of the many mandatory therapy sessions with the surrogacy counselor, I'd been advised never to resort to euphemism on the topic of surrogacy and egg donation with our hypothetical child. But I could read between the lines, and the consensus was not to secretly go out with said egg donor.

"Which one shall I open first?" Grace asked teasingly.

"This one!" Henry said, already starting to open the present. She tore at the wrapping paper to find a model of a red Fiat tractor, surprisingly like the one Henry had his eye on.

"Thank you!" Grace said with excitement. "This is *just* what I needed." Grace winked at Tom over Henry's head, then listened intently as Henry pointed out the cab and the warning lamp.

For a moment, Tom felt as though he were looking at his life through ground glass. Five years ago, he was alone in this house, bereft and considering suicide, when the phone rang and the hope of Henry became a reality. Then that letter led him to Grace, and he fell wholeheartedly in love with her. Why couldn't it be as simple as melted butter on toast and milky coffee in bed? Why couldn't they just be mum, dad, and baby?

"Open Daddy's next," Henry said. Tom ushered his gift towards her.

"I never told you it was my birthday," she said. Tom's hand stalled on her shin where he'd been rubbing it.

"Huh?" he said.

"I never told you it was my birthday."

"Didn't you?"

"No, I didn't. I never tell anyone."

"Really? Well, anyway. We have our ways, don't we, Henry?" Tom said. In the excitement of getting breakfast ready with Henry, Tom had forgotten she'd never actually told him her birthday was coming up. Tom knew it by heart, though, just like he did her donor number—Dunkirk—and the exact date the letter had been sent. As good as Tom was with numbers, he was weak on narrative, and now he was having to keep a mental spreadsheet of every little utterance.

"But seriously though? How did you know?" she said. Tom could feel saliva thickening in his throat.

"I saw it on your driver's license when I added you on the insurance," he said finally. Her eyes narrowed as Henry ran his tractor over a fold in the duvet. "I wanted it to be a surprise, of course," Tom said, ruffled again. "Anyway, I'm next."

He handed her his present, but as she unwrapped it, he could tell her mind was elsewhere. After she pulled off the paper, she sat with the red leather box in her hands. This wasn't the moment of bliss he'd imagined in Cartier, where he'd spent hours deliberating over which watch she might like best.

From downstairs, Duke barked and barked, demanding his morning walk. Grace looked from Henry to Tom and lifted the lid of the box, revealing an understated yellow-gold Cartier watch, circa 1970. Tom took it out of the box and fastened it around her wrist.

"Do you like it? I thought it would match your hoops," he said, as she moved the watch around her wrist.

"Yes, I do, thank you. I wasn't expecting a morning like this—and I love my tractor," she said, diverting her gaze from Tom and onto Henry, who was swiping incessantly at the wheels.

"Are you sure you like the watch?" Tom said. "We can exchange it for something else if it's not to your taste."

"No, no. I love it," Grace said, but he still sensed an undercurrent of tension. The perfect balloon of the morning had popped. Just a few hours ago, Grace had woken Tom up with kisses on his shoulder, which had led to slow sex in the dark before falling back to sleep. But the whole breakfast-in-bed surprise had taken an unexpected turn. Duke barked again from downstairs as Pat dropped the post through the letter box.

"Coming, Dukey! Be patient, my boy!" Tom said in the ridiculous, pompous voice that always used to make me laugh but this morning sounded strained. Grace fiddled with the watch on her wrist, as if trying to get used to its presence. Tom held back the urge to ask again if she liked it. He had a horrible feeling in his stomach, but maybe the morning dog walk would rid him of his paranoia. Maybe lunch would be better.

*

Tom had booked a corner table at Scott's for the three of them. Like Grace had predicted, the restaurant was packed. All the tables outside were full. She'd suggested lunch at Petersham Nurseries instead, somewhere more fun for Henry. But Tom had insisted on Scott's because it was her favorite. But then the service was slow because it was Saturday and after an hour and a half, they had only just finished their main course. Henry was getting impatient, entertaining himself by ramming his tractor repeatedly into the heavy silver salt and pepper shakers, which were sticky with fancy tomato sauce.

"How many times do I have to ask for the dessert menu?" Tom said in a hectoring manner, watching the old couple next to them tuck into their sticky toffee pudding. "Henry, watch the glasses. Please."

"I knew we should have eaten at home. I had a feeling it would be like this," Grace said, just as Henry spilled Grace's water all over her arm and her new watch.

"Henry!" Tom said.

"Don't take it out on him," Grace said. "He's sat here for two hours." Grace dabbed at her arm and rearranged the glasses. The way the older woman with the sticky toffee pudding was staring at them was starting to get on Tom's nerves. Parenthood seemed to invite unsought advice and opinions in every scenario. People felt as though they had a right to volunteer information on your parenting style at the most inopportune moments.

"Okay. I'm going to take Henry outside," Grace said, helping Henry into his coat. "We'll meet you out there."

"But I've ordered you a cake."

"I don't want a cake. Tom, please. Just stop."

Grace began pushing Henry forward in his little navy peacoat, clutching her birthday tractor. Just then, the older woman from the next table leaned over and said, "Now, you be a good boy for your mummy."

"She's not his mother," Tom snapped at the woman, and downed the rest of his wine.

"I wasn't trying to be," Grace said to Tom, her voice suddenly stern.

"Grace—I didn't—I didn't mean it like that."

"Then how did you mean it? We're going outside," Grace said, then turned to the woman beside them and added, "Enjoy your dessert."

"Grace, wait," Tom said.

It wasn't an outlandish assumption. In the seven months they'd been together, it had occurred multiple times, and Grace had always been quick to correct the misconception. It most often happened when they were at the park, when the sun was out, and people would comment on the striking similarity of Grace's and Henry's eyes—how they were a matching glacier blue. Were these constant comparisons to me beginning to weigh on her?

Tom asked for the bill and overtipped in the hope of erasing the shame of the whole mess—the naughty child, the tomato sauce, and then the argument to top it all off. He paid the bill and slammed shut his wallet, turning to the elderly couple on his way out.

"Sorry if I was rude before," Tom said to them, gesticulating. The woman looked up at him, her spoon dripping with custard.

Walking through the restaurant, he felt like everyone was staring at him, though nobody was. They were enjoying their oysters and cheersing over birthdays, too busy to notice a stranger's family squabble.

Outside, Grace was waiting, holding Henry's hand. The air was warm for May, but the sky above was dark, as if threatening to rain.

"I'm sorry. You know that wasn't directed at you, right?" Tom said as soon as he was beside her on the pavement. "I don't know what's got into me today." The outdoor diners sat in their prandial merriment. A champagne cork popped. A woman laughed, a long braying cackle. In an ideal world, their lunch hadn't gone to pot. Grace had blown her candles out. She loved her watch. Henry hadn't spilled Grace's water and the woman beside them hadn't mistaken Grace for Henry's mother.

"I think we need to have a talk later, when Henry's in bed," Grace said. She wasn't making eye contact. "Because I'm just letting you know that I really don't need reminding about who I am to Henry. From you or anybody else."

"Grace, I wasn't reminding you. I'm sorry. It's—that wasn't at all my intention."

"I told you I wouldn't get my wires crossed. I don't need reminding. Especially from you."

The color drained from Tom's face, and he looked up the road to hail a taxi. He felt like he was living in a video game and every time he broke through to the next level, it got harder and harder. There were points to be gained, but also more opportunities for sudden extinction. Grace and Henry were so simpatico. Aside from the connection Tom and I had orchestrated between the two of them, they'd built their own organic one. Would this same chemistry have existed without biology?

"Taxi!" Tom called at every passing cab. "Taxi!" Finally, one pulled up beside them. "Come on, Henry."

"But I thought we were getting ice cream," Henry whined.

"We'll have it at home," Tom said.

"But you said we would have it after lunch," Henry said, still holding Grace's hand.

"Henry, please. I promise you can have two scoops as soon as we get home. Daddy's not feeling that well. Will you please get in the taxi for me?" But Henry neither listened nor did as he was told. He turned away, yanking his hand out of Grace's, and ran up the road away from them.

"Henry!" they both shouted. As Henry looked back, his toe caught on the pavement, and he tripped and fell, hitting his forehead against the concrete slab. His cry was shatteringly loud and immediate enough that people stopped eating their fish cakes to look at the commotion. The blood ran down Henry's face, staining the Peter Pan collar of his shirt. A waiter from Scott's ran over with bundles of napkins and a champagne bucket full of ice.

"Could everyone please stand back," Grace said, kneeling on the pavement. She was calm, reacting with precision. Smiling down at Henry, even if her smile looked a little strained. "Henry, everything is going to be okay. Just keep looking at me," she said, but Tom stood there frozen. Since Paris, he'd convinced himself that he was mentally trained for disaster. His recurrent fantasy was of running into the Ritz lobby and pulling me and Chloe alive from the wreckage. Sometimes he imagined murdering the bomber. But looking at his son with blood running down his face, Tom was paralyzed.

The doorman helped them into the car and told the driver to take them to Saint Thomas's A&E. The waiter gave Grace a pile of fresh napkins for the journey, which she carefully pressed to Henry's head. Tom and Grace did their best to keep him from falling asleep. She pointed out two pigeons who were arguing over a stray french fry on the lip of the pavement. The sight of the napkins blotted in blood and Grace's bloody hands holding them to Henry's face was making Tom queasy. The metallic smell of blood sent him back to that moment he woke up on the gurney in Paris. Tom opened the taxi window for some fresh air, letting in the sound of a distant siren.

As soon as the taxi pulled in front of the hospital, Tom ran into reception, holding Henry like a baby, supporting his head with his arm. Tom hadn't been inside a hospital since Henry was born, and in that waiting room there'd been gentle music playing and framed Disney pictures on the walls. Unlike the maternity ward, there were no jolly faces nor helium balloons declaring "It's a girl!" Instead, it was carnage. Tom stood agog, lost in a sea of terrified parents and febrile, wounded children. He started to hyperventilate. Grace put her hand gently on his forearm.

"I'll check us in. Just try and find a seat," she said. But there were no seats and the waiting room only seemed to be getting busier. Grace went to the check-in desk and returned a few moments later with a clipboard and a pen attached with an absurd amount of Sellotape. While they waited for a seat, they stood by the wall, Henry still in Tom's arms. Grace fired questions at Tom about Henry: birth date, height and weight, allergies, parental medical history. Each question felt like a barbed arrow to his chest. He could see the list of questions from the corner of his eye, the word "mother" repeating like a mantra.

"Maybe it's easier if I fill out the form," he said.

"I've got it," Grace said. "Keep applying pressure. Does the patient's biological mother—"

"Does the patient's mother what?" Tom said, in the exact same tone he'd had at Scott's.

Grace didn't bite back this time. She looked at Henry and slowly rubbed her lips together; I could almost hear her giving Tom the benefit of the doubt. This was high-level stress. One of them had to keep it together, and it wasn't going to be Tom. "Does the patient's mother have any medical conditions?" she said.

"No," Tom said. "I—I mean, I don't know. I don't know." Tom looked around at the scene in the waiting room, at the tortured faces and broken wrists. The wolf was at the door. "I don't know who she is," he said. "What's the next question?" Sweat had gathered at his brow.

"I don't think you can just skip a question like that. I think in this situation, when you use a donor, you're given documents, a detailed medical history. Are there any documents at the house I can go and get?"

"No, there aren't. I—I threw them away," Tom said. Henry squirmed but Tom held fast. "Try and stay still, Tootle."

"You threw them away? You threw Henry's donor's medical records away? Why would you do that?" Grace said.

"I told you the other day, that was all Honor's stuff. I don't have it."

"Okay . . ." A little girl threw a handful of wooden bricks across the waiting room before breaking into a colossal tantrum.

"Maybe the GP has them? Honestly, Grace, I should be doing those forms. Maybe I'll remember if I see the questions." A woman next to them bounced a wailing, colicky baby on her knee.

"My head hurts, Daddy," Henry said. His eyelids were starting to droop. He'd thrown up in the taxi, and the vomit was turning crispy on Tom's jumper, the pungent odor wafting into his nostrils. The whole scene, and not just the rotten smell of stale vomit and the worry that Henry had a concussion, was sickening. Tom felt like he was being hung over a bridge. After I died, Tom had set himself one task: to be there for his son, to protect his child from all harm. But he hadn't anticipated the ripple effect of attachment. Henry had fallen in love with Grace as much as he had. What version of events would he tell Henry if Grace were to uncover the secret and run?

They waited in silence for nearly an hour. Tom was too terrified to say anything and potentially trip into another hole. If he said nothing, it meant there were no fresh lies to keep afloat. The lie regarding medical documents wasn't like the lie he'd told in bed this morning about Grace's birth date. This lie had legs, and it was running in unexpected directions. This lie had consequences. It involved Henry. It was a matter of life and death.

"Henry Wharton?" a different nurse called, holding yet another form.

"Here!" Tom called. His eyes were bloodshot and dry.

"I need to move you into a different waiting room," the nurse said. Grace handed her the form they'd filled out and the nurse quickly flipped through it. "You need to sign here," she said, passing back the clipboard.

Grace looked at the form. "Oh, no. I'm not Henry's mum," Grace said.

"My mistake," the nurse said, and clicked the pen shut. "Look, I'm sorry to do this, but we can only have one adult per child in the other waiting room. It's carnage back there."

Two paramedics rushed in, then with a seizing teenager on a gurney, slamming through the double doors and into the bowels of the hospital.

"I'll go," Grace said.

"Grace, wait," Tom said. "Miss? Can we make an exception?"

"I wish I could, love. But then I'm going to have to make an exception for everybody, and we don't have the space."

"It's fine. I'll go," Grace said. "Really."

"I don't want Grace to leave," Henry said, starting to cry.

"Darling, don't cry," she said. "It's going to be okay."

"You promise?" Henry said.

"Promise." The impatient nurse was already trying to usher Tom and Henry through the doors to triage. Tom leaned in to kiss Grace, but she wasn't responsive.

"I'll see you at home?" he said.

"I think I'm going to go back to my flat tonight," Grace said. "This is why I hate my birthday. Something always goes wrong."

"Sir, we're up to our eyeballs here. Can you please follow me?" the nurse said, checking her fob watch.

"Wait, Grace—you're not going to stay at our house?" Tom said. "I'm sorry about Scott's. This is all—"

"It's not about Scott's. It's this. You should be with your son," Grace said. "Just please, let me know he's okay when you're home."

Grace kissed Henry one more time, then turned to go. The thought of her not being in bed tonight, the idea that when he got home the house would be empty, without any lingering trace of her shampoo or her perfume, was enough to make him break down in tears, but he would never cry in front of Henry. His world was crumbling again: Grace was leaving, Henry bleeding.

How had he managed to create such a shit show? He'd always thought that if there were ever an emergency, he'd play the hero and save the day. Yet here he stood, alone, holding Henry, his eyes fixed on the back of Grace's head as she walked away from them.

CHAPTER TWENTY

At five o'clock the following morning, Tom threw in the towel and got out of bed. He couldn't lie there any longer tormenting himself, wide awake in the silent darkness. Throughout the night, in between half-hourly checks on Henry, Tom had managed to convince himself that Henry never would have fallen and smashed his face if he hadn't been so consumed with the logistics of his fraudulent existence.

Tom checked Henry again. He was sleeping soundly, snuffling in his bed with Pudding beside him. Luckily, Henry didn't have a concussion, but what if he did? Tom would never have forgiven himself for taking his eye off the ball. He splashed water on his face and went downstairs to let Duke out into the garden. The sky was still dark, an inky, foreboding blue. No matter which direction he looked—towards the dewy grass, the distant oak tree—he couldn't escape the image of Henry's bloody face or stop seeing the back of Grace's head as she walked away from him in A&E.

What a difference from this exact time yesterday morning in bed, when Grace had been holding on to his shoulders, their bodies intertwined as she came. Now he was alone in near darkness, running through possible worst-case scenarios: She didn't love him anymore. She was moving out. She knew he was a liar. She thought he was a terrible father.

Tom scrolled through their texts from last night again, a sterile exchange of niceties. It didn't sound like them. It didn't read like them. It was like two strangers, clinical and matter-of-fact, with no kisses at the end, so alien from their usual way. Once Grace had learned Henry was okay and discharged, that all he'd needed was a few stitches, she'd wished Tom a terse good night and that had been it.

How could he make this better? But no matter how Tom played it, there was no wrangling out of this one. In the waiting room, Grace had asked him directly about the egg donor's medical history and he had lied point-blank. There was no avoiding the repercussions. The lie would float to the top at every annual checkup Henry had, every appointment with the optician, and who knows where else. On top of that, for the rest of their lives, people were going to assume that Grace was Henry's mother. This existence was uninhabitable. He had to come clean. He'd been bouncing and bouncing on the diving board, and now he had to jump.

Between coffees, Tom had managed to persuade himself that telling Grace the truth was going to result in only a few rocky weeks, a lot of raking over the same ground, but that eventually they would be Tom and Grace and Henry again. All he had to do was to start at the letter. If he could just get hold of her.

But the early morning slogged by with no word from Grace. Tom texted and rang her incessantly. Firing off frantic, misspelled, nonsensical messages that repeated the same thing he'd already sent ten minutes before. He was so immersed in his phone that he burned the toast and set off the fire alarm, waking Henry.

After finishing his fourth cup of coffee, his blood thrumming with caffeine, he'd galloped towards the idea that Grace would forgive him.

Tom checked Henry's temperature once more before the two of them ate breakfast with all the windows open. Henry kept asking Tom to repeat what had happened with the toast and the fire alarm, finding Tom's reenactment utterly riveting. After breakfast, Tom sat with Henry in the drawing room while he watched *Cars*, absent-mindedly ruffling Henry's hair as he stared, unseeing, at the screen, rereading their text messages as if there were something he'd missed. In all my years married to this man, through tens of dozens of arguments, silent treatments, and missed calls, I'd never witnessed this intensity of erratic behavior.

It wasn't until Doc challenged Lightning to a race that Grace finally picked up, her unexpected "Hello?'" knocking Tom sideways. He'd become so used to the trancelike sound of her ringtone, then her voice saying, "You've reached Grace," that now he stammered over his words like a drunkard. "Grace—Hi, you're there. Hi, I'm so—pleased. You picked up. I was getting worried. Look, I—I want to—" he said, getting up from the sofa where he'd been sitting with Henry. He walked to the window, out of earshot.

"We should speak in person," Grace said.

"I agree," he said, just as a gaggle of teenagers walked past the window, obnoxiously blaring Gnarls Barkley out of one of their phones. There was a clogged feeling in his chest, reminiscent of the time he'd gone diving during his gap year and convinced himself he'd got the bends.

"I'll be there in ten," Grace said, her tone curt. He tried not to overthink the fact that she didn't say "I love you" when she hung up. In some delusional pocket of his brain, he could feel himself growing lighter as he mentally began to shed the letter and the lie.

Keeping an eye on Henry in the drawing room, Tom paced the hallway as he rehearsed his opening lines over and over. He would begin with the letter. Let the story unravel for her in the same way it had unraveled for him. If I'd been physically there, I would have told him to roll back his expectations.

When he finally heard Grace's key, it might as well have been a pneumatic drill. He yanked open the door, her keys swinging in the lock, her blank expression at odds with his overly caffeinated smile.

"I've made coffee," he said, though he'd clearly had enough. His eyes were like saucers and his hands had the shakes. "I'm so glad you're here. Do you—do you want a coffee?"

"I've already had some, thanks," Grace said. She didn't take off her coat. Instead, she followed Tom into the kitchen and sat down at the table. "How's Henry?"

"He's fine. He's watching *Cars*. I'm so sorry about yesterday. I have no excuse. I was being a twat," Tom said, tightening the lid on the Bialetti.

"It's not just yesterday," Grace said. She sat back in her chair and poked her tongue into her cheek. "Maybe me moving in pushed you into a weird place."

"Don't be absurd."

"It would be normal. You lived here with Honor and Chloe . . ."

"That's not what this is."

"Then why don't you look me in the eye when I talk to you about Henry?" Tom looked at her. With senses as refined as hers, of course she'd noticed his idiosyncrasies, and marked them down like a tasting note on one of her flash cards; she'd just, quite understandably, come to the wrong conclusion. Who could blame her? There was no behavior strange enough nor sequence of events that would lead her to think she was our anonymous egg donor. "You recoil every time someone thinks I'm Henry's mum. I see it." She put her hands together as if in prayer and pressed them against her mouth.

"That's why I was ringing you. Grace—You're more than a mother, you're—"

"You're picking and choosing what I do and don't know." Tom felt himself getting sweaty, his skin sticky from where he hadn't showered. "Like Henry's egg donor. You didn't tell me. Even when I told you I donated my eggs."

"I know I've been acting strangely," Tom began. "But I promise it's not about you moving in."

"I just don't believe you. And then you didn't want me to know medical information about him yesterday. You were so weird about those forms. Like it was sickening to have me there. I think—I think we need time apart," she said, rising from her chair.

Tom got up to follow her, his skin opaline white.

"I know why it feels like that," he said, tears gathering in his eyes. "But please, let me show you."

"Show me what?"

"It all started that first night I saw you in Sprezzatura. When I found you. I saw you through the window and I found you. I just— You'll see. I have something I need to show you."

"You're not making any sense."

"Just give me one minute." He bolted out of the kitchen past Henry who was still transfixed by *Cars* in the drawing room, up the stairs, and into the wardrobe. He was finally going to tell Grace everything, show her how fate had brought them together. His mind was whirling, going back in time, remembering the moment he'd seen her in the shop, his eyes locking onto hers, the same eyes as Henry's, with that unmistakable dark blue circle around the edge. Tom pulled his shirts apart like curtains at the break of day. There it was. The safe. The green light, blinking, blinking, blinking. Tom punched the code in for my birthday, his hands so shaky they misfired the first time. The second time he put the code in, the safe unlocked with an automated whirr.

Pushing past his dad's Rolex, Tom picked up my engagement ring in the red leather box, holding it in his hand as he grabbed the CD, accidentally knocking Hedgie onto the floor in the process. The sudden urgency to tell Grace everything was sending adrenaline buzzing through his body, shutting down his senses. So much so that he didn't hear Grace's and Henry's footfalls on the landing. Tom stood facing the safe, Hedgie by his feet. My ring box in one hand. The CD with Grace's baby picture on it in the other. The letter, still in the manila envelope at the back of the safe. He had only one thought: Tell her everything. Show her the CD. Show her the letter. So, when Grace and Henry suddenly appeared beside him in the wardrobe, he startled and froze like an amateur cat burglar.

"Henry can't find Pudding," Grace said. "I assume he's in here."

Henry let go of Grace's hand and went over to inspect Hedgie on the floor.

"Is this for me, Daddy?" Henry said.

"Yes," Tom said. "Yes, it's yours." Tom could hear the thud of his heart, beating and beating and beating. This was it. Any moment now, Grace would recognize her baby picture on the CD, and they would be free of the lie. There, in the wardrobe, among his freshly pressed shirts, he could prove how much he had wanted her from the very beginning, and they could start afresh.

"Oh my God," Grace said.

"I know, I know," Tom said. "It's exactly what it looks like." Grace put her hands to her mouth before swiping them through her hair.

"Oh my God, Tom," she repeated, coming closer. Tom had spent the whole morning preparing to tell Grace the whole truth and nothing but the truth. He'd been so sure that honesty was the way out. He'd even managed to convince himself of an outcome where Grace saw past the lie. Maybe there would be tears, an argument, then a moment where everything hung in the balance. Once the slate was clean, they would be even closer, starting fresh, without a single mistruth between them.

But Grace's eyes weren't focused on the CD at all. Instead, they were gimlet-trained on the red box that contained my engagement ring.

"Is *this* why you've been acting so strangely?" she said.

Tom didn't react well under pressure. He always needed a moment, but he was out of time. This wasn't *Pride and Prejudice*. Tom wasn't Mr. Darcy. There would be no coming back from a withdrawn proposal. Even though Tom endlessly fantasized about marrying Grace, he hadn't planned to propose this very morning. And certainly not with my engagement ring. The ring would be there glinting at him at *every* breakfast, every trip to the shops, every dinner party. It would be all she wore when they made love at night. How could he even contemplate telling her that it wasn't originally meant for her? That, in fact, it was the ring he chose for me.

But the genuine sentiment had always been there. Grace was the love of his life. It had been that way since he saw her through the window at Sprezzatura. Their meeting that evening at Sunday Blues might not have been fate, but the letter was. That was the part of the story he wished he could tell her—*wished he had told her*. He loved Grace so deeply. He would rather die than hurt her. He quickly slid the CD back into the safe and dropped down on one knee.

"Marry me," Tom said. He opened the box to reveal my engagement ring and proffered it to her like a monk with an alms bowl. "Marry me. It's you," he said, hoping he didn't look how he felt, which was deranged and euphoric, yet gutted. Tom had managed to compromise yet another wonderful moment between them. First their meet-cute, now their engagement. "Please say yes," he said. He took the ring out of the box and held it in his fingers. There it was. My ring. He hadn't looked at it since he'd received the box from the French authorities. The sight of it now made him take an involuntary breath, the air hitting hard against his throat, turning it dry. The platinum band vibrated in his fingers.

"Grace?" Henry said. "Why are you crying?"

"Because Daddy wants to marry me," Grace said.

Tom couldn't remember how to breathe. Just the simple act of inhaling and exhaling seemed gargantuan. There Grace was, wonderful, honest, perfect. Alive.

"Is that a yes?" Tom said. The sun through the wardrobe skylight illuminated the ring, casting tiny prisms all around them.

"Yes," Grace said. "Yes, I'll marry you."

CHAPTER TWENTY-ONE

I was absolutely dreading the weekend at Annie's in Scotland. On paper, her house was idyllic—right on the beach, with no neighbors for miles, and offering the kind of grandiosity one might associate with a bygone era. But the bedsheets always felt damp and smelled like mothballs, and Annie had a deep-rooted resistance to turning on any heating. I'd tried wholeheartedly to get out of it, but Tom was adamant we go.

When we finally arrived, I couldn't help but feel everyone was acting a little out of sorts. Tom more so than anyone. All weekend, he was in a state of constant readjustment. Tightening his belt, then loosening it again, claiming to have forgotten things in the car only to come back with nothing. I just assumed he was smoking again like I was, sneaking in the cheeky, odd cigarette out the window with Annie.

The journey to the Highlands took nearly six hours door to door. On arrival, Annie thrust a glass of champagne in my hand and kept clinking glasses with me every time I tried to take a sip. Perhaps she was overcompensating because she hadn't read the first draft of my manuscript yet or she had and hated it. Regardless, I did my best to slot in. I knocked back my drink, writing sentences in my head while chatting with Lauren's new boyfriend, Daniel, who was perfectly sweet but painfully dull. He fawned over Lauren, topping up her champagne and rubbing her back while Annie and I huddled in the kitchen, praying to the great Lord that this one would stick around. Lauren's need to be married with two and a half children before she turned thirty was greater than the national debt.

On our final night, Annie threw a dinner party in the dining room, and we all dressed up like we were in Brideshead, drank far too much, and danced till our feet blistered. The following morning, we woke up with blazing hangovers and a desperate need for bacon sandwiches.

"I think we should go for a walk on the beach. It will make us feel better," Tom said, running me a bath.

"A walk? Are you mad? It's pissing down with rain," I said. "I can barely speak, mind walk."

But later that morning, I diligently followed Tom along the beach while the gale hit me head-on, horizontal rain pelting my face.

"Don't you fancy going back? Having a cup of tea or something?" I shouted, holding up the hood of my raincoat, but Tom was in another world. I couldn't work out if he was constipated or walking me to my death on the cliffs.

"Just a bit farther," he said, looking behind us again. We walked another minute, but it felt like fifty-five. "Okay, this is good," Tom said, stopping and turning to face me, the sea alive behind him with white horses. "Right here."

"Why are you stopping? I've got to be honest. I'm not enjoying this as much as you seem to think I am."

That's when he got down on one knee in the pouring rain. "Marry me, Honor," he said, squinting where the rain was shooting into his eyes.

"What the fuck?" I shouted over the wind. I was laughing, then crying, then shaking. "Seriously? In this weather? In this jacket?"

"Are you gonna say yes or what? I'm freezing."

"Yes! Yes, you nutter. I'll marry you," I said, jumping on top of him.

"She said yes!" Tom shouted, the torrential rain hammering down into the sea. That's when everyone appeared from behind me: Oliver with more champagne, Annie with her camera up to her face, Lauren struggling to maintain control of a bunch of balloons, copious tears already streaming down her cheeks.

"Show us! Show us the ring!" Lauren said.

"Oh, bollocks," Tom said.

"Oh, ha-ha," I said. "Very funny."

"No. I'm not joking. I must have dropped it when you jumped on me."

"What?" I said. Lauren yelped and let go of her balloons, which floated up into a miserable sky. Now everyone was on their knees in the sand, searching for my engagement ring like ants at work. After twenty minutes, with Tom starting to sway a bit, Lauren popped up and let out a joyful squeal.

"Oh my gosh! Oh my gosh!" Lauren said, holding the ring tightly in her fingers. Thunder clapped and the wind blew off my hood. "I found it! I found the ring!"

We all applauded, and Tom grabbed Lauren's face, leaving a big smacker right on her lips.

"Lauren! I love you! I bloody love you!" Tom said. Oliver popped the champagne as Tom slid the ring on my finger. It felt like the rain stopped after that. I didn't even care that there was a moth taking a dip in my champagne. Except for when Chloe was born, it was the happiest day of my life.

*

The rest of the week somehow passed by without incident. Tom made dippy eggs with tomato and garlic toast. Grace watched Henry at tennis and reported his forehand was on fire. Tom and Grace fell asleep on the sofa watching *The Affair*. He'd even managed to avoid Lauren on his evening dog walks with Duke. It was only when he clocked my ring on Grace's finger every now and then that he was reminded how far he'd sunk. His whole body filled with corrosive dread. This wasn't one of my jumpers in the basement. This was something the whole world could see.

It was one thing to keep a secret from your fiancée behind a locked iron door, but now the chasm between his two lives was closing. He was conflating his worlds—and Grace was none the wiser. Like any newly engaged woman, she spent the week admiring her ring from different angles and calling Tom her fiancé at any given opportunity. When Grace showed Nellie the ring at the shop she'd screamed and congratulated herself for "picking up on the vibe," before popping open a bottle of cold Italian Cava from the shop's fridge.

As Sunday lunch approached, Grace's excitement to share the news with Tom's friends grew by the hour, while Tom longed to be struck by an aggressive strain of influenza. But there was no wangling out of this announcement or the obligatory viewing of my ring. No one had admired my ring more than Lauren. And Annie was at capacity. How was she supposed to react when faced with the added layer that Tom had not only proposed to Grace, but he'd also proposed to her with my ring?

Annie was quick to open the door as soon as they arrived for Sunday lunch, Lauren advancing close behind her with lashings of mascara and what appeared to be a push-up bra. Tom and Annie awkwardly kissed hello, both at sixes and sevens, resulting in Tom treading on Annie's toe.

"Shit," Tom said. "Sorry. That was an accident. Why are you wearing an apron?" Annie looked down at her unfamiliar attire as Lauren bent down to cuddle Henry hello.

"I'm fine," Annie said, her cheeks flushed, her hair pulled tight off her face. "I stupidly offered to help Oliver because we came back late from the theater and now he's bossing me around the kitchen like Gordon bloody Ramsay."

Annie and Oliver's had been such a respite for Tom in recent years, but today the sickly odor of wilting gardenias in the hallway was dizzying. He pulled Grace closer, feeling the platinum band against the inside of his hand. He knew he should have prepped them about the upcoming announcement, but how would that have gone exactly? *Please don't mention my dead wife's ring on the finger of my new fiancée?*

"We brought this dessert wine," Grace said, trying to shuffle off her coat, only Tom was holding on to her so tightly that she was forced to abandon the effort after only one side.

"Oh great," Annie said, admiring the bottle. "Thank you so much." She touched Grace's elbow. "It works perfectly. We've made trifle for dessert."

"I made the cream. It's organic," Lauren said, rising. Just then, Henry threw himself into Lauren's legs and swung for a moment.

"Daddy is marrying Grace!" he announced.

"Oh, what fun," Lauren said. "Were you playing dress-up? Am I invited?"

"Yes, you can come. Pudding is coming," Henry said.

"Well, in that case I must," Lauren said, looking down at Henry.

"Can I go outside?" Henry asked, running past the geranium plant and kicking up its scent as he headed into the garden.

Grace stepped in closer to Tom, looking at him with eyes verging on soppy.

"Actually, it's true," she said. "Tom asked me to marry him. We're engaged."

"What?" Lauren said, her eyes narrowed like she was looking for Venus through a telescope.

"Gosh, congratulations," Annie said, her hand gripping her glass so tightly I was expecting it to shatter it into a million little shards.

"When did this all happen?" Lauren said, her eyes flashing

between Tom and Grace, wandering around the hall like a perplexed Egyptian goose.

"Last week," Grace said. "It was such a surprise."

"Last week!" Lauren shrieked.

"Golly. Wow. Congratulations! Show us the ring then," Annie said, the skin of her neck mottling cherry red the more she spoke.

Grace wrenched her hand from Tom's grasp and pulled back the sleeve of her coat to reveal my engagement ring.

"The *ring*," Lauren gasped, Grace's hand still suspended in midair. "The ring," she repeated idiotically. Annie's face was frozen in terror, like a little girl who had lost her mother in a theme park. Not since J. R. R. Tolkien had there been a ring so fraught with meaning. Not since Elizabeth Taylor had an engagement ring sparkled with such insistence, catching every ray of light from the hallway chandelier.

"What on earth are you squawking at, Lauren?" Oliver said, coming into the hallway, the sleeves of his salmon-pink shirt rolled up to the elbow. "You sound positively deranged."

"We're getting married," Tom said, pulling Grace under his arm. Oliver looked from Tom to Annie and then back at Tom, his face breaking into a wide smile.

"Oh, bloody hell," he said. "Congratulations!" He kissed Grace on each cheek and gave Tom a hug, short and rough with a lot of manly slapping. "This is just bloody fantastic!" Oliver said. Was he welling up? He never cried at *my* engagement. "This calls for the good stuff."

Trapped in the hallway, doing his best to adopt a jolly sensibility, Tom was drenched with regret for the way he'd dealt with this pronouncement. He felt like the last six years of his life had condensed into this moment. He kissed Grace hard against her cheek, while Oliver insisted everyone follow him into the kitchen for a toast. Tom put one foot in front of the other. Grace was happy; that was all that mattered. No one had immediately dropped him in it, or burst into tears, condemned the merriment, and fucked his engagement. So far everyone was managing to keep a lid on it. The next thing he knew, Oliver was unscrewing the muselet on a bottle of Krug as Lauren hovered around Grace like a hungry mosquito.

"Let me see that ring," she said as the group gathered around the kitchen island. Tom stuck close to Grace, watching as Lauren took in the all-too-familiar diamond. "Gosh," she said, swallowing with exaggeration. "This ring. This *ring*."

"I know," Grace said. "Isn't it so beautiful? I can't stop looking at it. Where *did* you find it, babe?"

"Yes. Wherever did you find it?" Lauren asked, looking directly at Tom.

"It's a—it's a . . . *secret*," Tom said with emphasis, letting out a laugh that was strained at best. Annie didn't look up, polishing the already pristine glassware repeatedly as though that might save the day.

"Right, a toast!" Oliver said, passing around the glasses and filling them with bubbles. "To our wonderful friend Tom, and our newly wonderful friend Grace. I know I can safely say that we *all* wish you the world of happiness. To Grace!" he said, lifting his glass. *"Love sought is good; but given unsought, is better."*

Annie fiddled obsessively with her necklace. I'd never seen her down a glass of champagne so quickly. Lauren continued to fix her gaze on Tom, as if he were the only one in the room. *You're so lucky to have Tom. I'm making Tom's favorite. Tom works so hard . . .* Had Lauren so cunningly disguised her affections for Tom? Or had I just dismissed any inklings because everyone had a sort of crush on Tom, even Postman Pat? Had I been so caught up in my own life, my book, Chloe, and having another baby, that I hadn't clocked Lauren jonesing for Tom? Had this been gestating since university, or had my death been the kindling for a long-simmering flame?

"So, how did Tom propose?" Lauren said, her voice at a strange pitch.

"Yes. Let's hear from the bride-to-be," Oliver said. He bent down in his cranberry chinos to open the oven door and check on his Yorkshires.

"I was completely surprised, to say the least," Grace said, touching the back of her neck. "Tom came along out of nowhere, and changed everything." Annie rolled her lips, then pinned on a celebratory smile. "I never thought I'd be here again—a ring on my finger, a man I love, and a little boy who makes life worth living . . ." She glanced at Tom, who blanched slightly. "And I promise to love and take care of them—Tom with all my heart and Henry as if he were my own flesh and blood."

Annie's eyes filled with tears. Tom couldn't look at her. Oliver pulled Annie in closer and they all cheersed. I could see Lauren revving up to piggyback on Grace's speech, but thankfully for everyone, the timer for the beef Wellington went off and lunch was served.

*

"That really was the most wonderful beef Wellington," Grace said. "Mine always tends to turn out a little wet." Oliver told her his secret was plastic wrap, which made Lauren's face contort; she was on a zero emissions kick, which was slightly at odds with her Range Rover and her toxic overshare about her dead best friend.

After lunch, Oliver went on a long, in-depth tangent about the day he and Annie met. He had perfected this one. How she'd been so certain that his red Volkswagen Golf belonged to her even though he was sitting in the driver's seat. Lauren laughed too loudly, considering how well she knew the story, casting her eyes between Tom, Grace, and that diamond. Tom had inhaled his meal and was now suffering from acute indigestion and Annie didn't appear to be listening, picking at a silver platter of strawberries on the table. She had knocked back four glasses of champagne and was busy pouring herself a fifth from the warm bottle on the table. Tom watched her, feeling like a marshal. With each glass he became more worried that she would get drunk and blurt out the ring's provenance.

"Right, time for trifle," Oliver said as he stood up and began clearing the plates.

"I'll help you," Annie said, pushing back her chair.

"None for me," Lauren said. "Now that we've got a wedding coming up, I'm going on a diet. You probably won't get married until next summer, though, will you? I think winter weddings are a bit naff."

"We haven't really talked about it," Grace said. "I don't think either of us has a strong desire for a big wedding, though. We'll probably just go to the registry office." Tom nodded enthusiastically. A small wedding, a paneled, cold registry office, and a hostile receptionist sounded ideal.

"The registry office?" Lauren said, without blinking. "Oh, that's . . . niche. Tom and Honor got married here. In the garden." Annie twisted a tea towel into a truncheon, then swatted at a fly I'm not sure existed.

"Yeah, I don't know that I'm a big wedding person. I think we're both in a different place in our lives," Grace said, turning to Tom. He straightened his back but said nothing, longing for the subject to divert onto safer topics.

Oliver plunked the creamy, layered sweet onto the table. "Who's having trifle?" he asked, holding two silver spoons like he was conducting an orchestra.

"None for me. Well, just a tiny taste," Lauren said, pinching her waist. Oliver dolloped a large portion onto a scalloped-edged dessert plate and passed it to her.

"I've gone heavy on the cherries and light on the cream. The future Mrs. Tom Wharton? Do you want trifle?" Oliver said.

"Yes, please," Grace said, taking the plate from Oliver's hand.

Tom looked through the orangery at Henry playing in the garden. He could see the three of them at the registry office, Grace holding hands with Henry on the pavement, wearing something white, or perhaps not. She'd pick up her bouquet on the way from the flower stall near their house. It was how he wanted them to live their lives. Simply. The three of them, without a constant threat that someone was going to slip up, say the wrong thing and whip up Grace's suspicion in the process.

"None for me," Tom said, "I've actually got a bit of a headache."

"Oh no," Grace said, putting her hand on Tom's forearm. "I told you not to drink that dessert wine. I'll eat this and we can go?"

"Thank you," Tom said just as Jarvis yelled, "Tag! You're it!" from the garden.

As everyone wolfed down their trifle in silence, Tom felt as though he were in the final furlong of a race he hadn't trained for. *If only Annie could act more upbeat about the whole idea and Lauren would stop mentioning the ring . . .*

"I'll get Henry," Grace said, placing her hand on Tom's shoulder as she got up from the table. "That was delicious as always, Oliver. You outdid yourself on the Yorkshires."

The minute Grace was out of earshot, Annie leaned across the table and went for it: "I take it she doesn't know she's wearing Honor's engagement ring either?" Oliver stood flabbergasted by the sink.

"Wait, what?" he said, holding the neck of a bottle like a Viking.

"Don't you recognize Honor's engagement ring?" Lauren said to Oliver. "I would know that ring anywhere."

"Are we supposed to pretend that we've never seen it before?" Annie said. "It's not fair on her. And what, now you want us to lie to Grace too?" Tom threw his napkin on the table and stood behind his chair, holding the back of it. Annie was blinking excessively, a telltale sign she'd had one too many. Lauren licked her dessert spoon before dropping it loudly on her plate.

"Hang on?" Oliver said, scrunching his eyebrows. "You gave Grace Honor's ring?"

"Not intentionally. Can you all just stop? It's not like that," Tom said. The familiar golden light in the kitchen had waned, giving the room a morgue-like feel. "I didn't mean to propose."

"You didn't?" Lauren said.

"No, I did. Only—not with that ring," Tom said, rubbing the heels of his hands into his eyes. A vein throbbed at his temple.

"Okay, let's all just take a breath," Lauren said. She rose and moved towards him. "Let's talk about this rationally."

"Lauren, honestly, the last thing I need is more talking from you," Tom snapped. The room froze, suspended in time.

"Excuse me?" Lauren said, her hand at her neck.

"You told Grace about Honor and I using an egg donor with Henry. At what point did you think that was any of your business?" Tom demanded. Lauren's neck flushed deep red.

"Tom. I—I thought she already knew. You and Honor always said that you were going to tell people."

"She *knows*?" Annie said.

"Never mind that," Oliver said. "We're celebrating. Can I get anyone else some more wine?" Oliver said, as if nothing were awry. "Have this conversation another day."

Annie thrust her glass in Oliver's direction, and he hesitantly topped her up.

"No. Let's have it now," Tom said.

"You're living a lie, Tom," Annie said. "And it's not fair to drag us all along with you."

"Honestly, would you rather I was alone?" Tom said. "Is that what you want?"

"That's not what I'm saying. You know it isn't," Annie said.

"I'm not going to be made to feel bad for moving on with my life in the way I want to do it," Tom said. Through the window, he could see Grace kneeling down to tie Henry's shoe. "Henry adores her. I adore her. I'm happy again. It's just a ring."

"Of course, of course," Oliver said. "Absolutely. We're not going to say anything. Are we, Annie?"

"Why can't you just let me be happy, Annie, for Christ's sake?" Tom said. He felt as though he was on the verge of a seizure. His friends' eyes blinked and blinked, castigating him for all his questionable choices, even the ones they didn't know about.

"I'm not going to apologize for wanting you to be honest," Annie said, her eyes beginning to fill with tears. "I really like Grace, and of course I want you two to be together. But I can't sit here saying nothing."

"If you want us in your life, yes, you can," Tom said.

CHAPTER TWENTY-TWO

Driving home from Annie's, Tom sat stiff in his seat, while Grace and Henry played rock paper scissors. It should have been so cute, watching his fiancée play with his son, but his bid to hold on to Grace was being held together by a thin piece of tainted hardware. There was no room left for mistakes. He didn't need Annie to lecture him on the moral high ground, nor to be constantly faffed over by Lauren. Oliver was different, of course. He wouldn't say boo to a goose. Tom had his family safe in the car, but for how long? He briefly considered putting the house up for sale and moving to Wales, or to an actual island. Anything to relieve the constant pressure.

"Why don't we go away?" he said. "To celebrate."

"What? Now?" Grace said.

"I win!" Henry shouted.

"Yes. Why not?" Tom said, his eyes flicking between the road and Grace. "Just us." Grace raised her eyebrows.

"What about Henry's school? And it's a bit short notice for me to ask Nellie to cover the shop," she said.

"I don't need to go to school," Henry said, never one to miss out on a good bunking opportunity.

"Nellie can handle the shop for a week."

"It seems a bit hasty," Grace said. "Why don't we just wait for half term?" Her eyes still had that high shine. She turned from where Henry was in the backseat to look at Tom. He put down the window and immediately put it up again.

"Grace, Grace, it's your turn," Henry said, kicking Tom's seat. Grace contorted her arm into the back and resumed another round of rock paper scissors.

"Did you find Annie a little odd today? I know it's a lot for her to take in. But didn't you think she was a little, I don't know— aloof?"

"No, no. Annie was just a bit pissed. Everyone's *thrilled* for us. That's what we were talking about when you were in the garden."

Tom drove along the familiar route between Richmond and Notting Hill until they pulled into the drive. As Grace got Henry out of the car and raced up the stoop, he racked his brain about where they could escape to on such short notice. He would email Miss Rose about school, and if wherever they went didn't allow dogs, Lauren could look after Duke. She'd already texted Tom twice asking him to call her, proclaiming yet again that she was sorry and had never meant to tell Grace anything. He'd reply and apologize for his tone, and they'd put it behind them. Space would help. Perhaps by the time they got back, the shock of the ring would fade.

*

Tom watched Henry chase Grace along the wide expanse of Talisker Bay Beach. Finally, isolation. They hadn't seen a single soul since they'd arrived in Scotland, not even a fishing boat. There was just the sea occasionally kissing their ankles and the verdant cliffs looming behind them. Tom thought about taking a photo of Grace, looking sexy in her striped jumper and shorts, but whatever picture Tom took would never capture this feeling of weightlessness. Back home in London, he'd been so tense, but walking along the beach his shoulders dropped, and he could take in the feeling of sand between his toes. It was almost like they were the only family in the world. A world where he could be free of unsolicited interjections from our best friends observing him constantly, remarking how Grace was the spitting image of me or how I had folded the napkins or how morally bankrupt he was. They were in love—wasn't that the most important thing?

"It's definitely *not* Notting Hill," Grace said, walking backwards, her hair blowing like a windsock.

"It suits you," Tom said, jogging to catch up with her and Henry. He took Grace's hand in his and kissed the back of it, interlacing their cold fingers.

"Daddy, look!" Henry said, holding up a crab shell. "I found one!"

"Well done," Tom said. "Put it in the bucket, otherwise he might bite you. Five minutes more, okay?" Henry agreed and continued digging.

"I thought you were going for a dip," Grace said.

"My only incentive for swimming was to see you in your swimming costume."

"You should have just said," Grace said, lifting her jumper, her nipples hard beneath her costume.

"Right, okay, that's five minutes, Henry. Let's head back for lunch," Tom said, his mind no longer occupied with making smoked salmon sandwiches.

If a stranger had walked by who didn't know Tom's history, they might have found Grace and Tom's endless display of affection mildly nauseating. Barely a moment went by where one wasn't kissing the other. If he could, Tom would spend every second with his hands on her, his lips on her, picking up the raspberry muffin she liked from the local cafe, revising with her, teasing her, cooking her pasta carbonara, and warming up the cold skin of her legs as they wrapped tightly around him. Grace. His fiancée, his future wife. The woman I picked out of a catalog. The closest thing Henry would ever have to a mother.

When they got back to the cottage, Tom built a fire in the wood burner and Grace made Henry pickled cucumber sandwiches. Henry managed to get through about half before falling asleep on the sofa, the plate still resting on his knee. Tom pried the half-bitten sandwich from Henry's hand and scooped him into his arms. He kissed Henry's forehead before tucking him safely under the duvet in his bedroom.

On the way out, Tom bumped his head on the low beam for the fifth time that day, then left the door slightly ajar, the way Henry liked. Being cozy inside this little cottage with Grace, with crumbling walls and the distinct smell of damp, Tom had no desire to return to the well-trodden pavements of Notting Hill where tittle-tattle was the legal tender and privacy was frowned upon. The sound of Grace running a bath while Henry slept on a rainy day—this was life. This was how it was supposed to feel.

Tom followed the smell of Grace's rosemary oil down the narrow hallway, then knocked on the bathroom door.

"Come in," she said. Tom unlatched the door and peeked into the tiny bathroom that could barely even fit the roll-top tub. Grace was already in the bath with her hair up, steam rising all around her.

"That is an extremely appealing sight," Tom said. He walked into the bathroom and perched on the edge of the bath.

"It's amazing how simple life can be, isn't it?" Grace said, sinking farther under the water. Her skin glistened and her nipples sat on the surface.

"I was just thinking the same thing," Tom said, touching her wet knee. "I'm tempted never to leave. I've even got my eye on that rusty old fishing boat."

"You're actually serious, aren't you," she said, sitting up in the bath.

"Completely. I like this poky little place."

"I hate to burst the holiday bubble, but there's not even a cinema in this town. We are ten miles from the nearest shop and I'm not even sure the woman behind the till was alive."

"Screw the cinema—we can watch films on TV. And if that woman behind the till was dead, then we can grow our own vegetables. Apparently, the soil's brilliant here. I was just reading about its acidity in *Farming Scotland*."

"So, you're a farmer now too?" She flicked water on him, but he barely flinched.

"I could be a very good farmer, you know."

"You can do many things. Some extremely well, I'll give you that. Like your chicken pie. And a good impromptu lecture in the National Gallery. But a farmer you are not. You couldn't even keep the basil alive."

"I take your point. I could join the Scottish art council," he said, taking a wet hair from her face. Grace held Tom's hand against her cheek and began biting the meaty part, the way he sometimes did hers when they were making love.

"Now *that* is actually a good idea," she said. "Or maybe even go back to school. Put all that passion to good use."

"I can't think about all that right now," he said. Grace kissed Tom's hand, the front slowly, then the back. Careful, thought-out kisses, making his skin cover with goose bumps, before she leaned back in the tub, her hair up against the basin, slightly wet at the ends. She slowly lifted one leg after the other from the water, so they were on either side of the bath. Tom couldn't think about where he wanted to live or going back to school. He leaned down and kissed her lips.

"You really know how to shut me up, don't you," she said. The sea outside was beginning to get rough, and the rain was hitting hard against the small window. Grace shut her eyes as Tom's hand disappeared into the water and he slipped his fingers inside her. Listening to Grace moan with pleasure, Tom could forget everything—the lies he'd told, the lies he was telling. There was only this. Only now. This cottage. Safe inside Grace.

*

The weather only worsened over the next few days, but Tom and Grace didn't care. Tom read *The Philosophy of Andy Warhol* by the fire, his eyes barely lifting from the page, a cold, half-drunk cup of tea under his armchair. Grace found an old set of Monopoly under the sofa, and once she'd brushed off the long-legged squatters, it was as good as new. Tom oversaw cooking and the wood burner, while Grace went out and haggled with the local fisherman for the best price on his Scottish salmon.

A couple of days before they were set to leave, the sea calmed down enough to take Henry out on a fishing boat. Tom had forgotten what it felt like to wake up this well-rested. As they left the jetty, Tom looked back at the little white cottage they were renting, the chimney smoking, the glimpse of sun falling across the salt-battered front door. Tom could see the life he longed for, here, just the three of them, free from his friends' opinions and the school gates, the Vultures whispering behind Grace's back about the ring. But real life loomed.

"The cottage looks even more charming from here, doesn't it?" Grace said, taking a photo with her phone, her white dress flapping in the wind. In his peripheral vision, Tom watched Henry in the cabin with the captain, learning to steer, his orange life jacket on tight.

"He's already a better sailor than you," Grace said. Tom pulled Grace in closer as the boat began to roll in the swell.

"I think I might surprise you. I'm very hardy, underneath it all," Tom said.

"You nearly put your back out lifting Duke into the car the other day."

"That was only because of the angle," Tom said, looking down at his hands, which showed no sign of wear.

"Imagine how wonderful it would be to live here. We could literally get married at the weekend. You could even wear that dress."

"You want us to get married this weekend? Here?" The color of Grace's face was beginning to match the color of her dress, her lips tinged blue.

"Yes, I do," Tom said. "What do you say?" Grace glanced down at her ring, the stone catching in the sunlight.

"That's very romantic, but I can't think about this now. I really don't feel great," Grace said. She white-knuckled the rail, looking back and forth between Henry and Tom, then proceeded to vomit over the side of the boat. Tom held back her hair and put his arm around her shoulder, hoping it was the swell and not the talk of marriage that had made her ill.

"God, sorry," she said, wiping her mouth with the back of her hand. "I knew I felt a bit dodgy coming over those waves. I guess I'm not as boaty as I thought."

As soon as they were back at the cottage, Grace felt better. It was nothing a Coca-Cola and a packet of Walkers Salt & Vinegar Crisps couldn't fix. Tom made Henry his famous hot choccy and Grace read aloud chapter six of *Fantastic Mr. Fox*. At bedtime, Henry was out like a light. One of the many, gorgeous side effects the sea air has on children.

Later in the evening, Tom and Grace were lying on the small wrought iron bed beneath the eiderdown. Grace was wearing her woolly red socks and one of Tom's white T-shirts. The wood burner in their bedroom crackled and the glass door lit up in a hot orange blast.

"Fuck it," Grace said, dropping her book flat on her chest. She was looking straight ahead, but she could only have been talking to Tom. Tom was almost asleep, his eyes barely able to stay open on the page.

"Excuse me?" Tom said, readjusting his glasses, which had gone aslant.

"Let's do it. Let's get married. Here. Like you suggested before I vomited."

"Are you serious?" he said, turning to face her.

"We don't want a big wedding. We don't need people to see us saying our vows. What better place than here with Henry?"

Tom looked at Grace, her still-dewy skin. She looked so ethereal, so pure in his white T-shirt. It was like a dream that he'd stepped into. But suddenly, he was awoken by a harrowing, aggressive sound like an air raid siren on Grace's phone. She reached for it on the bedside table and peered at the screen.

"It's Lauren," she said.

"Don't answer it," Tom said. "Let it go to voicemail."

"Why?"

Tom felt his rib cage tighten, his defenses suddenly up.

"Did she try you? Do you think something's happened to Duke? I'm answering it," Grace said. She slid the phone open. "Hi, Lauren . . . Is everything okay? Oh, don't worry." Grace turned to Tom and covered the handset. "She set off the alarm by mistake. She's told the alarm company, though. Yeah, sorry. Tom's phone is out of battery . . . No, the weather's been a bit hit-and-miss but we're making the most of it . . . Yeah, Henry's great. He's taken to crabbing . . . Is everything all right with Duke? . . . Oh good."

Grace gave Tom a thumbs-up and sat up straight in bed. "On Saturday, well, originally, tomorrow but . . . Really? That's an idea." Grace pressed the phone to her shoulder and whispered, "She wants to throw us an engagement party on Saturday. At the house." Tom shook his head and Grace shrugged and grimaced.

"That sounds like a lot of work," she continued. "I'm not sure we want anything too grand on the day we get home . . . Oh . . . Uh-huh . . ." Grace put the phone to her shoulder again. "She's already sent out the Paperless Posts," she said.

Tom put his hands to his face. This was the last thing on God's earth he wanted. A room full of people gawping at Grace in the context of what was once my life. Lauren hadn't seemed that celebratory at Sunday lunch, so why the sudden urge to throw a party? "That's very kind of you. Just nothing too big . . . Yes, you too." Grace put her phone on the bedside table and fell back into the pillows.

"I guess we're not eloping," she said.

CHAPTER TWENTY-THREE

On the best of days, Tom hated a houseful of strangers, let alone when he'd just arrived home from a refuge in Scotland. By the time they got back, the house had been completely taken over by caterers. Someone had shifted the furniture in the drawing room to accommodate the buffet, part of which involved a flower wall in the shape of a heart. There was a chef preparing ill-conceived crabmeat canapés in the kitchen and a fleet of florists were swapping out my Boston ferns for huge white orchids, a botanical exchange that never would have happened under my watch. Any flower that needed a hair clip to stay erect was a no in my book.

"Lauren keeps texting me," Grace said from the wardrobe, pulling her dress off a hanger. "She's saying she needs us downstairs." Tom unbuttoned his shirt at a glacial pace, as though he could stave off the party if he remained undressed. "Babe, can you help me?" Grace said, turning her zip to face him.

"Sorry," Tom said. He zipped up her dress the way I'd trained him all those years ago, being careful not to catch Grace's skin. That morning, before they'd left Talisker Bay, he'd barely touched his food—even Grace had commented on it. He would rather have swum the Drake Passage than attend this party.

"I don't mean to press you, but I think you should start getting ready," Grace said, balancing on one leg as she put on her shoes. "You're very quiet. Are you okay?" Through the open bedroom window, Lauren could be heard squawking at a caterer.

Though it was half past six, it was still light out, the spring evening balmy and close.

"I've got a bit of a headache, to be honest," Tom said, scratching at the back of his neck. "Maybe I'm coming down with something. Do you think we should cancel? I don't want to get everyone ill."

"We can't cancel now. People are going to be here at seven o'clock. Do you want me to get you some paracetamol? If you're poorly, I'll go down by myself. I mean, I'll barely know anyone but—"

"I can manage. I'll see how I go—just for a little bit." Grace squinted at him, then went to her bathroom cabinet.

"Okay, take these," she said, handing him two tablets. "There's water by my side of the bed." He smiled at her weakly, wondering as she left the room how he was going to navigate the rest of the night.

In the shower, he let the hot water pound against his face, hoping the pressure would erode all his wrongdoing. Afterwards, he toweled off and went to put on his favorite shirt, but the bottom was oddly wrinkled, so he picked another and put it on, huffing when he noticed it was one that needed cufflinks. He keypadded into the safe to get a pair from the box. But when the safe opened, Tom could tell straightaway something wasn't right. He'd left it in total disarray when Grace had caught him with the CD the morning he'd proposed, but now it was tidy, even orderly. Hedgie was sitting atop the manila envelope beside his dad's Rolex.

His heart immediately started thumping against his chest. Someone had been in here. He checked for the CD and the letter, the way you might feel for your wallet when you think you've left it in a restaurant. He whipped the envelope out of the safe and rifled through its contents. The letter was there, of course. *Crisis averted.* But where was the CD? His heart dropped. The plastic jewel case with Grace's baby picture on the cover was gone.

Tom felt bile instantly burning his throat, his skin going clammy, then cold, though the room was oppressively hot. He shook out the envelope, dumping its contents all over the floor. He was on his knees now, paper everywhere: birth certificates, death certificates, travel documents, a clipping of my obituary from *The Times*. Begging whatever force existed in the universe that the incriminating CD might be hidden among the detritus, Tom shook the envelope one last time, but the CD wasn't there.

"Tom!" Grace called from downstairs. "Henry wants to show you something!"

In his mounting hysteria, as he gathered up the papers, stuffing them back into the safe, Tom convinced himself that Henry had randomly punched in the correct code, opened it, got hold of the CD, and taken it straight to Grace. Tom closed and locked the safe, but when he charged downstairs, Henry was merely holding up a card he'd been making with Rita. A picture of the three of them—Tom, Henry, and Grace in Scotland on the beach. A big, round, yellow sun in the corner and a navy-blue sky.

"Babe, maybe you *should* lie down for a bit," Grace said when he reached the bottom of the stairs, out of breath. "You really don't look well."

"I'm actually feeling better," Tom said, barely acknowledging Henry's drawing. Grace narrowed her eyes.

"This is one of your best, Henry. Thank you," she said. "Where can we put it so everyone at the party can see it? How about right here, by the drawing room door?"

The front door was fixed open as a regiment of cater waiters wearing understated T-shirts and aprons filed in carrying trays of inedible canapés. My mother was first to arrive, looking somewhat maudlin. Her lips were a lighter shade of red than usual and she wasn't wearing her dark glasses. She held her cigarette case with the silk tassel, the one I used to love playing with when I was a toddler. Tom hadn't told her about the engagement yet, but of course, right on form, Lauren got to her first. It must have been strange for my mother to hear the news that Tom was remarrying secondhand. Had she hoped Tom would tell her personally, like he had with our engagement?

As my mother walked towards Tom, he felt a rush of hot blood tear through him, his face and body suddenly clammy with sweat. Colette would recognize my ring instantly. Was this going to be the moment his life collapsed yet again? In the hallway, with Henry watching?

"Bonsoir, mon chèrie." She took Henry into her arms then kissed Grace on both cheeks. "Congratulations. Being engaged suits you."

"I was going to ring you. Obviously," Tom said. "It all happened so quickly, and then we went to Scotland. Lots of rain," he went on, waffling again.

"Pas de problème," she said, but I could tell there was a whisker of disappointment there.

"You look wonderful, Colette. I'm so—" Grace started, but Tom cut her off.

"Can you excuse us? I need to speak to Grace about something before people start arriving."

Tom pulled Grace into the drawing room. He couldn't see straight, his mind clouded by a map of potential land mines. My engagement ring. Grace's hand. The CD. The worst mistake he'd ever made was not snapping it in two the moment he'd found Grace.

"Babe, are you sure you're all right? Maybe you should go and lie down. Colette's here, and I'm sure Annie will arrive any minute. Go upstairs and rest," Grace said, but Tom had fused himself to her.

"I'm fine. Just—just don't leave me. Don't leave me the whole night. Please."

An hour later, the sky had turned a dark shade of slate, and the party was in full swing. The house was so packed it was as if Lauren had put an advert in *The Evening Standard*. The entire school pickup line was in attendance, even Miss Rose, who had put on some costume pearls for the occasion. Tom could have sworn Lauren promised a "low-key gathering" to Grace on the phone, but this fanfare was more like one of Elizabeth Taylor's weddings. Henry ran around the party, weaving his way through the throng of legs. Nellie arrived in a pair of rainbow platforms with Blanche, Jenny, and Marjorie in tow, each eagerly taking a glass of champagne from the tray and moving towards the buffet.

Meanwhile, Tom stuck to Grace like a barnacle on a hull as faces loomed in and out of his line of vision, rubbernecking from all corners of the drawing room. The Vultures huddled by the kitchen door, Camilla especially seemed riveted on it, waiting to jump on the tray of prawn toast as soon as the cater waiters emerged. The same thought kept slamming to the forefront of Tom's mind: *Where was the CD?*

Much to his annoyance, Lauren was in an etiquette frenzy. She kept bringing people over whom he had no interest in speaking to, all of them ambushing him with seemingly innocuous questions he had no desire to answer: *How did you propose? When's the big day? How did you two meet?* Each well-meaning interaction felt like a lit grenade rolling along the wood floor.

"I think Lauren and I have slightly different definitions of low-key," Grace said, sitting on the padded fender. Tom sat next to her, clutching her hand as she waved to Nellie across the room. "I must admit, I am rather enjoying it. It feels nice to have a little celebration."

Tom tried to mirror Grace's enthusiasm, but internally he was counting down the minutes until everyone left. Guests kept arriving, wave after horrible wave. By nine o'clock, it was as if the drawing room had split into two camps. On the sofas, by the open, double-height Palladian doors, were the Sunday Blues girls, while Miss Rose and the Vultures were gathered by the dining table, at long last getting their opportunity to nose around Tom's house. Lauren was shuttling back and forth between the two camps in a hideous pair of patent heels, still trying to get Tom to chitchat with this person or that.

"Have you introduced Grace to Mrs. Wilding yet? She's *essential* to the council. Really important to always have her on our side," Lauren said, readjusting the straps of her ruched polka-dot dress.

"Introductions to the local council are not high on my list of priorities tonight," Tom said.

"Oh, I was just trying to make Grace feel welcome," Lauren said. She removed the straw from her gin and tonic and took a hefty gulp.

"That's really thoughtful, Lauren," Grace said. "Maybe I'll say hi a little later. And thank you again for throwing this party. It's incredible." Lauren beamed at Tom.

"It's my pleasure." Lauren turned and walked away, picking up a gravlax canapé on her way to the kitchen.

"That was a little rude," Grace said. "I mean, she has organized this entire party for us."

"Sorry. It's my head. I didn't mean it to come off like that," Tom said, holding her hand even tighter than before. Henry ran through the drawing room, his head just visible behind the back of the sofa as he raced out into the courtyard. Rita trotted behind, reminding him to mind the candles. "Do you think it's too early to start winding down the party?" Tom asked.

"Already? Yes," Grace said. "Zara's only just got here. And she's with Katie." Tom looked up at Zara crossing the room towards them, holding the hand of a striking redheaded woman.

"You two certainly look the part," Zara said as Tom and Grace rose to greet them. "Bloody hell. This is some engagement party. How big is your wedding going to be? Tom. This is Katie. Katie—Tom."

"It's lovely to finally meet you," Tom said, taking Katie's hand. "The party wasn't our doing, I can assure you. And don't worry, we don't want a big wedding." Grace straightened the diamond on her finger. They hadn't discussed their wedding since Lauren had rung and put the kibosh on Tom's plans to elope. "Unless Grace has changed her mind?" Tom said. "I just want to marry Grace. I'll do whatever she wants."

"Can I get that in writing?" Grace said, kissing him.

"Okay, enough, you two," Zara said. Katie laughed, staying close to Zara. "There is such a thing as *too* in love. Can we smoke in here? I'm guessing not. Sproglets flying around and all that." She put her cigarettes back in her bag and picked up two champagne flutes from a passing waiter's tray and handed one to Katie. "I don't know what you were fussing about all those months ago when we met at Annie's."

"Fussing about what?" Grace said, but it was Tom, not Zara, who quickly answered.

"Oh, nothing. I was just nervous about asking you out, that's all."

"I always forget you two had met before we started going out," Grace said. Tom smiled at her nervously.

"And he gave me bloody good advice about Katie. I never would have had the courage to tell the truth and ask you out if it weren't for Tom."

"Quite the matchmaker," Katie said. "Cheers."

Through the Palladian doors, Tom could see Oliver in the courtyard, sipping on a viscous, icy concoction, talking to Nellie while Henry ran riot around the iron table.

"You're hurting my hand," Grace said, extracting hers from

Tom's. "I'm getting a drink. Do you want anything?" The dozens of candles on the ottoman flickered as she rose.

"I'll go with you," Tom said. Grace scrunched her face at him. Could she sense that he was on the brink of a nervous breakdown?

"Stay here with Zara and Katie. I'll check on Henry while I'm up. Are you sure you don't want anything?"

"Just some water, please."

Tom watched Grace cross the drawing room, like a beautiful, moving target, her hair catching the breeze from the open glass doors. Even in his mounting paranoia, he couldn't help but notice how ravishing she looked in her peach dress. On any other night, Tom would have been lusting over his beautiful fiancée, imagining her naked upstairs after the party, her dress rumpled in a heap on the rug, but tonight he was on watch, scanning every profile for a potential perpetrator. Whoever went in the safe had known what they were looking for. It could only be one of a handful of people.

Tom watched Grace on her way to the bar, stopping as she said hello to Miss Rose and Marjorie, who were standing by the door to the hallway. Within seconds, all three of them were laughing. Grace held out her ring, and they all admired it. Their show of sincere delight was so sweet and genuine that Tom had to look away. If only this engagement could have been the flawless one that Marjorie saw when she looked at that ring.

When Grace got to the bar, Annie was waiting there for a drink. Tom watched closely, tensing as they kissed hello. He tried to concentrate on what Zara was saying—something about her daughter's school—but he was too distracted by the possible suspects in the drawing room.

He knew it wasn't Rita. Tom's jaw tensed as he tried to make out Grace's expression. *Does Annie know the code?* She'd been banging on about the truth since day one. *Would she slip the CD to Grace at the end of the night? Has she finally had enough of being an accessory after the fact?*

Tom watched my mother moving in Grace's direction. Colette declined a glass of wine from a freshly shaved waiter. Tom still couldn't see Grace's face, but Annie was talking animatedly. *She wouldn't dare tell her here, would she?* Tom excused himself to Zara and Katie, scooching by people's legs as he tried to extricate himself from the seating area. Just as he'd made it halfway across the room, Marjorie and the girls accosted him, their plates piled high with nibbles from the buffet.

"These are the most delicious chicken satays I've ever eaten. Did you make them?" Marjorie said.

"No, I didn't, but I'll be sure to get you the recipe," Tom said, staring at Colette, who was now standing beside Grace.

"I can't fault you on the food," Blanche said. "But I draw the line at the flower wall. I didn't have you down for a flower wall person."

Tom faked a laugh, but his only focus was on my mother. He had to get Grace away from her before my mother saw my ring.

"You don't mind if we take a couple of these sausage rolls with us, do you? They're lovely," Jenny said.

"Fill your boots. I'm just—Excuse me, but I've got to pop over to Grace for a moment."

"Young love," Marjorie said. Tom smiled grimly and stepped away. He was almost at the bar when Lauren blockaded him.

"Tom, I want you to come and meet Jimmy's mother, Sandra," she said, pawing at Tom like some needy old spaniel. "She's head of membership at Equinox."

"Lauren, please. Enough."

"What? But you were saying the other day you wanted to join the gym."

"Can we wrap this up?" Tom said, his voice rising over the hubbub. "I don't know what possessed you to throw this ridiculous party."

Lauren's bottom lip began to quiver. "What is it with you and

Annie not wanting to celebrate things? Everyone's having a very good time," she said.

"Not everyone. I can't wait for this whole thing to be over," Tom said, leaving Lauren stunned and standing on the striped runner in the middle of the room. As Lauren turned, she crashed head-on with a waiter carrying a tray laden with half-drunk glasses of champagne, the dregs spilling all over her dress.

"My dress!" she cried. "How difficult is it to carry a tray?" The terrified cater waiter scrambled to apologize, patting her with napkins, but she pushed him off and stormed out of the drawing room.

At the bar, Tom hastily kissed Annie on both cheeks. He wanted to take Grace's ring hand in his, but she was holding her drink. My mother gave him a tight-lipped smile.

"Colette was just asking if we've set a date," Grace said.

"Soon, very soon," Tom said, rubbing his forehead. Was he shouting or had Lauren put the music on too loud? He felt like someone had plunged his head into a hive of working bees. The noise of one question buzzing on repeat: *Who has the CD? Who has the CD?* Just then, as if in slow motion, Grace lifted her drink to her mouth, her ring finger wrapped around a cold, glistening glass of champagne. Colette's eyes widened.

"Mon dieu," Colette said. "Honor's ring."

"Excuse me?" Grace said, tilting her head at my mother. The blood rushed in Tom's ears like a tsunami. His lungs were filling with water and any second he'd be taken under.

Grace looked at the ring and then back at Tom. "Is this—Colette, what did you say? One of you, say something."

"I told him to tell you," Annie said.

"Annie, don't," Tom said.

"Did you say this is Honor's ring?" Grace said. My mother didn't respond. She stood there, shell-shocked, clutching her cigarette case. Tom gripped Grace by the arm. This was it. He had finally run out of road.

"Grace, please come upstairs, I can explain," Tom said, almost pleading.

"Please tell me she's mistaken," Grace said. "Please tell me that's not what I'm hearing right now."

Lauren reappeared through the drawing room door, looking over the party like a proud lioness. She'd apparently run home to change her champagne-sodden dress for a puff-sleeved, floral number and was now moving across the room. Annie began to look faint, her eyes blinking slowly as she looked at Lauren, kneeling to fiddle with the music. Annie had warned Tom this would all end in shit, but I doubt in her wildest dreams she had imagined a public spectacle like this.

"Okay, okay," Tom said, shaking his head. "Technically, *yes,* that *was* Honor's ring. But hold on, let me, let me . . ." Grace pulled her arm away and started backing away from him towards the hall as Tom followed close behind. "Grace, please!" She stopped on the striped runner in the middle of the room and turned to face him, her eyes filled with tears.

"You proposed to me with Honor's ring? Why would you do that? Does everyone know? Is that why Annie was acting so weird at lunch?"

Tom scrambled for the last shred of truth. The party was peaking around them. Glasses were clinking and people were mingling. Tom could hear laughter and snippets of conversation, like a radio being tuned. He had to tell her the truth. All of it.

"Grace, I never meant to—One morning, I was making shepherd's pie for Henry when I got a letter. I wasn't paying much attention to it, and when I opened it, I noticed it was addressed to you, and—"

Grace interrupted his story. At first, Tom thought he was hallucinating because, though he heard Grace talking, her mouth wasn't moving. The music had stopped. My mother turned to look in their direction. Annie stood dumbstruck.

In slow motion, Tom watched Grace glance up at the speakers in the ceiling, a look of terror dawning on her face. The realization of what he was hearing hit him like a speeding train, the words as familiar to him as a nursery rhyme. He could barely breathe. Even the waiters stopped their circulating.

"Can I ask you to repeat your donor number? And can you speak up a bit?"

"Yes. Donor number 1940GG." Grace's voice blared through every speaker in the house.

"Please confirm that you're a closed donor and you've requested to remain anonymous for the entire donation process."

"Yes. I'm a closed donor."

Lauren leaned against one of the pillars in the drawing room as if butter wouldn't melt. Her face was blotchy, and her upper lip slightly wet.

"Oh my God," Grace said. "No. No. No." She shook her head back and forth. "You lied to me," Grace said, tears pouring down her face. "You horrible fucking person."

"So, you're donating these eggs in Italy, is that correct?"

"Oh *shit*," Nellie said, setting her plate on the buffet.

". . . I'm five foot eight on a good day. My eyes are blue. My hair was blond as a child. I don't know what you'd call it now. Brown-y blond maybe."

"Grace," Tom said, stepping towards her, but she backed away from him. "You have to let me explain. I was going to tell you."

Each second the CD played, he could feel Grace receding, the love in her eyes extinguishing. Her belief in everything decimated— their life, their future. Everything had been orchestrated from the start, and Tom had been the conductor. There were no coincidences. No serendipity. No miraculous love story.

"I told you everything and you already knew," she said. "Were you laughing at me?" Tom reached for Grace's arm, but she recoiled, turning away from him before running out of the drawing room.

"Grace, wait!" Tom said as he followed her into the hallway.

"Do you come from Heaven or rise from the abyss / Beauty? Your gaze, divine and infernal . . ."

"Lauren, turn off this noise!" Annie said, pushing her way through a gaggle of gawking Vultures. Annie scrambled in a bowl of remotes by the window, aiming them at the ceiling, frantically pressing every button—only none of them worked.

"You walk upon corpses which you mock, O Beauty! Of your jewels Horror is not the least charming . . ."

In the hallway, Grace stood facing the front door, her hands at her diaphragm like someone was pulling her corset too tight.

"You let me read this poem to you in the car," she said. "Every word of it. And you didn't think to mention it?" Grace shouted at Tom over the sound of her own voice.

"If your regard, your smile, your foot, open for me / An Infinite I love but have not ever known?"

Hearing the poem of his life, it was as if Tom could no longer discern the speaker. Was it Grace or me? Was this Paris or London? Was that fireworks or smoke? He saw a bride in her long white veil, confetti, and a funeral procession, dirt landing on the lid of a child's coffin. Henry screaming in the delivery room, or was that Chloe in the hotel? Was that Grace's scar on my face? Henry in the morning eating porridge in the kitchen, or was that Chloe with her crêpes? He heard his feet hitting the risers as he ran down the stairs to search for us in the lobby of the Ritz. Was that a violin screeching or me screaming? Tom felt the heat against his face, the thick smoke, choking him, the obliteration of his world as he knew it. It isn't your life that flashes before your eyes when you're about to die. It's the life you thought you were going to have, just before it's snatched away from you forever.

Finally, the recording stopped. The sudden silence of the party felt violent, like a floodlight on an escaping convict.

"It makes no difference what I knew," Tom said. "It was you I fell in love with. Despite the facts. I never meant to give you that ring."

"*What?*" Grace said.

"I didn't mean it like that. That's not what I meant. I—"

Grace ripped the ring off her finger, pressing it into Tom's palm.

"You let me talk to you about being an egg donor. You looked me straight in the eye when I said I was curious about what happened to my eggs when Henry was sleeping right above us. You let me put him to bed. You let me love Henry. You made me Honor's replacement. You're such a liar."

"You're not a replacement," Tom said. "Why I fell so in love with you has nothing to do with the fact that you're Henry's egg donor. I love *you,* Grace. Please. You must know that."

"This isn't love," Grace said. "It's fraud!"

Marjorie marched through the drawing room doorway, Nellie stomping behind in her platforms, car keys in hand, her pink puffer coat over her arm.

"Grace. Don't say that. I—Please let me explain how this happened. It isn't the way it seems. I didn't seek you out. Well, I did—but it wasn't—I didn't mean to trick you. I was going to tell you at the museum, at the cafe, but then—"

"The *museum*?" Grace said.

"This is dark," Nellie said. An errant waiter ambled into the hall before quickly retreating to the kitchen. Tom reached for Grace, but Marjorie was quick to block his way.

"You leave her alone. You, of all people," she said. "Come on, Gracie. We're leaving."

"You never would have told me if I hadn't found out," Grace said. Her voice sounded raw. "It's one thing to lie to me, it's another thing to lie to Henry. Don't you dare follow me!"

Nellie opened the door, and as quickly as the letter had arrived, Grace was gone. The sudden draft caught Henry's drawing of the three of them on the beach in Scotland. It fluttered to the floor, the three happy faces smiling at Tom. He felt like someone had pressed rewind on his life. The last time he'd had this many people in his house, he'd been in mourning. Tom didn't care that he had a houseful of guests. He needed to curl up on the bathroom floor and be alone. When he turned to go upstairs, he saw Henry sitting on the landing, his lip trembling. He'd heard the whole thing.

CHAPTER TWENTY-FOUR

After an hour and some light persuasion, Tom eventually managed to get Henry to sleep. Henry knew Grace was gone; he'd watched her walk out the door, but Tom wasn't ready to face the bombardment of questions his son was asking. *Why was Grace crying? Why isn't she sleeping at home? Why was Grace crying? Why was Grace crying?* Tom could hear the waiters downstairs deflating his engagement party at speed and Lauren braying at them to be quiet, though she was the one making the most noise. It seemed so strange that life was still going on around him when such a huge part of his had just vaporized in an instant.

He'd always known he would have to explain to Henry where he came from, but where did the story start? Was it now or in Paris? Did it begin with me or with Grace? There were so many crossed wires. So many dead ends and complications. But like children's books and memoirs, we don't write from the very beginning; one simply chooses a place to start and that becomes the first chapter of the story.

As Tom gently closed the door to Henry's bedroom, my mother sprung at him from across the landing, accosting him like a leaping hare. She must have been waiting there since Tom had run upstairs. Her lips looked pasty, and she'd picked the nail varnish off her pinky.

"Is Henry all right?" she said.

"I've managed to get him to sleep for now," Tom said, his voice hushed. "I need to find my phone." He turned down the dimmer on the landing.

"Tom," she said, her face pale. "I'm so sorry—for mentioning the ring. I should never have said anything. I just—"

"I don't give a fuck about the ring," Tom said, a little louder than he intended. His mind pinballed between his phone and the malevolent DJ, as if he wasn't the one to blame. "I have to call Grace. I was going to tell her."

"I feel terrible. I had no idea what was going on." She opened her mouth as though about to say more.

"Yeah, well, neither did she," Tom said, and charged down the stairs, leaving my mother baffled on the landing. In the front hall, Lauren was ushering the dregs of cater waiters as they bustled out the door with an assortment of bin liners and plastic crates.

"Have you seen my phone?" Tom demanded. "I thought I left it here. On the table."

"I haven't," she said, tottering over to him on her cloven hoof. "Tom, gosh. I'm so sorry. I can stay the night. Help with Henry? We have tons of eggs and I have a nanny till the morning. It's no problem. Let me make you a chamomile?"

"No. Fuck the tea. I just need to find my phone."

He flung open the door to the drawing room, where Annie was sitting on the sofa by the fire as though waiting for an execution while Oliver paced around the ottoman.

"I need to talk to you. *Now,*" Annie said, vaulting over to Tom by the door, Lauren in step beside him. Annie glared at Lauren as she flopped down on the armchair nearest Tom and kicked off her mules.

"Are you going to confess?" Tom said to Annie.

"Steady on," Oliver said. "I know you're upset, but don't speak to my wife like that. She didn't even tell *me* what was going on."

Colette came into the drawing room and began lifting cushions from the sofas and plunging her hands down the back of every chair. Tom did a panoramic sweep of the room before thundering towards the CD player and jabbing at the eject button. When the caddy slid open, he caught sight of his reflection in the CD, Grace's words echoing in his head. Her intonation, the way she left, the finality of it. He ripped the disc out of the player and snapped it in two, before throwing it into the fire.

"You can't truly think I would do something like that," Annie said. "You've got this so wrong." The acrid smell of smoldering plastic hit the back of Tom's throat, the heat of the fire cooking his cheek.

"What am I supposed to think?" Tom said. "You were the only person who knew. You kept going on about it, badgering me to tell her. Fuck knows how you even got hold of it?"

"Wait, Annie knew?" Lauren said. She rose out of her seat and moved over to the fireplace. "She *knew*? That Grace was your egg donor? You told Annie and not me?" A log spat out a spark, narrowly missing Lauren's shin.

"Just shut up, Lauren," Annie said, her voice breaking. "Shut up. *You* especially! Tom, I need to speak to you right now. In the kitchen. Alone."

"I'm not doing anything until I find my phone!" Tom shouted. Annie shot a sharp glance at Lauren. The room was oppressively hot, a jostling scrum of conflicting smells. Tom felt along the marble mantelpiece, blowing out errant candles as he went.

"I'll call it," Oliver offered, scrambling in his pocket for his own phone.

"We don't need to call it. It must be here somewhere," Lauren said. "Unless someone picked it up during the party by accident?"

Oliver pulled out his horn-rimmed glasses and held his phone to his ear.

"Fuck it. Lauren, are you going to tell him, or should I?" Annie said.

"Excuse me?" Lauren said.

"It's ringing," Oliver said, perched on the edge of the sofa. A very faint sound emanated from the hallway. While the four of them stood there, my mother was hot on the scent, tracking the ringtone like a hungry foxhound.

"Colette, I can help you find it if you give me a second," Lauren called.

"I saw you, Lauren." Annie said. "I saw you drop the disc. I saw you press play. I watched you. I watched it all." Tom's blood ran cold, the full extent of Annie's accusation spreading across his brain like a deadly virus.

"*Me?* Play the CD? Oh my God. She's gone crazy," Lauren said, her neck turning a beetroot red. "Don't listen to her. She's covering her tracks. Honestly, I don't know where she's gotten these ideas from."

My mother walked into the drawing room holding Lauren's clutch bag, glaring at her with the warmth of a deep freeze.

"Your bag's ringing," she said, and dropped Lauren's clutch onto the ottoman. As it landed, the clasp fell open, Tom's phone ringing inside the bag, the screen saver of Henry shedding a much-needed light on the CD case. Everyone stared at the bag for a moment, as though Colette had just dropped a malignant tumor onto the ottoman.

"You," Tom said, his voice hoarse. His mind fired back to those dark days right after Paris when Lauren was always at the house with a freshly baked lemon drizzle cake or a chilled bottle of wine. The patron saint of the playground, the sleep-training scholar, always there at the ready with a spare pack of WaterWipes. The one who insisted we clean as we go. The one who always left things neat and tidy, just like she had the safe. She had the spare key and the alarm code. She'd plotted every moment of this from the start.

"You broke into my safe? You played the CD?"

"It wasn't like that. I did it for us," Lauren said, her hands beginning to tremble against her dress.

"Oh, *Christ,*" Oliver said.

"For us?" Tom repeated. "How?"

"Yes, for us. I came back from walking Duke and he just . . . ran upstairs to your bedroom. I followed him, and then I saw the blanket on your bed. You still have it. On your bed. The green blanket I bought you in Harrods. It's on your bed. Then I saw all Grace's *stuff* in the wardrobe. Her shoes, her jumpers. She was everywhere."

"What do Grace's things have to do with going into my safe?" Tom said.

"I saw the light on the safe flashing in the wardrobe and I didn't even think you'd have the same code anymore but then, well, it just popped open. And I saw the CD, with the baby picture. I'd listened to so many of those things with Honor. How was I supposed to know this was Grace? I just played it. Then everything made sense. Why Grace came out of nowhere. How perfectly she fit the part. I didn't go looking for it. I just took it without thinking. I was going to talk to Annie about it."

"Yeah," Annie said. "And I'm a banana."

"I was just worried about you," Lauren continued, her voice pleading. "You looked so tense all the time. I wasn't planning on playing the CD that way, but then you shouted at me, and you just looked so unhappy, I knew I had to do something. I knew you were terrified. I know you, Tom. Tom, look at me," Lauren said, gobbling sobs. "I love you—you and Henry. I've been with you since day one, since Honor and Chloe died. We spend more time together than anyone else. I'm the emergency contact in your passport. Pat drops your packages at my house when you're not home. We basically share custody of Duke. We live two houses apart. I pick up your dry cleaning. I helped with all Henry's birthday parties and taught you my trick to bring down a fever. I get double kitchen rolls when I go to Costco. Henry, Jarvis, and Basil are like brothers. It was *me* Oliver meant to set you up with, not Honor. You kissed me. You told me you loved me. On the beach. It was raining and you kissed me."

"Kissed you on the beach?" Tom said. "What are you talking about? I've never kissed you in my life."

"You did. Don't you remember? When I found the ring in the sand? In Scotland?" Tom gripped his head in disbelief.

"What?" he said.

"On the beach," Lauren said, jabbering like some nonsensical teenager reading aloud from her junior school scrapbook.

"At my house?" Annie said. "The weekend he proposed to Honor? Are you off your head?"

"I love you, Tom," Lauren said.

"Oh, *Christ,*" Oliver said again.

"I always have. And Henry *knows* me. I'm more of a mother to him than Grace could ever be. Or Honor. She was never really Henry's mother anyway. She died before he was even born." Lauren's embittered venom took Tom by the throat, but before he could retaliate, my mother interjected.

"Don't you dare speak my daughter's name," she hissed. "You could never be a replacement for Honor, no matter how hard you tried. My daughter was loyal. She was brilliant. And she is Henry's mother. Get out. Get out of this house before I drag you by your neck."

"Tom? Is that what you want?" Lauren grabbed for his arm, wailing like a toddler having a public tantrum. "You were lying too. You were keeping something from Grace, and I was keeping something from you. We're the same, don't you see?"

"We are not the same. Please leave," Tom said. "You can keep your key. I'm changing the locks," Tom said.

Bellowing pathetic sobs, Lauren took Tom's phone out of her bag and left it on the ottoman. Her eyes swollen and snot running out of her nostrils, she picked up her shoes from the rug and scuttled out of the drawing room. With Lauren gone, the house fell into a monastic silence. The events of the night hung pendulously above them.

After the front door slammed, Tom felt the gut-wrenching pain of grief descend, his friends' pitiful eyes upon him all over again. When Tom and I fell in love there was no jumping when the telephone rang or strained proposals, there were no secrets or locked safes. But he'd been on a collision course with Grace, whether Lauren had pressed play or not. The gun had rested there, locked and loaded, night after night, pressing against his heart.

"I know I deserve this," Tom said to Annie through a torrent of tears. "I'm sorry. I'm sorry for everything. For accusing you. Grace is gone, Annie. She's gone . . ." He trailed off. "You were right," he said as Annie moved closer towards him. "I don't know what I'm going to do."

"You don't have to know," Annie said, hugging Tom's body tight. "We'll figure this out together."

CHAPTER TWENTY-FIVE

"Okay, chérie, but this is the last time. We really need to get home to Papa," Mummy said as I made my way to the top of the slide. She'd promised me a trip to the playground after we'd finished her routine doctor's appointment. Her cheeks were still glowing from a week in Normandy and her mint chocolate chip ice cream was melting down the cone over her fingers. It was a memory I would later trot out in front of a slew of highly paid psychologists: my mother licking her ice cream, the tips of her hair like the color of a lion's mane dusted with gold. How the tulips were pushing through the soil, hopeful shoots of butter yellow and lilac. How exciting it felt to visit the playground with my mother when we were sailing so close to dinnertime.

When I reached the top of the ladder, I looked up at the elderflower trees, budding open above my head, flat-topped clusters of creamy-white flowers like clouds against a blue sky. The air hit my face, thick and warm. I was about to go down when I felt a force hit my back so hard that I tumbled from the slide, my sticky hands attempting to break my *fall. But my mother was there to catch me before I even had a chance to touch the ground. Sitting in those therapy sessions decades later, I could still smell the sickly-sweet mint chocolate ice cream she dropped running to catch me. I could still feel her hair on my cheek.*

"You're okay," she said, scooping me into her arms and kissing my head repeatedly. "I'm here. You're okay."

After assessing my body, she looked up at the impatient little boy at the top of the ladder. "Don't you ever, ever push my little girl. Ever," she said, her eyes wide, her ice cream splattered and melting on the ground beside us.

*

In the days following his disastrous engagement party, Tom managed to get out of his pajamas only when my mother suggested it might be time to wash them. He flooded the bathroom, burned the crumpets, and did pickup in a questionable tracksuit. There seemed to be no imminent plans for my mother to go back to Paris and after a while, the conversation of her departure just petered out. They took turns doing the school run and on the odd occasion Tom dozed off in the afternoon because of a particularly rough night, he'd wake to the smell of freshly baked madeleines and the sound of Colette and Henry chatting in the kitchen. Henry still asked the same question on repeat: *Why was Grace crying?*

My mother banned Tom from curling up on the sofa until the early hours, sending him and Duke up to bed instead. Tom would sometimes lie there all night, the loss of us all engulfing him. Only now, he didn't reach for the remote to drown out Chloe's laughter or the sound of her calling for him. He just lay beneath the duvet of his own grief. Some nights he couldn't stop the tears and others he couldn't get them to start. But when they came, he welcomed the relief. When I died, Tom became a widower, a word that needs no further explanation. But there is no word in the English dictionary for a parent who loses a child. They remain the same: a father, a mother, suspended in time. Forever explaining, forever retelling, forever tethered to an indigestible loss.

Some mornings, Tom woke with a damp pillow and red rims around his eyes and reached for his laptop, composing long, meandering emails to Grace he never sent. And after the umpteenth time getting Grace's voicemail, he turned to calling Marjorie, continually leaving her long, rambling, apologetic messages overflowing with remorse, until one day she left him one of her own, telling him bluntly to give it a rest. *I was rooting for you. We all were. We let you in and you betrayed us.* He forced himself to listen to her message countless times before admitting that the only thing left to do was fold his hand and hope the weight of his lie would eventually dissipate.

Any delusion Tom might have had of Grace's return was short-lived, because barely two weeks after she left, Zara emailed to say she had organized movers to pick up Grace's things. When Zara arrived to oversee the packing, Tom offered her a cup of tea, but she politely declined, and when he'd asked after Grace, she'd replied with a look that told him not to bother.

He'd sat at the bottom of the stairs as strangers carted box after box of memories out the front door. Maybe Colette had been right, maybe he should have gone for a walk with Duke during the agonizing process, but Tom thought witnessing it might help him make sense of this sudden readjustment. There had been something so wonderfully torturous about still having her things around the house, but now every physical trace of Grace was gone. Her Post-its, her architectural prints, her wine books, even her red duffle coat. Zara didn't leave a single item behind.

*

A few weeks later, London was in full bloom, the city donning its cape of lush green and blossom. Colette and Tom had just got back from the school run when a gargantuan package arrived.

"What is it?" Colette said, staring at the manila beast lying in the hallway.

"Erm, it's a rowing machine," he said. Duke gave the box a good sniff before collapsing beside it.

"*C'est très grand.* Where are you going to hide it?" she said, raising her eyebrows in disapproval. Exercise is not something French women ever discuss.

"I hadn't thought that far ahead," Tom said, walking round the package as if surveying it from all angles might make it smaller. "I definitely underestimated the size when I ordered it."

"Having these things on sight—so tacky. Why do the English so adore the exercise? *Alors,* I think you put it in the basement," Colette said. My mother was becoming more lovable by the day, but still more irritating by the hour.

"I'm not sure about the basement," he said. The muscles in his neck tightened. "There's a lot of—stuff down there."

"So? We move it," Colette said.

"It's not that easy," Tom dropped his head back in his hands and looked up at the skylight. "It's—it's Honor's and Chloe's . . . things. All their things. I didn't know what to do with them."

Colette touched her neck, her enthusiasm for the project visibly plummeting.

She went to the kitchen and came back with a bottle of red wine and two glasses. *"Alors,"* she said. "We start now."

The air turned fusty and damp as Tom followed my mother down the steps to the basement. Just the thought of revisiting the relics of our life again gnawed at his gut, but Colette was already at the bottom of the stairs, pulling at the light.

She poured herself a modest glass of wine and opened the first box. Tom watched in wonder as she nuzzled her nose into one of my jumpers before folding it beside her like she had when I was a newborn. If I'd known there was a way of reigniting my mother's tenderness, I would have faked my own murder years ago, and kicked off this whole surprise before returning one Thursday. *"I'm back, I know you love me, really!"*

Tom couldn't bring himself to untie even a single bin bag, his arms leaden at his sides. "It feels wrong to get rid of these things," he said, surveying the mountains of boxes. "What if—what if—what if Henry turns to me one day and asks for something from his mother or his sister? And I've got rid of it all?"

"I don't think you have to worry about that," my mother said. "He doesn't even know Chloe's name. These belongings are just things unless you talk about them. This jumper I'm holding is just a jumper to someone who didn't know Honor, but I'm sure you can tell me about a time when she was wearing it." Tom did know that vintage Gap jumper. I had it on when my water broke and I went into labor with Chloe.

My mother picked some stray lint off one of my many navy-blue jumpers. "Talk about them. Tell Henry funny stories about Chloe. Tell him how much his mother would love him. That's what keeps their souls alive, not all this"—she gestured—"this lovely *désordre*. Take it from me, I didn't handle things well when Honor's father died."

As Tom began to reacquaint himself with my things, our memories rose to the surface. My navy Birkenstocks under a taverna table in Corfu, the sheer black dress I wore the last time we went to the River Cafe. He didn't need the program for *La bohème*. He hated opera anyway. By the third box, he found a rhythm. He made a pile for the charity shop, and even though he didn't open it, he put the original manuscript of *The Ice Cream Zoo* in a special file for Henry. My mother wanted my notebooks and Tom kept my red Gap jumper.

"I don't know what to do with her laptop," he said while my mother was beginning to sort through a box of Chloe's books. "There's stuff on here. Stuff she was working on. I think she was writing a memoir. I'm guessing—I could only read a few lines. She never told me about it." My mother looked understandably nervous.

"I think I should be more worried than you," she said, forking the collar of her crisp pink shirt with her fingers. Tom shot her a tight-lipped smile; she wasn't wrong. The document on my laptop was half of a first draft, vomited out with zero self-reflection. I never got the chance to light the burner and boil down my prose. Had I known my first readers would be my characters, I might not have written so candidly.

"I found the CD of Grace in here," Tom said. "Where Honor left it. It was like she was waiting for me to find it—to find Grace." Tom stalled. "Honor knew something was happening. Somewhere in her imagination, she set me up for survival. At least, that's what I want to be true. Not that she died unhappy. Not that the last thing she ever said to me was go fuck yourself.'"

Colette took in a sharp breath.

"I told her I was never going to try for another baby," Tom continued. "But I didn't mean it. I was just being a dick. I would have tried forever if that's what she wanted." The exposed light-bulb by the stairs flickered. "I didn't kiss Chloe goodbye," Tom said. "I didn't even tuck her in the night before. When I close my eyes, I don't see Chloe dancing on the bed or bossing us all around. I don't see her wearing one of her tiaras or having a tantrum. She's just standing there, waiting for me, wondering why I didn't save her. Wondering why I'm not there." Tom wept without regard, the tears coming thick and fast down his face. "How dare I grieve? I got to go on with Henry. They didn't," Tom said, finally unsubscribing from his lethal English stoicism.

Colette looked at Tom, her eyes soft. "Do you want me to read it first?"

Holding my laptop, Tom wondered if I would mind my mother reading my manuscript. But there's an old cliché that suggests you should write your memoir as if your mother's already dead. I wrote mine as if I were dead, and then I died. Or perhaps Tom was right, maybe I did know something was going to happen. Was that why I'd had such an unshakable urge to document our life, against all professional advice? *Honor, your readers are children. They want to read about your ice creams, not your miscarriages. There is no place on the shelf for this book.* But had my agent been wrong? Was there a place for this book after all?

"I'm going to take these books up for Henry," my mother said. "Whatever he already has, we can give away."

Tom nodded, knowing full well that the only books in those boxes Henry didn't already have were the ones I'd written, the ones Tom had avoided for years.

"I know this is going to sound really, I don't know, odd," he said. "But I sometimes worry that Chloe doesn't have Hedgie or her books. You know, up . . . there. If her things are here, then what's *there,* you know?" Colette stopped on the stairs and turned to face Tom.

"Chloe doesn't need books in heaven," she said. "She has her mother."

*

A few weeks later, Henry was at the kitchen table, hunched over a pickup-truck coloring book. The windows were open, letting in the sound of the swifts' call, as Tom stood by the Aga with a saucepan in hand, adding the final finishes to a rather impressive full English breakfast.

"We might have to buy another fridge to put up all these pictures you're coloring, Tootle," Tom said, sitting down beside Henry at the table, where he cut Henry's sausage into edible pieces.

"I'm doing this one for Grace," Henry said, moving it aside, his eyes prized on the sausage. "See, I wrote *Grace*." Tom looked at the picture, the written words illegible as a doctor's prescription.

"Oh—great. Yes, good idea. Lovely idea."

"I want to give it to her when she comes back," Henry said, stabbing his fork into a slice of pre-cooled sausage. There was a short pause. The only sound Tom could hear was Henry drinking from his water glass with both hands, his elbows akimbo.

Tom had spent the last few weeks trying to find the right moment to tell Henry the truth about Grace. But there was no right moment. There was no right entry point. How could he boil down Henry's life to an age-appropriate parable? Every time Tom tried to find the words, usually in front of the bathroom mirror during one of his many rehearsals, he would get himself in a muddle and quickly abandon the idea. But here it was, over eggs and beans before he'd even washed his face: an opportunity to tell Henry the truth from the very beginning, the way he wished he had with Grace. To tell Henry about the role Grace would always play in the creation of his life and the role she no longer did. To speak about it like anything else, the way he spoke about bath time or driving to school.

"See, that's the thing, Tootle. I'm not quite sure . . ." Tom took a bite of his toast and washed it down with a big swig of tea. "I'm not sure she is coming back."

"Why?"

"Why?" Tom said, unfolding Henry's napkin and placing it on his lap. "Because . . . Well, it was Daddy's fault. It—it was because Daddy wasn't honest . . . wasn't truthful. About something . . . about something important."

"You told a fib?" Henry said, looking somewhat intrigued.

"Yes. Yes. I did. I told a fib," Tom said. "And I wish I hadn't." The sun came through the window, lighting up the dark blue rim in Henry's eyes. "Grace was upset because I didn't tell her something about you," Tom said. Henry used his finger as a knife to load up his beans. "You see, I knew something," Tom continued, resting his elbows on the table and leaning towards Henry. "And I should have told her. I should have told Grace."

"Is she upset with *me*?" Henry said.

"No, gosh no. Promise. It was Daddy that was the silly sausage. Silly sausage," Tom said, lifting a sausage and taking a bite. Henry laughed. "It's a long story, really. It starts with Mummy—Mummy, your mummy. You know how I tell you she wanted you, so so so much—"

"How much? This much?" Henry had begun to love this part of the story about me. The part where Tom stretched his hands as far as he could to show Henry how much I wanted him. Henry never asked why I was dead. Sometimes he asked where I went, but he was always more interested in the love I had for him before I even knew he existed.

"So, in a strange, sort of roundabout way, Mummy knew Grace very well," Tom said.

"My mummy?"

"Yes, your mummy. You see, Mummy liked Grace a lot. And when Mummy's tummy broke and she wasn't laying eggs anymore—basically, Grace helped me and Mummy make you." Henry stared at him intently. "The thing is, Grace didn't know—" Duke barked suddenly, storming to the back door and growling at a squirrel that was springing across the lawn. "Duke, stop that," Tom said.

"Did you say sorry?"

"Did I say sorry? To Grace? Yes, I did. But, sometimes, when you're older, sorry isn't always enough." Henry looked at his beautifully colored pickup truck, then at Tom.

"Daddy, you know the other day? When you asked me if I put toothpaste on my toothbrush and I said yes? Well, I put it on, but there wasn't as much as normal," Henry said. Tom leaned back in his chair.

"That's all right. Next time, just put a little bit extra."

"Finished!" Henry said, lifting his plate off the table, his knife just narrowly managing to stay on the plate.

"Right, yes, finished. Okay." Tom tried to conceal his disappointment, but what did he expect from a five-year-old? What reaction was he really looking for? Was it silence? A screaming tantrum akin to the previous day because he had started peeling Henry's banana when Henry had wanted to peel it himself? Had he chosen the wrong words? Had the tone been off? Had the idiotic mention of laying eggs made Henry think I was a chicken? But children have a superpower we often overlook. They trust every word of the story. Then they ask us to tell them the story again. Preferably in the exact same way.

*

After breakfast, Tom was scraping the plates into the bin when Henry suggested Tom color a picture.

"Okay," Tom said. "Pick me a good one."

"And then you can post it to Grace," Henry said. "Then she'll know you're double sorry."

Tom looked at his son, knowing that this imperfect perfect moment, scraping congealed beans into the bin, would be forever etched onto his hard drive. The moment hadn't passed to tell his son everything. All the boxes weren't going to be ticked over breakfast. That wasn't the point. There would be further questions at different stages of Henry's life; it would ebb and flow. But Tom would always be there, ready to tell the truth, however painful and difficult it would be. There would be days when the questions about us would seem relentless. Then years would go by when Henry wouldn't mention us at all.

Tom didn't end up sending Grace a picture. But Henry was right. Tom did need to send something to Grace: the letter. Her letter. He posted it the following morning outside the White Horse Bookshop, in the same format as he'd received it. A white envelope. No explanation, no editorial, no return address, no sappy apologies, no fate. Maybe now they could revert to factory settings like she'd originally asked. Henry could be my baby, Tom could be Tom, and Grace could be Dunkirk.

SIX MONTHS LATER

It was late November and Richmond Green was covered with the lightest touch of frost, just enough to make that glorious crunching sound underfoot. The clocks had gone back, and those hideous, papery-leaved poinsettias were popping up in droves all over town. Annie had already started on the Christmas decorations and the fireplace in the hallway was dense with tartan baubles and bracken.

"Great goose, darling," Annie said, wearing an oxblood velvet dress that I would have bought in navy and never worn. She pushed her thick brown hair behind her ears and leaned over to kiss Oliver. Tom topped up Henry's sparkling apple juice and congratulated him on winning yet another round of Uno against his grandmother.

This was the first year Henry had been properly excited about Christmas, practically shaking with elation at the prospect of his Advent calendar. He'd shot up like a rocket in recent weeks, eating everything in sight, even his Brussels sprouts. Christmas was never going to be straightforward. The anniversary of our death would always be the dominant thought. There is no knack to grief. It's like the sky—it hangs over everything. Sometimes the sun peeks through the clouds, other days it rains, and some days it pours.

"Please, can I have a chocolate cat tongue for dessert?" Henry said.

"I don't see why not," Oliver said, reaching behind himself for the pastel-pink chocolate box. Duke came plodding into the kitchen and nosed into Tom's hand.

"I'm strangely proud of you," Annie said to Tom, passing him a wooden box of glacé fruit.

"Don't be vulgar," Tom said. He winked at her across the table.

"You're certain you don't want to spend Christmas Day here?" she said. "With us?"

"I'm sure," Tom said, attempting to peel the paper wrapper off his glacé pear. He looked down the table at Henry and Colette holding their cards. "I want to start making our own traditions. Henry deserves a proper Christmas. Tree, decorations, the whole shebang, at home. But thank you."

"I think that sounds lovely," Annie said. "Did you get a card from Lauren, by the way? We did."

"Yeah, I did. And she sent a present for Henry. Which was nice." Annie raised her eyebrows and shot a look at Colette, who pursed her lips.

"Come on, darling. . . . you can't reheat a soufflé," Annie said.

Tom shook his head. "Look, I know what you're all thinking. What she did was awful. And you're right, it was. And I can assure you, I have no plans on going round for tea and shortbread anytime soon. But I see her twice a day at the school gates, and Henry loves the twins. I don't want him to get caught up in this mess any more than he already has."

"Well, you're a lot more forgiving than I am," Annie said, which I knew translated to something a lot less ladylike. If I'd fallen out with Lauren while I was alive, I would have immediately put the house on the market and changed Chloe's school.

"Do you want me to order you a goose from my supplier?" Oliver said, pushing his glasses up the bridge of his nose. If Annie was pragmatic, Oliver was diplomatic. He always knew when to change the topic. "They always have the best birds."

"No, better not," Tom said. "I actually don't like goose."

"You're joking? You just ate it?" Oliver said through a mouthful of chocolate.

"Well, not quite. I sort of danced it around my plate and Duke likes it, so I've been passing it off to him. But delicious potatoes as always," Tom said.

As he spoke, Tom could feel that heavy swelling in his throat, but no desire to divert the conversation or make a joke. "And on the topic of Christmas and New Year and all things new, I don't want to get sentimental over a heavy lunch, and I know I've been a little somber the last few months, but I feel like I've turned a corner, and I can safely say I'm not feeling quite so sorry for myself anymore." Annie leaned across the table and squeezed his forearm. "I'm rowing twice a week and I'm even going back to university, hopefully, provided I get in."

"A master's in contemporary art will look rather swish on your Tinder profile," Oliver said.

"Let's not jump the gun. But seriously, I feel a small part of my old self again, which is astounding considering I've ended up living with my mother-in-law."

Colette laughed, balling up her napkin and throwing it at him. "Not only that, she spends most of the day quoting Honor's memoir," Tom said. "It's like I'm living with both of them."

Ever since my mother got her hands on my memoir, she'd printed it out, and read it multiple times. After each sitting, she would come trotting into the kitchen or the drawing room to point out to Tom something new she'd discovered: how much I wanted her to tell me stories about my dad, how it felt like he died all over again every time I came home from boarding school, how I noticed her shaky hands and how her hair had gone strange. How from my earliest days, I found comfort and safety in stories—writing them, telling them, imagining them. She finally understood why I created a fictional family of ice creams. She was Madame Choc Chip, and my dad was Mr. Mango Sorbet, except in my version, none of us melted in the end. We had no expiration date.

"I thought it would be sad," Colette said. "To read it. But it's not. Not in the way you think it would be."

"I still can't do it," Annie said.

"I said the same for ages, but it's oddly reassuring," Tom said. "It's like she's talking to you."

I had never foreseen my raw and unfiltered prose bringing comfort to the people I was writing about. I didn't know reading my words would one day free Tom from the mistaken belief that our life boiled down to that last argument in the Ritz. Our love was all there in black and white, an empirical piece of evidence. Every page was our love story.

"Granny, you're taking ages," Henry said. "It's your turn."

"*Mon tour? Allons-y,*" Colette said, turning her attention back to Henry.

"I suppose Grace will be doing her exam pretty soon, won't she?" Oliver said. He stood and poured Colette a glass of port. "Annie reminded me this morning."

"No I didn't. Not really," Annie said, making a face at Oliver. "I was just wondering about it, that's all."

Tom nodded, as though trying to recall the logistics of Grace's exam, when he knew full well it was this afternoon. Grace had circled the date on the calendar in the kitchen. He'd thought about Grace more than once that morning, wondering if it was Marjorie who had driven her to the exam, if she'd slept well, if she'd eaten enough breakfast, but he was no longer privy to the details of her life. When he was walking Duke last week, he even swore he saw Grace across the park. He'd often thought the same about me every time he saw a long, navy cashmere coat and a bedraggled barnet.

"Yeah, anytime now," Tom said. "But let's not get into it. I've mentally decamped."

"So, you don't think about her anymore?" Oliver said.

"Erm, I wouldn't go that far," Tom said, dropping his hand to fondle Duke's silky ears. Colette cleared her throat and adjusted the silk scarf around her neck.

"Uno!" Henry said with a degree of relish.

"*Zut!* You win again," Colette said. Henry began shuffling the cards back into a pile, seeming rather pleased with his loot.

"Look, call me a soppy old bugger," Oliver said. "But you haven't contacted Grace for . . . what is it? Six months? Maybe she's ready to talk now. Now that everything's calmed down. It's worth a try."

"*Oui*," Colette said, nodding enthusiastically. "He's right." Tom swallowed, trying to excavate the glacé pear from his back molar.

"As tempting as it is, I'm not going to chase Grace down again when she so clearly asked me not to. And can I at least try to digest this meal before we dive into my questionable behavior yet again?"

"Aren't you curious if she passed the exam?" Oliver said. "I'm dying to know."

"Of course I want to know," Tom said. "I want to know everything. But . . . Anyway, she didn't reply to the letter. So, that's that."

"Because you didn't give her anything to reply to," Colette said. "You ignored my advice and you didn't write anything with it."

"Listen," Annie said. "I'm not suggesting you rock up at her exam and spin her round and whisk her off her feet. That would be appalling. But who knows? Oliver is right. Six months is a long time. It would be nice to clear the air. And if not you, she might want to see Henry."

At the mention of his name, Henry turned his head.

"I don't know," Tom said, trying to imagine himself walking into the Hilton, where Grace would be standing in her red duffle coat, only this time she would turn to smile rather than walk away from him. "I've probably missed her by now anyway . . ."

"Not if you take the M25 and come off at Watford," Oliver said. Even the mere discussion of Grace's whereabouts was making Tom fidget in his seat. He looked over at Colette.

"What do you think, Grandma?" Tom said.

"Honor would want you to go," she said firmly. Tom didn't take any further convincing. He squeezed Henry goodbye, stuffed a lone cat tongue in his mouth for the road, and buttoned up his coat.

The traffic was light as Tom flew down the M25 towards the hotel. He didn't turn on any music; he just focused straight ahead, his thumbs tapping the steering wheel. As much as he was trying to convince himself that he was simply on his way "to clear the air," he wasn't convincing me. I'd spent more time than anybody looking into those eyes. I'd written half a book about this man. He was going in search of forgiveness, hoping, in time, she might one day consider at least meeting up with Henry. But that was all a foil. Because I knew he was still utterly in love with her.

When Tom shot through the doors of the Hilton, the lobby was packed wall-to-wall with pompous, rumbling men, all of a certain vintage, talking about wine with the utmost pretension. Tom waded his way through the soup of dense cologne and ill-fitting suits until he reached a young gentleman sitting at a computer with a lanyard round his neck, surrounded by a mass of laminated name tags.

"Sorry to trouble you, but has Grace Stone checked in yet?" Tom said, trying to catch his breath.

"Are you taking the exam today, sir?" the gentleman said.

"No, definitely not. But she is." The man turned and commenced a brief conference with the colleague beside him. "What did you say the name was?"

"Grace Stone," Tom repeated. The young gent began furiously tapping away on his computer.

"There's no Grace Stone in the system," he said. The room was thick with radiant heat, sucking every drop of moisture from the air.

"That can't be right," Tom said. "Are you sure?" His shoulders drooped. He felt like he'd been struck by a javelin.

"Quite sure. Says here she withdrew months ago."

*

As soon as Tom arrived home, he charged up the stairs without taking off his coat and shoes, desperate to seal in the night with story time and snuggles. When he walked into Henry's bedroom,

Henry was sitting on the armchair by the window with my mother, the curtains drawn, the lamp above them dimly lit. The soft timbre of her voice reading the final page of *The Snail and the Whale* reminded him of me doing the same with Chloe. He'd seen me in that chair with her on so many occasions. But for the first time, the ghost of guilt didn't follow him into the room. He'd been so gutted at the Hilton, but instead of continuing to track Grace down, he'd driven home to his family. Regardless of how his story with Grace ended, he would always have a happy ending because of Henry. Our son.

"Daddy!" Henry said, launching himself off his grandmother's lap and into his father's arms. Henry was all dopey after his bath, his eyes blinking slowly as he rubbed Pudding's ears against his cheek. "Can you read me a story?"

"How many tonight?" Tom said. "Six hundred and thirty?"

My mother peered over her glasses at Tom as if to say, *Well?* But he shook his head.

"She withdrew," Tom said. My mother looked forlorn.

"But she was so determined. It doesn't make any sense," she said. "I'm sorry, I should never have encouraged you to go. Are you all right?"

"You know what? I actually am," Tom said.

My mother got up and kissed Henry good night. "I think I'll take Duke for a walk," she said.

Tom sat beside Henry on the armchair and looked at the books on the pedestal side table. On top of the pile was Chloe's copy of *The Ice Cream Zoo*. He ran his finger over my name on the cover, the corners bent from years of bedtime mileage.

"Why don't we read this one tonight," Tom said, pointing to my name. "Do you remember how I told you Mummy wrote stories?"

"Yes . . ." Henry said, sucking his thumb, the soft glow of the lamp casting its light on the butter-yellow front cover.

"This is the one she wrote when she was pregnant with your sister." Tom opened the book and underlined the dedication to

Chloe. "That was your sister," he said, the word still caught in his throat, but he didn't rush to swallow it down. "Chloe. But we called her Coco."

"Oh," Henry said. The blessing of logic at Henry's age is that it's yet to be affected by experience or context. "Would Coco like me?" The question nearly stopped Tom's breath.

"She would love you," Tom said.

When I originally pitched *The Ice Cream Zoo* to Tom over a cappuccino, he immediately started intellectualizing: *But why didn't someone notice the freezer was unplugged? Wouldn't someone have opened it and realized things felt soggy? Is "Zoo" really the right word?* I never pitched him another book after that.

But with Henry on his lap, as Tom turned each page, the story I'd told him about all those years ago finally came to life for him. Every nuance, every word choice. Over the brow of the book, he could see us—Chloe and me, dancing around Henry's bedroom, Chloe twirling in my arms, in her ruby-red tiara, bossing me to jump higher.

"'. . . *And Mr. Mango Sorbet was refrozen just in time for tea.*' The end," Tom said. Henry rubbed his eyes and looked up at his father.

"Can we read it one more time?" he asked. This time Tom started at the dedication.

"Of course," he said. "'*For Coco . . . Once, in the depths of a deep, deep freeze on the outskirts of London . . .*'"

CHAPTER TWENTY-SIX

Potty-training your child means you spend an inordinate amount of time sitting on the floor of the bathroom inhaling the fricassee of toddler farts. Whenever Chloe needed to "honk," as we called it, we would charge to the loo like two superheroes heading into Gotham. At her request, I'd make up stories on the fly like my dad once did for me. Every now and then, Chloe would let out a perfect little "poof," and I would enthusiastically remind her to push.

"Where does the boy live?" she said, referring to a red chalk drawing by Augustus John hanging above the mirror in our bathroom. He was my chosen protagonist for a story that had gone on for the best part of twenty-five minutes.

"London, most likely. Or Bath?" I took the picture off the wall and turned it over to see if there was any information on the back, but there was only a crumpled auction sticker.

"Can we go and see him?" Chloe said, looking over my head at the picture.

"Erm . . . That's probably a bit tricky, because this picture is nearly a hundred years old." She looked at me curiously.

"Where is he then?" I'd written myself into a corner, but I tried not to seem as though I wasn't willing to talk about it.

"I imagine he's in heaven, darling," I said.

"Where's heaven?"

"It's up there, in the sky . . ."

"Are there toys there?" she said, her face turning red from a terrific push.

"Oh yes, plenty. And pancakes. And chocolate."

"Will I go to heaven?" she said.

"Yes, we all go to heaven eventually, but not for a very, very, very long time."

"When? A thousand years?"

"Oh, even longer than that." I glanced at the geranium plant on the windowsill, its leaves velvety and green. Chloe was quiet for a moment.

"Will you be there, Mumma?" she said, looking straight at me, her chin resting in her hands now. The question hit the back of my throat.

"Yes, my darling. Of course I'll be there."

*

"Crikey! You haven't been shy with the brandy," Tom said, having sloshed back a generous mouthful of my mother's mulled wine.

"Really? I was thinking maybe it needed a little more," she said.

"No . . . I think we're good," Tom said as the warm liquid scalded his throat. He stoked the fire in the drawing room, sending sparks dancing up the flue. Much to Henry's delight, the snow had started falling earlier that morning, and by lunchtime the pavement resembled a clade of water lilies across a frozen lake.

As marvelous as the house looked, the tree rich with every manner of gold and crimson, Christmas Eve would always leave a bitter aftertaste. Every cracker pulled, every present exchanged, every passing scent of pine still had a loaded kick. But this year Tom refused to plow through the holiday on autopilot. Henry deserved an untainted Christmas. The wreath was up, the turkey was brining, and the house was thick with greenery hanging from every trestle.

Tom stuck his nose into one of the green felt bags with the bulk of Henry's presents. "I think that's the last of the sacks," he said. "I keep thinking I'm forgetting something . . ."

"Does your road get blocked off when there's this much snow?" Colette said, glancing out the window like a child on the lookout for a passing sleigh. She seemed almost mystified by the snow's rhythmic descent—either that, or she was plastered.

"I don't think so . . ." Tom said as Duke trotted towards him and performed an enviable Downward Dog before readily collapsing beside the ottoman.

"Do you think there will be other road closures?" she pressed.

"Why? Are you planning on going somewhere?"

"No, no. You know, I just find it fascinating, this one-way system," she said. I'd never known my mother to have such a deep interest in the implications of England's climatic conditions.

"Maybe you shouldn't drink too much more of that wine," Tom said as he moved towards the fireplace to adjust Henry's stocking. "You've been a little . . . I don't know—*off*—today."

"*Non, c'est ne pas vrai,*" my mother said, though she'd been in a perpetual state of readjustment since she woke up.

"Right . . . okay," he said. He picked up a stray water glass from the side table and went into the kitchen, where he plated a carrot for Vixen and gave Father Christmas an overly generous tipple, breathing in the smell of dried clove and cinnamon from my mother's infamous mulled wine simmering on the Aga. He couldn't help but wonder what I would make of it all, my mother with her slippers on drinking mulled wine in the drawing room, Henry, our son, nearly six years old and thriving.

Tom walked past my mother, who was now in a near nosedive,

scruntling under the tree in the hallway. He set the plate on the fender and took the obligatory bite from Vixen's carrot.

"Everything all right?" he said, looking awkwardly past her backside.

"*Voilà,*" she said, bolting upright, her hair a little askew. "I found it." She handed Tom a small, wrapped box, about the size of a coaster.

"You want me to open this now?" he said. My mother nodded. Tom let the ribbon fall away as he undid the paper.

"*Attention.* It's delicate," she said. Tom cautiously opened the box. Inside was a white ceramic star with "Chloe" faintly etched across the body in looping cursive.

"It's for the top of the tree," my mother said. Tom held the box in his hand, a galaxy of emotions coursing through him.

"It's perfect," he said after a moment, gripping my mother's hand tight. She tried to stifle her tears as Tom gingerly took the star from its box and put it on top of the tree.

"There she is," Tom said. "How does she look?"

"Perfect," my mother said, dabbing at her nostrils with a white cotton hanky. Tom stood beside my mother and took in the sight of Chloe on top of the tree.

"I really mean it, Colette, thank you. Who would have thought it, me and you?"

"Yes. I just wish you wouldn't have the heating up so high all the time."

Tom laughed. "Maybe lose the scarf. Just an idea."

Outside, a group of carolers spread festive cheer with a rendition of "O Holy Night." The amber glow from their lanterns reflected off the snow as they walked slowly towards the house before ringing the bell.

"Tom, the door," Colette said. Tom opened the door to seven insistent mouths stretched open in harmony, each jolly caroler wearing a different variation of bobble hat and half-stitch. A whopping sphere of mistletoe hung from the pendant light in the

porch, diligently put up by Tom at my mother's insistence; there
are some traditions with which the French simply won't part. After a song or two, Tom dropped his donation into the basket and
the carolers drifted off to another unsuspecting neighbor.

"You know what?" Tom said, closing the door. "I think you'd
really enjoy a caroling group. What about joining one next year?
Or a local community choir. You'd fit right in. They're an insistent
bunch."

"Don't be ridiculous," my mother said, knocking back the last
of her mulled wine. She readjusted the curtain and picked the orange slice out of her glass.

"I'm knackered," Tom said, yawning.

"Don't go to bed yet. We can watch *Elf*. It's about to start." Tom
squinted at my mother. The prickly pear had come a long way.

"You want to watch *Elf*?" Tom said.

"Yes, I—I love Will . . . Smith?"

"I think I'm going to take Duke for a walk, then hit the hay,"
he said.

"I've already walked him!" my mother retorted.

"*Okay,* but I don't cap his walks. Plus, it's snowing. He likes it."

"I think it's too cold to walk now. Sit down and I'll bring out
those mince pies Annie made and some more wine."

"Right. How much of that concoction have you drunk?" Tom
said, just as another batch of carolers came knocking. "How can
there already be more carolers? Honestly, I really don't think Jesus
had all this warbling in mind."

"Answer it. They'll be freezing," Colette said. "I would, but I
think I'm coming down with something."

"All right, Mother Teresa," he said, heading for the front door.
"The only thing you're coming down with is a monster hangover."
He turned the deadlock and then the latch. But when he opened
the door, he wasn't met with a sea of gawping strangers holding
songbooks. It was Marjorie in a brown beret and red lipstick.
Blanche in a pair of green mittens and matching bobble hat. It was

Nellie in her pink puffer. Jenny. Edith. All the Sunday Blues girls. Except one.

"Sorry, wrong house," Blanche said, before breaking into a smile. The sight of the Sunday Blues brigade at his doorstep on Christmas Eve had thrown him drastically off-kilter. Was Tom imagining this? What did that drink have in it?

"We hope you don't mind us turning up like this," Marjorie said.

"Mind? I—I'm thrilled," Tom said. "I mean, I'm flabbergasted, but thrilled. Please, come in. Come in."

"All of us?" asked a familiar voice.

As the gaggle of women parted, Tom saw her: Grace, her face lit from above by the sodium streetlamp. He almost dared not blink. The falling snowflakes were catching in her hair, before slowly sintering into ice. It couldn't possibly be real. Grace, standing in front of him in her red coat, her radiant face in stark contrast to all those months ago when she'd so rightly stormed out of his life. Angels don't have wings. They have bobble hats and mittens.

"Is that actually you?" he said, almost too scared to speak in case it was a dream.

"*Ooh, la la,* you took your time," Colette said, suddenly appearing beside him at the door.

"Merry Christmas to you too, old girl," Blanche said, stepping into the house. She unraveled her scarf and handed it to Colette. "We're here *now,* aren't we?"

"Wait. You knew they were coming?" Tom said, his eyes fastened on Grace.

"Of course," Colette said. "Someone had to go to the shop and talk to Grace."

"Colette's our newest member of Sunday Blues," Marjorie said. I knew there was something dodgy about those Sunday life-drawing classes my mother had suddenly signed up for.

"And Jenny's got a boyfriend," Nellie said. "He's younger than her. The tart."

"Oh, stop it, Nellie," Jenny said. "It's true, though. Lowell's three years younger. Colette, is that mulled wine I can whiff?"

As Grace followed the girls into the house, Tom fumbled for something to say, suddenly confused and shy. She looked so happy and so well, bundled in her scarf and duffle coat. The vision was agonizing yet utterly wonderful. And even if she stayed for just a moment, he told himself he could go on knowing she was safe and smiling again.

"You look incredible," Tom began, after the girls had settled themselves in the drawing room with what was left of the mulled wine. "You look so happy."

Grace stood opposite Tom beside the padded fender in the hall, the fire crackling behind them.

"You've put up a tree this year," she said finally, the fairy lights reflecting in her eyes.

"I should have done it sooner. Henry won't believe it when I tell him you were here. Listen, Grace—"

"Tom, Colette came to Sunday Blues. She walked in just like you did. And I was speechless. We were all sitting there. You know the form. She's very determined, your mother-in-law. It was hard to argue with her reasoning. Especially when you're surrounded by a group of meddling romantics."

"I never asked Colette to do that—to go and find you." Tom said, glancing towards the drawing room, which had grown suspiciously silent. "I know you're listening in there!"

"No we're not," Marjorie called.

"I know you didn't," Grace said. "We talked for hours. She told me everything. Not just about what Lauren did, but all of it. We talked about Honor, about Pietro, about Henry, about you. About the letter and the CD and the ring and your intention to tell me right off the bat that first Sunday. She called my every bluff. She kept asking, '*If you'd known the truth from the start, wouldn't you have run?*' She said when there's doubt, there is no doubt. That running away doesn't cure anything. Nor does burying myself in Post-its."

"Not telling you will always be one of the greatest regrets of my life," Tom said. "I had a responsibility—to be truthful."

"But you never asked to know who I was in the first place. You just got a letter. You didn't hatch some master plan to track me down." Grace faltered. "I tried so hard to fall out of love with you. I had this idea that I'd move back to Alba, run away, and start again. Hide somewhere else this time. To what end? For months, I ruminated and obsessed over everything that happened between us. I tried to convince myself that none of it was real. But something imaginary could never hurt that much."

"It was real. Every second of it."

"If you had told me the truth in the beginning, I could lie and say I would've listened, but I know I would've run a mile and never let myself fall in love with you and Henry." Grace put her hand on his, her familiar skin soft and warm.

"Grace, I've played over every possibility relentlessly in my head, hundreds, probably thousands, of times." One of the girls had put on "Fairytale of New York" and Tom could just make out the lyrics *"I turned my face away and dreamed about you."*

"Then it's time to stop," Grace said. "This isn't like before for either of us, a reel of regrets that we play and play—because something that I thought was my biggest regret turned out to be Henry. And your biggest regret brought me back to life."

"But you pulled out of your exam. Was that because of everything that happened?"

"No. Well, sort of. You see, you can't take the exam if you're pregnant."

Tom felt his heart fly off in all directions. Euphoria, shock, Grace, a baby. He stumbled backwards and put his hands to his mouth in prayer, tears gathering in his eyes. The Christmas tree lights grew bright behind Grace. She moved even closer towards him, his heart beating tenfold, as she put his hand on her burgeoning bump.

"You're pregnant?" Tom said.

"Yes," she said. "And I want my family to be together. I want plan B." She slid her hands around his neck and nuzzled her face against his damp cheek before kissing his lips. The girls clapped and hooted in the drawing room and Nellie yelled, "More tongue!"

Standing with Grace by the fire, Tom thought of something my agent, Eva, had said on the phone when he called her frantic about my half-written memoir a few months earlier. He'd suggested that Eva might try to publish it as a collection of personal essays, but she'd disagreed. She'd simply said, "Some manuscripts are meant to remain unfinished." At the time, the idea had been hard to swallow, the notion that yet another part of me was out there floating, incomplete, in the void.

But love wasn't measured by its ending. It was every cup of coffee, broken boiler, empty crisp packet, and train ride. It was every hangover, stubbed toe, high temperature, nasty splinter, and burned tongue. Every eye roll, private joke, and piece of burned toast. Every morning cuddle and blunt pencil. Every kiss good night, every lost key, sore throat, afternoon nap, and sip of tea. Every birthday, hot shower, cold swim, paper cut, chesty cough, mosquito bite, and bee sting. Every lost bookmark, orgasm, funeral, traffic jam, and bite of cake. Every missed flight, snarky comment, haircut, and unmade bed. Every first step, endless holiday, mediocre film, sunrise, and poo-bag. Every missed connection, miscarriage, and resentful walk. Every wobbly table, broken heart, treasured photograph, and lingering kiss. Every wedding, toothache, and waiting room. Every school drop-off. Every single day.

Tom felt transported, not to the past but to the future—his future, a life that was honest.

"We're having a girl," she said.

THE END

ACKNOWLEDGMENTS

The production of a novel is a biblical team effort and the author is simply one of the team. Thank you to Jennifer Enderlin, who was a huge advocate for this book from day one. To my supremely wonderful editor, Sarah Cantin. You are so thoughtful, clever, empathetic, and brilliant. Thank you for the time and love you put into these pages. I would like to thank my impeccable agents, Christy Fletcher at UTA and Jonathan Lloyd at Curtis Brown. You are marvelous. Your guidance and attention to detail have been exceptional from the very beginning. A big thank-you to Dori Weintraub, my publicist at St. Martin's Press, for your care in getting this book out into the world.

A huge thank-you to everyone at SMP who helped build my idea into a reality: Lisa Senz, Drue VanDuker, Erica Martirano, Brant Janeway, Alexis Neuville, Robert Allen, Mary Beth Roche, Elishia Merricks, Althea Mignone, Diane Dilluvio, Lizz Blaise, Kiffin Steurer, Jen Edwards, Michael Storrings, Jonathan Bush,

Tom Thompson, and Kim Ludlam, and everyone in the Creative Studio. Jason Richman and Olivia Fanaro at UTA.

Thank you to Emily Stone, my utter ally, mentor, and teacher, who taught me everything I know about craft. Thank you for caring as much about my writing as I do.

So many conversations with people have shaped this book. I am especially indebted to Jim Mallinson for proofreading my work nearly a decade ago and telling me it was "pretty good," and Tara Summers for our early-morning workshops and for naming this book (echoed by Sarah Cantin!). I adore you.

Thank you to my wonderful sister, Olivia, and my brother-in-law, Jason, for always ensuring I stay well rooted on planet Earth.

To my incredibly supportive mother, for allowing me to have unlimited books as a child.

Special thanks to ÖMK for Baudelaire, Rebecca Gradinger, Claire Yoo, Katie O'Donnell, Olivia Edwards, Rachel Goldblatt, Downtown Writers Workshop, Kati Spencer, Laura Lekkos, Leigh Goldstone, Richard Louderback, Lena Wald, and Amanda Smith.

I thank Barry Manning for talking to me in Heathrow Airport that day and Roma Downey for reading an early draft and boosting my self-belief.

I'm thankful to the artist Cecile Davidovici for making the most beautiful embroidery for this cover.

My best friend, Robin, who I love unconditionally. I treasure what we have so deeply. Thank you for giving me endless material to steal and countless things to love.

Most important, I'm grateful for my family. Thank you for coming in whilst I'm writing to ask if I'm finished. My darling husband, Nat, who patiently waited for me to write this book. To my beautiful son, who insists I make up stories whilst he's honking. Thank you, my love, for telling me when a story doesn't have a very good ending. Your existence will forever be my finest work.

ABOUT THE AUTHOR

Jane Mcleish-Kelsey

Loretta Rothschild is originally from London and currently splits her time between the UK and Italy. She lives with her husband, Nat, their young son, and their beloved dogs. *Finding Grace* is her debut novel.